D0217236

HIDDEN DEPTHS

EMMA HOLLY

Copyright © 2011 Emma Holly

Hidden Depths

Emma Holly

Discover other exciting Emma Holly titles at: http://www.emmaholly.com

All rights reserved. With the exception of quotes used in reviews, this book may not be reproduced or used in whole or in part by any means existing without written permission of the author.

This story is a work of fiction and should be treated as such. It includes sexually explicit content that is only appropriate for adults—and not every adult at that. Those who are offended by more adventurous depictions of sexuality or frank language possibly shouldn't read it. Literary license has been taken in this book. It is not intended to be a sexual manual. Any resemblance to actual places, events, or persons living or dead is either fictitious or coincidental. That said, the author hopes you enjoy this tale!

This book contains mf, mm and mmmf scenes.

ISBN-10: 0983540276

ISBN-13: 978-0-9835402-7-4

cover photo: shutterstock.com/luxor

OTHER TITLES BY EMMA HOLLY

The Prince With No Heart

The Assassins' Lover

Steaming Up Your Love Scenes (how-to)

The Billionaire Bad Boys Club

~

Hidden Series

Hidden Talents

Hidden Depths

Date Night

Move Me

The Faerie's Honeymoon

Hidden Crimes

Winter's Tale

Hidden Dragons

Hidden Passions

CHAPTER ONE

AN isolated beach on a clear spring day was a wonderful place to think. As Olivia Forster lazed on a towel in her red bikini, the thought she worked on was this: She and her husband James were different from their married friends.

Olivia couldn't say why exactly. They all had similar high-powered jobs and comfortable houses on Long Island. They'd all been married around two decades and were within a stone's throw of forty from either side. In Olivia's opinion, all of them were attractive, though some of the women obsessed about their weight. They weren't necessarily intellectuals, but neither were they idiots. Their marriages had reached the vintage where they knew relationships needed work. More importantly, none were so lazy or uncaring that they wouldn't put in that work. All of them had at least one child who'd reached adulthood more or less in one piece.

Despite these similarities, Olivia had observed that although she and James were happy, their friends were—to greater or lesser degrees—habitually dissatisfied with their lives.

Her inner perplexity must have showed in her expression. James, her darling husband of mumble-mumble years, rolled toward her on their shared beach towel. He was tall and dark and just as handsome to her as he'd been when he was twenty. Every day, they worked together at the multimedia firm they'd founded twelve years ago, which could have been awful but turned out to be the best job either of them ever had. Olivia still loved seeing James in his suit and tie, though—as head of accounting—she rarely wore anything fancier to work than a blouse and jeans. He teased her about that, but never angrily. He seemed to like that she couldn't be swayed from her favorite things.

Since he was one of those favorite things, she supposed that made sense.

"Hey," he said now, tapping her furrowed brow. Hardly minding the interruption, she turned her head toward him. As she did, he gave her the killer grin that had seduced her the day they met. It was boyish and crinkly and genuinely affectionate. Every time she saw it, her heart warmed impossibly.

She was so lucky he'd fallen in love with her.

"I know we're playing hooky," he said, "but now you're playing hooky from me."

She wriggled around until she lay on her side as well. Her wavy red locks fell forward, reminding her she could use a trim. Despite their unkempt state, she didn't sweep them back. Like a background that was meant to lull them into intimacy, the Atlantic waves broke foamingly on the shore. Olivia felt as if she were dreaming when she spoke.

"I was wondering why I look at you and feel happy, when Sherri looks at Mark and sees everything she wishes he'd fix about himself."

"That's easy. Clearly, I'm perfect."

"You are not," she said, shoving his admirably buff chest. "No more than I am."

"You're perfect to me."

"What about my shyness? Or the way I need to organize everything?"

James shrugged one muscular shoulder. "Neither of those things is worth getting upset about."

"Why aren't they, though? Why does Dan go ballistic when Kim buys a pair of shoes he thinks she'll never wear, and you and I let stuff like that roll off us?"

James's dark brows puckered above his hazel eyes. "Are you suggesting we ought to fight about those things?"

"No. I'm just wondering why we're different."

"I believe I told you why we're different the day I proposed. You and I are soulmates. We've been married in lots of lives before."

Olivia rolled her eyes even though she loved hearing him say this—as she was sure he knew. James was endearingly proud of being romantic. "How do you know our friends aren't soulmates as well? Can't soulmates be grumpy?"

James cocked his head, his expression the one he got any time he heard an idea that started his gears turning. His willingness to entertain other people's viewpoints was part of what made him an excellent CEO.

"I suppose they could be," he said.

"And," Olivia said, encouraged by his attitude, "how do you know for sure *I'm* everything you need in a partner?"

And then she saw it: the tiniest shadow shuttering his friendly hazel eyes. At first, she thought the emotion the shadow inspired in her was fear. Her chest did go tight, and adrenaline certainly surged into her veins. When she looked inside herself, however, fear wasn't what she found. James loved her. That she knew as surely as the earth going round the sun. Strange as it sounded, she thought her reaction to the idea that James had a secret might be excitement.

Intrigued, she sat up and looked down at him, her hand pressed to the place where her heart pounded in her chest. They both liked to swim every morning before they drove to work, and she was nearly as fit as him. Her red bikini wasn't something she was embarrassed to be seen in. On the other hand, the way her nipples beaded painfully tight beneath it made her a tad self-conscious. Luckily, James was peering into her eyes right then.

But maybe it wasn't nice to call that lucky when his expression was so concerned.

"There *is* something," she breathed, giving voice to her suspicions. "Something you want that I'm not giving you."

"Liv," he cautioned.

"Is it the games?" she asked, her pulse drumming harder. "Do you wish we played them more often?"

He blushed, something he almost never did. His coloring was naturally dark, and usually it hid embarrassment. She glanced at his Speedo, which he carried off a good deal better than most men half his age—and never mind that his choice of swimwear sometimes gave their twenty-something daughter conniptions. If Violet had been around, instead of minding the store at Forster Media, he'd have had to cover himself. His cock was swelling inside the stretchy fabric, the swiftness of its rise and his not insignificant size creating an effect that was thoroughly X-rated.

Apparently, he couldn't make it go down by reciting baseball scores. As soon as he saw her notice, his hard-on jerked bigger.

Olivia bit her lip and laughed. "You know I like our games, right? I have made that clear to you?"

"I never want to pressure you."

She cupped his erection gently, hoping the touch was reassuring as well as pleasurable. The latter certainly seemed to be true. His entire bulging package jumped in her hold, his heat and hardness causing her to liquefy.

Violet wouldn't have wanted to know about that either.

"You never pressure me," she said. "Some of my favorite memories of us in bed are watching you go wild from me taking charge. What turns you on turns me on. It's as simple as that."

To her amazement, tears glazed her husband's eyes. "I feel the same," he said huskily.

"Oh sweetheart!" she cried, because he was almost too emotional to get the declaration out.

In that moment, she couldn't think she was wrong to take such joy in pleasing him. She wasn't a fifties throwback, as Sherri sometimes accused. James deserved every bit of adoration she gave him.

She swung one leg over his thighs even as he sat up to meet her. He took her face between his strong olive hands. Everything fell away but him, her universe filled with his tenderness. "I love you, Liv. Even more than you understand. I couldn't bear to lose you."

He kissed her before she could swear that would never happen. He might like being dominated, but the way he kissed was all man. Twenty years hadn't dulled the magic of his lips pressing hers open, of his tongue sliding sleek and hard against hers. He had the best lips ever, narrow but expressive, with smooth skin and firm muscles. Employing them to good advantage, he drew a sound of longing from deep within her throat.

She pushed him back and he let her, both their breath coming quicker with anticipation as he fell back against the towel. James's diaphragm went in and out, emphasizing the development of his upper chest. Somewhat lower, his erection prodded her bikini bottom, tempting her to roll on it. Feeling completely wicked, Olivia untied her bikini top.

"Liv," he breathed. "Here?"

She'd always been on the slender side, her shoulders slightly broader than her boyish hips. Fortyish or not, her breasts sat prettily on her ribs. James's eyes snagged on them, then rose admiringly to her face. Olivia admitted she liked both stares.

"Why not?" she said, flinging caution to the winds. "We're behind a dune. And we have the beach to ourselves."

"What if someone comes close enough to see?"

"Then we'll run back to the cottage, and some old codger walking his dog will have a story to tell his friends."

James laughed, his hands coming up to cup and caress her breasts. His strokes were sure, the tips of his fingers deft. In seconds, he had her nipples achy and hard. He liked seeing them that way. He wet his lips as he watched himself tug them out.

"I think you should let go of me," she said, her voice not as steady as before. "I need to tie your wrists together."

He inhaled sharply, his hands stilling. His whole body seemed to help him hold his breath.

"Above your head," she said, pushing his strong arms there.

He didn't resist as she bound them with her bikini top. He breathed more raggedly instead and got so hard he started leaking inside his Speedo. James had been her first lover, and she'd always been fascinated by his cock: the size of it and the heft, the way it responded so readily to almost anything she did. Their first game—which had happened by accident—had surprised her, because she hadn't known he could enjoy sex more than he already did. She'd always thought one of his finest qualities was how much he loved fucking. She did too, and it was nice to be kept up with.

"Lift your hips," she said, wanting to admire the picture he was making.

James lifted and she dragged his snug black swimsuit far enough down his ass to bare him. Digging between his thighs, she pulled his balls up so the elastic cradled them. His testicles were about half drawn up, and she knew she had time to play. Maybe he did too. He moved his hips restlessly, like he was trying to dig a deeper depression into the sand underneath the towel.

Rather than succumb to what she wanted, which was to plunge her aching pussy over that tall thick rod, Olivia stood and skimmed her swimsuit bottom down her legs.

When she stepped out of it, completely nude in the open air, James let out a groan that said better than words how sexy she was to him.

Because she thought it would flip his switches, she stepped over him like a Valkyrie, one bare foot firmly planted to either side of his hips.

"I am your queen," she said, the words oddly natural.

"Yes," he agreed.

"You're here to serve me."

"Yes."

"Anything I ask of you, you must obey."

His eyes dipped to the triangle of curls that declared her a true redhead. In her legs-akimbo pose, she was certain he could see her sexual moisture glistening.

"Anything," he said hoarsely, making it a plea.

She dropped to her hands and knees so quickly he couldn't help but gasp. She was crouched over him like a cat, unmistakably predatory. As she'd hoped, this flipped his switches too. "You won't come until I say, no matter what I do."

This time, her darling husband could only groan.

She kissed him too quickly and too sharply for him to kiss her back. With the in and out rhythm of the waves as accompaniment, she nipped a stinging path down his long lean body. His nipples tightened for her biting kisses, and chill bumps broke out across his skin. His strong legs kicked when her fingers stroked the ticklish spots on his abdomen, and again when she stuck her tongue into his navel. The one thing he didn't do was laugh.

He was too involved in what she was up to for that.

She'd reached his gorgeous erection. The thing stretched thick and flushed and veiny up his belly. It and he shivered when she blew on it.

For just a second, she wondered what other men looked like when they were this aroused. The thought disturbed her, and she shook it off. She didn't need other men when she had James.

"I think my servant needs a bit more restraint," she said.

They'd brought a little picnic down to the beach. Nothing elaborate, just sandwiches and salad and soda pop, bought ready-made from the small local grocery store. Olivia dug into the plastic bag to retrieve a rubber band she thought was the perfect size and thickness.

"Liv," James said when he saw it, the word wrenched from him.

Liking that, she stretched the band between her fingers. "Tell me if it hurts."

She bound it twice around the base of his balls. Their skin got tighter and darker, partly from the way the rubber band forced it taut and partly from his excitement. She petted his fullness gently, trying to gauge if she'd gone too far. She hoped not. She really liked the way he looked trussed up and on display.

People were so wrong about women not being visual.

"Too tight?" she asked.

He shook his head jerkily.

"Will the constriction make it harder for you to come?"

"I don't know," he whispered. "It's *really* turning me on."

A shiver ran across her shoulders, his excitement heightening hers. Her pussy was squirming, like it was trying to rub itself. His eyes held hers when her gaze lifted, their gold-green-blue darkened by the expansion of his pupils. He was no stranger, and yet she'd never seen him as pushed to the edge as this. She felt as if she were a stranger herself, as if together they'd crossed the barrier into Neverland.

Her mind flashed back to the odd second when she'd wondered what other men's cocks looked like. Outside of magazines and X-rated movies, she'd never encountered one close up.

Momentarily nervous about what *her* eyes might reveal, she shifted her attention to James's erection. Surely there couldn't be a better visual than this. His hole was leaking more than before, the clear fluid trickling down the swollen crest onto his hard belly.

"I want to lick your cock," she announced.

"My queen should do as she wishes," was his breathless response.

Slick wet heat ran out from her sex. She wanted James to see it, wanted him to know what this game of theirs did to her. She turned her body to face his feet.

"I want you to pleasure me while I lick you."

"Yes," he sighed. "That's what I'd like too."

His bound hands settled on her butt, urging her down to him. Once she'd lowered, he shifted them between her legs, his corded forearms pushing her thighs wider. When his mouth settled over the spot he wanted, his thumbs reached back to work her clitoral hood up and down. Since his mouth was also working her, this meant his thumbs were pushing under his lower lip.

Olivia temporarily forgot what she'd meant to do to him.

Oh he was good at giving head, strong and quick and very sure of himself. She groaned at how close to coming one hard suck pulled her.

"Don't," she said, fingernails digging into his muscled thighs. "Don't make me climax so soon."

He backed off, and she could think again—enough to take in the view anyway. His cock and balls stared her in the face, a feast of the first order.

Olivia was no porn star. She couldn't deep-throat a man James's size. She couldn't moan cinematically or even toss her hair around like one. She'd have felt too silly. Her main advantages were willingness, curiosity, and knowledge of her partner's sweet spots. And love. That was probably an advantage when it came to driving a man crazy.

Olivia crooked her little finger under the cinch of the rubber band, then let it go with a snap.

"Christ," James cursed, his body jerking as his mouth fell from her pussy.

Olivia didn't ask permission. She snapped the band again, drawing a wild cry from him. Then, before the sting on those sensitive nerves could fade from his consciousness, she took the swollen head of him in her mouth. She pressed the soft warm flat of her tongue against it, made sure her teeth were covered, and sucked him once as hard as she could.

He nearly came. The taste of precum flooded her mouth as his body writhed under her. She slapped her arms on his thighs, bearing down with her weight and not coincidentally increasing his sense of being restrained.

Then she sucked him again.

His cry was garbled, pain and ecstasy and shock all rolled into one. She gentled her suckling, but that wouldn't matter now. She'd already pushed him to the edge, nor would he have forgotten that she'd ordered him not to come.

"Oh God," he gasped, twisting both to and from her suckling mouth.

"Stop," she ordered. Instantly, he froze, giving her a heady sense of power. As she paused to decide on her next order, James sucked in a great gulp of air, no doubt hoping to recover his control. "No more thrashing, servant. I want my hands free to work on you."

"Yes, my queen," he said in a thready voice. His body tensed but didn't thrash as she moved her hands to his twitching balls.

She didn't hurt him again. James responded well to variety and surprise. She cupped and compressed his scrotum, then ran three fingers firmly over the smoothness of his perineum. He had nerves here that liked massaging. Sure enough, his back arched off the towel, and he groaned more luxuriously. When she sucked the upper half of his cock back into her mouth, he returned his lips and tongue to her. His bound hands rested compliantly on his belly, fisting and then relaxing as she did things to him that felt good. She wasn't sure he knew she could see. His reactions made a handy sexual litmus test.

She used this to lull his worries that he'd disobey her by climaxing. Letting him relax, she nuzzled his balls, then licked his penis repeatedly. Down and down she swiped her tongue on his underside, over and over like a metronome. Using her saliva to make him glisten, she painted the stretch between the sweet spot under his rim to the cinch of the rubber band. This would feel good, but it wouldn't push him over. The muscles in his thighs stopped bunching.

"Liv," he sighed, the sound pure sensual indulgence.

Deciding it was time for a change of pace, she licked four fingers and pushed them behind his balls, back onto his perineum, where the structure of his cock rooted. His bound hands didn't fist up again until she teased her rubbing around the pucker of his anus.

He tried to cover the reaction, or possibly deflect her from noticing by stabbing his tongue into her pussy. Olivia was far too accustomed to focusing on him to fall for the ploy. Anal play was a game they hadn't tried, but she'd seen signs before that he was interested. Perhaps he'd feared she'd find it distasteful, and hadn't dared bring it up. Whatever his reasons, Olivia decided she'd stop waiting to be asked.

She pushed one wet finger into him to its first knuckle. He jerked and gasped, but in a way that made her think he welcomed the intrusion. Made bolder by this reaction, Olivia pushed the finger to its second knuckle and rotated. James choked out a sound, but she couldn't doubt he liked what he was feeling. His cock swelled and his hips lurched up, shoving him farther into her mouth. A single pull of her cheeks had more of an effect than she anticipated. Suddenly he was thrusting with more purpose, his promise not to come forgotten.

More than willing to let him enjoy himself, Olivia wrapped one hand around his throbbing base to prevent him from gagging her. Going on the theory that two fingers were better than one, she drove a second into him. His anal muscles were more relaxed than they'd been initially. Far from resisting, his passage seemed to suck her probing in eagerly.

"No," he gasped, but Olivia didn't listen.

He felt smooth in there and warm. She scooted forward for a better angle, pulling her pussy out of reach of his mouth. Way too excited to mind, she started fucking her fingers in and out of him.

She didn't even know how she knew to do it; maybe these things were instinctive. She felt weirdly sure of herself. *This* was the speed that felt good. *This* was the pressure that got to him.

"Fuck," he swore, thrusting faster in and out of her mouth. The hard, slightly awkward rocking of his pelvis intensified the working of her fingers. Somehow knowing he would like it, she scissored her fingers wider and twisted them in half circle.

Despite the grip she had on his base, he shoved the head of his cock nearly to her throat.

"Damn it," he said at the small uncomfortable sound she made.

She didn't mean for him to stop. She'd have recovered in a few seconds. She didn't get a chance to convey that to him. He wrenched out of her without warning.

Cloth snapped—her bikini top, she thought—because suddenly he'd twisted their bodies around in two directions and he was looming on top her.

Before she could figure out how he'd done it, her wrists were trapped by *his* hands beside her head. His eyes burned furiously down at her, the blue-green drowning out the gold with anger. Angry or not, he was so excited his cock was dripping precum on her belly. He seemed ready to do anything to her, as long as it involved getting off.

Olivia abruptly understood why being dominated was arousing.

"I'm sorry," she panted, her pulse pattering in her throat. "I thought you were enjoying that."

He growled in answer, his teeth grinding. "God, Olivia. I can't hide anything from you."

Apparently, he could, or she wouldn't have been confused. "Do I need to apologize?" she asked unsurely.

With another animal rumble, he crushed his mouth over hers.

She didn't think he'd ever kissed her like this. He was assertive, yes, but this kiss was meant to overwhelm. Before she had a chance to adjust, to let him know she accepted it, his knees butted hers open. His hips came down in the space he'd made, his body as hot as a barbecue.

His grip tightened painfully on her wrists as he probed between her labia with his cock. He must not have wanted to release her hands. After a push or two he found her entrance, grunted into her mouth, then slung inside in one hard thrust. She was so wet, so hungry that all she felt at his roughness was relief.

He gasped her name, tearing free of her mouth.

That was all the pause she got before he started fucking her like a maniac. A second later, she was meeting him with abandon, her hips bucking up at his. They went at each other so hard it felt like they were fighting.

"Yes," she groaned, hitching up her knees and spreading her thighs wider. He shifted both her wrists into one big hand, then shoved the other under her bottom, controlling her thrusts to move her in better synch with him. She quivered so close to coming she knew she didn't have much time to do what she still wanted.

"Let go of my right hand," she said, trying to tug it free.

He shook his head and pumped into her harder.

"Yes," she insisted. "I'm your queen, and I'll do to you what I please."

"Liv," he said miserably.

She didn't care. She knew he wanted this. The next time she tugged, her hand flew free of his. She spit on two fingers, then decided three would be better. His breath grew choppy as he watched her.

He closed his eyes and shuddered when she pushed all three into him.

He loved it. That was clear from the way his spine arched and his expression grew dreamy. The fact that he'd wanted to hide how much he craved this sweetened her victory. She began to move her fingers inside of him.

The look on his face grew truly beatific.

"I'm fucking you," she whispered, some demon genius taking control of her vocal chords. "I'm fucking you like a man."

"Oh God!" he cried.

Suddenly, he was fucking her twice as hard, really slamming into her, as wild and desperate as if the only way to save both their souls was by coming in the next ten seconds. Maybe the rubber band did make it more difficult to ejaculate. He seemed like he was reaching for it hard and couldn't quite get there. The twisting of his facial muscles pushed more of her buttons than needed it. She started to go, and finally he did as well. She moved her fingers faster and was rewarded by a ragged shout of pleasure.

The shout was only the beginning. His ejaculation gushed heat inside her as he strained to hold as deep as he could. She felt herself clamp around him, and that made them both come harder. The orgasm felt like pleasure was stabbing through her womb—no subtlety to it, just a hard-core explosion of sexual nerves.

Olivia made a sound like she was sobbing. Maybe she was. Even though he'd come, James had started thrusting again, taking advantage before his cock softened. Helpless to stop her sex from reacting, she went over a second time.

Half a dozen jabs more, and it was all over.

"Jesus," she gasped as he sagged down on her. She felt like a hurricane had blown through her, one that swept everything before it with a storm surge of ecstasy. When she tugged her fingers from James's body, her hand and arm were shaking. He shivered, and she wasn't certain it was with pleasure. "God, James. Did I hurt you?"

He moaned, his sweaty face turning back and forth across the crook of her neck. "You—" He stopped for air. "You did that perfectly."

How did he know? Had he been finger fucked before? She'd been singularly inexperienced when they met in college, but she'd heard young men sometimes experimented, just like young women did. Maybe he hadn't been fucked by *fingers*. Maybe he was comparing what she'd done to something else entirely.

She pressed her lips to his temple, unable—or, she guessed, unwilling—to ask him to clarify. Did she want to hear his answer?

He lifted his head and smiled softly down at her. For a second, she drank him in. He was never so beautiful as when he'd just climaxed. His eyes were brighter, his sensitive mouth relaxed. His thick dark lashes blinked lazily.

"Olivia," he said as if she'd done something to amuse him.

"What?" she asked him defensively.

"You're organizing your thoughts again. Trying to force everything, immediately, to make a sense you're comfortable with."

"It's what I do."

He kissed her lips so gently her mouth might have been the Holy Grail. "Whatever you want to know, I'll tell you. Just let it be until tomorrow."

She searched his sleepy eyes. He seemed a little rueful, but not afraid. Whatever he was going to tell her, it wasn't too terrible. The tension that had taken hold of her ribcage eased.

"All right," she surrendered. "Go ahead and enjoy your post-coital nap."

As he laid his cheek against her breast in his favorite spot, she felt him grinning.

CHAPTER TWO

One month earlier

HIS Majesty, Lobodon Vitul was dying.

The ruler of the wereseals lay in his sumptuous chamber in his enchanted palace beneath the sea. Heavy embroidered curtains—some blue, some green with eel-like silver patterns—were drawn across porthole windows that overlooked the innermost courtyard. A single candle burned within a pierced metal lantern, the star-shaped holder dangling from the painted ceiling many meters above his bed.

They had electricity in Oceana, powered quite reliably by the ceaseless currents around them. The golden flame was simply the only illumination the king's failing eyes could bear.

"Not . . . long now," he said with a rasping laugh to his son.

Anso, the crown prince, sat on a cushioned stool beside him and took his hand. The king's carved cedar bed—which normally was set in the floor—had been propped on stands to spare the ancient court physician from having to stoop to treat him. Ironically, the dying king was decades younger than the old doctor, far younger than the age their race should have anticipated living to. His disease was one that ran in families, noble lines in particular. Lobodon knew exactly what to expect from it. Because he did, and because he'd never liked being lied to, Anso didn't contradict his words.

"Glad," his father said, confusing him. "About marrying your mother. In spite of . . . how it ended for her. At least I . . . brought new blood into the line for you."

Anso's throat choked tight. His mother had killed herself on his fifteenth birthday, within an hour of his naming ceremony as official heir to the throne. He wasn't sure why she'd waited that long. For as long as he could remember, she'd been desperately unhappy.

"She tried," his father said, his cold hand giving Anso's a feeble squeeze. "She loved us as well as she could. She just missed her home Outside too much."

By *Outside*, he meant outside the borders of the Pocket, the fae-created cross-dimensional territory that was not quite mundane or purely magical. The Pocket began at a modestly sized city called Resurrection on the eastern seaboard of North America. Once past land, it dove through a corridor under the ocean floor, then rose and spread out again to host the cities of the Atlantic League—the foremost of which was their own.

Anso had traveled to Resurrection and also to Manhattan, New York. Both metropolises were too dry for his taste, though people claimed the weather was better in summer. He'd been an adult when he took the journey and not a child. Nonetheless, he remembered feeling more hurt than he'd been prepared for. Oceana was more beautiful in every way than either landlubbing city. Moreover, Oceana had given his mother him.

Evidently, neither of those things had been enough to inspire Denise Vitul to go on living.

As there was little point in bringing any of this up, Anso pressed his forehead to his father's shoulder, hiding the tears Lobodon probably knew were there anyway. "I always knew you loved me, Dad."

His father let out a sigh. Anso sensed him gathering his reserves and sat up to face whatever he wished to say. Recognizing this, his father gave him the slanting half-smile Anso had seen so many times in his own mirror. "I'm proud of you, son. You're going to make a fine ruler. I know you'll do what you must for your people."

"Father—"

"You *will*." He nodded in emphasis and warning, then settled deeper into the bolster and closed his eyes. "Probably don't even need me to tell you to. It's . . . the blessing and . . . curse of the Vitul line . . . that our instincts are strong. Like salmon." He laughed again breathlessly. "You'll be . . . driven to it soon enough."

As he spoke, his respiration had grown labored, seams of pain deepening in his face. Anso laid his hand on his father's heart, willing his own warmth to him. "I'll call Pinni. He'll give you something to help you rest."

"Call . . . the Magus too. Like to . . . make my peace."

All shapechangers were magical beings, though few had the ability to perform spells. The wereseals were fortunate their coalition of city nations had been adopted by a faction of the fae, who transported the cities whole from their shared native land. Back in Faerie, the cities of the seals had been in danger of falling into magical anarchy, a condition that had spelled the end to other civilizations there. Here in the Pocket, the energy that powered all magic was both less potent and more stable. The rules by which it functioned one day were almost certain to apply the next.

Without the fae, life on the seafloor could not have been sustained at this level of sophistication, the drawback being that wereseals were now dependent on a race that did what they did for their own reasons. That knowledge might not be comfortable, but it couldn't be changed.

Anso bent to kiss his Father's brow. "I'll get them both," he said.

Naturally, the physician and the spiritual leader were waiting in the antechamber. All Lobodon's advisers and relatives had gathered for his death vigil. The pair Lobodon requested were his closest friends, their loyalty proven many times during his reign. Anso was glad for that. He knew his father didn't want his son at his side right now. He was in too much pain for his pride to welcome that.

"He's asking for the pair of you," Anso said.

They went in without questions, their expressions calm, their gazes meeting his with quiet understanding. As a pureblood faerie, the Magus's age was difficult to pin down. Pinni, the old physician, was an elf and consequently lower on the magical prestige scale. His kind often chose medicine or technology as careers, not being as standoffish as pure fae. Pinni gave Anso's shoulder a gentle rub as he passed. The gesture was enough to fill Anso's eyes with tears.

To his dismay, his cousin Ellice ran forward at this sign of his emotions. She was a pretty woman—tall and strong, with the dark gold hair and deep blue eyes the Vitul family was famed for. She and Anso had grown up together, had shared their first shifts into seal form. Anso couldn't count how many times they'd played naked in the surf off some pristine beach. In all that time, Ellice hadn't done him a single cruelty. Never laughed when he was embarrassed. Never failed to sympathize when he was sad. She'd lost her mother too, when she was only ten. Nonetheless, since they'd reached adulthood, Anso found he couldn't be comfortable with her.

His unease stemmed from more than spending time close to a female. The prince was used to handling that. All noblemen learned to. Male wereseals had strong sexual drives. Females did too, of course, but it was the males' responsibility to ensure they didn't father pups indiscriminately. Among a closed society like theirs, the perils of inbreeding couldn't have been realer. The means to prevent pregnancy existed, but given the potency of wereseal semen, it couldn't be counted on. While a commoner might be allowed to slip up, noble males refrained from sex with women until marriage. Even then, they only married those whose blood the mages tested first for weakness.

The temptation this resulted in could be overwhelming. They were men. They had urges. To be forbidden to satisfy them only increased their power—a fact Ellice wasn't as sensitive to as she should have been. Anso's lack of romantic feelings for her hardly mattered to his desires. She was fruit of the secret tree. She had breasts. And a pussy. And a bottom so much lusher than a man's. She shouldn't have made a habit of touching him.

"Anso!" she cried now, catching his face between graceful hands. "Dear,

dear cousin. How sorry I am for you!"

He took her wrists to pull her touch away, which somehow resulted in her tangling their fingers together. "I'm fine, Ellice. We knew this was coming."

"Of course we did, but still . . ." She leaned closer, speaking so only he could hear. "If there's anything I can do to make you feel better. *Anything.* I know how close you and your father were."

Are, he thought. How close we are.

"Anso," interrupted a welcome voice. Anso's best friend Tykon Otari had just stuck his head around the antechamber's dark paneled door. He grimaced as the room's inhabitants turned to look. "Sorry to interrupt. Need to steal the prince away for a few."

"*Ty,*" Ellice said in the gently scolding tone she used a lot on his friend. More than once she'd warned Anso against spending so much time with an Otari. As noble families went, they weren't the most prestigious. "Anso needs to be with his family now."

Ty shrugged at her, his face impassive. "Guard business. I'm afraid it can't wait."

Anso disentangled himself from Ellice as carefully as he could. "It's all right. I could do with a distraction."

He moved away before Ellice could pet his sleeve. She said something behind him, but he was too focused on his relief at getting out of there.

"*Thank you,*" he said the moment the door was shut behind them.

Ty chuckled under his breath. "Thought I might have picked up a silent distress call."

He might not have been joking. Tykon did sometimes intuit what he was thinking. Anso's best friend was very intelligent, a trait Ellice didn't value as highly as Anso did. It was true Ty wasn't as kind as Ellice. He had a temper and spoke thoughtlessly now and then. He'd slept with a lot of men besides Anso, but the prince had long since gotten over being hurt by that. Males their age had sex together out of necessity. They weren't meant to form heart attachments. Ty was a good friend—not perfect but as dear to him as a brother.

Anso felt more at ease walking down the hall in his company than he'd have felt if he were alone. They followed the march of electrum-rimmed porthole windows that provided ever changing underwater views into the courtyard. Like the city around it, the royal palace was octagonal. As rulers, the Vituls commanded its central ring. Beyond that ring, each noble family had a wedge-shaped portion where members lived. They had their own coral gardens, their own decorative fisheries, but the courtyard Anso's father nurtured was best of all.

The sound of bubbles rising through the sunlit waters was a balm to his wound up nerves.

"How is your father?" Ty asked as they reached the final turning to

Anso's rooms.

Anso shoved his hands into his pockets, not wanting his friend to see how they shook. "Close to the end, I think. I'm not certain he'll last the night."

Ty stopped and turned to him. "Do you want to go back? You know I made up that bit about needing you for guard business."

"I know." Anso smiled at Ty, their faces perfectly level. Ty was as muscular as Anso and just as tall. He was better looking, Anso thought, with shining sand-colored hair and thick-lashed yellow eyes. His skin, which always looked like he'd been sunning, bore a barely visible pattern of darker spots—as if his bloodline ran back to leopard seals. Like Lobodon's illness, the coloration was a symptom of inbreeding. Fortunately, the Otaris didn't suffer from health problems.

Ty didn't shy from Anso's gaze, though a pain he didn't usually let show darkened his yellow eyes. "You're lucky," he whispered, "to have a father you're going to miss."

Ellice would have clucked her tongue and called him insensitive, but Anso understood. Ty's father was a drunk—and a mean-natured one at that. His mother could have counterbalanced her spouse's failings, were she not so caught up in trying—endlessly, it seemed—to establish herself as Someone Who Mattered in were society. Anso occasionally clicked past the *Real Housewives of New York City* on the Import Channel. From what he could tell, Sabra Otari would have fit right in.

Understanding what her shallowness did to Ty, Anso squeezed his friend's hard bicep. "I know I'm fortunate."

"I shouldn't have called you away. You should go back. Spend every minute that's left with him."

Anso shook his head. "He's in pain. He doesn't want me to see it. We—" He swallowed his emotions back as they rose. "We said what we needed to."

Ty covered the hand he'd put on his arm. The deep furrowing of his brow gave him a haunted look. "Tell me how to comfort you."

His offer wasn't so different from Ellice's, but Anso's response to it was. Heat flashed through him and his pulse quickened. His cock had only been half retracted, but it slipped from its protective sheath in a long smooth thrust, thickening fast with the blood that pumped into it. The very speed of its emergence supplied a sensual pleasure. Anso was fully erect in seconds, the throbbing head tenting his snug hide trousers.

Ty read his blush of course. "Well," he said with a sexy chuckle. "If *that's* all it takes to make you feel better . . ."

"Shut up," Anso laughed, smacking his friend's shoulder.

"Only if you *open* up," Ty ran his tongue around his full upper lip, causing Anso to blush harder.

They were both laughing by the time they barred Anso's door behind them.

The instant their privacy was assured, Ty kissed him, deep-tongued and hot. Men who slept together didn't always do this, but he and Ty liked it. Their saliva contained a mild aphrodisiac that added *oomph* to their encounters. Happily, they liked lots of things in common. Every inch of Ty's tall hard body pushed Anso's back into the wood. Anso stood that for about five heartbeats, then started tearing at Ty's clothes.

"Hurry," Ty urged, his own hands busy on Anso's garments. "Mo-*ther*, I've been crazed all day."

Anso had too, embarrassing though it was to admit. Something about facing his father's mortality made him want to hump everything in sight.

"Fuck," he said, struggling with the laces that closed Ty's trousers over his genital bulge. Zippers were considered lower class, and most royals eschewed them. "Why do you have to tie these so well?"

Ty closed his eyes and rolled his hips forward. "Can't let just anyone get in there."

Plenty of people wanted to, that was sure, though for the moment Ty was focused on him. His hands roamed Anso's now bare chest, thumbs zeroing in to circle his tight nipples. The massage wasn't helping Anso's coordination. He snorted at his susceptibility, then gave up on opening his friend's trousers. This caused Ty to lift drowsy eyelids and give him an accusing stare.

"Ty, that's a fucking sailor's knot you've got there."

"Fine," Ty huffed, taking over the task himself. "I'll do mine and you do yours."

Anso knew Ty wasn't truly annoyed. He was grinning broadly as he backed up, retreating on the glassy basalt floor toward Anso's bedroom. Anso's excitement kicked higher. One of the first erotic favors they'd exchanged was masturbating in tandem.

"I know what you're thinking," Ty singsonged.

"Do not."

Ty shucked his trousers and wagged his brows, maybe to mock Anso for his childish answer, or maybe because he knew damn well how delicious he looked naked. His erection was very long, very thick, and very flushed where tiny vessels fed his blood to the swaying head. He hadn't been exaggerating about being crazed. The edges of his penile sheath were already sealed tight around his base.

Wereseal genitals retreated into their bodies when they relaxed, serving as streamlining and protection for swimming in man form. Ty was the opposite of relaxed as he stood framed by the bedroom doorway, his balls full enough to bulge in their normally tucked up sac. Anso licked his lips, helpless not to run his gaze along his friend's body. Ty's shoulders were broad and well developed, his long legs dropping gracefully from tight hips. The ridged muscle of his abdomen testified to hard training, and his golden skin looked every bit as smooth as it was. The faint leopard spots that marked it darkened near his groin, the pattern extending into the short sand-colored fur of his pubic triangle.

Anso's thatch was as dark honey. He'd never forget how aroused he'd been by his first sight of their complementary coloring.

"Oh I *so* know what you're thinking." Ty's laugh drew Anso's gaze to his amused face. "Jacking off together that first time. Coming so fast, so hard, we practically spattered each other from head to toe."

Anso couldn't mind Ty's teasing, not when Ty's hand moved to his own erection and fisted it leisurely. The memory aroused him too.

Anso decided to play along. "What about the first time I tried going down on you? You squealed like a dolphin the moment I tightened my lips and sucked."

"You had quite a gift for a neophyte."

Despite the humor sparkling in his eyes, Ty's voice had gone husky. With a wonderful sense of freedom, Anso kicked off his trousers. He always enjoyed being undressed with Ty. Anso had many duties, but with his friend he was not constrained. Two long steps put them chest-to-chest, gazes locked, heat pulsing one to the other in time to their heartbeats. Ty's hand bumped Anso's erection as he continued to jack his own. A slow stroke was all he needed to remain at the peak of hardness. Both their bodies were ready for pleasure.

"Remember the first time you fucked me?" Anso murmured, loving how Ty's face flushed. "I thought I'd gone to heaven, you felt so brilliant inside of me."

"I remember playing sick for days so we could skip training and do it around the clock." Ty's gorgeous eyes were soft. "You've no idea how cute you were, my sweet eighteen-year-old virgin prince, suddenly in love with taking it in the ass. Neither of us could get enough, though I recall trying manfully."

"I thought you were being nice for fucking me that much."

Ty chuckled, letting go of his cock to touch Anso's cheek. "Nice had nothing to do with it. You might not have been my first lover, but you've always been my best."

Anso hadn't known that. Ty had been *his* first, though—bless him—he'd never mocked Anso on that account. The back of his eyes burned in reaction.

"Shh," Ty said. "None of that tonight."

He kissed him, wrapping him in his arms and moaning when Anso did the same. Ty's lips were hard, his tongue pushing greedily inward. Anso relished his aggression. Lust blotted out emotion, rising in thick hot waves. As was customary, Anso's bed was set in the floor, the comfortable mattress flush with the shining tiles. They dropped to it on their knees, still kissing, arms exploring each other like octopi.

Ty's ass was firm and tight. Anso couldn't resist squeezing it.

"Oh God," Ty breathed, rubbing his cock more urgently along Anso's. "I need this so much."

"Me too," Anso groaned.

They toppled onto their sides, muscled legs scissoring together to give their swollen ball sacs access to rub each other.

"Fuck," Ty cursed, rolling Anso beneath him.

Anso recognized his tone—and the way he was suddenly grinding himself more forcefully against him, as if no matter what they did he couldn't get close enough. They'd been together so many times each man knew the other's preferences. Ty had one particular kink that never failed to amuse. Anso's fellow guard was so masculine it should have been the last thing that steamed his windows.

Then again, maybe that was why Ty found the practice so alluring.

Unable to stop himself, Anso burst out laughing.

Ty pulled back from him and frowned.

"I know." Anso's chest shook with amusement. "You can't control when the mood for that *special little act* hits you."

"You like it too."

"Of course I do, but you do realize it's perverse, right? If other people knew we did this, they'd think we were as twisted as Outsiders."

"It feels good," Ty said, the hint of a pout pushing out the heavy shape of his lower lip. "It's the only thing that really gets me to relax. And it heats up the gland in my anus, the one *you're* always moaning for me to pump over harder."

"You don't have to defend yourself to me. I admitted I like it too." Anso petted Ty's lean tanned cheek and then across his shoulder.

"Sometimes it gets in my head. I can't think straight until you do it to me."

His voice sank on the last part of his confession, his brows drawn together above his nose. He looked concerned for Anso's opinion, which wasn't necessary at all. Touched but smart enough to hide it, Anso nipped his chin playfully. "Roll off of me, you pervert. I need to get the oil. The last thing I want is you chafing yourself to death."

Quick as magic, his compliance turned the tide of Ty's mood. Ty rolled off him onto his back, stretching every inch of his aroused body and letting out a sound like a purr. His arms were above his head, his toes curled like a diver about to plunge. His thick hard cock extended up his belly, his veins blue ropes, his tip beginning to leak precum. The display of muscle and meat was gorgeous, something Ty absolutely knew. Anso bit his lip to prevent laughing. For all his intellectual prowess, Ty was sometimes childishly simple.

He kept the oil in a low mother-of-pearl inlaid cabinet beside his bed. When Anso removed its stopper and the spicy fragrance wafted out, Ty let out an actual whimper.

"You could *try* not to get so excited before I start. You know you like to last through an actual session before you come."

Ty bit his lower lip. "Please. You can see how much I need it."

"I don't even know how you do it. I'd go in two seconds if I got as aroused as you."

"You're the one who makes me that way," Ty said throatily.

Oh Ty knew how to get to him. Anso's prick jerked between his legs, the ache of need tightening. Suddenly he was breathing harder, nearly panting with excitement. He poured the oil into the cup of his palm . . .

"Lick me first," Ty whispered. "The harder it is to hold off the better I like it."

Anso's fingers trembled as he corked the oil again. He curled his hand around the lubricant he'd already poured, not wanting to waste it. "Two minutes."

"Three," Ty bargained and undulated against the bed.

Anso gave him four, deep-throating his thick erection until Ty clutched wads of bedcovers in both hands, his entire body writhing with pleasure. Anso put more pressure on his hipbones.

"Fuck," Ty groaned, obviously struggling not to climax. "*Anso*, you are so fucking good at this."

He was good, better than Ty, who'd never quite caught the knack. He swallowed one last time, his relaxed throat closing softly around Ty's glans. Then he backed up to catch his breath.

Ty's brick-red erection shuddered like he'd slapped it.

"Want a sampling of what's to come?" the prince offered, because a slap wasn't something Ty would mind.

"Better not," his friend said breathlessly.

Anso thought it funny how Ty always ruled these bouts, despite Anso being the one who was meting out punishment.

Smiling, he rubbed his still oiled left palm against his right, then smoothed both around the base of Ty's cock. Ty tensed, probably worried he'd go over from even this careful stimulation, but Anso knew how to skirt his limits. Gently, slowly, he coaxed his lubricated little finger down into Ty's penile sheath, relaxing the constricted passage enough to let the tip of the digit in. His pubic fur ended at the pocket's edge. The interior skin was baby-smooth, rarely touched as it was.

Nerves ran through it, not as many as in Ty's cock, but they were receptive to pleasure. Ty trembled, and squirmed, and bit his lip on a tortured groan. To let Anso touch him this intimately was quite a sign of trust. Their instincts, which *were* part animal, resisted exposing such vulnerable spots.

"Shit," Ty said.

Anso laid a hand on his thigh. "I can stop."

"No. I like when you do this." High emotion brought a glow into shapechangers' irises. Ty's yellow eyes burned into Anso's, so bright they should have conveyed actual heat. He seemed to mean he liked it more than physically.

Few things could have excited Anso more than watching Ty struggle to find his inner submissive. But maybe it was time to give him more help. Submissives needed dominants, after all.

He pulled his touch away from Ty and gazed sternly down at him. "I want you to turn over now."

Ty groaned.

"Now," Anso insisted.

Ty rolled onto his belly, taking hold of the mattress edge with both hands.

His ass was muscular and narrow, its golden skin dappled with the faint leopard spots Anso found so enchanting. Two deep dimples framed his tailbone where it dove into his anal crease. Those smooth depressions begged for kisses, but that wasn't on tonight's program.

"Please," Ty whispered, wriggling and clenching at the same time.

"Lift your ass," Anso ordered, the assumption of command naturally deepening his voice. "You're not to rub yourself against the mattress until I say you can."

"I won't," Ty promised.

He meant the promise, but sometimes he forgot, which was why Anso had oiled him. The skin of their normally protected penises was susceptible to bruising. Before Ty could bruise his, Anso unleashed a rain of smacks on both of his butt cheeks. When he stopped half a minute later, Ty's skin was rosy and blazing.

Ty was panting, but not as deeply as he could.

Because he was in charge, Anso bent and licked him. His skin was saltier than before.

"Don't," Ty pleaded. "Hit me some more."

Anso let him feel the edge of his teeth. "You're not my master, Ty."

"I want you to master me."

Did he? Sometimes Anso wondered if Ty knew his own desires. Not what they were, but why he felt them. As promiscuous as he was, he had to be searching for something he hadn't found. Had it been in Anso's power, he would have given whatever it was to him. Ty's happiness mattered more to Anso than Ty might have been comfortable knowing. Now and then, Anso wasn't comfortable with it himself. One day, he'd give his heart to a woman—or at least he'd try to. When that day came, he didn't want his friend to be hurt.

"I brought you a present," he said aloud.

Ty tossed a raised-brow look over his shoulder. Male lovers didn't give gifts to each other, not romantic ones at least.

"Don't worry," Anso chuckled. "It isn't a bunch of flowers."

It was a rubber coated wooden paddle, easy to wield and more effective than Anso's palm. Ty's breath came faster when he saw it.

"Okay," he said. "That's a nice present."

"On your back again," Anso instructed. "Pull your knees to your shoulders. I want you to watch me smacking you."

The position was more intimate than their usual, but Ty only hesitated for a few heartbeats.

"Wrap your arms around your thighs to hold them. I don't want you touching yourself. Tonight, no one's getting you off but me."

Ty complied with this as well. Once he had, his eyes were wider, his handsome features more deeply flushed. Not only were his buttocks bared by his position, but so was his asshole. For once, he actually looked docile.

Anso wasted no time taking advantage. The paddle made a lovely resonant crack on his ass muscles. It felt good in Anso's hand, each impact running warmly up his arm. Ty was already pink, so Anso couldn't hit him long. He stopped when Ty let out a sound that was suspiciously close to a whimper.

Now he was panting the way Anso liked to hear. Dropping the paddle, he spread one palm over Ty's hot ass cheeks. Ty's eyes had been tightly closed for the paddling, but at the caress they flew open.

Their sessions, when they indulged, generally finished with Ty taking charge and fucking him mightily. Right then, he didn't seem capable, and not because he wasn't plenty hard. His cock was huge, its slit trickling steadily. No, Ty seemed incapable because his expression was so stunned.

"Put your feet on the bed," Anso growled.

His voice was rough, as if he too were shaken. Ty dropped his feet, his arms releasing the hold they'd taken behind his knees. His hands fell to the sheets as if they'd lost their ability to move without orders. He didn't budge as Anso swung over his torso, one knee to either side of him. Because Anso hadn't let him touch his cock, his skin was oiled and ready. If Anso wished, he could take him without delay.

Ty's eyes glittered up at Anso as he shifted over it.

In all their years together, they hadn't fucked face to face. Other things they'd done that way, but not penetration. Anso saw Ty was aware of this.

"I won't last," Ty rasped. "I am so fucking ready to go."

Anso swallowed, feeling ready to go himself. "Put your hands on my hips."

Ty wrapped his fingers around him there, warm and sweaty and tight. Praying he'd last long enough to get Ty inside, Anso placed the head of Ty's cock against his asshole. He was so aroused he barely had to push before it went in.

As it did, his head fell back and a groan of ecstasy tore from him. Ty felt so good gliding into him, so hot and smooth and alive. His flare pressed Anso perfectly as it squeezed past his prostate.

"Oh Lord," Ty moaned, his grip pincering his hipbones. "Do you think it feels this good to fuck a woman?"

The question wasn't conducive to self-control. Abruptly desperate to come himself, Anso started humping him up and down. Ty cursed and joined the motions as well as he could with his back arching off the bed. Wanting more stimulation and afraid Ty was about to shoot his load, Anso slapped a hand around his own cock.

"Unh-uh," Ty said and slapped his hand there too.

He rubbed Anso's prick faster than he did.

The double-speed double handjob was more than his nerves could take. Sensation crested and crashed outward. Anso cried out hoarsely, ejaculating with such volume that his seed immediately turned both their grips slippery. The rubbing felt even better then, intensifying the orgasm. Maybe Ty knew. A second later, he made a snarling noise and filled Anso's ass with warmth. He came in successive waves, each punctuated with strangled groans.

The evidence of Ty's pleasure sent aftershocks through Anso. Ty always came with abandon after he'd been dominated. This time, though, he outdid himself. His nails dug into Anso's hips so forcefully they stung. Finally, he relaxed.

"God," he sighed. "I don't think I've come that hard since the first time you sucked me off." His chest went up and down while Anso eased off him. "Considering I was eighteen and insanely horny, that says something."

Anso couldn't speak yet, he was panting too hard. He collapsed beside his friend and patted his chest soothingly.

"I'm okay," Ty assured him. "My ass is a little sore from the paddling, but strictly in a good way."

Anso rolled his eyes. "You might not be eighteen any longer, but you're still insanely horny, from what I can tell."

"And you're not?"

He was where Ty was concerned. At his quiet exhalation, Ty squirmed onto his side to face him. His hand trailed down Anso's centerline to his groin. With a gentleness he didn't let many see, he stroked the knuckle of one bent finger along his cock. "You're still a little hard. I would have thought that would finish you."

The truth of his words made Anso uneasy. What they'd just done should have left him completely limp. He'd noticed nothing did lately. The forces that drove his sexuality were rattling their cage. Every day they shoved the bars a little harder, until even his sleep was broken by torrid dreams. Knowing this and facing it, however, were separate things.

"Spring is coming," he mumbled, eyes closing drowsily. "You know what that does to everyone's hormones."

Ty seemed to accept this explanation. His gentle knuckle continued to tickle him up and down, ironically increasing his sleepiness. "You're the only one I play these games with, you know."

"Good," Anso slurred. "You need to be careful who you trust yourself with."

Ty's hand shifted to his hip. "Anso?"

"Mm?"

"Are you going to mate Ellice when your father dies?"

Anso dragged his eyelids up for that. "Lord, no. What makes you think I would?"

"She talks like you will. I mean, she doesn't say it exactly, but other people understand what she means. The Vituls do have a tradition of marrying cousins."

"Which is why my father is dying before his time!"

"I think people figure your mother being human brought enough new blood into your line."

Anso stared at him. Ty was too sharp to be mistaken about prevailing opinion. Could Ellice believe they were going to marry? Surely she'd noticed him pulling back from their old closeness. Unless she explained it away as him not wanting to risk temptation. Maybe everyone, Ty included, thought that was why he treated her distantly.

He sat up to look down at his friend and lover. For once, Ty's gaze wasn't meeting his. Anso found he didn't like that at all. "I'm not attracted to Ellice, or not more than any normal male could help. She's a sweet female, but in your worst mood your company appeals to me more than hers."

Ty plucked at the rumpled bedcovers. "She'd be a good political choice."

He almost sounded jealous, which wasn't possible. Ty was the bull all the wereseals wanted, male and female alike. Hell, if they'd known what he liked to do in secret, spanking probably would become the next big fad.

"I'm not marrying her," he said, the words emphatic. "I want a queen who makes me happy."

He'd never said that aloud before. It sounded childish. Kings didn't marry for happiness. Ty pressed his lips together against a smile, but at least he didn't laugh.

"Good," he said. "Because *I'd* be happy if you picked a queen who liked me."

Anso didn't mention that his father thought he was going to spawn, which would render picking of any sort irrelevant. Preferring to put dealing with that off, he wriggled back down and nudged Ty's shoulder. "Angling to be my third?"

Ty shook his head and smiled faintly. Wereseal kings often ruled in triads: a queen, a king, and a trusted male intimate. Anso certainly would have offered Ty the position if he weren't so easy with his favors. Politically speaking, with so many partners, Ty's loyalties would always appear suspect. Fair or not, appearances mattered. The kindest thing was not to ask him to change his ways. Indeed, the idea of Ty restricting himself in bed made Anso snort softly.

"I know I'm not *your* third," he said, his eyes drifting shut once more. "What is my spot on your dance card? Two of twelve? Five of thirteen?"

"One of six," Ty answered, which Anso suspected was no more than the truth. Ty drew up his knees to bump Anso's companionably. "I'm slowing down as I get older."

Anso laughed. "As long as I'm number one."

"Always," Ty swore, the ring of honesty in it.

Anso let that vow nudge him into slumber.

~

He woke to the sound of low conversation in his outer chamber. One of the voices belonged to Ty. The other was Lord Noth's, the head of the King's Council. Along with an elected legislative body and the king, the Council formed Oceana's government.

Anso sat up abruptly, the blanket Ty must have covered him with dropping to his waist. It had happened then. His father was dead. From newborn pup to grayfur, Anso was responsible for Oceana now.

He scrambled out of bed and nearly fell over. Had he been screwing Ty when his father passed? Did Lord Noth guess that was why Ty was there? Ducking into the bathroom, he scrubbed a wet washcloth up and down his chest, removing the remains of his own semen. He still smelled of sex when he pulled on and tied his robe.

Well, too bad, he thought. He'd taken comfort with a friend at a trying time. Lord Noth was married, but presumably he'd done as much himself when he was younger.

Anso squared his shoulders and drew a long calming breath. If he truly needed his people to think him perfect, he was in trouble.

Despite knowing he was king now, the sight of dignified Lord Noth dropping to one knee took him aback.

"Your Majesty," the noble said, his head bowed respectfully. "Please allow me to offer my sincere condolences on your loss."

The words weren't empty. Lord Noth and his father had been known to butt heads, but he'd been a staunch ally.

"Thank you," Anso said. "I'm sure your guidance shall be as valuable to me as it was to my father."

Even with his head inclined, Anso saw Lord Noth's involuntary smile.

"I know," Anso acknowledged. "I expect you and I will disagree sometimes too. Do rise. I'm not used to talking to the top of your head."

Lord Noth rose with a shorter bow. With a start, Anso realized he was waiting for orders.

"Have the Council gather in an hour," he said, the decision coming more easily than he expected. "My father kept me apprised, but the ministers can brief me on outstanding matters. It's important they know I'm listening to them. We can also go over what needs to be arranged for the funeral. My father deserves full honors."

"Very good, sire." The Council head betrayed no sign he'd noticed Anso's voice had gone throaty. "I'll advise everyone to be . . . succinct."

Because some of the ministers were long-winded, Anso appreciated that. Lord Noth left in the same unobtrusive fashion that he'd arrived.

"Well," Ty said, sounding as dazed as Anso felt. "Long live the king."

Anso's eyes spilled over. When Ty's yellow irises met his, they shone with sympathy. "Shall I bow as well, Your Majesty?"

Anso shook his head, unable to speak right then. In bed, mastering his friend was fine. In real life, he preferred them to be equals. To his relief, Ty came to him and held him. His embrace was gentle, his shoulder warm.

"You'll be fine," he said, giving him a slightly awkward pat. "More than fine. I have no doubt of it."

Anso hugged him once, then pushed back from him.

"Thank you," was all he managed to say.

CHAPTER THREE

ANSO'S first month as king brought many changes into his life. Shortly following his father's elaborate funeral at sea, he'd been moved into the royal apartments and assigned a retinue of servants. Despite being waited on hand and foot, he'd never had so little time for himself.

He'd barely had a chance to mourn.

There were meetings to attend and dinners and endless stacks of reports. Lord Noth assured him his duties would lighten as he gained experience—if only because he'd decide which tasks he truly needed to perform personally. Anso tried to take his word on this. In the last thirty days, he and Ty had been together precisely twice.

He'd had other offers—more than he knew how to handle. He simply couldn't trust the males' motives for wanting to sleep with him.

Bedding Anso Vitul had become a political act.

Alone for the moment, Anso stroked the courtyard porthole in the blue salon and let his lungs empty. Apart from refurnishing the bedroom with his own things, he'd left the royal suite as it was. This room included settees and tables his great-great grandmother had chosen, creating the odd sensation that he was adrift in time.

Outside the window, night had fallen. The royal coral garden bloomed beneath the soft phosphor lights, the flowerlike polyps opening to filter drifting food. Anso watched a tiny crab fend off a bright blue fish that was trying to nibble the branches that formed the crustacean's home. Again and again the fish darted forward, only to be driven back by the crab's sharp claws. Neither combatant seemed to tire of the battle. Anso wished he could claim as much.

Ty had promised to come by this evening, but because he'd taken over running the guards from Anso, that promise might not be kept. Anso wasn't certain how he'd react if his lover cancelled. Along with the rest of his life, his body was exerting new and disconcerting pressures, pressures he found difficult to ignore.

Each time he neared the palace's sea gates, his blood would thicken and his steps would slow. He couldn't prevent the reaction, though he tried hard enough. No matter who was with him, his groin would tighten and his prick slide free. He could feel the call of the warming ocean, just as his father warned. Someone was out there, some distant female whose blood was a match for his. He wanted to fling himself into the water and swim until he found her, wanted to fuck her amongst the waves and fill her womb with his pup. His dreams had grown increasingly explicit, laden with images of acts he'd never experienced in life. He'd wake hard as iron and wishing he'd had a wet dream.

He craved the touch of a woman more than he'd known he could crave anything.

*Not **a** woman*, he corrected, his hand forming a fist on the thick window. ***The** woman.*

If he hadn't witnessed his mother's sadness, he'd have long since obeyed the urge. What his blood craved didn't justify the crime involved, nor did it guarantee anyone's happiness. Moreover, Anso wasn't a damned salmon. He was a modern person with a conscience.

And a responsibility to continue my ancestral line, the opposing side of him reminded. His blood carried magic that had lent generations of Vitul rulers better ruling instincts than the norm.

"Your Majesty," his butler interrupted from the doorway behind his back. "Lady Ellice has come by. Shall I tell her you're in?"

Anso opened his mouth and turned, but Ellice was already entering the salon.

"You don't need to do that," she laughingly told the servant. "Anso and I don't stand on ceremony."

"Actually," Anso said, deciding this conversation was overdue, "he does need to. I have too many demands on me to let anyone, no matter how old a friend, stroll in at their pleasure."

Ellice's smile faltered. "You can't mean me."

"I do," he said softly but firmly.

"Oh." She blinked rapidly, her hands clutched together before her narrow waist. She looked especially nice, draped in a rich blue gown that made the most of her Vitul eyes and her fine cleavage. Anso's sole consolation was that tonight he was unmoved by the display. "I'm sorry, cousin. I didn't mean to offend. My father and I were wondering if you'd like to join us for a late supper. We couldn't help noticing you barely ate two bites at the state dinner."

Anso doubted her father had noticed anything of the sort. His Uncle Phoca was a jovial man but not particularly observant. Anso enjoyed his company, especially his stories of the Pelappo Wars. If the invitation had come from him alone, Anso would have accepted gladly and enjoyed a relaxing meal. Sadly, Ellice had the habit of treating her father like an addled child. While Anso admitted she was cleverer than her sire, he didn't like watching it. Less intelligent or not, her father was a war hero.

"I'm afraid I have plans," he declined politely.

"Oh," Ellice said. "Well, perhaps another—"

Anso's butler reappeared at the door. When he cleared his throat, anger flashed across Ellice's normally sweet face, tightening her rosebud mouth into a flat line. The expression startled Anso enough for his jaw to drop.

"Forgive me, sire. Your ten o'clock has arrived. You did say you wanted to be informed."

He hadn't, but you'd never know it from the servant's grave manner.

"Thank you, Harrison," he said. "Show them to my office and assure them I'll arrive shortly."

"Well," Ellice said with a brittle laugh. "I suppose those are my walking papers."

Anso resisted the urge to apologize. "Please give your father my regards."

Ellice rolled her eyes and turned. "I'm not giving up," she threw over her shoulder. "Being king is no excuse for never taking off your crown."

The butler came back as soon as he'd closed the door behind her. "Forgive me, sire. I didn't mean to presume. Or to let her slip by me."

Anso realized the man was worried he'd be disciplined. "You did fine, Harrison. Lady Ellice should be treated with respect, but it's true I don't want her traipsing in as she pleases. Er, did anyone actually arrive?"

The butler's mouth gave a little twitch. "Lord Otari, sire. I put him in your office as requested.

The warmth that spread through Anso's chest was probably too grateful. Not inclined to play games, he didn't keep Ty waiting but went immediately to greet him.

"Hey, stranger," Ty said, pushing off his desk and grinning.

Anso hugged him and slapped his back before letting go. "Your timing is impeccable as usual."

"Ellice, eh? She's not going to become less determined now that you're king, you know."

Anso grimaced and dropped sideways onto the office's antique red sofa. The furniture was mostly scarlet, the room's walls lacquered black and stenciled with the Vitul family's signature silver eel patterns. The effect was heavy, but here too he'd decided he'd rather leave the decor alone. Lobodon had often worked here, sometimes late into the night. When Anso had been a boy, he'd liked to hide in the storage compartment beneath a drinks trolley, because he'd wanted to remain close to his father. Looking at the trolley now, he marveled he'd ever been small enough to fit.

On the other side of the room, behind the large carved desk, the king's private sea gate was set into the wall. The hatch and wheel were fashioned from an alloy of gold and silver known as electrum, which retained magic well. The mechanism was slightly tarnished but still functioned after centuries of use. Oceana's mages renewed the spells that powered the city's gates periodically, ensuring the outside water stayed where it belonged. This particular hatch led to a pressurized changing tube whose further door gave into the royal courtyard, which then accessed the sea. Given the effect the gates had been having on him lately, Anso had avoided the space. He only told the butler to stash his guest here because he'd spoken without thinking.

He thought that was the reason, in any case. To have brought himself here on purpose would have been stupid.

"You . . . don't look right," Ty said unsurely.

He didn't feel right. Maybe it was because he hadn't eaten or how busy he'd been all day. His head swam with dizziness, and his hands and feet tingled. If he hadn't known how fit he was, he have sworn he was going to faint. Suddenly too heavy to move, he closed his eyes just for a second.

He dropped into a dream like a boulder through dark water. The wheel to the hatch was stuck. All his strength wouldn't open it. He had to open it. She was out there. Waiting. Only she could complete him. His body burned with awareness, every pore opening to catch her scent. He knew he would recognize her. All he had to do was slip out into the spring currents . . .

"Anso. *Anso.*"

Anso shuddered awake. To his amazement, he was on his feet. Ty stood behind him, hauling him back with both arms. Anso resisted, his grip seeming welded to the big electrum wheel. He'd been trying to turn it, exactly as in his dream.

"Good Lord," he said, dropping the handles like he'd been burned.

As he gawked at the thing, Ty placed himself between Anso and the hatch. This probably was a good idea. Anso belatedly realized his cock was hard as a rock.

Ty folded his arms and glared. "Care to tell me what that was about?"

Anso really didn't want to. He barely wanted to tell himself. Shaken in more ways than one, he ran one hand back through his honey-colored hair. "My father warned me this might happen."

"*This* being?"

"I think . . . my instincts are trying to tell me I need a human wife."

He couldn't stand this close to the hatch. It was making every inch of his genitals itch. He walked back to the couch and forced himself to sit. Ty followed, standing over him in a posture that said he was prepared to block him if he made a run for the sea again. His expression was wary. "Have you blacked out like this before?"

Anso shook his head. "I've been feeling odd, though, whenever I get close to an ocean door. I've been dreaming as well. About women. *A* woman. And not the usual sort. These dreams are as vivid as if they're happening." He shifted uncomfortably on the cushion, a few of the situations from those dreams making his prick pulse harder. "I thought I could resist it if I made up my mind."

Ty sat gingerly on the couch beside him. "It looks to me like resisting it might not be the best idea."

"I can't give in! Just abduct some human because my body decides I need to? Look how that turned out for my mother."

"Have you talked to Pinni? Maybe he's got a potion he can give you."

"I suspect he'll take the same position as my father. Needs must, and all that."

"Perhaps the mages then." Ty's hand was warm on his knee, too warm considering his arousal. "I confess I find them as creepy as you do, but if a spell could help maybe you should try. You know you can't afford for this to happen in front of someone else."

Anso did know it. Mad kings tended not to have long reigns. And people were already flapping their jaws about how young he was for rule: not yet forty—as if being thirty-eight rendered him an infant. "I don't like putting myself in the mages' debt. My father trusted the Magus, but I don't even know his real name. You know how faeries are about those things. If he were just an elf, it might not be so bad. God." He covered his face and rubbed it. "I think I have to do this."

"Then you do."

Anso dropped his hands to look at his friend. "Maybe I just think I do because my blood wants me to."

Ty laughed at him. "You're not your father. If you were, you wouldn't be fighting this."

"I loved my father."

"Of course you did. So did we all. He was a good strong ruler. The thing is, he never really tried to understand your mother, not that I recall. He never figured out how to make her love him. I think you would. I think you look more deeply into people's hearts than he did." He cocked his head and offered a winsome smile. "You'd also have me to advise you. You know how big you're always saying my brain is."

Anso wasn't sure women fell for brains, but how could he know? "You'd help me do this?"

"I'm the captain of your guards. I could hardly let you swim off alone. Drylanders are eccentric, but they're as likely to defend their women as we are."

Of all the responses he'd imagined, Ty offering to go with him wasn't one. Maybe he hated the idea of Ellice snaring Anso more than he'd realized. Whatever the reason for Ty's helpful attitude, Anso's heart thumped faster inside his chest. If his friend came with him, he'd have a safety net against his blasted instincts doing something terrible. *Could* Anso inspire a woman from a different race to love him? It seemed too much to hope for. He barely understood were females.

"You'd stop me," he said. "If it looked like I was going to commit some act my conscience wouldn't be able to live with afterward."

Ty pulled a dubious face. "You're my friend, Anso. And my liege."

"You have to promise."

Ty held his gaze, thoughts flittering like baitfish behind his eyes. "I promise I wouldn't let you do anything *my* conscience couldn't live with afterward."

Anso sensed this concession was the best he was going to get. The sea gate loomed behind him, unseen but certainly not unfelt. "Kiss me then. I could really do with a distraction."

Something else flickered through his friend's eyes, one more minnow of a thought.

Then Ty distracted him.

~

Ty didn't generally let men bugger him. He preferred being the active party in sexual exchanges. Anso was the exception to that rule. Right then, he was exploiting his favored nation status with a vengeance.

Ty turned his head sideways on the red sofa cushion while Anso went at him from behind, able to do little more than take what Anso was dishing out. Fortunately, the king was good at fucking even when halfway out of his mind. Ty groaned at his building pleasure. The crest of Anso's penis thumped the aching swell of his anal gland every single time he went in.

"*God*," Anso gasped, thrusting ever more urgently. The sharp slap of his groin into Ty's buttocks was driving him crazy, like a spanking but not. As if he knew this, Anso's hand fumbled under Ty for his erection. When he found it, his grip was tight enough, not to mention rough enough to sink Ty's teeth down into his lower lip.

This was good. Anso was jacking him with the precise fervor Ty's kinks required. Sometimes Anso was overly careful with him.

"Shit, yes," Ty said, arching his spine to encourage Anso to go deeper. This seemed to be appreciated. Anso's second hand dug into his hip like a claw.

"God." Anso slammed in again and held. He strained so hard, Ty assumed he was coming, but then he drew out and repeated what he'd just done. The solid, bull's-eye blow to Ty's prostate had his eyes crossing. Anso dragged his prick to the brink, and once more he drove in. His ball sac ground against Ty's butt like he was trying to push his testicles in there too.

"Fuck. *Ty*."

His hoarse desperation sent Ty over. Ty came with a suddenness that startled, the rush of it strong and sweet. He wasn't certain Anso noticed. His hand continued to work his shaft so fast it was clicking in his wetness, dragging the orgasm well beyond its usual limit.

"Ah," Anso cried. "*Ahh—*"

Heat flooded Ty inside. Anso was coming, the ejaculation both long and hard. Perhaps the cause was their weeks apart, or maybe Anso's desires were more feverish from his urge to spawn. When the wet pulses finally tapered, Anso sagged over him.

"Sorry," he panted, his hot cheek on Ty's shoulder. "Couldn't stop myself for a minute there."

Ty wished he could take credit for Anso's extraordinary loss of control. Alas, he feared he'd simply been a stand in for Anso's mysterious future mate. This sort of thing was more Ty's style than his friend's. Ty often became obsessed with people he hadn't seduced yet. The turning of the carnal tables caused more discomfort than he expected.

When Anso pulled out of his pummeled ass, the muffled moan Ty let out was precariously close to wistful.

"Sorry," Anso said again.

His legs not yet up to rising, Ty slid back, turned, and sat next to him on the cold tile floor. Both their backs rested on the couch, both their faces matching shades of red from the vigorous sex. Anso's mouth was swollen from their earlier kisses, his hair stuck with sweat to his broad cheekbones. Ty didn't usually think of Anso as beautiful, but in that moment he was. His honey-lashed eyes were closed, his mind probably on anything but him.

"No need to apologize," Ty made himself say lightly. "What's a friend for if not to take a jolly rogering now and then?"

Without opening his eyes, Anso snorted out a laugh. "That was the best distraction I ever had."

Ty knew Anso didn't mean this as an insult. Somehow, though, in spite of Ty's own profligate habits, it damn well felt like one.

CHAPTER FOUR

ANSO had hoped his mating instincts would lead him to Resurrection, a Pocket city in New York where humans were aware his race existed. He should have known he wouldn't be that lucky.

His mother had been a native of New Jersey.

He and his three-man escort swam in seal form. Ty had chosen the Corlier brothers to round out the squad. Nico and Mark were close-mouthed as well as tough, ideal recruits for a mission Anso was trying to keep under the radar. If their king's quest to find a mate ended in shipwreck, the fewer people who knew the better.

Once they emerged from the Helike Tunnel, they continued south along the Atlantic coast, avoiding boats and tankers as best they could. Outsiders liked seals as a rule, but they couldn't be sure some idiot wouldn't take a shot at them. If the mundane human was drunk or nearsighted, they might be mistaken for sharks. Their lack of dorsal fins aside, they were the same size as some.

The further they swam, the harder it was for Anso to remember dangers. Even in seal form, his body was aroused. He couldn't precisely smell his mate, but by God he could sense her. Every nerve in his pelt was twitching, every whisker spread at full alert. He worked his tail and hind flippers harder, willing his already swift body to cut faster through the water. It wasn't long before the others were struggling to keep up.

When he hit a hundred yards out from one particular sheltered beach, he braked so abruptly with his tail that his seal body rolled backward. His bones hummed like tuning forks as he righted himself.

This was it. She was here. His awareness of his mate was strong enough that his more rational human half simply couldn't doubt it was real. His pulse was rippling beneath his skin, his genitals so erect it embarrassed him. Unless his kind was *very* adventurous, wereseals only had sex in human form.

Given that Anso knew this, Ty shouldn't have had to grip his scruff and shake him as a reminder to transform. The others had already done so, while Anso hung there quivering. Changing took almost more concentration that he had. He visualized himself in man form, with arms and legs and the other accessories of bipedal life. *Slo-ow-ly*, the tingling sparkle that signaled he was successful rolled down him.

By the time it finished magically unpeeling him, he had a human body and a full erection. Anso didn't think he'd been this hard ever. No way on land or water could his companions miss seeing it.

"Well," laughed Nico, the older Corlier brother, his voice distorted by the murky sunlit water. He shrugged back into the small supply pack he'd volunteered to carry. "To judge by your reaction, I guess this is our last stop."

"Are you sure?" Ty asked. "I mean, of course you're sure, but we're past the borders of the Pocket. This is going to be tricky. Your mate won't have a clue why you're kidnapping her."

Anso met his friend's yellow eyes. "You can wait here," he said, knowing damn well Ty wouldn't. "I can collect her on my own."

Ty flinched, probably because Anso's tone was icy. Anso didn't know what had happened to his conscience either. He only knew his mate was here, and he was claiming her—preferably in every way possible very soon. If she was pregnant by the time they reached Oceana, that would be fine by him.

Come to think of it, being this focused on a goal was a pleasanter sensation than he'd have predicted.

"*I'm* not waiting here," Nico Corlier announced. "I've got to admit this is my idea of fun."

"Mine too," Mark said with a quiet laugh.

Under other circumstances, this might have been more than Anso wanted to know about his guards. Under this one, he was grimly satisfied.

The more overpowering force he could muster, the less chance his mate would be harmed in a struggle.

"All right," Ty said. "I guess we're all going ashore."

The transition from sea to air was necessarily an unpleasant one. One moment he was buoyant, and the next he was heavy. At first, he breathed rich smooth fluid, which he traded for desiccated gas. Once he reached the edge of the waves, Anso gave a great cough to clear his lungs, wishing as always that there was a nicer way to do this. For a second, his entire breathing apparatus burned, his eyes tearing violently. Then he recovered.

He noticed his discomfort hadn't lessened his erection. Ignoring that for the moment, he took in his unfamiliar surroundings. No one seemed to be on the beach, which was clean and white and overlooked by a single weatherworn gray cottage with cedar shingles and a white back porch.

Was his mate inside that building? He wasn't getting an inner ping as he examined the square windows. He knew she was near, not farther inland, because the rest of his body was going wild. Then his eyes lit on one of the taller dunes. The hair on his arms stood up.

There, he thought, his soul seeming to jump along with his cock. She was behind that small hill of sand. He strode toward it without hesitation, barely aware that his escort followed, spreading out behind him and scanning the land for threats.

Despite the handicap thrusting from his groin, Anso reached the goal first.

His heart nearly stopped. His mate was beautiful.

And naked.

And she wasn't alone.

She and a rugged looking dark-haired man were curled in sleep on a blue-striped towel, snuggled into each other as trustingly as pups. That they'd been doing more than sleeping on the beach was obvious. Smears of semen had dried glossily on the woman's slender thighs. With a sense of unreality, he noticed she was a true redhead.

Oh God, he thought, half surprised he didn't say it aloud.

His mate was married. She wore a gold band and diamond on her left hand.

Ty jerked to a halt beside him, drawing Anso's stupefied gaze to his. Of all the problems they'd imagined, this had not been one. Ty didn't speak any more than Anso, but his eyes were definitely saying *what now*?

What now indeed. His mate was married, and clearly not unhappily. If Anso's mother had been miserable in Oceana, what would stealing this woman from her spouse do to her? Anso *couldn't* take her, and yet he couldn't not.

As if they'd been dragged there, his eyes returned to his sleeping mate. How delicate she looked—and how kind, cradling her sleeping husband's head against her breast. It almost hurt to witness their entwined pose, to see how much they loved each other. Distantly, he sensed Ty looking at them too. Considering who Ty's parents were, Anso could imagine what he was thinking.

His friend's feelings didn't matter as much as they usually did. Faint lines curved around his mate's mouth, due to her smiling a bit in sleep. Anso was glad she was old enough to have laugh lines. A teenager wouldn't have suited him at all. Pleased, his eyes drank her in like food: her soft round breasts, her muscular curving legs. She had the velvety skin wereseals weren't ever born with, as if one-natured humans were more touchable than normal folk.

Despite his dismay at finding her with a companion, Anso's blood hadn't stopped thundering through his cock. The thought of touching this lovely woman sent an itchy tingle through his balls. There was only one way to solve this, one narrow strait through which all of them might pass safely.

"Take them both," he said harsh and low to his men.

CHAPTER FIVE

OLIVIA dreamed someone was easing her off the towel and lifting her in his arms. The sensation was very pleasant, like being a child again. Probably James was carrying her back to the cottage.

Smiling at his sweetness—because her husband's lower back wasn't twenty anymore—Olivia opened her eyes.

Life as she knew it turned upside down.

A stranger was carrying her. He was quite good looking, his dark gold hair slicked around his head by water, his cheekbones broad and slanting like a Russian prince. His eyes looked straight into hers. They were an unlikely shade of blue, the same shade as the London blue topaz necklace James had given her last Christmas. Olivia doubted she could have matched the color even with contacts. She didn't think it was her imagination that the stranger's eyes were glowing.

They stared at her adoringly.

Alarming as all this was, it didn't compare to the shock she felt at her own reaction. Neither terror nor outrage seized her. Instead, she felt precisely as she had when she was a freshman at NYU, the first time James grinned at her in the hall outside her dorm room.

This was her man. The one who'd keep her safe and help make her life a joy. The one she wanted to sleep with, the one she hoped would father her child. She and James had tried to have another after Violet, but a little brother or sister hadn't been in the cards. Some primitive part of her sensed this man could fulfill that wish. Her pussy squeezed with excitement, heated moisture dewing its walls. In a single heartbeat, she was fully aroused, her clit swelling like a berry between her labia.

As she recalled, James had been an instant panty-wetter too.

"Holy crap," she whispered, realizing she didn't have panties now—or a single other scrap of clothing.

The stranger's adoring regard softened. "Don't be afraid," he murmured tenderly. "I've no intention of hurting you."

He had a slight British accent, which Olivia admitted to having a weakness for. That weakness didn't explain why her hand lay quiescent on the stranger's rock-hard chest. He wasn't very hairy. The fine gold peach fuzz that overlay his pecs felt a bit like fur. She should have been struggling to get away, but all she could think was that she wanted to pet him. Olivia's mouth fell open in horror at herself. James was her husband—her soulmate, if there was such a thing. She'd never in her life wanted to cheat on him.

The stranger's gaze slid to the pebbled tips of her breasts, which had drawn so tight they ached. "I know how you feel," he growled, his voice as low as before. "I'd kill to make love to you right now."

That startled Olivia into shoving at his chest. "I don't—"

And then she heard James wake up. She jerked around in the stranger's arms so that she could see. Three big naked men were struggling with her naked husband, who hadn't quite made it to his feet. James was trying to fight, but they had him at a disadvantage, both in numbers and experience. James was fit, but he was no trained warrior—as these men seemed to be.

Navy seals? she wondered, but that didn't make much sense. Forster Media specialized in corporate presentations—flash and sparkle for shareholders or employees. They had no sensitive accounts. She and James had never worked for their government or anyone else's. No one from any military organization would bother coming after them.

"Olivia!" James cried frantically as he wrestled with his attackers. "Put my wife down, you cocksucker!"

I should say something, Olivia thought. *Do something*. But she'd gone quiet in the stranger's arms again, as if her body knew something her mind did not. It was like being in a dream where you'd forgotten how to scream. The three naked attackers were wrapping her husband in some sort of semi-sheer white tape, trapping his arms so he'd stop fighting. The man who held her observed this as if their actions were no surprise. She concluded he was in charge.

"What are they doing to him?" she forced her mouth to say.

"Olivia!" James cried again.

"Silence him," the man who held her said.

Olivia expected them to gag him. They had that tape after all. Instead, one of the men, whose skin bore the faintest pattern of leopard spots, clapped his hands overtop James's ears and kissed him full on the mouth.

Their profiles faced Olivia. She could see the spotted man shoving at James's lips with his tongue. James resisted that for about six seconds.

And then he kissed him back.

The shocks were piling on faster than Olivia could absorb. Did James know this man? Was this some sort of joke? But it couldn't be. Pranks weren't James's style at all. She also didn't think he'd be moaning with arousal in front of her—not if he could help himself. That he couldn't help himself seemed clear. Bound though he was, he was pushing back at the spotted man, forcing the kiss deeper, which the other man appeared eager to allow. Beneath all this, her husband's cock was swelling, the curve of it lifting, straightening, then thrumming thick as a flagpole toward the tape that wrapped his torso. Olivia knew James liked bondage, but more than that had to be behind his reaction.

She should have been hurt or frightened—especially with her recent suspicions about his sexual past. Perversely, Olivia thought she'd never seen anything as erotic as those men frenching each other. Her pussy was so aroused it hurt.

"We've gone mad," she murmured. Someone at the grocery must have spiked their root beer.

"Ty's from a noble line," said the man who held her. "Among other things, he has an aphrodisiac in his saliva. Once his hormones absorb into your . . . husband's blood, it will make traveling easier."

Olivia had no idea what he meant by this. She returned her attention to him and was caught again in the spell of his deep blue eyes. "You didn't kiss me," she said.

Her captor smiled and—oh God—he looked so beautiful her heart momentarily stopped. His strong arms tightened under her. "No, I didn't. I guess you naturally want me."

"I think my husband secretly likes men." The instant the words were out, she wanted to take them back. She shouldn't be blurting out their private business.

Her captor's smile deepened. "Luckily, my friend Ty won't object."

"What do you want with us?" her sanity finally permitted her to demand. "Who the hell are you?"

Her captor's face sobered. "I am His Majesty, King Anso the First of Oceana, and you are my mate in blood. I'm sorry not to take more time to explain, but your husband's shouts may have attracted attention. I think we'd best get this show on the road."

He had amazing diction for a kidnapper.

What show? she thought belatedly. *And what road?*

The second question was answered when King Anso—if that really was his name—began striding into the water's edge.

"No!" she cried, this at last awakening fear in her. Olivia liked *gazing* at the ocean. The roughness of the surf always frightened her.

Her captor's steps faltered but didn't stop. "No?"

"I'm afraid of the waves."

He did stop then, the choppy water splashing up his naked thighs, spraying her just a bit. She realized he was hard. As her weight had shifted, the silky tip of his cock bumped her bare bottom. Lord he was huge, like, porn star huge—an observation that filled her with a very inappropriate curiosity. She squirmed over an assortment of mortifying responses. Maybe worst of all, she couldn't look away from his beautiful blue eyes. She knew her own gaze was pleading. Some part of her wanted *him* to forgive her phobia.

"I love to swim," she clarified stupidly. "I just have nightmares about drowning in the ocean."

His eyes flared with the strange glow she'd noticed earlier. "You're with me now. You never have to be afraid of the sea again."

~

Anso was amazed his mate had barely struggled—and also reassured. On some level, she must know what he was to her, and her instincts calmed her body.

Holding her in his arms was extraordinary. It was as if, unbeknownst to him, his life had been in pieces until that moment, and she'd drawn the fragments into a whole. He loved that her eyes kept coming back to his, even loved the confused pucker between her dark red brows.

"Tell me your name," he said.

"Olivia," she murmured dazedly.

"Olivia," he repeated, thinking it beautiful. "We're almost at the depth where I can't hold you above the breakers. I need to kiss you now."

Her mouth fell open, so he took it.

A groan ripped from him at his first taste of her. This was a woman's mouth. This was *his* woman's mouth. He pushed his tongue into it gently. Oh she was soft—petite and succulent. His mouth watered.

She didn't know it, but her fate was sealed the second she swallowed.

"Mmph," she said, perhaps a teensy bit protesting.

Anso changed angles and went deeper.

As he did, she started kissing him back. Her response was tentative but miraculous to him. Maybe his hormones hit her. Maybe she simply couldn't resist the lure of her bloodmate. All he knew for certain was that his prick clanged between his legs, ringing for him to attend a life or death appointment. He swung her around to face him, her cushy naked body pressing his full on.

She liked that too. They moaned down each other's throats. Olivia kissed him harder.

A wave crashed over their heads without her noticing. Anso dove them under the next together, smoothly submerging them. Olivia didn't stiffen, perhaps because she was busy winding her arms and legs around him.

Fuck, he thought, wanting to do precisely that more than he'd have thought possible. His hand dragged down her back to clamp over her little ass. This squashed his near-bursting length into her soft belly. The pressure almost made him come, the stab of pleasure through his groin intense.

Fortunately for his pride, the next wave's under-torque spun them around like kids rolling down a hill. Olivia struggled and pushed back from his mouth, then realized she was still breathing.

The expressions that crossed her pretty face were comical.

"Wha—" The last land air from her lungs came out in a stream of bubbles.

Holding her firmly with one arm, Anso stroked her cheek with his other hand. The red waves of her hair spread out in the currents like a portrait of Temptation. He knew then she'd always be his siren.

"You're breathing water now," he explained. "It's a gift our nobles can share with other races."

"What the fuck race are you?"

He understood her impulse to curse. "I am King Anso the First, ruler of the wereseals."

"Wereseals."

"Yes."

"Wereseals."

Her disbelief frayed his patience. "Yes."

She narrowed her sunny blue eyes at him. If he hadn't been holding her too close to do it, he suspected she'd have crossed her arms. "I'm dreaming."

"You're not."

"Then I'm drugged."

"Maybe a little, but not the way you mean." He wrapped both arms behind her waist, gratified by the way she once again forgot to struggle. "We're bloodmates. Our bodies can't help calling to each other. That's how I tracked you so far from my home."

"I'm married."

"I know." He tried to sound calm. "I'm very sorry about that."

He'd have been more upset if her calves hadn't been sliding restlessly behind his, as if even in the midst of this argument, her body longed to open itself to him. He fought the groan that wanted to rise in his chest.

"What do you want with me?" she asked.

He wished he had more experience with females. Perhaps there was a more romantic, or at least a smoother way to put this.

"I want to mate you. Need to, actually. You're the best possible mother for my children. And I'd like to make you my queen."

This last declaration didn't impress her. Olivia rolled her eyes. "What if I refuse?"

Since her knees had crept to his waist, he didn't take offense. "Refusing is no longer an option."

"Look, buddy—"

"Try releasing me if you doubt my words."

She tried, she truly did, but she could no more let go of him than he could have let go of her. The more she tried to resist, the more her hands slid over him, her touch-hunger impossible to fight. The craving for skin-to-skin contact was a defensive mechanism. Her body wouldn't allow her to do something so against its basic interests as putting distance between them.

"Oh God," she gasped, the pain of longing twisting her face.

Anso took pity on them both and cupped one of her sharp-tipped breasts. A quiver ran down her body as she arched to him and whimpered. Anso understood how she felt. Her velvet skin seemed to bespell his palm. As he caressed the curve, sculpting it in his hold, the scent of her arousal filtered strongly into the saltwater. She blinked when he rubbed his thumb across her nipple.

"Oh God," she repeated.

Her hand was slithering around his hipbone, heading straight for his cock. Anso stopped it reluctantly. "We need to leave. We'll be safer once we reach the tunnel. I'll take care of you then."

"Take care of me?" she asked faintly.

He looked deeply into her eyes, his own glowing brightly enough to illuminate tiny motes in the water between their faces. "I'm going to penetrate you. I'm going to spill my seed in your pussy and make you come. Then I'm probably going to do it a lot more times."

Her mouth fell open in amazement, her cheeks turning raspberry.

"Climb onto my back," he ordered before he succumbed to his painful need to kiss her again. "If I hold you like this much longer, I'm going to make love to you here and now."

She jerked and moved behind him a bit more quickly than he could be grateful for. Annoyed, though he told himself it was for the best, he reached back to coax her legs around his waist once more. They clamped on him tightly, but she didn't grind her pussy against his back.

Never mind that, he thought. He knew the desire to rub herself over him would drive her crazy soon. The crazier she got, the easier she'd be to take once they reached the protected tunnel under the sea floor. Force was something he never wanted to resort to. To his relief, she wrapped her arms around his chest without being told, leaving his arms free to swim. Her cheek she tucked close against his neck, her soft breasts flattened against his skin. When she wriggled just a little, as if her nipples were itching, his mood brightened.

No doubt it was childish, but he also appreciated her not asking where her husband and the others had swum off to.

~

At first, Olivia tried to keep track of where they went. She was always the navigator on family road trips. Sadly, there were no street signs or K-Marts to serve as landmarks. When they veered away from the shoreline, the terrain became even less decipherable.

It didn't help that the man whose back she clung to was incredibly distracting. His immense erection thrust up from his groin above where her calves were crossed. She kept wanting to stroke it, to see if it really was the best part of him to touch. He kept steering her hand away before it got there. Olivia wasn't sure she could stand being put off much longer.

The frustration in her body grew by insane degrees, until her pussy felt like it was on fire. Helpless not to, she rocked her pelvis against his glutes, which were conveniently tight and hard.

"Christ," he said after a minute of this treatment. "We're almost there. Just hold on a bit longer."

Olivia ground her teeth together. If this was a dream, shouldn't she be allowed to come? She rubbed her mouth across his shoulder, searching out his pointed nipples with roaming hands. He moaned when she found the little projections and rubbed them. His body writhed so extravagantly in her hold that his swimming momentarily lost its astonishing momentum.

"O-livia," he growled.

Something about him saying her name, as if they knew each other, shocked her into stopping. He shuddered when she did.

"Thank you," he panted.

Was it panting when you were underwater?

He hadn't been lying about them being close to their goal. The tunnel turned out to be a giant hatch set into the side of a rocky trench in the ocean floor. Though the entry was sheltered, Olivia didn't understand how it could fail to be noticed. They weren't that far from the coast, and the sunlit surface of the water was still visible above them. That sparkle grew more distant as Anso allowed their combined weight to sink down in front of the immense door.

He must have sensed the tension this spurred in her. He rubbed one of the arms she'd wrapped tightly around him. "The hatch is cloaked by magic. You can see it because you're with me. We'll be perfectly safe inside."

Of course the tunnel was cloaked by magic. What else could have done the trick? Anso checked a cryptic readout beside a control panel. That wasn't magic. That was a computer.

"The others have gone in already," he said.

The others meaning James. The reminder of her husband's existence should have done a better job of subduing her hormones. Her ability to think was overwhelmed by Anso's promise to take care of her in there. Anso punched a code into the panel, his fingers fumbling as if all this rattled him too.

At last, he hit the right sequence of numbers. A smaller door swung open within the larger one. Anso pushed away from the panel and swam them both through it. Lights lit the huge space inside, long twinkly lines of brightness that curved away into the distance. The walls of the tunnel were gray but not concrete. She thought they might be high tech ceramic tile. The tiles looked wet, which of course they were. They glistered as if they contained mica. Though the passage was currently empty, it was large enough to accommodate multiple lanes of car traffic.

James and the others were nowhere in sight.

Anso's lungs went in and out faster. Olivia became aware that the small door had shut behind them. As closely as she clung to her captor's back, she couldn't help but hear him swallow.

"Olivia," he said, sounding strained as he gave her forearm another rub. "You and I both know this is going to happen. Our bodies have decided that for us. If you prefer, however, there's a maintenance room for staff farther down. We could go there and be more comfortable."

If Olivia waited another second, she was going to combust. She ran her hand down his rippling abs and took hold of his swollen cock, which was even silkier than she expected. As its unbelievable texture registered on the greedy nerves of one palm, she cupped and squeezed his ball sac with the other.

The back of Anso's head hit her shoulder, his neck and spine arching as she stroked. His hand slapped over hers to drag her grip to his tip.

"Oh Lord." He pushed it downward and up again. "Don't do that. I *have* to come inside you."

Before she could point out *he* was moving her hand, he wrenched around in her arms. Since Olivia was somewhat reluctant to let go of what she held, he probably hurt himself as he turned.

She wasn't sure that mattered to him.

Anso kissed her, and she kissed him back, both their tongues immediately dueling. His groan of pleasure-pain was thrilling, and the octopus-like quality of his arms. She thought she'd seen him move fast before, but when he suddenly swam her into the tunnel wall, his velocity stunned her.

"Yes," she groaned, loving that now she was braced for him to shove against her. Her hand reclaimed the prodigy he'd squashed between their bellies. God, it was like her hand was in love with touching him. She pushed the pad of her thumb around his meltingly smooth crest. His precum must have been thicker than most men's. It didn't dissipate in the saltwater. She rubbed it back and forth until it coated him.

"God," he said and shoved two long fingers inside of her.

Her mouth formed an *O*, but no sound came out. His fingers stroked her, gently, deeply, and it felt so good she forgot how much she wanted to play with his big penis.

"I'm sorry," he said harshly next to her ear. "I want this to be enjoyable for you, but I've never had a woman before."

He could have set a bomb off inside her pussy and not had as great an effect on her. Her inner muscles clenched around his fingers, abruptly desperate for a different part of him to fill her.

"Put your cock in me. Make me your first woman."

He jerked back to stare at her.

She didn't care how crazy she sounded. "*Now*," she insisted.

His deep blue eyes flared white, the flash almost bright enough to blind her. He pulled his fingers from her body, grabbed her upper thighs in both hands, and wrenched them apart. She reached for his cock to put it where it belonged. The crest felt large against her.

Good thing she'd lubricated it really well.

He grunted and shoved once as a kind of test. Finding no resistance, he thrust to her end in a single stroke.

Olivia couldn't have said which of them was happier about that.

He made a strangled sound at being surrounded, then pulled out halfway so he could plunge in again. "Jesus. You feel . . . God, I don't even know how to describe it."

Thankfully, he stopped trying. It wasn't long before his half plunges turned to full length pumping, maximizing the smooth thick drag of every inch of him against every inch of her.

Apparently, he felt compelled to accompany this activity with groans of praise. Olivia was right there with him on the overwhelming excitement scale. Either of them could have gone in two seconds, but neither wanted to let go. This was too delicious to cut short. Anso stretched one arm toward a metal handhold sticking out from the glittering gray wall, using it to power more forcefully into her. Perceiving the benefit of this, Olivia grabbed it too, their white-knuckled fingers wrapped next to each other. They were anchored well and good then. They could fuck as hard and fast as they were able.

Their gazes met even as their bodies jolted. Olivia had the strangest impression that her eyes were glowing too.

"Thank . . . you," he said, his words broken by the force of their impacts. "I need you . . . with me on this." His eyelids squeezed shut as some blissful sensation threatened to send him over. His second hand tightened on her bottom to better guide her movements. "Please. Come with me, Olivia. I can't . . . I can't—"

She quickened her thrusts, which might or might not have been what he intended. Normally, she needed clitoral stimulation, but her pleasure was so sharp she felt like she was almost coming already.

Anso was closer than almost.

"Liv," he cried, high and wild.

He slammed into her as his seed flooded out, his eyes flashing bright as his head pitched back with ecstasy. His semen detonated her sexual nerves, an explosion of pleasure no force on earth could have stopped. A climax this strong couldn't be natural. Her inner muscles gripped him with such violence she feared she'd hurt him.

But maybe *fear* wasn't the word either of them would have chosen.

He growled, pleased, as her sheath clamped his cock. His hips jammed tight to hers as he continued to shoot in her. That felt amazing too, delicious spurts of heat that contrasted perfectly with the cool water. His threat that he was going to make her pregnant didn't trouble her at all. In that moment, another child was her dearest wish. *His* child, a priceless gift from the other man she adored.

Her eyes flew open at her own thoughts.

His exotically handsome face was inches away, its muscles gradually relaxing as the fervor of his bliss faded. He'd stopped thrusting while he came, but now he pulled back gently to his flare and glided in again.

He was only a bit softer than before.

Olivia must have relaxed as well. Her hand was stroking up and down his spine, from his muscular shoulders to his tight buttocks. Her calves slid up and down the back of his legs the same way she liked to do after she'd had sex with James.

"You okay?" asked the stranger who'd literally rocked her world. His eyes were as warm and loving as any she'd ever seen. For all she knew, hers looked the same.

Olivia swallowed and nodded.

He smiled, the fingers of his free hand fanning around and fondling her bottom. Olivia realized two things simultaneously: a) she was meeting his lazy thrusts, and b) they both still clutched the metal handgrip beside her head.

"You look like you were hit by a train," he said.

Olivia cleared her throat. If his cock were that that train's engine, one had definitely hit her. She squirmed around the hot pole inside her, causing Anso to suck in a . . . a breath of water, she supposed. His cock twitched thicker between her walls, stretching them pleasantly. Apparently, he liked the constriction. He gave an extra push deeper.

"Um," he said, suddenly sounding less sure of himself. "Do you think you could stand to go again straight away? I mean, I *think* I could let you rest a bit, but I'd rather, you know, scratch the itch some more without waiting."

His hopeful words were all it took for a renewed ache to coil around her sex. Olivia wanted to groan. She *couldn't* want him again. He'd just given her—God forgive her—the best orgasm of her life. At that thought, the itch he'd spoken of flared in her.

She had to have it rubbed again or she'd die.

"Shit," was all she managed to say aloud.

Anso's eyes took on the brightness of compassion. "You think you're being unfaithful for wanting me."

"I am. I love James."

He flinched, which made her feel confusingly guilty. "Olivia, I promise I'll do my best to make sure he's happy too."

Olivia pressed her lips together and looked away from him. She wasn't sure how she felt about what making James happy might entail.

"We're going to do this again," he warned. "Bloodmates need regular intercourse. We can have sex now, or we can have it later, but trust me we'll have it. Lots and lots of it, whether we like it or not, for as long as we both shall live."

His tone had turned oddly grim. When she returned her gaze to his, his expression was guarded. Was he hoping she'd fall in love with him? Was he as much of a heart-and-flowers guy as her husband?

Lord help me, she prayed, aware that the responsibility for her decisions was going to be hers. Now or later might be a small choice, but it was a choice all the same.

"Take me now," she said with a sigh that wasn't wholly regretful.

As his blue eyes widened, she pressed her mouth to his.

CHAPTER SIX

JAMES Forster was so horny he couldn't think. Okay, he could, but he didn't want to. This whole . . . double abduction scene had to be a nightmare.

He didn't understand why Olivia hadn't fought that cocksucker—that *king*, according to the man who'd kissed him. James's kidnapper had shoved him into a break room inside the underwater tunnel, and was even now performing the swimmer's equivalent of pacing. The speed with which he zoomed from one tiled wall to the other was eye-popping. James didn't know why, but he'd sent the other two men ahead, leaving him and James alone.

Ty, the man called himself. God help James, but he was hot. Tall and well proportioned, with muscles that were for more than show. His chest was the sort women swooned over, his butt the definition of a nice ass. In their way, his legs were as sexy as Olivia's.

James tried not to picture nuzzling his way up them.

He'd entertained the occasional fantasies about having sex with men. They troubled him a little, but he thought he knew where they came from. Since the day they'd met, Olivia had gotten him too revved up to question that he was straight. Apart from one buddy he'd traded hand jobs with in high school, he'd never had sex with another male.

That seemed like an oversight now.

The Man From Atlantis had a huge hard-on. James could hardly keep his hands off his own, given that it itched like crazy and felt three inches longer than normal. He hung by the wall, out of the other man's way, one arm crooked through a handy sway strap to keep from floating around. Ty had removed his gag and bindings once they'd entered this room. James supposed it didn't matter if he screamed down here. That Ty could overpower him any time he wanted he'd already learned.

"You're making me dizzy," James complained to his captor.

He shouldn't have thought that word, *captor*. The reminder that he was a prisoner sent a shudder of excitement down his spine, one that didn't stop until it zinged out his cock.

As if it had taken him a second to hear, Ty stopped whizzing back and forth. He looked at James with his strange burning yellow eyes.

"Anso is fucking your wife," he said, striving for a cool demeanor he didn't quite pull off. "It's going to be the best sex they've had. No matter how much she loves you, she's going to want more of her new favorite drug. Now's your chance to work on getting used to that."

He had the voice of a British rocker, his looks appropriately golden. Golden hair, golden skin, slightly darker golden spots gilded over him. His pubic thatch resembled fur, the hair pelt-like rather than curly. His cock stood straight up from it. Had all that swimming back and forth felt good on his skin? Was that why Ty wasn't touching himself? James wanted to touch him. James wanted to lick him up and down like a freezer pop. To him, Ty's prick was as beautiful as his face.

James wrenched his gaze away with an effort. Jesus, how long had been staring? He focused on Ty's eyes.

"Are you in love with the king?" he asked.

Ty blanched, his golden skin going pale. "Get real," he said, recovering a second too slowly to be believed. "I'm Lord Tykon, the Great Whore of Oceana. I'll never settle for one partner."

Olivia often complimented James on being a good listener. James was never as impressed by this as she was. He knew he was naturally interested in other people's stories—born nosy, he supposed. In spite of the situation, this man's story intrigued him.

"The great whore," he repeated. "Do people pay you to sleep with them?"

"No, they don't pay me," he snapped angrily. "What's the matter with you? Your wife is fucking another man. Are you so dickless that doesn't bother you?"

"It bothers me," he said, though he felt oddly calm. Maybe his CEO half was coming to the fore. What was done was done. He and Olivia had to find a way out of this, whatever *this* was.

Ty stared at him. The other man was hanging there in the water like he was used to it. His gaze descended to the stingingly hard erection that bobbed between James's thighs. The corners of his sensual mouth turned up. "That boner should have worn off by now. I kissed you a while ago."

James blushed hot enough for his cheeks to burn.

Ty's smile broadened mockingly. "Maybe you *are* interested in payback for that pretty king-fucking wife of yours."

James should have been furious. Instead, a thrill surged through his pounding veins as a quart more blood squeezed into his penis.

"Jesus," Ty breathed, watching that. "I could eat you up for breakfast."

And then he put his words into action. He zipped to James in that insanely speedy way and gripped James's hips in hard golden hands.

"Yum," he said, licking his beautiful spoiled-boy mouth.

James meant to push him away, meant to say *get off me* or *what the fuck do you think you're doing?* But the road to hell was paved with *meant to*. Somehow, his free hand fell to the back of Ty's gilded head and pulled him closer. When Ty's sleek tongue swept across his glans, James shook so hard he could have been suffering from a fit. When Ty engulfed the knob in his big warm mouth, the instant explosion of pleasure shoved him to the verge of coming.

"Not yet," Ty growled. To enforce this, he gripped the base of James's ball sac and pulled down sharply.

The pain forestalled him from ejaculating, but not from enjoying what Ty was doing with his mouth. Possibly, given James's kinks, the pain made him enjoy it more. He'd never had a man suck him off. Ty's mouth was harder and bolder than a woman's.

It also took more of him.

Moaning and unable to stop himself, James bucked his hips forward.

"That's it," Ty praised, rising up to drag his warm tongue around the head. "Give me more of that. Fuck my mouth like you're going to die."

He was going to die, and soon, if Ty didn't yank his balls down again. James dug his fingers deeper into Ty's hair, which floated teasingly around them. His body was really get into this. Ty set up a steady rhythm. Up and down. Sucking and licking. Wonderful sensations gathered in James's groin, like weights were massing there. He remembered Olivia kissing the king as he'd held her above the waves. She hadn't been resisting. She'd been eating at his mouth like she did with James if it had been a while.

Did Ty and the king fuck each other? Was the ruler of Oceana truly a cocksucker? That made more pictures in his mind. A cry escaped his chest as Ty's head started bobbing faster. James was writhing now, unable to control himself. The currents caressed his body with each movement. God, he'd never experienced a rush like this. His balls were going to turn inside out.

He clenched his teeth and tried to hold onto the pleasure.

He might have succeeded if he hadn't opened his eyes to watch his captor going down on him. There was a reason Ty hadn't tugged his balls. His right hand was occupied with his own erection, pumping it up and down as fast as he'd been swimming. The head of his cock was reddened, the shaft veiny and swollen. Even as James watched, precum welled from the slit.

His scalp prickled so strongly, it could have been peeling off. James gasped a second before he came. Ty's answering grunt around his penis said he was coming too. That really kicked James around the bend. His ejaculation shot out so hard it hurt—and James enjoyed that fine. Images rolled across his mental movie screen as ecstasy roared through him. Olivia coming. The handsome king suckling her breasts. The four of them forming an eight-legged monster as they fucked each other in someone's bed.

James's climax spiked until he was screaming silently.

The pain-pleasure turned to heaven as Ty sucked down every drop.

When the earth settled back into place, Ty leaned his golden brow against James's belly. Slowly, James forced his fingers to relax in Ty's hair. Ty was probably lucky he hadn't yanked him bald. He didn't know what to say. *Thank you* seemed as inappropriate as *what the hell was that?*

He knew what it had been: the hardest orgasm ever, a release he felt like he'd been craving for ten lifetimes. As dearly as he loved Olivia, and as incredible as sex between them was, she'd never wrung him out like that.

The peculiar thing was, thinking about her brought his exhausted cock to stirring life again.

I've gone mad, he thought. Stark raving sex-crazed mad.

This wasn't something he'd expected to do at forty-five.

Perhaps shock caused his hand to fall to Ty's bowed shoulder. The gentle touch caused the other man to jerk back.

Ty rose stiffly, so much wariness in his eyes James couldn't help feeling sorry for him. In his experience, people with eyes like that hadn't been loved enough as children.

"We need to go," Ty said coolly. "Nico and Mark will have reached the palace by now."

There seemed no purpose in objecting. James was pretty sure he'd just taken Stockholm syndrome to a whole new level.

CHAPTER SEVEN

KING Anso had a private entrance into his palace, located in a gorgeous aquarium garden. Olivia might have admired the colorful fishes more if she hadn't been changing over from breathing water to breathing air. Suffice to say, the changeover was uncomfortable but quick. When she'd finished hacking out her lungs on her hands and knees in his depressurizing tube, Anso helped her up. He handed her a small silver cup to drink.

"Sip this," he said, steadying her shaking hand with his. "You don't want it to go down the wrong way."

No kidding, Olivia thought. She was relieved to discover the drink wasn't alcohol but something cooling and slightly sweet. It soothed her throat perfectly. Having Anso coddle her felt like her first morning after with James. Anso hovered on the edge of fussing just like James had. She found it awkward and yet weirdly endearing.

"It gets easier," he said. "The first time is always the hardest."

She knew he didn't mean the first time one cuckolded one's husband. Given that she'd initiated their second no-holds-barred erotic session, she felt almost as guilty as if that had been his meaning. She nodded in acknowledgment, her eyes on her bare wet feet and her head hanging.

Anso's hand settled gingerly on her shoulder. "I know this must be difficult for you, now that our heat has backed off. I promise you weren't imagining the connection between us."

She nodded again, unwilling to look at him for fear she'd feel the same magnetic pull as those other times. Were wereseals like vampires? Could they compel you with their eyes?

Oh God. She was jolted by a new possibility. If wereseals were real, what else was?

She almost looked up, almost drew breath to ask. Stubbornly, she closed her mouth. There was a sensible explanation for all of this.

Anso squeezed her shoulder and then let go. "I guess—" He looked behind him at the old-fashioned submarine-type hatch. "I guess we'll go in. Your husband and Ty are most likely in my apartments."

At least he was still calling James her husband.

His handprint was required to open the hatch to his rooms—to safeguard his royal person, she assumed. Did getting out require a handprint too? Would she have the nerve to attempt an escape if she got the chance? They'd swum quite a ways to reach here, and at Anso's super speed. The exact length of the tunnel she couldn't judge, or what underwater perils they'd avoided by taking it. Olivia always had to leave the room when James watched *Shark Week*. She seriously doubted she'd like meeting them in real life.

On the bright side, she and James didn't have to find their way back to Long Island. They only had to reach ordinary humans. Anso's people lived in concealment. Probably they wouldn't want to expose themselves. Olivia simply had to make sure she was never, ever alone near the sea again.

Anso sighed as he tugged the heavy hatch open.

They stepped—still dripping—into a handsome office. The color scheme was dramatic. Striking silver eel patterns danced across black walls, and silvery-gold portholes provided views of the water garden they'd just left. The mostly scarlet furnishings were good quality antiques—shabby chic for people with long histories and high incomes. The floor was a shiny glasslike black stone whose smoothness delighted her bare feet.

She realized Anso was watching her take in her surroundings.

"Many things here will be what you're used to," he said. "Our cultures aren't entirely alien."

She looked at him, trying to gauge his mood. *Cautious* was the best description she came up with.

"Anso," she began. He said her name at the same time. Before they could sort out who'd speak first, a knock sounded on the door.

"Sire," said a veddy British voice. "If I might take the liberty, I brought Her Majesty something to wear."

Her Majesty. Olivia's brows lifted. Anso pulled a face like he hadn't meant for this to happen, then went to open the paneled door. He didn't crack it far enough for Olivia to see who was there, a consideration she should have been grateful for. She *was* in her birthday suit. Anso accepted a small bundle from his unseen male caller.

"Thank you, Harrison," he said, more formal than he was when he spoke to her. "I take it the others have arrived?"

"Lord Tykon and his companion are in the blue salon."

"Very good. If you'd be so kind, please order everyone a meal."

Olivia's stomach growled. She guessed she'd . . . worked off the sandwiches she and James had eaten at their eons-ago picnic. Anso must have heard the reaction. He was smiling faintly when he passed her the pile of clothes.

"I hope this isn't like one of those pirate books," she said unthinkingly.

Anso had the gift of quirking just one eyebrow. "Pirate books?"

Because Olivia's accountant nature was incapable of giving half explanations, she assumed a pirate voice. "Wench, put on this low-cut gown. I want to see how you look in it."

Evidently, the king was acquainted with these stories. Anso's grin slanted up on the opposite side from his eyebrow, an expression that made him look like the naughtiest boy in the neighborhood. He'd been so serious till now that it startled her. "It's a lounging robe. Perfectly modest."

It was more than modest, it was the most amazing garment she'd ever slid her arms into. The robe's silk was cool and heavy, the embroidery clearly created by an artist. The silver eels that swam across the rich blue cloth seemed to writhe. Olivia tied the waist belt and stroked the pattern, amazed by how velvety smooth the stitching was.

"Vitul family symbol," Anso informed her. "Done in enchantable electrum thread. The robe is spelled to protect you from magical attacks."

Olivia's jaw dropped and hung open.

"I'm not expecting attacks," he hastened to assure her, misunderstanding her reaction. "I'm sure my people will accept you, just as they did my mother. In any case, the palace hasn't seen a misuse of magic incident in years."

"Magic," she said.

His brow furrowed before it cleared. "I thought you . . . Olivia, I'm a wereseal. We were both breathing underwater. I told you magic was what shielded the Helike Tunnel from discovery."

He had told her. She'd simply preferred to deny it.

"Vampires?" she burst out.

"What about them? Oh. You mean are they real? Yes, and a great many other creatures besides. Faeries. Elves. I've never met a weretiger; they don't like water, so they don't visit Oceana, but I hear they're wonderfully fierce and charming. Any race is welcome in the Pocket as long as they abide by fae law. Faeries are top dogs when it comes spells. They created the half-magic territory where most supes live. While the different city-nations rule themselves, the fae have the final say on what goes."

Because her knees felt a trifle wobbly, Olivia sat on a bright red couch. It was firm and comfortable. "Do they sparkle?"

"Vampires or faeries?" He flashed a grin when she gawked. "I saw that *Twilight* movie on the Import Channel."

"Faeries," she clarified breathlessly.

"Yes," he confirmed. "Quite beautifully, as it happens. Real faerie dust is a sight to see. Vampires don't sparkle, I'm afraid, though other things Outsiders write about them are true. *Outsiders* are what Pocket residents call people who live beyond our borders. It's bit of an insult, but we also call them mundanes."

Olivia pressed her palm to her pounding heart. Anso dropped beside her on the couch, his knee bumping hers as companionably as if they'd been lovers for years. He laid his hand gently on her leg. A warmth she couldn't control suffused her thigh.

"Wonders abound here, Olivia. More than you can imagine. I hope you'll open yourself to enjoying them."

She saw he meant it, which didn't make him less of a kidnapper.

"Could I speak to my husband now?" she asked politely.

He didn't wince, but his eyes searched hers. "Of course," he said. "Just let me grab my clothes."

When he rose, he was smart enough not to hold out his hand to her.

~

As near as Olivia could figure, Anso's rooms were laid out in a bending line around his octagonal coral garden. The color scheme for his salon was pale blue and silver, the furniture faded old French in style. The light that shone through the portholes made it look like a normal day outside, if you ignored the wavery reflections. The wereseals must have known how to replicate sunlight. A line of potted palmettos interspersed the round windows, their fronds lush and vigorous.

James was dressed in lace-up buckskin trousers and a full white shirt—which was either piratical or medieval, depending on your perspective. He leaped to his feet from a silver loveseat the instant Olivia and the king came in. He and Olivia hurried to each other and hugged tightly, a response she doubted either of them thought twice about, despite the eyes on them. To her relief, the love that welled up inside her was a strong as ever. This was her man, holding her in his arms. She closed her eyes and laid her cheek on his broad shoulder.

James's embrace tightened. "God, Olivia. I'm sorry."

This wasn't the most reassuring greeting he might have uttered, though—admittedly—Olivia owed her own apologies. She pushed back a little to look at him. His eyes were slumberous beneath their worry, his mouth relaxed. He looked the way he did after they'd had one of their Wild Sex Weekends—a tradition they'd established the first summer their daughter Violet begged them to let her attend band camp. They told their friends they were going out of town but really stayed in bed. Though Violet's skill with the trumpet never took off, the Wild Sex Weekends did.

To see that pleasured look on her husband's face when she hadn't put it there was a shock. Olivia shot a glance at the tall golden man who stood with his back to one of the round windows. Anso's friend met her gaze without expression. She did notice his fingers curling toward his palms, his hands not quite making fists. The black centers of his yellow eyes jumped bigger.

Because she couldn't very well ask him why, she returned her gaze to James. "Are you all right?"

"Yes. You?"

She nodded, and he stroked her damp hair behind her ear. His hair was dry. How long had she and Anso's . . . activities kept the others waiting here?

"He didn't hurt you?"

Olivia blushed and shook her head.

"All right," James said, seemingly to himself. He hugged her again. "All right."

She sensed James looking over her head at Anso, his hand stroking up and down her back through the blue silk robe. "She's still mine," he said to the king. "You can't undo that."

The calmness of his voice surprised her. Anyone who heard him would have recognized both truth and confidence in it.

"I'm hoping we can reach a compromise," Anso responded.

The man by the window bit out a terse swear word.

James tensed but didn't let her go. "My wife and I need some time alone."

Olivia didn't see Anso's measuring stare, just felt a buzzy prickle at the back of her neck. "Fine," the king said after a brief pause. "Meet us in the dining room when you're done. It's two doors further from this chamber."

James stood where he was, holding her, until the other men exited. Only then did he push back and clasp her hands.

"The spotted man sucked me off," he blurted. "And it felt really good."

In spite of everything, or perhaps because of everything, Olivia let out a breathy laugh. "You always did like to get your confessions out first thing."

"And you always prefer to think them through." His eyes asked questions his mouth wasn't ready to.

"We had intercourse," she said. "Twice. He didn't have to force me."

"And you enjoyed it? No." He wagged his head. "You don't have to tell me. Of course you enjoyed it. He's probably a stud and a half. You have that look you only get after one of our Wild Weekends. At least . . . At least tell me he used protection."

"I'm afraid he didn't." Olivia sighed resignedly. "At the time, I was hoping he'd give me a baby."

James closed his eyes, though he had to know she wasn't playing Hurt You Worse. Their doctors hadn't identified which of them was responsible for her problems conceiving a second time. After a few rounds of inconclusive tests, she and James decided they didn't want to know. The daughter they did have was more important to focus on.

James opened his eyes slowly. "Maybe he could get you pregnant. He is younger than me."

Olivia clasped his face, hating the hint of bitterness in his tone. "We need to get home. To our life. To Violet. I know she's grown up, but she still needs us."

James was silent for longer than she expected.

"You want to stay?" she burst out in disbelief.

"Not *want* to. Or not exactly. But I'm not sure we have a choice. That king fellow isn't going to let you go. He thinks you're his mate in blood. His friend claims you two need to have frequent sex, like it's an addiction."

"People recover from addictions."

"Yes," he said. "But until we figure out how to get out of here, we might have to play along."

"It wouldn't just be play. These people make us feel things."

"I know," he said.

They looked at each other. She watched his pulse throb at the side of his neck, just like her own was doing. This, at last, frightened them.

"I love you," he said huskily. "Nothing that's happened can change that."

"Even knowing I've been with another man?"

"Even that. I wish—" Her husband's voice sank lower. "I wish I'd seen you with him. I wish I'd been there to help."

This confession plain stunned her. James wanted to watch another man fuck her? A second pulse started thudding between her legs, where her clit was palpably swelling.

Her amazement must have been apparent. James's hazel eyes turned shy. "Wouldn't you have wanted to watch Ty go down on me?"

He called the man by his name, and that startled her as well. She ordered herself to be as honest as James had been. "Yes," she said. "When he kissed you at the beach, when I saw how much you enjoyed it, my body was excited."

"Then maybe we can get through this. This place is pretty amazing."

Genuine amusement rose in her. "My adventurer."

"You're one too, or you wouldn't have married me."

She stroked both sides of his face, his hint of dark afternoon bristle rasping her fingertips. One of them had to think like an accountant. Set terms and things like that. "We don't let them separate us."

"No," he agreed.

"And we get a message to Violet ASAP, enough to keep her from worrying."

"They have computers here. Maybe we can connect to the internet."

Olivia's heart fluttered, the emotional drag of fear changing to excitement. Had they really decided to do this? James's hands tightened on her upper arms. The sudden light in his eyes kicked her pulse faster.

"God," he groaned. "I would kill to fuck you right now."

His words weren't an exact match for Anso's from earlier, just close enough to send a shiver skipping like a pebble along her spine.

~

Kings, it seemed, didn't eat simple snacks. Thanks to the butler, a table large enough for twenty was at least half-filled with platters. James and Olivia were lucky they liked seafood, since every sort James could imagine was laid out—including an array of sushi.

Anso poured wine for everyone, seeming to enjoy playing host. "You have to have wine with fish," he said, a smile playing around his mouth as he noted James's surprise. "If the fish finds too much water in your stomach, he might start swimming around again."

It occurred to James that the king might be trying to get them drunk, but apart from his joke, he didn't push the alcohol. Anso and Ty both were well-mannered eaters, and apparently familiar with lots of forks. Neither was shy about digging in while their "guests" were still studying the offerings.

"Weres have fast metabolisms," Anso explained politely. "Yours are likely to increase as well. Both of you easily accepted the changes required to breathe water."

Because Anso was being civilized, James decided he could too. "Genetic changes, you mean. Do wereseals transmit a virus through saliva?"

And will it wear off? he wondered privately.

Anso offered Ty half the lobster meat from his claw. Ty accepted it without fuss, demonstrating that these two were indeed long-time companions. A sensation James didn't want to identify tightened in his chest.

His friend's stomach taken care of, Anso addressed James's question. "Our mages and scientists have tried to pin down the factor that causes the partial change, but neither has succeeded. We do know only royals can pass it on. It's been used a time or two to verify a particular king or queen's bloodline."

Olivia sat beside James, as Ty sat beside Anso. She scooped some red caviar and sour cream onto a cracker and slid it onto James's plate. His eyes widened, but he didn't think she was consciously echoing the king's gesture with the lobster, just being her usual thoughtful self. Oddly disconcerted, James spun the loaded cracker in a circle.

"If you—" He stopped, momentarily unable to push the question out. "If you and Olivia had a child . . ."

The king's deep blue gaze settled quietly on his. "The child would be a were, fully royal in every way. Another of the mysteries we're unable to explain."

Rocked by that answer, James took a swallow of the pale yellow wine. It was light and delicious, the product of a grape he couldn't identify. It managed to oil his brain into working.

What would he and Olivia do if she was pregnant by the time they escaped? Raise the child in seclusion? Keep it in a bathtub? Would they even be able to figure out what wereseals needed to grow up? Would the baby look human when it was born?

Something of his thoughts must have shown in his face.

"She's not pregnant," Anso said, setting down his own wineglass. "I can read her energy. I'll know the instant it happens."

Now James heard a male challenge in his voice, and no small amount of royal pride. James supposed he'd chapped Anso's ego when he'd said Olivia was still his.

"I *am* in my forties," Olivia put in. "Me having a baby might not be possible."

"It *is* possible," Anso said, turning stern eyes to her. "In truth, the ideal age for conceiving among our people is fifty or later. To breed before one is thirty is considered scandalous."

"But I'm not *your people*," Olivia pointed out.

James didn't think she meant to hurt him, but the king appeared taken aback by this statement.

"Oh boy." Ty laughed into his napkin.

"You have something to add?" Olivia asked him in the cool voice she'd invented for Violet's teenage rebellion stage.

Ty stopped laughing, but his eyes sparkled. "Only that you are his people. No one more so in the whole universe."

"Ty," Anso said warningly. "Give Olivia a chance to adjust."

"Adjust to what?" she huffed.

The currents in the room had definitely gotten strange. The king looked vaguely guilty, while Ty seemed both bitter and amused. Anso frowned at his friend, which caused him to guffaw outright.

The warm rolling sound made James's cock twitch inside his pirate pants.

"Adjust to what?" Olivia repeated.

"Ty only means you need not have health concerns. Living in Oceana is beneficial for most humans."

Anso wasn't lying, but he wasn't telling the entire truth. Twenty-five years in business had tuned James's antenna for evasions. He reached under the table to squeeze Olivia's hand. As was usually the case, she squeezed him back and calmed. They'd always steadied each other.

"I'm not forgetting this conversation," she said evenly to the king.

Someone rapped lightly on the door to the dining room. The king gave his man, Harrison, the okay to come in. Unlike the other men, the butler was resplendent in a black and white penguin suit. Thinking the term more appropriate here than ever, James smiled softly to himself.

"Sire," said the butler. "I'm afraid there's been a . . . leakage of information in the kitchens. The dessert course has arrived early, and Lady Ellice has come with it."

"Shit," said the king, which implied Lady Ellice wasn't a welcome guest. "Can't you get rid of her?"

"I can, sire. However—" If possible, the butler looked even more constipated. "You need to inform me if the judicious use of force is permissible. When I tried to guide her away before, she clung to the doorway."

"Good Lord!" Anso exclaimed as Tykon once again burst out laughing. Anso spun to him. "This isn't funny. Ellice must have lost her mind."

"Ellice is too smart to lose her mind." Ty's sardonic manner served nearly the same function as his laugh. "She's just guessed your iron is hot, and now is the time to strike."

Anso's bluffly handsome face turned pink. "My iron is spoken for!"

"She doesn't know that," Ty said.

"Crap," Anso said, then turned resignedly to Olivia. She was watching all this with interest. "I'm sorry. I had intended to . . . to . . ."

"- have time to sort things out?" Ty archly suggested.

"Yes, to have time to sort things out between . . . all of us . . . before news of your existence became public. Unfortunately, my cousin Ellice cannot—at least not decently—be manhandled out of here by my butler. I need to receive her. You should feel free to withdraw to the other room."

This last was said hopefully. James rolled his lips together to hide his smile. Olivia might be shy, but she was no doormat. No way would she make Anso's life that easy.

"I'd rather stay," she said demurely, her hands folded like a schoolteacher's on the table. "I'm sure it would be an honor to meet your relatives."

Anso heaved a weary sigh. "Fine. Just, please, don't pay Ellice too much mind. Your position is unassailable, as is . . . as is the respect with which I already regard you."

James suspected he and Olivia wore matching expressions of surprise. Naturally, Olivia deserved admiration. Olivia was awesome. The thing was, neither of them expected the king to be professing *respect* for her. Ty didn't either. His golden lashes blinked rapidly in front of his yellow eyes.

~

Olivia watched the occasional soap in the company break room on her lunch hour. Ellice's type wasn't hard to peg. She was the fake-sweet frenemy who snuck around causing trouble while pretending to be a nice person. Olivia was more relieved than she should have been that Anso didn't seem to buy what she was selling.

It was hard to respect a man who fell for that kind of thing.

Unaware she'd been seen through, Ellice tinkled out a bunch of baloney about how surprised she was that Anso would disappear without telling anyone. He *knew* he was supposed to file travel plans! *And* take a proper vehicle. Did he think this was the middle ages to be swimming God knew where under his own power? It was barely spring outside. She was *so* glad he'd returned safely, and wasn't it nice of the royal kitchens to help her prepare his favorite dessert for him?

That nonsense delivered, Lady Ellice got down to the brass tacks of what she'd come for: discovering why the hell another female was sitting at the king's table.

"I don't believe we've met," Lady Ellice said, holding out an elegant hand to her. Anso's cousin was taller and curvier than Olivia, but also very strong. Her sleeveless yet vaguely Victorian gown bared arms that could have competed in Olympic sports. Her eyes were the same gorgeous blue as Anso's—a family trait, she presumed. Despite her apparent strength, her skin was delicate enough to look translucent.

Olivia was childishly pleased her fingernails were currently in good shape. They got ragged if she neglected them. Accustomed to shaking hands with men, she gave Lady Ellice a firm but not over-assertive grip. "I'm Olivia. I'm a guest of King Anso."

"And a mundane," Lady Ellice observed, using the term Anso had warned her was insulting. "That's . . . extremely interesting. His Majesty didn't tell me he wanted to meet Outsiders."

It was too bad this wasn't a soap opera. Olivia would have asked Ellice if *she'd* have offered to introduce him to some.

"Olivia is being modest," Anso said.

They'd all risen for his cousin's entrance, and somehow none of them had sat again. Olivia suspected that would be too much like letting down their guard around his relative. Anso was standing a foot from Olivia. As he spoke, he took her hand. Olivia met the subtle question in his eyes with an equally subtle nod. She'd back his play if he wanted to make one. James would want her to. He'd never liked fake people.

Satisfied, Anso turned back to Ellice and dropped his bomb. "Olivia is my mate."

"*What?*" Ellice's horrified expression was the first honest one she'd displayed. "She can't be. She and this other mundane are married. They're wearing matching rings! I assumed you'd tired of balling Ty and brought her here to play with."

Olivia gave the woman credit for deductive reasoning—minus a couple debits for not watching her tongue better. Without looking away from Ellice, Anso's thumb caressed Olivia's knuckles.

"You're my cousin," he said calmly. "And royal in your own right. Nonetheless, it isn't proper for you to speak of your queen that way."

"My queen!" Ellice was sputtering with anger. "Never!"

"Our union has been consummated. It cannot be annulled."

Olivia hadn't known this, and it gave her a turn. She'd thought there had to be a ceremony—a ritual exchange of sardines at least. James hand came to brace the small of her back from the other side. The gesture was small, but Ellice noticed it.

"She's married," she repeated, her eyes pleading for him to concede her point.

"Similar cases have occurred in the course of our history. You know as well as I do that blood law rules supreme."

"But why would you mate a married woman?" Ellice's confusion seemed sincere. "You saw what happened between your mother and your father, and your mother's affections were free to give. Don't you want a queen who loves you?"

Whether Ellice loved Anso as much as she loved the idea of ruling was questionable. All the same, she knew him well enough that her question struck a nerve. Anso flinched, his hand jerking slightly in Olivia's.

"I shall love Olivia enough for both of us," he said.

His dignity—or perhaps it was humility—astonished Olivia. The way he pulled himself straighter and met his cousin's gaze caused her throat to tighten. But she couldn't promise to love him. That would make her as false as Ellice. She wasn't even planning to stay. She squeezed Anso's fingers instead, oddly comforted when his squeezed hers in answer.

"You're crazy," Ellice said. "And this isn't over."

That made Olivia smile, because it was precisely the parting shot a good soap opera villainess would fire off. Ellice's sharp eyes caught the flicker of movement at the corners of Olivia's mouth. She stopped and stared hard at her. Olivia just knew the other woman wanted to warn her not to get too comfortable.

Sadly, Anso's cousin had rediscovered her self-control. Lifting her chin—which really was regal—she strode without another word from the dining room.

"I thought you wanted dessert," Ty tossed after her. At some point, he'd sat back down in his chair. He lounged in it lazily, the perfect picture of bad-boy insouciance.

"Ty," Anso scolded. "There's no need to bait her."

"Sorry." Ty grinned so they knew he wasn't. "Watching Ellice get her comeuppance was the most fun I've had in a while." His eyes cut to James and gleamed brighter. "Make that the *second* most."

James made a low sound beside her. He covered it by clearing his throat and turning to address the king. "What will your cousenemy do?"

"My what?" Anso asked.

"You know, a frenemy but a cousin."

"Ah." James had made Anso smile, which pleased Olivia in complicated ways. "I expect my *cousenemy* is heading straight for the family lawyer."

"There *are* precedents for what you've done," Ty confirmed grudgingly. "William the Second's queen was a pre-married Outsider. And Conjugus the Magnificent's—though that was prior to Oceana being magically transplanted to the Pocket. The legal parallels might not apply perfectly."

"Blood law trumps everything," Anso said. "The legalities at least I have no worries about."

He sighed, which suggested he had worries on other fronts. He released Olivia's fingers, freeing her from the dilemma of whether to comfort him again.

"Your mother was an Outsider?" she asked, too curious not to.

"From New Jersey. Her name was Denise."

He sounded tired when he told her. *Queen Denise.* Perversely, she thought *Queen Olivia* had a nicer ring.

"Well, I want dessert," Ty announced. "Say what you will about Ellice, this apple crumble looks delicious. Who besides me wants some?"

"I could have a bite," James said tentatively.

They all could, evidently. Their appetites whetted by the drama, they sat down together and polished off the treat.

~

The king excused himself from the table before the others, returning as the kitchen servers finished clearing the plates. James believed he'd spotted the leak among them; one young man was especially shifty-eyed. Telling Anso could wait until James discovered what the punishment for blabbing was. If the man's tongue was going to be cut out, he'd keep his identity to himself.

"Forgive me," the king said as he came back. "I don't wish to abandon you on your first night here, but I need to speak to the head of my King's Council. It's important that I ensure my cousin isn't spinning the news of your arrival to suit herself. Ty, I've pulled together some viewing material in the library. Could you show the . . . Forsters how to work the machine?"

Ty rose, the deference in his manner seeming very natural. Sardonic ways aside, Ty respected his friend's position. "Of course. Do you want me to join you with Lord Noth when I'm through?"

"No. I'd feel more comfortable if you stay here to watch over them."

Did he mean *watch over* or *guard*? James couldn't tell from his demeanor.

"Are we in danger?" he asked aloud.

Anso looked at him, and James understood why those deep-blue eyes affected Olivia. They weren't just beautiful, they were soulful, as if the man behind them were both sad and kind. Right that moment, the expression in his eyes was very serious. James wondered how old Anso was. He'd implied he was over thirty, but he could have passed for younger.

"Generally," Anso said, "we're a peaceful people, but no one close to a throne can truly claim to be safe. If you'd remain within my apartments, that would be best for now."

"For now," James said.

"For now," Anso repeated.

The king was definitely taking his measure with that steady stare. Interest coiled in James, centering on an organ lower than his brain. Pushing that aside as more than he could deal with right then, he watched Anso nod at Ty and leave.

"Come on," Ty said to both of them. "I'll show you how to work the digital viewer."

The library was everything the name suggested: dark wood, dark leather, floor to ceiling shelves packed with old and new volumes. Someone was a fan of Ian Fleming. His books occupied an entire shelf. Ty settled James and Olivia on a long leather Chesterfield. He pushed a button to elevate a large flat screen from the center of an old carved table. Then he handed James the remote. The device very much resembled ones he was used to.

"If I know Anso," Ty said—and assuredly he did, "he'll have put the serious documentaries at the front of the queue. If that gets boring, skip ahead to the sexy ones."

"Because that's what you'd watch first?" James teased.

Ty didn't laugh, and James recalled Ty calling himself the Great Whore of Oceana. Had his joke been too on the mark?

"Sex always matters," Ty said. His face was difficult to read, his gaze holding James's with an intensity that threatened to make him squirm. God, this man ignited his pilot light. "I'll be in the room next door, if you need anything."

"Ty," Olivia said as he turned to go.

He faced her with a small but noticeable reluctance.

"Thank you for being so considerate of us," she said.

This seemed to strike Ty as unexpected—perhaps as unexpected as Anso's declaration of respect.

"Anso is my king," Ty said hoarsely. "To be considerate of you shows the same to him."

"Nonetheless, this situation is challenging for everyone."

"For Anso as well. When his father, King Lobodon died last month—" Ty shut his mouth, perhaps thinking this too much information to give them. He had a harder time restraining his eyes. Now that he'd finally looked at James's wife, he couldn't seem to wrench his stare away. A blush stained his cheeks, and his lungs went in and out more quickly.

James's brows went up as recognition struck. Ty desired Olivia. He wasn't solely attracted to men, though clearly he wasn't as comfortable interacting with women. A serious erection was even then beginning to strain the leather laces on his trousers.

Realizing this himself, Ty offered a jerky bow. "Forgive my inappropriate reaction, Your Majesty. You're very beautiful."

"I am . . . not insulted," Olivia responded carefully.

Ty exited, leaving both of them dumbfounded.

"Well," Olivia said shakily. "I wouldn't have guessed I could strike him speechless."

"Neither would I," James admitted.

Recovering her humor, Olivia waggled her brows at him. "Jealous?"

He laughed and elbowed her. "Just for that, I'm not sharing the remote."

It was good to joke with her, to know that however awkward their circumstances, neither of them was as freaked out as they could have been. James slung his arm around Olivia's shoulders and flicked on the viewing screen.

Ty had been right about the documentaries coming first, though they certainly weren't boring. Fascinated, James and Olivia both leaned forward to take them in.

In some ways, Oceana was like cities they were used to. Housing half a million souls, the underwater metropolis was home mainly to wereseals, though other races did live and visit here. One documentary examined why elves so often went into medicine. Another was an architectural tour of different areas of the city, touting their appeal for magic historians.

Plain old historians would have liked Oceana too. The older parts resembled Venice, side-by-side palazzos packed with baroque porthole windows that stretched along twisty streets. The difference was that here the canals had swallowed everything. The buildings and the graceful bridges contained the air. In the underwater streets, people swam or rode in black gondola-shaped submersibles. There was also a modern monorail, which presumably was more economical.

James couldn't deny he *really* wanted a ride on it.

Once he and Olivia had finished blinking over the half-familiar, half-alien old city, they moved on to a news clip of a two-hundred-year-old market hall being saved from the wrecking ball. Its defender was a preservation society that was exactly the cardigan-wearing crew he'd expect . . . apart from being led by a dragon.

The society's president was a very big lizard. She had intelligent dark red eyes and could stand upright, topping off at perhaps nine feet. Gills allowed her to breathe underwater, and a pirate-treasure-type medallion hung on a heavy gold chain around her neck. Her wings were both alarming and attractive, with gleaming brown-gold scales and claw finials. As she complimented King Lobodon (Anso's father, he gathered) on sparing the historic hall, her Irish accent was raspy. James wasn't ready to attribute that to her breathing fire. Some things he had to resist believing on principal.

By joint astounded consent, he and Olivia replayed the segment of the dragon with the brogue half a dozen times. James knew more about special effects than Olivia, but if this creature had been created by CGI, he couldn't pick out how. Giving up on that for the moment, they clicked on Anso's next selection.

This showed the perpetrator of a string of thefts at a shopping mall leading police on a high-speed chase. Both the thief and many of the cops zoomed through the city in seal form, the drama recorded by a quick-thinking aquatic news camera. A graphic at the end of the piece claimed the chase had sixty thousand views on something called WooTube. When the criminal was finally apprehended, both shapes of police herded him gently into a secure-looking metal cage.

Seeing this, James decided the loose-lipped kitchen server's tongue probably wasn't going to be cut out.

More respect for justice was evidenced by news coverage of an elected legislature, which he supposed balanced out Oceana's hereditary king. From what James could tell, its members were as big blowhards as any New York politician. Though the attitude wasn't democratic, he thought Anso seemed as fit to lead as them.

Most of all, Anso's viewing selection made it increasingly difficult to doubt this place was for real. No one could fake all that footage. It would have cost millions. Nor was the talking dragon the last of the marvels in store for them. He and Olivia gasped like gunshots at their first sight of a faerie. Even in two dimensions, the sparkly-skinned man was breathtaking.

The fact that he was mending a giant rupture in a sea wall simply by chanting some foreign words was almost less of a shock than how beautiful he was.

"Wow," Olivia said with a wonderment he seconded. "Where do you suppose his wings are?"

"Maybe he doesn't have them."

"Well, that would be disappointing. Maybe they're folded up underneath his shirt. Like faerie-wing origami."

James laughed, because Olivia's logic sometimes took sidetrips into whimsy. Her hand rubbed his thigh and he covered it.

"Click on the one called *Baby's First Change*," she said.

James had been avoiding that title, but she was correct about them needing to see it. Given who had kidnapped them he doubted this piece had to do with diapers.

Baby's First Change was also culled from WooTube. It opened with an ad for a pediatric clinic run by what else but pointy-eared elf doctors. Immediately after that, a home movie rolled. A boy about five years old was splashing around in an indoor pool that looked like it might have been filled with saltwater. James's throat clenched, because the boy was all kinds of cute. Happy, healthy, with eyes so brightly green they could have been emeralds. He was acting the way kids do when they have their parents all to themselves. *Watch this, Mommy! I'm going to touch the bottom. Look out, Daddy! I can splash you from here.*

He swam with the fearlessness of a kid who'd been in the water since infancy, which he probably had.

His parents, who seemed to be filming him, made the approving noises fond parents do. Then a strange expression came over the boy's face, a startled look that quickly turned to excitement.

"Oh Mommy!" he exclaimed, his eyes as big as saucers. "Watch me do *this*!"

A sparkly circle sprang into being on top of the boy's head, like he was wearing a halo or magic crown. The sparks got bigger and brighter and then the ring rolled all the way down the boy's body. As it did, everything it sparkled past turned into part of a seal. It didn't take even thirty seconds for the boy to change fully.

As soon as he did, he started whizzing around the pool like an act at Sea World.

"Oh my *God*," Olivia exclaimed, her hand pressed flat to her chest.

She seemed caught between delight and amazement, and James didn't think those were the only emotions she was feeling. The kid had been cute as a little boy. In seal form . . . holy smokes, he was adorable. It was all James could do not to coo like Olivia was. Those big liquid eyes, that sleek silver fur, the plump little body that swam about so excitedly. They didn't have to anthropomorphize this baby seal. There was so obviously a little kid's soul in there: smacking its flippers to get attention, wriggling and racing through the water so it could shoot out like a cannon ball. The camera shook as its parents laughed at its antics.

James's stomach sank. He totally wouldn't blame his wife if she wanted one of those. He kind of wanted one himself. He revised his estimate of Anso as a basically decent but over-entitled guy.

King Anso was a good deal more than over-entitled. He was quite possibly the cleverest, and maybe the most devious person-with-power James had ever met.

"I didn't know," he said, when he found his voice again.

"Know what?" Olivia asked, wiping tears of laughter and maybe more from her eyes.

"I didn't know you still wanted another kid that much."

"Oh." She paused in the midst of taking the remote from him, probably so she could watch the kid change again. Her expression turned serious. "I'd like one, James, but not having one doesn't make me miserable. And it might have been for the best. Violet loved having all our attention. You notice *she* never pleaded for a sibling."

"That was then. This is now."

Olivia covered his mouth gently with her fingers. "Let's not borrow trouble."

He let her silence him, but his heart remained knotted. He wanted everything for her. To give her a child himself. To be a big enough man to let her have one with Anso. In that moment, he wanted so many things they were confusing him. Her eyes were soft as she stroked his cheeks.

"I love you," she said. "Always and forever."

That at least wasn't confusing.

CHAPTER EIGHT

LORD Noth hadn't liked being left out of the loop about Anso's mating any more than Ellice. Unlike her, the head of his Council arguably had a right to be kept informed. Anso hoped to make up for this by not withholding pertinent details now.

To his relief, Lord Noth took the news that Anso's queen came with a previous husband in his usual low-key way.

"I'll keep a lid on it as long as I can," he said. "For myself, I can't say you were wrong to do this. The call of a blood bond is compelling. And the health of future Vitul generations certainly is important. It's simply . . . tricky that Her Majesty is already married. I don't mean to overstep my bounds, but is there a chance you could make the husband your third? The commoners might find that more palatable. You know how they get about family values."

Anso sat back in the deep leather chair Lord Noth had offered him. Their conversation was taking place in Lord Noth's apartments, in his private study with the anti-eavesdropping spells turned on. The fact that Lord Noth's suggestion hadn't occurred to Anso momentarily shook him.

"I expect you were considering Lord Tykon for that position," Lord Noth went on. "Otari wouldn't be a bad choice. His bed-hopping aside, he's intelligent enough to make any triad a useful third. I'm hearing good reports on how he's led the guards this last month. I don't mind telling you that surprised me. I didn't think he'd be so responsible."

"Ty's always trustworthy when it counts."

"And he's your friend," Lord Noth said sympathetically. "Which adds to the difficulty. I do think, however, that people would appreciate the fairness of giving the husband the third seat, regardless of whether he's qualified to fill it. Do you know if the husband is open to intercourse with men?"

This was a more direct question than Anso expected. "I think . . . it's too soon to discuss that."

Lord Noth nodded. "I understand. And whether a whole triad sleeps together is rather a neutral factor in approval ratings. The liberals like it. The conservatives not so much. I just thought it might ease the unavoidable tugging of loyalties between you three. Unless the wife, uh, Her Majesty dislikes that idea." Lord Noth rubbed the center of his forehead as if it hurt. "Well, not my business. I'm sure you'll sort it out." He shrugged his shoulders before resettling them. "The important thing is not to have to face the public before you can present a united front, even if you're faking it somewhat to begin with."

"Yes," Anso agreed. "We could use some breathing room."

"I'll see that your schedule is cleared of all but necessities, as far as Council business is concerned. I can also recommend a good relationship counselor. After the second pup, my wife and I . . . had a bit of craziness all around."

Noth pulled a humorous face that made Anso like him in a new way. He rose from his chair, sensing they'd covered what they needed to. "I'll think about that," he said.

They shook hands, and Lord Noth showed him to his front door. "I'm glad you're on the throne," he said with unexpected diffidence. "I worried about your age at first, but you've proven to be a steady goer."

"I'm not sure how steady this state of affairs makes me look."

"Some kings wouldn't have the nerve to go after their true mate. They'd have the mages fix them up a 'cure.' I've always thought the path to the highest end lies in following your inner voice. Sometimes, living in the Pocket, we try to be too much like mundanes. We forget to have faith in the other half of our heritage."

Lord Noth's tone had gone gruff at speaking words he obviously believed deeply. Anso clapped him on the shoulder. "Thank you for your support. I'll be in touch if there are further developments."

Lord Noth's relatively painless acceptance of Anso's news made him feel buoyant. He strode back through the corridors of the palace with a bounce in his step. Night had fallen in the upper world, a change reflected by the fading of the virtual sunlight outside the portholes. Other royals greeted him as he passed, nothing in their manner indicating Ellice had spread the tale of his hasty match. She would spread it of course, once she figured out how to leverage it to her best advantage—and how to disguise herself as the source.

He shook his head at that realization. Ty had been right about his cousenemy all along.

Engrossed in these thoughts, he was halfway to his chambers before he noticed his cock was sliding slowly from its protective sheath, as if anticipating where he was going. Naturally, noticing made the erection emerge faster. By the time he reached the royal apartments, the thing was painfully stiff and demanding it be seen to. Anso was all for that, if only it could have been as simple as locking himself and Olivia in a bedroom for a week or two.

The thought of shutting themselves away sent such a spasm through his penis he couldn't fight back a groan. His queen had already made it clear she wouldn't consent to that.

He found Olivia and James in the best of his eight guest rooms. They were sitting on the floor-level bed, their heads together over one of the tablet computers he equipped all the chambers with. They were both wearing Vitul robes, and mirrored each other in their slightly frustrated body language. He felt a pang to see them so in harmony. This was the amicable partnership he'd longed to find with a mate. Too bad for him it increased the challenge of wooing Olivia.

The couple looked up when he knocked on the doorframe. He wondered if they'd kept it open so they'd see him coming. He didn't like the idea of being someone they were on guard against.

"Oh," Olivia said. "We've been trying to get onto our Internet. We need to send our daughter a message. So she won't worry."

"I'm afraid that's not possible," Anso said gravely.

"You mean you don't want it to be," James countered.

Anso met his cool gaze, unaccountably reminded of Ty in his more serious moments. "I wouldn't want you taking impulsive actions we all might regret later."

"Like contacting our government."

"Do you think they'd believe you'd been kidnapped by wereseals?"

"If you're so sure they won't believe us, why not let us do as we please?"

Anso smiled. Olivia's husband argued like a lawyer. He lowered himself to sit cross-legged on the edge of the bed. This caused his tightened trousers to pinch his cock, but he was next to Olivia, and she smelled scrumptious, so it was worth it. "I'm responsible for the safety of a lot of people. Mostly sure isn't sure enough."

He was aware of—not to mention gratified by—Olivia's gaze darting to and then away from his trouser bulge.

"We only want to reach our daughter," she said, as reasonable as James had been. "You could type the message for us. Make sure we don't say anything you don't like."

Anso considered this even as he took in the hectic color that had risen into her cheeks. He doubted the cause was just seeing his erection. The relief their last coupling had provided was nearing its expiration. On top of that, being this close sent their hormones into overdrive. He could scent her arousal rising, though she seemed to be trying to conceal its effect, no doubt to spare her husband's feelings.

Her consideration pleased him. Her love for James might be a thorn in his side, but he thought better of her for protecting him. Wives ought to be loyal to their spouses.

"All right," he said, conscious of the irony of his musings. "Tell me what you'd like to say."

He held out his hand, and she passed him the mini-computer. In addition to a password, accessing the Outnet required his eyeprint, which the tablet had a special scanner for. James and Olivia debated what to say for a minute, then traded off dictating lines to him. Their email described a fictitious trip to Manhattan to see a Broadway show, an apology for not returning to Forster Media as soon as planned, and a promise to touch base once they stopped having so much fun. They sounded like they were close to their daughter, and that they trusted her—within limits—to take care of herself and their business.

Anso filed all this away. He didn't forget to log off the Outnet before returning the tablet to Olivia.

"Satisfied?" he said.

Admittedly, his choice of words was loaded. He was a bit surprised that both members of the couple blushed. He wondered if it would be too crass to suggest that Ty satisfy the husband while he saw to his growing yen for the wife. He knew he hadn't imagined the chemistry between James and his friend.

As if her sexual parts were itching too much to hide, Olivia wriggled on the mattress beside him. Her nipples pushed out the silk robe she wore, adding new appeal to the embroidered electrum eels. "About you and I being together . . ." she said.

Anso lifted his brows at her. Her pretty face was prim and embarrassed at the same time. And aroused of course, though he wasn't holding his breath for that to rule her actions. He braced for what she'd say next.

"James and I decided we're not going to separate. If you want to have sex with me, he stays too."

This wasn't a complete surprise. Anso glanced at James. His flush was fainter than Olivia's, but it was there.

When Anso looked back at Olivia, she was scarlet. "I know you're not shy about other men seeing you naked."

"That's true," he conceded, trying to understand what she was really saying, and why her husband was going along. "Because royals are highly fertile, we don't sleep with females until we take a mate. We do have strong libidos, and doing without intercourse isn't feasible. Well, we could masturbate a lot, but wereseals are social creatures. We like connecting physically with others. Traditionally, our outlet of choice is were males."

"And Ty is your choice."

Was this a question? "He's been my most frequent partner, yes. Our arrangement isn't exclusive." Olivia's hands were curled on her thighs. Anso covered one gently, pleased by how warm it was—and that she didn't pull away.

"Olivia," he said carefully. "Would you enjoy it if I brought your husband pleasure? It's you my body craves—needs, if it comes to that—but if you both wish this, I wouldn't be averse."

"Would *you* enjoy it?" she asked.

She seemed to care about his answer. "I would," he said, a tiny bit surprised this was true. He'd always assumed his interest in men would ebb or even disappear when he found a mate. At the moment, that didn't seem to be the case. James's presence added another layer to his desire. "I . . . I confess I find your husband attractive." Now he was blushing, which he didn't much like at all. He straightened his shoulders. "I have experience pleasing men. I'm told my bed skills are competent."

James snorted. "You're told they're *competent*."

"Well, I was a prince, and now I'm a king. It's possible my partners were flattering me."

"What does Ty say about your skills?" James's voice was rough. Anso searched his eyes, but couldn't read them. James was right about Ty being unlikely to lie, suggesting he was a fair judge of character.

"Ty says I give the best head he's ever had." Said aloud, the words sounded obnoxious, but James didn't snort this time.

"Ty was no slouch himself," he observed.

Is that what the pair had done when they'd swum off on their own? Why did James want him to know this? Was it tit for tat? Anso slept with his wife, so James bragged about getting head from the king's lover? Anso's groin grew heavier, images of Ty going down on James flashing through his mind. What Ty lacked in technique, he made up for in interest. Anso remembered how James had looked sleeping naked on the beach: lean and lanky and long. He had the same velvety skin Olivia did, skin that begged for caressing. His human-style body hair made him seem extra masculine. At the time, Anso hadn't realized he noticed, but his cock had been substantial.

"Have you ever been fucked?" he blurted. At the question, Olivia's hand touched her husband's thigh. Perversely, the little gesture made his cock throb harder.

James shook his head. "I've daydreamed about it now and then, but Ty sucking me off was the farthest I've gone with a man. I didn't want to stray. Olivia always kept me satisfied."

Anso's breath was coming almost too fast to speak. What would it be like to initiate a man the way Ty had initiated him? *Good*, he thought. Maybe better than he was prepared for.

Especially if Olivia was watching.

Lust slammed through him at that idea.

"I have to take her first," he rasped. "Before I see to you. Otherwise, I won't be able to think straight." He turned to Olivia. "I'm happy to please you by pleasing your husband, but I promise I'm not exaggerating about needing you right now."

She shuddered and—as if she and her husband shared a few nerves in common—a second later, James did too.

For one incredible thrumming moment, he felt like they both belonged to him. Olivia found her voice.

"I'm not inclined to argue," she said faintly.

~

When Anso hooked one arm behind her neck and pulled her to her knees to kiss her, Olivia couldn't keep a moan inside. God, she wanted him. Her body had been on simmer since before he returned, as if sex with him truly was a drug she'd become addicted to. The push and pull of his tongue, the hunger he was clearly trying to keep a handle on, turned her sex to sun-warmed honey. Her fists came to press his sides, her hands not quite ready to clutch him.

He didn't seem satisfied with her half response. Growling, he shoved the robe she wore down her shoulder, baring one breast to his possessive palm and fingers. The way he squeezed her was something else, like she really did belong to him. She moaned at how good it felt, then tensed. James was watching. It didn't feel right to let go in front of him.

But Anso wasn't the only one who disapproved of her holding back. "Don't fight it," James said hoarsely. "I want to see what he does to you."

Did he, though? Did he understand how intense this was, how ready her body was to acknowledge Anso's claims? She groaned as James slid his hand under her robe too, where its gap gave access to her inner thighs. Okay, maybe James had a few claims too. His touch was gentler than Anso's, perhaps because Anso was used to fondling men. Gentle or not, James knew exactly how to get to her. He found her pussy and massaged his fingers up and down her slippery folds, rubbing either side of her clitoris.

She squirmed, unable to stop herself, at the multi-layered jolts of sensation that shot through her. Her clit felt like it had doubled in size.

To her dismay, Anso wrenched his mouth from hers. "Help me," he said to James. "I want her stretched across the mattress."

That was it for her. The idea that James was going to help Anso fuck her didn't just slam down her buttons, it invented all new ones. She thrashed and made helpless sounds as they eased her together onto her back, each one taking charge of a different writhing limb. They made sure she wasn't hurt, but they didn't let her stop them from arranging her as they liked.

James freed her arms from the silky robe, leaving her naked and the men dressed. Her legs were sprawled, her sex exposed in glistening detail. The ache in her pussy was painful.

"I've got her wrists," James said, holding them stretched securely above her head.

This wasn't some endear-yourself-to-your-captor strategy. Olivia was pretty sure James got a vicarious charge from this. She saw Anso's gaze go to him. Whatever he found in her husband's face seemed to make him recalculate his plans. Not in a bad way either. His tongue came out briefly to wet his lips.

"Okay," he said, his hands going to the stretched laces at the front of his buckskin pants. "I don't have the patience to undress. I'm just going to open these."

Opening them turned out to be a production. His erection had swelled so big the knots must have tightened. Olivia fought to keep her demand that he hurry unspoken. She couldn't remember ever being this desperate to have sex. Her hips were arching off the mattress, her wrists tugging uncontrollably at James's hands. Not that he minded. He was panting like an old-style steam train.

"I know," Anso said in response to her swallowed moan. He set his shoulders, dug his fingers under the ties, then took a deep breath and pulled.

The laces snapped liked they'd been thread instead of leather. He used the same determination to pop the buttons on his white flowing shirt.

"Wow," James said, sparing Olivia the need to. "I guess you weres are stronger than normal folk."

"Somewhat," Anso said tightly, occupied in digging his swollen cock from the remains of its confinement. "Pound for pound . . . seals are stronger than human beings." He groaned as he won his erection free, and again when he stroked and squeezed it from base to crest with both hands. His eyes closed with pleasure, like he was so hard up he needed soothing right away.

"God," Olivia said, because *she* wanted to do that.

"Sorry," he said, as if he had something to be embarrassed for, as if her tone hadn't been utterly envious. "I didn't realize I'd like you both being here this much. I'm more excited than I was prepared for."

James made the same small sound he had for Ty earlier.

"You okay?" Anso asked him. "I promise I'll . . . do whatever I can to make this up to you."

James swallowed noisily. "I'm okay. I, uh, I guess this is more exciting than I expected too. I'm afraid your fancy robe is gonna need some dry cleaning."

Anso gave James a look Olivia had only seen a man give a woman. It was cross between a smile and a warning. It dipped to James's crotch, where he probably had a wet spot, then rose again to his face. *I'll get to you later* was what the expression said. It turned her on insanely, though it was gone in a heartbeat. Anso dropped his eyes to hers then, their blue fire flaring for her alone.

That was a turn on she might never recover from.

He didn't ask her if she was ready. The answer was all too obvious. He planted his elbows beside her, nudged her legs wider with his own, and pushed his tip straight between her folds like the thing had radar. The hot wet touch, so close to where she wanted it, drew a longing sound from her. Anso's smile curved up.

"Now," he said. "Why don't we see if I can do this better when I'm not weightless."

He'd done it fine when he was, but apparently practice was good for everyone. Her knees twitched up as he pushed the head past her entrance, triggering a reflex she simply couldn't control. Her body wanted his, and it didn't care who saw.

"Oh God," she moaned. He was halfway in and still pushing. He was so long and thick, and she needed him exactly where he was. She crooked one leg around his hip, leaving her other foot on the bed so she could push up him.

Between the two of them, they made short work of getting him inside. Anso shuddered as he sank home, the tip of him nudging at her womb. Olivia undulated, wishing she had hands inside her pussy. She settled for tightening her sheath on him.

Anso must have liked that. He cursed and rubbed his face from side to side in her red wavy hair. James knees bracketed her head. Olivia suspected he enjoyed the motion too.

"Please," Anso whispered, his hips writhing deeper into her. "Please let go of her wrists. When we're in heat, we get touch-hunger."

James let go. Freed, Olivia laid both hands on Anso's back, underneath the looseness of his open shirt. The tingle that ran from him into her palms was powerful, as if new floods of hormones were releasing from this contact. Anso made a crooning sound that seemed more seal than man. It had an innocence, a purity of pleasure most humans were too self-conscious for. Wanting to hear it again, she ran her hands along him.

He arched his spine like he couldn't not, his hands feathering her shoulders. His upper body had drawn back slightly, and his blue eyes glowed into hers. "Your skin is velvet," he said huskily. "It makes my bones hum when I touch you."

She gasped, because he'd pulled his hot thick shaft back inside of her. She didn't have the breath to tell him his skin was satin.

"My cock likes touching you too," he said. He pushed it in, and Olivia went straight to heaven, a heaven she got to stay in when he started repeating the motion. Maybe he was taking a cue from James. His strokes were gentle but deep. They felt like he was trying to learn her from the inside, pressing harder first one way and then another, searching out her shape and her responses. She longed for him to go faster, and probably he did too. The sheer deliciousness of what he was doing kept her from saying so.

"Mmm," he moaned, his face sinking to her hair again. His right hand slid down her side to her left butt cheek, where her bent leg was pushing her up him. His hand squeezed under her, his eyes drifting shut with pleasure as he stretched his fingers across her.

"Women are so *soft*," he marveled. "I could spend all day just nuzzling your ass and breasts."

She laughed, because she was proud of how firm she was in both those places. Everything was relative, she guessed.

"Is that wrong to say?" he asked, half opening his bliss-glazed blue eyes.

"No." She touched his flushed face shyly. "I like how hard you are compared to me."

Her saying so sent a flicker of movement through his cock. "Maybe I could go a little faster?" he suggested, his eyes gone dark despite the banked glow in them.

"I wouldn't mind." She bit her lip, then decided *what the hell*. "If you could make me come soon and hard, I might be calm enough to let you play with James for a while."

James sucked in a breath above her.

"You, then him," Anso confirmed, his eyes firing brighter as they held hers.

"And then maybe me again? If that wouldn't be too greedy?"

Anso grinned. "That doesn't sound greedy. Most were males have more than one go in them."

"James does too," Olivia confided. "Once you get his kinks wound up."

When Anso smiled at her, the fondness in his eyes reminded her of when she first woke to him carrying her on the beach: how he'd looked like he adored her. This time she thought more than pheromones might be behind his expression. Was she someone he could have liked if they'd met some other way? If she was, was it wrong of her to be pleased by that? Her heart didn't think so. Her heart wanted to adore him back.

"I'll do my best to keep winding them," he said drolly.

She hoped he meant it. However this bizarre situation ended, she wanted tonight to be a good memory for all of them. Anso lifted his brows at her. She understood he was asking if he could start going faster now. She nodded. He inhaled, his big swimmer's chest expanding, and then he went at her full out. There was no warm up, just him plunging straight into the deep end. In and out he pumped, fast, hard, his rigid organ slicked by her wetness. He fucked her like she imagined men fucked men and—God—it felt wonderful.

With a groan of pleasure, Olivia gave up on hiding anything.

~

James wouldn't have thought watching Olivia go crazy for someone else would be this exciting. Hell, if he were honest, watching the king go crazy was exciting too. Anso's body was a gladiator's, and it acted like he hadn't had sex in years. His thrusts were so wild, so *impassioned* they almost pulled him out of

Olivia.

James suspected his size and length were what kept that from happening.

Anso's cock was titanic, nor did it seem to have finished hardening. Each time he drew the shaft from Olivia, it curved upward more, until James thought the tip might be pointing up. James wanted to touch it all over, to see if Anso's veins were as distended as they looked. Maybe the angle skewed his impressions, but his balls looked different from James's. They were full but their pouch seemed snugger. Maybe James would like giving head to a man. He was sure the acts were different, but he'd always gotten off on going down on Olivia. Trading off power in bed was one of his favorite things.

Anso grunted, drawing James's attention farther up his sweaty heaving body. The king had shifted his left hand onto Olivia's breast, his weight balanced on his elbow and his knees. That was always the dilemma for a man on top: how to touch everything you wanted and still get traction for your thrusts.

James braced Olivia's shoulders to help prevent Anso's vigor from shoving her away.

Both the pair made a swallowed sound at the sudden strengthening of impact.

"Yes," Olivia gasped, then bit her lip and dug her fingertips into Anso's bunching back muscles.

James recognized the signs of how close she was to coming. "Faster," he said to Anso. "Rub your tip against her harder on the side where your cock curves up."

The king jerked in surprise, but he didn't hesitate to follow the advice. Evidently, he liked the new angle too.

"Oh God," he said, his pelvis churning more forcefully.

James's penis tightened, sympathizing with Anso's responses. He could only imagine how it felt to have your first woman when you were old enough not to screw it up. Anso's face looked like he hadn't gotten over the miracle, like everything he felt was a couple times too intense.

"Fuck," the king growled, yanking his hand from beneath Olivia's bottom. With more desperation than delicacy, he mashed his thumb across the base of her clit, where rubbing her wouldn't interfere with his crazily pumping thrusts.

Luckily, Olivia didn't need delicate. She cried out just as Anso's upper body reared back and arched. She was coming, and he was slamming through her contractions with a series of guttural grunts. Olivia's hands shifted to his hips, mutely urging him to join her in the climax. Anso gasped, his face twisting with ecstasy as his body succumbed.

Some instinct neither could control must have had them in its grip. They both held Anso as far into her as he could go, seemingly using all their strength. James couldn't even want them to stop, despite Anso pouring so much seed into his wife as they strained together that it overflowed her pussy. The moment was too primal, and part of him wanted Olivia pregnant. Why shouldn't she mother a king's children? She was a queen to him.

Jeesh, he thought, his body trembling with its own manic responses. *I really have lost my mind.*

Anso and Olivia sighed in harmony as their mammoth orgasms eased. Murmuring with pleasure, Anso bent to kiss Olivia's neglected breast, which inspired her to rub her cheek in his gold-brown hair. Her tenderness forced James to acknowledge that his wife liked this man. Olivia wasn't good at lying with her body. With her mouth sometimes, out of politeness, but physically she was a truth teller. It wasn't hard to tell if she was angry or afraid or aroused. When she loved, that too was obvious.

James knew in his heart that she could come to love Anso.

He waited for this to decimate him, but all he experienced was a twinge—not much worse than when he'd observed the closeness between Ty and the king. That was unnerving, but what could he do? Olivia and the king were blazing hot together—like the best cast, most authentic porno he'd never seen. A guy would have to be dead not to feel something watching them.

He hoped watching Anso and him together turned Olivia on half as much.

James shivered, because Anso chose then to lift his head and look at him. James's cock was pounding right in his field of vision, leaking precum and making confessions James didn't have the option of concealing. Anso smiled slowly and heatedly.

This didn't calm James's the slightest bit.

CHAPTER NINE

NO one saw Ty leave the royal apartments after Anso returned. Certainly, Ty didn't announce his departure. Slipping out unnoticed might be his best chance to avoid being pimped out to James Forster.

Ty hadn't missed the hopeful glances Anso had been turning between them. If only the Whore of Oceana could snare Olivia's husband in his net, all knots would unravel! Olivia and the king could paddle along together in mated bliss, and the scandal of her previous marriage would magically dissolve. All would be well . . . as long as Ty didn't forget what he was good for.

If Anso wasn't already considering making James his third, Ty would eat clamshells.

He frowned at the dead end of the corridor he'd strode down in his anger. He was in a section of the palace that housed service personnel. The halls were dark and narrow, the plain stone tiling worn down by many feet. A concrete bench outfitted the alcove at the hall's termination, allowing for gazing out a murky but large porthole. No garden enlivened the view outside, just the uncultivated sea.

Ty accepted the bench's mute invitation to sit down.

He'd been here once before when he was a boy, dragged along by his mother. She'd come to rant at a low level mage. The fellow's failure to correctly animate an ice sculpture for a party had ruined—so she'd claimed—her latest attempt at becoming palace society's doyenne.

Ty traced his finger across the glass as the memory of her shrill screams returned to him. His father had drunk his way through that party, providing rather a greater embarrassment than an ice swan that failed to dance. Ty's mother hadn't yelled at him. Far easier to abuse someone who depended on you for his livelihood. And wasn't it funny the things one remembered years afterwards?

The mage had bowed to Sabra Otari even as she shrieked her insults, his slender body bobbing over and over. Work visas could be strict for the magical rank and file. Ty guessed he hadn't wanted to be sent back to Faerie.

But Ty was avoiding what really bothered him with this detour down memory lane. He thought he'd resigned himself to not being the third in any triad Anso formed. If Anso had married Ellice, Ty would have been shoved aside in every possible way, as soon as she figured out how to do it without looking malicious. Ty understood his promiscuity might create political awkwardness. He simply wanted Anso to acknowledge, just once, that Ty *had* committed himself to him. Ty's erotic nature was what it was, but he'd saved the foremost place in his heart and bed for his closest friend.

He snorted softly, amused by his self-deception. Anso admitting "just once" that Ty could be counted on would never satisfy him. When it came to Anso, *just once* was never enough.

Swinging sideways, he drew his comfortably booted feet up onto the bench, his shoulders and toes now braced by both walls of the alcove. It was time to get real, before he returned to Anso and his involuntary guests. Ty admitted he liked James Forster. The man was hotter than a volcanic vent: tall, dark and ruggedly handsome. He seemed smart and not lacking in passion. For a man of Ty's jaded tastes, his humanity added to his appeal. Introducing him to more man-on-man adventures would hardly be a hardship. No neophyte had ever popped Ty's cork like Anso, but James came close. Indoctrinating virgins was a favorite game of his. James being older made him feel less guilty for being into it.

A quiet sigh gusted from him, impossible to hold in. Ty knew he liked sex with men more than he was supposed to. The thought of fucking women also drove him crazy, but who knew if the reality would live up to his imaginings? For that matter, who knew if any noble female would consent to marry an Otari? For now, he enjoyed the pleasures he had access to. He liked that James had a similar edge to Anso, as if he might take charge if given an opening. Ty never knew for sure what would happen in Anso's arms, and that made taking the lead exciting.

He shifted on the bench as his cock stirred restlessly in its sheath. He wasn't hard, just close to going there. He'd been childish to storm out of Anso's rooms. He could have been fucking James right then. Or teaching James how to fuck him back.

His regrets were cut short when two ruby-red glowing eyes drew his focus to the porthole. A mini sea dragon was outside, its tiny-clawed front paws and nose pressed curiously to the glass. Its hide was jet black with gold markings, its wings half open as it hung there. Its long black tail curled like a baby fern.

"Hey, little guy," Ty crooned, instantly forgetting his troubles. From nose to tail the dragon was no longer than his forearm. Unlike full size dragons, this species didn't speak. They were intelligent, though, possibly as intelligent as dolphins. Apart from their famous roosting colony at St. Mark's Basilica, they weren't a common sight. The priests at the basilica fed them the shrimp they liked, and they interacted—if they cared to—with Oceana's other residents there. Their shyness and the way their mouths looked like they were smiling made Oceanans adore them more.

"I wish I had a treat for you," Ty murmured, though he couldn't have pushed it through the porthole.

He flattened his palm against it, slowing his breathing and telling his mood to calm. As he succeeded, his life energy swelled brighter. That part of him could radiate through the barrier. Feeling it, the sea dragon chirped and rubbed its shoulder against the glass, like a dog rolling in a smell it wanted to take home.

Ty laughed, and it wriggled around some more. Apparently, some beings couldn't get enough of him.

After a few more wiggles, the sea dragon stiffened, staring intently over Ty's shoulder with its bright ruby eyes. A second later, it darted away so quickly the motion was just a small black streak.

Ty twisted around to see what had startled it.

His stomach couldn't have sunk harder. A nearby door was opening in the corridor, and Ellice stepped out of it. She wasn't any happier to see him.

"What are *you* doing here?" she demanded.

He might have asked her the same, but the fancy perfume vial in her hand told its own story. He'd always suspected she had her fragrances spelled. They smelled too good and lasted too well to be natural. Luckily, love philters were against the law. Using them on a king was a jailable offense.

He answered her question with a shrug. Sometimes Ellice went away if he didn't spar with her.

This wasn't going to be one of those occasions. She came closer, her gaze sliding over him where he sat, her mouth curving up smugly. She stopped a few feet away. "Kicked you out already, I see. I guess your charms don't hold up next to a real woman's."

"Maybe not, but that doesn't explain why *your* nipples always harden when my charms get close to you."

"Hah," she said, though they were hardening even then. A blush she probably hated spread across her precarious decollete. She looked ready to pop out of her corset-style red silk bodice. The trousers she'd paired with it were tight black leather—not her usual style. Ellice favored queenly gowns, her subtle way of telling Anso she was up for the role. Privately, Ty admitted she looked hot.

"Oh my God," he said, realization hitting him. Her flush was due to more than him. "You just fucked someone. You screwed the mage who spelled your cheater's perfume. I'll bet he gave you a discount. Anso's pure-as-snow cousin is a cheapskate *and* an interspecies lay."

"Don't be ridiculous," Ellice sniffed. "Just because you spread your legs for anything with a penis doesn't mean the rest of us do."

Enjoying this, Ty pushed to his feet and prowled around her. "I can smell it on you. Your real smell, not the one he tricked up. Used a rubber, I gather, or I'd scent more semen. I bet you love it that a faerie can't knock you up as easily as a seal. Faeries are hung, aren't they, Ellice? And they've got plenty o' carnal energy."

Ellice shoved him when he dropped his nose closer. "You would drag everyone down to your level."

If she hadn't denied it, he'd have liked her better for having needs like a real person. Because she did deny it, he drew back and smiled coolly. Ellice was tall, but not as tall as him. She seemed to resent having to glare up at him.

"I don't know who you remind me of more," she huffed. "Your drunken self-indulgent daddy or your pathetic social-climbing mum. All you Otaris belong in the gutter. Fortunately, I've no doubt you at least will topple in there soon."

There were plenty of ripostes he could have made, home truths about social climbing Ellice was conveniently ignoring. Right that moment, he didn't have the energy. Ellice was careful to keep this side of herself hidden from Anso, but Ty knew from experience she wouldn't stop jabbing at him until she'd drawn blood. Since her last words tonight were arguably on target, Ty decided to let them stand.

Sure enough, she nodded in satisfaction and stalked off down the corridor.

~

Anso's queen was watching her king consider her husband's cock. Anso saw her do it from the corner of his eye. Even if he hadn't seen it, he'd have heard her breathing hasten. Gratification over this joined the other pleasures he was feeling. Anso's body was loose and warm from its recent climax—not sated; that would take more effort, but relaxed enough to give him an unusual sense of well being.

Sometimes Anso was nervous with new partners. The people who'd propositioned him expected things of a future king, and they weren't always confident themselves. As a result, Anso's sexual history wasn't substantial. Ty mostly, and five or six or others. How comfortable he felt with James and Olivia surprised him. Though they had their own relationship, he didn't feel excluded. Against all logic, what he felt with them was safe.

That was surely an illusion, unless you were talking physically. Neither seemed likely to hurt him that way, despite their obvious wish that he hadn't abducted them. Anso realized he was looking forward to introducing James to his most highly praised bed skill.

If he wasn't volunteering to release them, the least he could do was sweeten their captivity.

"Why don't you hold him for me?" he suggested to Olivia.

She'd been sprawled on the covers, not so surreptitiously eyeing him. At this, she scrambled up and grinned endearingly. "Oh yes. James likes it when I restrain him."

James snorted, but didn't seem annoyed.

"Ty's fond of spanking," Anso confided, his heart secretly aching at her entrusting him with her spouse's preferences.

"*No*," Olivia responded, the light in her eyes intrigued. "Your friend seems so dominant."

She blushed a moment later, and didn't *that* startle him a bit? Was Olivia attracted to Ty as well? His downstairs friend didn't mind. It hadn't relaxed enough to retract after blasting off in her. At her words, it twitched and began to re-stiffen. Ty had never had a woman. Would he want Olivia? Would Anso enjoy watching him take her as much as James seemed to? His balls joined the affirmative chorus by growing fuller and pulsing.

O-kay, he thought. This was getting complicated. Strictly speaking, his desires should have been targeting Olivia alone. That's what mating hormones were for. He needed to remember fantasies weren't necessarily meant to be lived out.

Unaware of his thoughts, Olivia waved for James to lie back. She scooted around to sit behind his shoulders.

"Hands," she said, and he gave them to her.

Her smile for Anso turned his blood molten.

"Wait," James said. His voice was hoarse enough to draw both their attention. He looked at Anso, his hazel eyes beautiful. They were also worried, like he wanted to ask a favor he wasn't sure was okay. "I'd like to touch you. Before. If you wouldn't mind."

Anso could have laughed at how polite he was. Sensing this wouldn't be strategic, he restrained himself. "Spread you legs wider apart," he said.

His tone of command elicited compliance and the erotic shiver he'd hoped for. James spread his strong hair-fuzzed legs like someone who enjoyed submission. Anso moved on his knees into the new space. Though the blue Vitul robe still covered James's groin, his erection made an impressive tent in the silk. The wet spot over the bouncing crest had grown. Anso's mouth watered at the idea of tasting him.

"Release his hands," he said to Olivia.

She released them. James's hold came without hesitation to Anso's cock and balls, like he'd been longing to touch them. One hand surrounded each, the hand on his shaft gripping and pulling, the one on his testicles supplying a finger rippling massage. Anso's breath rushed out of him with pleasure—and a bit of surprise.

"I've done this before," James confessed. "When I was in high school. A friend and I used to trade hand jobs."

"You—" A grunt of enjoyment cut off his words. "You got good at it."

"Isn't his skin silky?" Olivia asked her husband. "You'd think wereseals moisturized their penises or something."

"Mm," James agreed. "It makes me wish my hands were smoother."

The two of them talking around him was weird—especially since Anso knew why his sexual skin was smooth. The conversation was also strangely arousing. He'd never had two people so focused on him in bed.

Deciding feeling was easier than thinking, he let his hips roll forward, encouraging James to continue. His touch was gentler than he was used to but very deft. Anso's balls were soon whimpering at James's well-targeted squeezes. His hands were big, his fingers long enough to reach back and tease his perineum. Anso's neck rolled when he did that. God, his hands were golden. Coupled with the care he took, the slight roughness of his palms was perfect. The only thing that could have made the sensations better was if Olivia's mouth had been on his tip, her pink tongue lapping over the little hole. Anso wouldn't have minded kissing Ty at the same time. He loved sucking his friend's tongue.

Anso groaned with longing, and his eyes flew open. What was the matter with him? Could he be that greedy?

He was glad the others couldn't read his mind. James's caresses combed through his pubic fur, bringing him back into the moment.

"You're as soft as a cat," James marveled. His fingertips skimmed around Anso's base, almost discovering the seam where his seal sheath clung to his root. Anso thought a tour of those anatomical differences was better left for another night. He covered James's hands with his own, lightly stroking their backs and at the same time guiding them away.

"My pubic thatch is fur," he said. "Wereseals don't have the same body hair as humans."

James ruffled it backwards, making him shiver. "Does our hair seem coarse to you?"

Anso shook his head. Strengthening tingles ran up his cock as James continued to stroke his sexual pelt the wrong way. "Some wereseals wouldn't like it, but it appeals to me."

"It's exotic," James said.

"Yes," Anso agreed. His cock had begun to well with excitement, so he stilled James's hands. If he got too wound up, he'd start zeroing in on Olivia again. That might be less confusing but not ideal. He was hoping to keep both of this pair happy. "Why don't I concentrate on you for now?"

"You don't have to," James said. "I mean, I've already experienced getting head from a guy."

"And having experienced it, you're not interested anymore?"

Olivia laughed at his drollery, smiling at him even as her hands squeezed her husband's shoulders affectionately. A warmth spread through Anso that he couldn't put a name to. He only knew it felt good to be on the same page with her. She gave her husband's dark bangs a tug. "Let the king show off, James. I have a feeling you won't be bored."

She stretched down her husband to untie his robe. Her dangling breasts were gorgeous: flushed, full, with pretty dark pink nipples. Their current pointy state distracted the men from the otherwise simple process of getting James naked. She laughed when she noticed what had flummoxed them.

"Men," she teased, kneeling back and gathering up James's hands. "Go on then, Your Majesty. Show us what you can do."

Anso wasn't intimidated. With a grin for them both, he backed up on his knees, planted his hands on James's thighs to control them, and bent forward for his prize.

Odd chills tingled through his spine at his first taste of Olivia's husband. James's cock was different from a wereseal's, very smooth but with an underlying impression of toughness. Could Anso play with him harder? Would he perhaps last longer? Those possibilities made his own cock tighten. But better not to experiment too much. Tried and true was likely his best approach.

"*Mmm*," James hummed at the gentle pressure he began with. His hips rolled from side to side, maybe over of the pleasurable stimulation and maybe because Anso wasn't letting him move freely. When Anso looked up James's body, he saw Olivia manacling his wrists. If James got off on restraint the way it appeared he did, this could get interesting.

"Oh God," James said as Anso swallowed him deeper.

The key to giving good head was relaxation and attention to detail. Nice wet tongue work was a plus, along with controlling your partner. Strength was helpful but not necessary, because one could always add one's hands. Patience, stamina, and a fondness for driving other people to painful states of desire definitely didn't hurt. Anso used all those assets on James.

Then he brought out his ability to deep throat.

"Jeez," James moaned, his spine arching off the bed as Anso swallowed gently against his tip.

Pleased by this reaction, he drew up and swirled his tongue around the head, giving James and himself a moment to recover. The saltiness of near ejaculation flavored his mouth, and he wondered if James could take much more play. He seemed to want to. His thigh muscles were knotted like steel cables.

James panted hard before he spoke. "Can you do that again?" he asked, his cock trembling on Anso's lips. "Maybe after . . . Olivia helps me sit up so I can watch."

Olivia laughed as Anso backed off. He guessed she was used to men and their fondness for visuals. With James's rugged body propped back on hers, her hands slid soothingly up and down his chest, taking care to cross his sharp red nipples with every pass. Evidently, James liked her closeness as much as he'd liked Anso sucking him. By the time he was situated, the little slit in his penis was seeping more quickly. Anso looked at it, then up at the man it belonged to.

"You're going to come in my mouth," he said. "I'm going to suck you and suck you until you can't hold back. My queen is going to watch, and you're going to feel her heart pounding in her breasts. You're going to know how excited she is by your pleasure."

"Jeez," James breathed, and Anso smiled at him.

This time when he lowered his head, he knew his work would soon be over.

~

Ty walked in on quite a scene. Everything considered, it wasn't surprising that no one looked up at him.

"Don't stop," James Forster was moaning, his tight hips straining upward as the king sank on him. "Oh my God. Your tongue . . ."

His wife was hugging his lean torso, her forearms providing an anchor for his gripping hands. Her legs hugged him too, and they were amazing: long, smooth, their muscles taut with tension over her husband's struggle not to come. The dark red waves of her hair spilled across her husband's shoulder, adding to the visual drama. Ty envied her the front row seat for watching Anso in action.

To judge by the way James's cock was disappearing, Anso was deep-throating him.

James moaned as if this killed him. He began reaching for Anso's head.

"Don't," his wife said firmly. "Leave your hands where they are."

"Fuck," he moaned, her order seeming not to help him back off from orgasm. Anso was bearing down on him with his weight, but the tightening of James's buttocks pushed him higher into his mouth. Clearly overcome with pleasure, he arched his neck back over his wife's shoulder. "Oh God, that feels *good*."

Anso cupped his ball sac and sucked him harder. Then all that came from the Outsider's throat was sound.

Groans of climax were different in air than water. James's rang loud and clear, its roughness scraping every one of Ty's sexual nerves. He knew how it felt to come like that for Anso, to have your brain swallowed up in bliss as Anso swallowed you. Swallow Anso did. James's hips shook with pulses of ejaculation, his groans interspersed with gasps. This went on for a while.

Once he judged the peak was ebbing, Ty stepped through the guest room door. His tone was as dry as he could make it. "I guess no one missed me while I was gone."

Anso jerked back from his final suck, pulling a mournful sound from James. The king of all the wereseals dragged his forearm across his talented mouth.

"Ty," he said, his voice understandably hoarse. He had just taken a load of semen against his vocal chords. Ty took a certain small-minded satisfaction in how dismayed he looked.

Telling himself he wasn't sorry, he crossed his arms and smirked. "I see I was wrong to worry the husband would be fobbed off on me."

"Ty." James speaking up took Ty by surprise. His eyes weren't insulted by his talk of fobbing. His expression held something more dangerous: it held compassion.

That was more than a proud man like Ty could stand.

"No," Anso said as Ty spun on his heel to leave. He was at Ty's side in three strides, his hand gentle on Ty's arm. His kindness was bitter comfort, a cruel reminder of what Ty seemed destined to lose.

"What do you even need me for?" he asked.

The hand on his arm tightened. "You can't believe I could bear to lose your friendship."

"I'm more than your friend." Ty looked into his king's concerned deep blue eyes. *I love you*, he thought, letting himself admit it for the first time. *I've loved you from the start.*

"I know we're more than friends," Anso said. Ty heard the words . . . and the fact that this conversation was catching Anso flat-footed. That told him pretty clearly Anso didn't feel the same. Ty tried to tug away, but Anso held on. "*Ty.*"

"I should go," he said.

"No, you shouldn't. Damn it." Anso ran one hand through his sex-tousled hair. He'd come himself at some point. Wereseals had a sharp sense of smell. The scent of his semen was as familiar as Ty's own. "I can't do this without you."

"You looked like you were doing fine a minute ago."

"I don't mean the sex. I mean being king. If you aren't with me . . ."

That brought Ty's eyes back to him. "I'm always with you for that."

"Then don't storm off. Stay."

His eyes were pleading. Uncomfortable with that, because he didn't know what it signified, Ty looked at the couple sitting hand-in-hand on the guest room bed. They weren't pretending not to listen, but they were quiet. Ty knew they had the kind of partnership Anso had hoped to find someday: true compatibility, support as well as love.

Ty lowered his voice. "You could make them both fall for you. People lust after me, but you earn their devotion. All you need is time, and they can be everything you want."

Anso was the same height as Ty, and his eyes met his steadily. "They can't be everything I want if part of what I want is you."

Ty's heart leaped inside him. He wished he could pry a window into Anso's mind and know exactly what he meant by this. Did Anso love him? Did he plan to save a place for Ty in his bed? The intensity with which he hoped for that both alarmed and embarrassed him. Loving people rarely ended well for Ty.

Another hand touched his arm, the last one he'd expected. Olivia Forster had moved quietly to join them. Anso's mate was petite. Ty lowered his head to look into her face. Her expression struggled as she tried to compose her thoughts.

"I'm not sure what to say," she began. "I don't know what, if anything, you want from me and James. I do know Anso shouldn't lose his friends because he . . . just because we showed up. If he wants you to stay, and if you'd like to yourself, I don't think you should let pride or anger get in the way of that."

She set her jaw as she finished, as if she thought he'd argue. Ty was too astonished. How had she understood what was inside him, and in so short a time? Her husband had as well. James had been the first to accuse him of being in love with Anso. No one else thought him capable.

Not even Ty, to be honest.

"You want us all to stay together?" he blurted.

Her brows went up and her eyes widened. "If that's what both of you would like."

She'd spoken as if her wishes were a lesser priority. That's when Ty realized she wasn't thinking of herself as Anso's queen. She was sharing mating heat with him, and she certainly seemed to like him, but in her mind they weren't a bonded pair.

Maybe Anso wouldn't wrap this situation in a bow as easily as he'd thought.

"I'll stay," he said, his attention half caught up in this conundrum, which led him to speak unthinkingly. "Not here, though. Anso's bed is bigger."

Olivia's cheeks flushed an attractive shade of rose, an interesting combination with her red hair. "I didn't mean . . . I'm not necessarily expecting *all* of us to have sex."

Ty's groin tightened and went warm. His mouth curved in his best Casanova smile. He didn't know whether Anso wanted to share her, but he couldn't let a blush that pretty pass unremarked.

"Don't turn shy now," he teased, watching the color deepen. "A man like me enjoys his fantasies."

~

Olivia couldn't help it if she had a thing for bad boys. Ty's teasing grin would have wet her panties, if she'd been wearing them. As it was, her clit was still squirming from watching Anso give James that amazing blowjob, the ache in her body not ebbing in the least. Anso took one look at her reaction and started pulling off his already disheveled clothes.

Once he did that, no way could she muster up enough politeness to refuse.

James's jaw dropped as Anso stripped naked. The king's physique was a cross between a football player and a competitive swimmer, with a touch of something sleeker than either of those thrown in. Even wrestling with his garments, the king was graceful. Olivia didn't blame James for being a bit dazzled.

They both were startled by how speedily he scooped Olivia into his arms. "Sorry," he said over her shoulder, for James's benefit. "I understand you want to come along, but please don't touch her this time. My body is starting to react against all this company. I'm feeling a little . . . instinctive."

He meant possessive, and Olivia totally got it. Her hands were roaming his beautiful arms and shoulders, little moans escaping her as she dragged open lips across his sweating chest. He was hers, no one else's, and she wanted him to herself. The last time she remembered feeling this way was on her honeymoon. She licked salt from Anso's clavicle, then caught his descending mouth with hers.

They kissed so deeply, so hungrily, he bonked them into a doorframe.

Anso tore from the kiss, his eyes blazing blue fire at her. His arms tightened around her. "Be ready for me," he warned.

He tossed her onto a bed she hadn't realized they'd reached. To save her life, she couldn't have said what else was in the room. The sight of him dropping to her—flushed, intent—was all she had eyes for. She sprawled her legs for him to come closer even as he kneed them apart.

He knew where he was going. Foreplay wasn't an option for either of them right then. Olivia moaned as he lowered and drove straight in, her gratitude unbelievably. What followed his swift thick entry might have shocked both of them.

Anso screwed her so hard, so fast, that it should have hurt her and him. Instead, they reacted as if neither could get off unless he was pounding her. She wailed at how good the absolute wildness felt. True to Anso's request, James kept his distance. She was only dimly aware of Ty and him standing shoulder-to-shoulder at the foot of the mattress.

She came twice before Anso quivered and let go.

"God," he swore, slamming all the way in to shoot. Her body strained to pull more from him, as if his seed were a medicine she needed. Maybe it was. Maybe that's what his mating heat did to her.

Once again, she hadn't thought of asking him to wear a rubber.

When this round's ejaculation petered off at last, she was hugging him to her with her face buried in his neck. His pulse thudded strongly against hers, the matching rhythms causing her pussy to tighten helplessly. Forcing her arms to loosen was not easy. As she did, Anso stroked her damp hair back from her forehead.

This was a different kind of possessiveness, one that said he had the right to be tender. Deep in his eyes, she saw sadness. That might have called to her most of all. He thought he loved her and knew she didn't feel the same. Saying it aloud couldn't have made it more obvious.

"Okay?" he asked.

She nodded, afraid to trust her voice.

He drew back within her, but couldn't seem to pull out all the way. With a groan, he rocked back in just as his penis would have slipped free, his still-hard shaft forging slowly, deliciously into her.

"Sorry," he panted. "I can't stop quite yet. This heat is making me crazy. I think I need to spill at least one more time."

Olivia bit her lip, really, *really* not wanting to turn him down. Anso pulled back and pushed again, dragging a groan of desire from her.

"Maybe you should change positions," Ty said. "You might make her sore if you keep going at her the same way."

She didn't know when Ty had dropped to his knees on the edge of the bed. She certainly hadn't noticed him taking off his clothes. Anso's mattress was set flush into the floor, and was twice as big as the one in the other room. Ty knelt on the rumpled covers, his tight butt resting on his heels, his cock sticking up like a flushed pink pole. His pubic fur was lighter gold than Anso's, and she couldn't help thinking the colors would look nice side-by-side. Ty's strangely beautiful yellow eyes gleamed at her. The faint leopard spots on his skin looked completely strokable.

"I never saw a man take a woman before," he said. "Not outside of a porno flick. I wouldn't have thought it was okay to be that rough."

He seemed to want information for himself.

"Rough feels good when it's him doing it," she said.

He nodded. "I like it when he's rough too."

She didn't think he was hoping to make her jealous, just sharing a fact with her, almost as if he wanted to make friends. Did either of these men know how to be intimate with women? For that matter, how good were they at being intimate with each other? They were giving off a definite shortage-of-communication vibe. Ty looked at Anso then, and both men's Adam's apples bobbed.

"Take her again," Ty whispered. "From behind, so I'll have a clear view of you going in."

Maybe from someone else, this request would have been presumptuous. Anso was the king after all. He pulled out of her, possibly so he could clear his head and consider the suggestion. Olivia doubted hers were the only eyes to sneak to his rock-hard, cream-licked cock. Anso seemed not to know he was attracting admiration. His attention stayed on Ty. As it did, James's fingers curled around hers from the other side. He'd knelt on the mattress too. Olivia's head jerked to him. She had just enough time to take in the calmness of his eyes.

Her husband certain had sides she hadn't known were there.

"Okay," Anso said, sending involuntary thrills cruising up her spine. "If Olivia is agreeable, we'll do this as you suggest."

Olivia's limbs were shaking, but she had no objection. Anso and James both helped her turn onto her front. Ty found a bolster pillow with the ideal firmness for propping up her hips. All this assistance made for an odd team sport. By the time she was in the desired position, all three men were breathing more heavily.

That was a sound she didn't think she would soon forget, no more than the singular buzz of being watched. Some impulse made her rest her right cheek against the mattress, so that her eyes faced Ty. When he noticed her attention, his breathing went choppy. She smiled, and she was pretty sure he saw.

"Give me your oil," he rasped, more or less in Anso's direction. "I want to share it with James."

She didn't know if she'd ever get used to another man saying James's name in that tone, but she couldn't deny it was a turn on.

"Please do," she said to Anso, perhaps emboldened by Ty's daring. "I'd like to watch your best friend jack off while you're taking me."

Anso's hands had been smoothing around her bottom, admiring the softness he'd commented on earlier. His caresses stopped at her words. She thought what she'd asked was fair, but she hoped she hadn't offended him.

She hadn't, apparently, or his hands wouldn't have resumed circling her.

"All right," he said, a hint of a shake in it. "I think I'd like that as well."

~

Olivia wouldn't have believed it, but this bout topped the previous one. She and Anso seemed to get more lost in having sex every time they did it, though her awareness of Ty and James kneeling on either side of them was acute. There was nothing smooth about the way their audience pulled at their well-oiled cocks. They misshaped them, and made noises, and yanked at their balls unself-consciously. These were private habits, used because they were what felt best, and because their attention was so focused on Anso driving his cock in and out of her. The king wasn't as crazed as before, but by God, he was intense.

The moans of pleasure he let out were as arousing as James or Ty's.

Ty, she noticed, like to play with his balls a *lot.*

"Is she tight?" Ty gasped between tugging strokes. Olivia suspected he wanted to know exactly what Anso was feeling more than he wanted to take his place.

Anso groaned, momentarily incapable of answering. "She's a . . . fucking fist." He worked himself into that fist more emphatically. "Maybe—" He grunted as he hit her end. "Maybe she and James . . . will let you feel for yourself."

The offer was unexpected—and possibly she'd been wrong about Ty not wanting to take Anso's place.

"Shit," he said, abruptly stroking himself so quickly his hand was a blur. "Why did you tell me that? Now I can't wait at all."

James and Anso both let out low pained noises. They were going faster too, Ty's dilemma exciting them. Olivia probably felt the same as they did. Though her pussy was being pummeled better than it ever had in her life, she kept her eyes open and on Ty. She knew he was the one worth watching.

"Shit," he repeated, seeing her attention. "Just touch me. Just put your hand on my cock."

Ty was kneeling right beside her, but Anso had to ease some of his weight up so she could reach to him. When she gripped his quivering erection, Ty slapped his hand over hers. Even with her fingers squashed to him, she could tell his skin was as petal soft as the king's. Her palm fell in love with it just as thoroughly.

Ty seemed to like her grip in return.

"*Agh*," he cried, forcing it up and down his length. "God. Liv."

He'd used her nickname. James's nickname for her. The coincidence gave her goose bumps. Hadn't Anso done the same thing in the tunnel? It wasn't the only circumstance that sent a thrill through her. Anso slung in hard and started shooting in that extraordinary God-let-me-drill-an-inch-deeper way he had. A second later, James cried out and came like a geyser, hot seed spattering on her back. Ty gasped at that, obviously excited, though he seemed determined to hold on.

"Oh yeah," he rasped, his hand and hers rough on himself, as if masturbation was better when it felt like a punishment. "You . . . are the . . . hottest female ever."

She came like his voice made her, like she was a wine press, and his praise slammed all the juice out at the same time. She gushed cream around Anso, the pressure he was exerting suddenly registering twice as strongly on every nerve. She couldn't even scream, the orgasm stole her breath.

"*Now*," Ty growled.

His hips bucked forward as his seed shot from him as lengthily as the other men's.

When they all were finished, she was covered in jism.

She began to laugh, because she knew she must look a fright. The stuff was all over her. Down her legs. Across her back. Some even dripped from her hair.

"What's wrong?" Anso panted, pushing shakily back from her.

Olivia collapsed. "Something about . . ." She couldn't get it out; she was dissolving into giggles, rolling up on the bed.

"*Something About Mary*," James finished for her, chuckling.

"The sequel!" she gasped, and both of them snorted.

"The horror sequel!" he came back.

"I saw that movie," Ty said, though he seemed mystified as to why they found it hilarious. "You don't like having semen on you?"

Olivia's laugh quieted with a sigh. "I like it," she said, smiling reassuringly up at him. "Maybe I'm not as . . . natural about being messy as you seals are."

"It looks sexy," Ty said. "To me, anyway."

Oh this one had a sweet streak she could get used to. She'd let go of him in the aftermath, but she reached out now to rub his thigh. She sensed he'd learned to be sweet from his own vulnerability.

"I'm not being polite," he said, his yellow eyes narrowing. "Seeing you like this really is a turn on."

She laughed, but her eyes stung without warning. She liked this man, and she liked Anso, but this whole thing was impossible. She was married. James was her real husband.

As if he knew she needed their connection, James took her elbow and helped her stand—or at least sway on both feet. "We'd like to borrow a shower," he said. "Just the two of us."

"Of course," Anso said. He pushed to his feet and looked at her. "Make yourself at home in mine. And please come back afterward. It would make me happy if . . . if we all shared this bed for sleep tonight."

His words seemed to surprise Ty. James, by contrast, had a good poker face—one of his most valuable CEO assets.

"We'll talk it over," he said. "We appreciate being invited and, um, thank you for the sex."

The moment they were alone in the mile-long white marble bathroom, Olivia shoved his shoulder. "*Thank you for the sex*?"

James's boyish mouth split into a grin. "What was I supposed to say? Orgasms that extreme deserve to be acknowledged."

Olivia hugged him and sighed into his chest. They had been extreme. Maybe too extreme for comfort.

CHAPTER TEN

BECAUSE the Forsters were using Anso's bathroom, he and Ty cleaned up in one of the guest chambers. They didn't horse around the way they might have before. Anso expected they each had too much to think about. Ty finished first and left, seeming to want to be alone. Respecting that, Anso took his time drying off and donning pajama pants.

He didn't realize how worried he'd been that Ty would leave altogether until he found him in the casual sitting room that adjoined his king's bedchamber.

WQON's midnight news was on the TV, the sound low but audible. Ty was watching sprawled on the well-stuffed couch, having grabbed yet another blue and silver Vitul robe for himself. He didn't keep his own robes here, though Anso would have made room for them.

Wondering if Ty's choice had a deeper significance, Anso stepped into the room. Ty sat up as he entered. He didn't pat the cushion beside him, but Anso dropped to it anyway. Kevly Manning, the wereseal newscaster they both liked was covering a dry but important story on recent volatility in the stock market. Manning had interviewed Anso more than once, and he'd been smart but fair. Though Anso tried to pay attention to his talk of fluctuating prices, the words slipped right back out his ears.

"Hey," Ty said, his hand coming to his shoulder. "When did you last get a good night's sleep?"

"Don't know," Anso said, then shook with a mighty yawn. "Not since my heat started, I think."

Not since his father died, but that sounded too sad to say. He looked at Ty, who probably guessed anyway. "Sometimes she looks at me," he said, "and I can see it in her eyes. She knows she belongs with me."

"You *just* found her," Ty reminded him. "I'm relatively sure it takes more than hormones for mates to fall in love long term."

"My mother never did." He didn't feel better for saying it, just like he had to.

"That was her. And that was your father. You're your own man."

Anso looked down at his hands. He'd flattened them on his thighs, atop his plain blue pajama bottoms. For one strange second, he didn't recognize who his hands belonged to. "I'm in love with her already. I look at her, and I ache. I know it sounds ridiculous, and maybe I'm imagining it, but it feels absolutely real."

Ty released a near silent sigh. "Maybe it is real. I guess people fall in love like that sometimes. Olivia doesn't seem like a bad person. She's kind enough. And quick. And certainly game in bed. Complications aside, you could do worse for a mate."

"You want her too."

"She . . . attracts me," Ty admitted, his chest rising and falling a little more shallowly, though his gaze remained steady. "Were you serious about me taking her if she's willing?"

"I think I was. My instincts are veering around. One minute, I can't stand the thought of anyone touching her. The next, exactly that sounds unbelievably exciting." The idea was making him hard even as he spoke. Ignoring that, he finished telling Ty what he needed to. "I thought when I mated I might stop wanting you, but that isn't happening."

The yellow iris around Ty's expanded pupils flared. He blew out a ragged laugh. "I can't say the fires have sputtered for me either. The question is, what are we going to do about it?"

Anso didn't know, and it didn't seem right to guess. Then his mouth took a sidestep he hadn't planned. "You probably can't get her pregnant. She's already behaving as if her body is keyed to mine."

"That's true," Ty said. Anso hadn't known he needed this concession until he felt a primitive satisfaction well up in him. Maybe Ty saw the reaction. The corners of his seductive mouth quirked up. "You know, not being able to knock her up won't make me any less motivated to have sex with her."

An erotic land mine went off inside his groin. In his mind he watched Ty take her, saw the face his best friend made when he came. Ty's hand was resting behind his shoulder, both their knees turned slightly toward each other. They sat close enough to kiss. In spite of the mammoth relief his body had recently enjoyed, Anso didn't think he'd ever wanted to fuck Ty more.

"I'm too greedy," he burst out. "I want all of you."

Ty laughed softly, the light in his eyes dancing. "Some would say that's the prerogative of a king."

"It can't be. My blood makes me fit to rule, not to take advantage. I—"

"Sh," Ty said and pointed at the wall TV.

"This just in," Kevly Manning was saying, two fingers to his earpiece. The graphic of a black and gold mini-dragon was displayed behind his shoulder. "Earlier rumors have been confirmed. All the Meimeyo dragons have unaccountably disappeared from the campanile at St. Mark's. Keepers postulate the dragons figured out how to work the locks on the outer door, stating that their intelligence is similar to that of wereseal four-year-olds. Why the dragons would want to escape is a matter of ongoing speculation. According to folkloric tradition, as long as the Meimeyo reside in the basilica, Oceana cannot fall. We've brought in a specialist from the city's university to comment on this."

The newscaster turned to address a tweedy-looking blue elf who'd appeared on the screen behind him. His black wool turtleneck looked like it must be hot. Perhaps to counter this, the elf's dark blue hair was scraped with painful neatness behind his pointy ears.

"Professor Darty," Manning began, "what do experts in your field make of this development?"

Anso groaned behind his hand. He had an inkling where this was leading. When he'd been crown prince, Professor Darty had asked him to fund a grant for studying the parallels between ancient Outsider myths and those of the weres. Anso would have been happy to do so if the elf hadn't twice been accused of fiscal malfeasance. The charges hadn't stuck, but the professor himself had set off Anso's bullshit meter. Six months later, he'd awarded a similar grant to one of Darty's rivals. Despite his attempts to present a sober facade, the professor's glee at this lovely chance for revenge was close to bursting from him.

"Obviously, it's a curse," he said. "Someone high up in Oceana's administration has offended the magical balance. Nothing less could trigger an ill omen of this magnitude."

"What do you mean by *high up*?" Kevly Manning inquired.

"Prime Minister high," Darty said, somehow managing to convey primness and gloating at the same time. He paused to look portentously into the camera. "The offender might even come from the royal house."

"Crap," Anso said. There could be no doubting Darty meant to implicate him.

"It couldn't be a coincidence?" Manning asked. "Maybe the Meimeyo snuck out of their roost to chase a nice school of shrimp."

"This is the Pocket," Darty said, peering down his long blue nose at the newscaster. "Most people know coincidences mean something."

Overcome with disgust, Anso flicked him off with the remote.

"Well," Ty said, flopping back on the sofa. "I guess we don't have to ask what Ellice's opening gambit is."

"Come *on*," James's voice protested behind them. "They're talking about a *curse*."

Anso turned to find James and Olivia standing beneath the sitting room's archway. Like Ty, they'd dressed in Vitul patterned robes following their shower. The entire trio was wearing his family symbol. Anso's brain swooped in a manner he didn't have time to make sense of.

"Okay," he said to Ty, "a) we can't be certain Ellice is behind this, and b)"—sighing, he turned to James—"while enacting curses is illegal in the Pocket, they aren't unheard of and they can be real. It's within the realm of possibility that the Meimeyo constitute a reservoir of good fortune that protects the city."

"That professor implied you're the reason the dragons left," Olivia broke in indignantly. "I haven't known you one whole day, and I know you care about your people too much to put them at risk. *Oh*!" She covered her mouth as puzzle pieces fell into place. "If your cousin is behind this, she must be laying the groundwork for claiming you violated the magical balance by mating me. Maybe she thinks you'll give in to public pressure to cast me off."

At least she wasn't denying they were mated. "I'm afraid that might be her train of thought. *I* know you really are my mate, but you being married isn't ideal."

"What a bitch," Olivia exclaimed, the heat of her defense warming him. "And an irresponsible bitch to boot. She could cause a panic. And what about those cute little dragons? If she arranged for them to be lured from the home they're used to, they might be in danger from predators."

"She has a point," Ty said. "We'd better contact the Oceanic Wildlife Patrol. Make sure they're looking for them. Chances are OWP has been notified, but it wouldn't hurt to check."

"Tell them I'll cover overtime and extra personnel myself." Anso was cynically aware that this would look like a PR stunt, but that was just too bad. Like most of Oceana, he'd adored the Meimeyo since he was a boy. His favorite Sunday morning cartoon had been *Mini-Dragons to the Rescue.*

Ty had dug up a cell phone, and was already speaking to someone. Anso pressed his temples between his fists, trying to think what else he ought to do. Contact Lord Noth? Try to talk sense to Ellice? He couldn't give her what she wanted, so that seemed unlikely to produce good results. The mini sea dragons were a protected species. If she admitted what she'd done, the consequences would be uncomfortable for her.

"Damn it," Ty said, knocking the now closed cell phone against his brow. He looked as frustrated as Anso felt. "I should have known something was up when I saw that dragon outside the service wing. I told OWP where I spotted it," he added. "They'd been notified straight away by the St. Mark's keepers, but they appreciate being able to put extra squads on the search."

"Good." Anso sagged back on the sofa. To his surprise, a small pair of hands settled on his shoulders, kneading gently to either side of his neck.

"It's late," Olivia said. "And you both look exhausted. Is there anything else you really need to do tonight?"

Anso looked at Ty, who pulled a face and shrugged. "Apart from confronting Ellice, who has too much to lose to tell the truth, we could probably tackle this tomorrow."

"Then do," Olivia said. "You'll make better decisions after a good night's rest."

She sounded like a caring mother. That made Anso smile until he remembered she was one.

"You'll stay?" he asked, doing his damnedest not to let it come out a plea.

Olivia looked at James, who nodded back at her.

"We'll stay," she confirmed to Anso.

~

Anso's bed was big, but with four of them in it—three of whom were large males—body parts necessarily touched each other.

Anso's protective instincts demanded that he spoon Olivia. She, not surprisingly, curled up behind her husband, who rolled around to face her. Anso discovered he didn't mind the pair exchanging quiet glances, or them twining their fingers together before they closed their eyes. Ty filled the stretch of mattress behind Anso. At first he lay on his back, but when Anso reached backward to rub his arm, he sighed and rolled into him.

Anso's reaction to Ty's weight settling at his back was extraordinary. A strong flush of heat spread out from his center, as if a new array of hormones were releasing. The effect wasn't sexual. Though he took pleasure in being surrounded by beautiful bodies in silk robes, he didn't grow more aroused as the endorphins or whatever they were spread through his bloodstream. Instead, his body became totally peaceful. The feeling was more profound than mere relaxation. It was as if, in that moment, every atom in the universe was in its proper place—including the atoms that made up him.

Olivia murmured in her sleep, her soft little bottom wriggling closer to his groin. Her movement didn't break the spell. In truth, Anso felt it deepening.

In some seal species males collected harems, if they were strong enough to defeat rivals. Perhaps this situation had triggered those responses inside of him. He couldn't doubt he had a bigger atavistic streak than most. He *had* gone spawning to find his queen. Smiling, he settled his arm more comfortably around Olivia's waist. As he did, his hand came to rest on James's forearm.

The man didn't stir. No one was awake but the king. Bubbles ticked soothingly in the courtyard garden, a lullaby he'd known his whole life.

*They're **all** mine*, he couldn't help thinking.

Because he couldn't help it, he let that be his final thought before he sank into slumber.

~

Neither James nor Olivia was morning people. This was one reason they liked to swim first thing. They could do it slowly if they wanted, and they didn't have to talk to each other in the meantime.

James was at best half awake when he extricated himself from the sleeping bodies on the low bed. The floor was the same smooth black stone that ran through most of the royal suite. He shuffled across it as well as he could toward the sound of a pounding shower, praying to every god he could think of that Oceana served coffee. His nose must have been more alert than the rest of him. Anso's rooms smelled amazing, as if a bed of spicy-sweet summer flowers were blooming just around the corner.

The tantalizing fragrance followed him into the huge marble bathroom, which boasted a toilet stall and a urinal. James grumbled at his unusually stiff morning wood, something he thought he should have been too old for. Ignoring an incipient urge to rub one off, he gave his penis an annoyed pinch, waited a couple seconds, then emptied his bladder.

Maybe he'd slept longer than he realized. The stream was strong and went on for a while. Done at last, he turned to wash his hands.

He didn't look at himself in the mirror. Whatever age Ty and Anso were, they were as fit as if they were twenty, with the perfectly developed muscles of pro-athletes. James had eye circles in the morning, not to mention patches of gray whiskers. Olivia always gazed at him like the most gorgeous man on earth, but his own eyes could be less kind. He'd stare down his reflection after he'd had caffeine.

With a grunt of private approval for this decision, he dropped his robe and stepped around the white Carrara dividing wall for his wake-up shower.

Someone was using the big enclosure, but it wasn't Olivia. Ty stood under the pelting spray: tall, golden, and steamier than the chamber in which he stood. James's gaze dropped helplessly down his naked body. Ty's soapy hand was around his penis, tugging it by the flare from his groin. At first James thought he was whacking off, which made his previously discouraged morning wood slap back against his belly.

Then James squinted harder at what he was looking at. Ty was indeed tugging on his penis, but the organ wasn't jacking-off erect. He seemed to be holding it out from some sort of smooth skinned pocket, which was surrounded by his wet pubic fur. The open slit sent a shudder down his tailbone. James honestly couldn't tell if he were repelled or aroused.

"What the fuck?" he exclaimed hoarsely.

Ty was too startled by the intrusion to maintain his hold on himself. The crest of his penis slipped through his soapy fingers, the whole thing flipping back and disappearing into the fold of skin. His pubic pelt sealed together, creating the appearance that he was wearing a generously filled fur jockstrap.

"What. The. Fuck," James repeated, starting to back away in alarm. His heart was pounding so hard he nearly had to swallow it.

"Oh for Christ's sake," Ty snapped, his hand flashing at faster than normal speed to catch James's arm. "I'm a wereseal. Of course I'm built differently. The penile sheath protects my genitalia when I'm swimming. Wouldn't want the lobsters nipping my favorite bits."

"But—" James said, then couldn't decide what he wanted to object to.

Ty sensed his confusion. He smiled at him, his annoyance sliding away. "Okay," he said. "You weren't prepared to see that. I wasn't prepared to see you. I thought you were Anso out there, peeing like a racehorse."

Now James felt stupid for having cursed at him. The spray of the open shower was catching him on the arm, but he couldn't seem to move away. "I assumed you were Olivia."

"That was *quite* an assumption." Ty's eyes were glowing now, and not only with amusement.

"My brain doesn't wake up until I've had coffee."

"Some parts of you appear lively," Ty observed.

The crazy erection he'd woken with was bouncing in front of him. Ty smiled more broadly, tugging James half a step closer. Then he wrapped his hand around him.

"Oh God," James moaned, because Ty's hand was soapy.

"Put your hand on me," Ty said, low and intense. "Feel my cock slide out of its sheath when you make me hard."

James's eyes had closed with bliss, and he was afraid to open them. What if his libido decided this was too weird? Despite his trepidation, he couldn't resist cupping Ty's crotch, feeling the silky seal fur, and the seam, and the swelling head starting to push out. This time when he shuddered, he knew he was aroused.

"This is crazy," James said. "This shouldn't turn me on."

Ty's mouth was grinning when he kissed him.

The kiss was full out—no shyness, no you're-a-straight-guy-so-I'll-go-easy-on-you restraint. Maybe James wasn't so straight anyway. Maybe he was closer to half bent.

He was getting used the strangeness of Ty's equipment, or at least very interested. He stroked his penis as it emerged, loving its growing hardness within his palm. He was almost sorry when it was out all the way. Apart from his ball sac not dangling the same way, Ty's cock felt like a normal erection.

Not that feeling other men's erections was normal for him. Anyway, it hadn't used to be.

"I should stop," he said, tearing free of Ty's very active kiss. The other man's lips were temptingly reddened.

"Should you?" Ty slanted his mouth over James's again.

James remembered Ty had hormones in his saliva, which acted as aphrodisiacs. That reminder couldn't make him stop kissing him. Truthfully, he enjoyed it so much he couldn't convince himself he was coerced. He groaned as Ty backed him into the buffed marble tile, his slightly greater weight holding James prisoner there. Wound up plenty by that, James stretched to align the few inch in their heights. Though it was a sacrifice at first, he let go of Ty's cock in favor of rubbing their soap-sluiced erections together. As soon as those hard rods touched, Ty writhed against his front like a sex-crazed eel.

"Mm," James hummed, clamping his hands on Ty's buttocks to get more pressure.

As good as this felt and as wildly as they were rubbing, what he really wanted, more than anything in the world, was for Ty to fuck him. His hole felt like it was burning, his ass cheeks clenching as if that could give his rear passage the friction it was longing for.

"God," he gasped, his head falling back at the strength of his desire. Right that moment, he'd have paid Ty quite a sum to give him a good reaming.

Despite how much he wanted it, he couldn't quite bring himself to ask.

"Turn around," Ty said, his sure hands already moving him. "Brace your palms on the tile. If I don't fuck you this second, I'm going to go crazy."

It was exactly what he wanted, but he couldn't accept.

"I should—" James groaned as Ty sucked what felt like a monster hickey on the back of his neck. The sting of that cranked him even higher. "I should really . . . clear this with Olivia."

Ty's hand slid down James's heaving chest to grip the base of his throbbing cock.

"Really?" he said, his upward tug so fierce James's kinks had to race to catch up to how good it felt. "You think you should *clear* this with your wife?"

He sounded angry, and that was exciting too.

Before James could find his voice, Ty's tip probed between his cheeks. It was broad and hot, and as it searched for a home, sparks shot straight up James's spinal cord. A gush of what had to be pre-ejaculate joined the last of the soap on Ty's dove-soft crest. James didn't have the moral fiber to resist the allure of that. The need inside him was too brutal.

"*Ty*," he said, the man's name tearing from him. "God. Yes. Shove your dick into me."

Ty shoved, and grunted, and the head of his prick squeezed in. This turned out to be the key to opening James's personal anteroom in heaven. Ty's cock was better than a set of fingers. It filled James like he imagined men filled women, stretching and massaging nerves that seemed like they were only then being born. James arched his hips to let him deeper.

"More," he moaned, not caring how it sounded.

Ty wrapped one arm across James's chest and plunged.

James nearly came from that single penetration.

"Shit," Ty breathed, clearly on the edge himself. His prick was pulsing hard inside James's ass, suddenly feeling twice as big as before. He dragged it back within him. "Try to hold on for me. I want this to last a bit."

James tried so hard his brain hurt. Ty kept his pace on the slow side, but each thrust felt so good, so thick and alive and hot sliding past those awakening nerves that his slowness didn't help James much. Ty wouldn't let go of James's penis either, though he was more feeling him up and down than stroking. When even that began to seem like too much stimulation, James tried to push him away. Ty wasn't having it.

"I need you in my hand," he said, his whisper impossibly intimate. "I want to feel what I do to you."

With talk like that, it was no wonder James was soon groaning with desire. This, it turned out, was what Ty had been waiting for.

"I like holding off," he confided burningly beside James's ear. "I like it when I need to come so badly my balls feel like knots of pain."

James's erotic switches were too damn similar. His hands fisted on the shower's marble cladding, his hips pushed toward Ty as far as they would go. His legs trembled almost too badly to hold him up.

"You're killing me," he panted, which made Ty's next thrust sling in harder.

"Okay," Ty said, his own breath ragged, his powerful hips drawing back for another drive. "Why don't we die together?"

When Ty started hammering into him triple time, the fucking felt so insanely wonderful, James thought he honestly might expire.

~

Ty hadn't planned on falling on James like this. There was such a thing as seduction, and Ty generally enjoyed it. He'd simply been overcome by an urge to claim James for himself.

Anso had his new favorite. Why shouldn't Ty as well?

Letting his inner Viking loose felt like flying, as if this man's ass, and maybe this man's nature had been created just for him. Ty loved sex, but Anso was the only partner who'd ever felt this in synch with him. Even better, James wanted him exactly as he was. Ty didn't have to hide a thing.

Ty's climax shoved against the dam that held it. He was going to obliterate it, going to crash through like a missile. James strong back arched, his hand fumbling for Ty's hip as he improved his angle for entry a fraction more.

That little movement spelled the finish to Ty's control.

He came even harder than the night before. He gulped for air as the orgasm broke, clutching James to his front while he drove as deep as possible into him. His own heat rushed out of him.

Ty would never tell, but James mewled like a cat when he went over.

"Oh God," the man said, the last of his climax dripping down Ty's hand.

"Are you sure I'm still alive?"

Ty laughed, pulled free of him with a wince, and let him turn around. They'd moved farther from the spray than they'd started, to the edge of its clouds of steam. As James blinked his dazed eyes open, Ty got one of the bigger shocks of his life.

James's eyes were no longer hazel. From swollen pupil to clear bright white, they were the drowning blue of the best sapphires.

Vitul blue.

Anso's blue.

The sense of betrayal that squeezed Ty's throat was worse than any he could recall. He hadn't claimed James; Anso's majestic genes had already marked the man.

"What?" James said, his hand flattening gently over Ty's breastbone. "You look like you've seen a ghost."

There was no point in not telling him.

"Come," he said, leading him to the one of the bathroom's three marble sinks. There, he cleared a circle on the steamy glass and waved for James to see for himself.

"Holy crap," James said once he'd leaned close enough. "What the hell happened to my eyes?"

"This is the mark of mates. Apparently your genetic makeup thinks it belongs to Anso too."

"Too?" James turned to him uneasily.

"Olivia's eyes are certain to look the same this morning."

"Oh my God," James said. "How will we—" He stopped talking with a strange expression on his face. He clamped his jaw, a muscle ticking hard in it. "I need to see my wife."

"I'm doing nothing to stop you," Ty pointed out.

"Did you know this would happen?"

"To your wife, yes. Your transformation has caught me by surprise."

James's newly blue gaze held his, seeming to search for some answer. Ty would have paid good money to know what he was looking for.

He said what he did next because it was fair. "Anso hasn't done this to hurt you or her. The process is an involuntary one."

"You said it's genetic."

"With some magic thrown in."

James's mouth twisted as he turned away. Ty noticed he was no longer denying magic existed. "All right," he said. "We'll find some way to handle this."

~

Olivia enchanted Anso by the simple act of lifting her dark red lashes. Her eyes were no longer the blue of a sunny sky. They were his blue. Vitul blue.

Her body had fully accepted their mating.

"What?" she asked, her sleepily smiling face an inch from his on their shared pillow. They had the bed to themselves, which was a miracle in itself. In that moment, they could have been any two new lovers.

"You're beautiful," he said, brushing the tip of her nose with his.

She bit her lower lip and grinned.

Enjoying that, he slid his hand down her side to the dip of her waist. She was his now. No one could deny it. No one could take her away. "How do you feel this morning?"

She thought about that with her nose wrinkling adorably. "Very good," she decided. She stretched and wriggled, which had a predictable effect on his lower parts. "I must have slept well. I feel like someone peeled ten years off me."

Actually, it was more, but he felt no need to enlighten her right away. "I told you Oceana would be good for you."

"You did." Her deep blue eyes had gone serious, simply staring into his. The back of her hand came to rest lightly on his bare chest. "Why do you move me? Why do I feel like I could happily gaze into your eyes all day?"

"Because I'm your mate. Because I love you."

The words came naturally to him. She didn't protest, but her eyes turned worried before the fans of her lashes dropped. She was biting her lower lip in a different way from before.

"It's all right," he said, chafing her shoulder through the robe. "I hear these things take time."

"Is there coffee?" she asked shyly.

"There can be. I'll tell Harrison to call for breakfast."

She nodded and rolled out of the bed. His body seemed tied to hers by a string. He followed her to one of the porthole windows where artificial daylight poured in.

"Those sunbeams look real," she said, craning her head to see upward. "How far above us is the surface?"

"Many leagues." This line of inquiry made him uneasy. "Olivia, it isn't out of the question for you to visit the upper world. It simply isn't advisable right now."

She turned to look at him, and his head reared back in surprise.

"What is it?" she asked, startled by his reaction. "Do I have something on my face?"

Her pupils had shrunk dramatically in reaction to the bright light, revealing a second color on the inner ring of her irises. The narrow striated circle was bright yellow.

The same yellow as his best friend Tykon Otari's eyes.

For two long seconds, Anso was incapable of any response but shock. Then resentment came. And fear—because how could she belong to him when another male had marked her? Finally, and most unexpectedly, a glimmer of the rightness he'd felt last night returned. He wasn't sure the feeling would last, but he clung to it.

He pulled Olivia's smaller hand into his and rubbed it. "Come with me. I need to show you something."

A full-length mirror hung beside his bedroom door. Olivia grabbed a robe on the way—his robe, as it happened. The sleeves dangled quite a ways past her hands. This inconvenience was forgotten when she got a look at herself.

Her gasps of revelation at her changed reflection were what he'd have predicted. She was disbelieving, and suspicious, and then simply confused. She peered at her face from one angle and then another.

"My crow's feet!" she accused. "What did you do with them?"

"Your genes are different now, sweetheart. Their clock got turned back and slowed down. You'll age as Ty and I do. Chances are you'll be healthy right to the end of your life."

"I can't do that," she said, surprising him. She turned from the mirror, wringing her hands in plea. "I have to be a normal person. I have to grow old with James."

Anso truly didn't know what to say to that. Most females seemed to prefer staying youthful, or why did humans buy all that wrinkle cream? Now that the issue was on the table, he realized of course she'd want to age at the same rate as her husband. Anso was being self-centered to think he'd come first with her.

He was spared from stammering more than a moment by Ty and James's emergence from the bathroom. Her husband had his own news to share, which led to another round of gasps and exclamations. The dilemma Anso had just discovered existed seemed not to after all. James's eyes weren't the only part of him that was different. He looked younger, just as Olivia did, though thankfully he hadn't lost the friendly crinkling around his eyes. At Anso's gentle request, he submitted to having his irises exposed to the porthole's light. When his pupils shrank, the same yellow ring that had appeared in Olivia's eyes showed in his.

Ty's mouth went slack with amazement. Anso was childishly glad for the company.

"I don't understand this," Ty said, his face fighting not to show his strong inner emotion. "I've never heard of two people marking the same person, much less doing it twice." Ty looked at Olivia and blinked rapidly, most astonished at having affected her. "I don't . . . understand what to make of this."

"I expect it means there's a bond between all of us. Maybe—" Anso rubbed his jaw and spoke carefully. "Maybe the four of us are meant to be together."

James was flushed—and recently ravished if Anso's heightened senses were to be believed. No matter what had transpired between him and Ty in the shower, he held Olivia's hand as if it were his lifeline. "How do we know you two didn't manipulate this change in us? You're asking us to take your word that this mystical mumbo jumbo means what you say it does."

Olivia squeezed his tense fingers. "James, you usually know when people are lying. Does it feel like Ty and Anso are conning us?"

He turned to her, his expression helpless. Anso could tell he wanted to deny it all. Olivia lifted her free hand to stroke his cheek. "I know, honey," she said. "I know this is difficult."

James bent and embraced her. He whispered something in her ear as she hugged him back, maybe about his recent activities in the shower. She patted him. "We'll figure it out," she murmured.

When James straightened, they both seemed steadier. James squared his shoulders, which might have been a teensy bit broader. He looked more rugged than before—and handsomer, which should have troubled Anso more than it did. Seeing his own blue eyes in Olivia's husband's face, feeling the primitive tug on the parts of him that were wired to respond to that, should have set warning bells clanging. Never mind his theory about the four of them bonding. It *couldn't* be a good idea to fall for both members of this couple.

Risking one heartbreak was quite enough, thank you.

"Olivia looks like your mate now," James said.

"Yes," Anso agreed cautiously.

"I know a few things about PR. If you and Olivia were seen in public, and her eyes could be caught on camera, you might counteract the lies your cousin is planning to spread."

In spite of everything, James's devious turn of mind made him smile. "We might," he said. "Perhaps we could discuss it over coffee."

CHAPTER ELEVEN

JAMES loved solving other people's image problems, especially unearned ones. Kidnapping aside, James's assessment of Anso's dedication to his subjects ran in line with Olivia's. The king's sense of responsibility seemed deep enough to call old-fashioned.

The challenge of managing spin in a brand new culture engrossed him so much he nearly forgot the problem involved him.

The three men hashed it out over breakfast and coffee. Olivia was mostly quiet, the black and white of numbers more her style. Not that she didn't have a grasp of psychology. James was aware of her watching them. She was taking in their dynamic, making her own assessments. He found his hand straying to her more than usual: rubbing her shoulder, brushing her sleeve. He needed the touchstone. Because of what he'd done with Ty, because his and Olivia's bodies hardly seemed their own anymore, his emotions were tumbling inside of him.

He didn't feel able to face all that. Having Anso's PR challenge to chew on was a godsend. That the other men heard out his opinions came as a pleasant surprise.

By the time they'd eaten the last scrap of toast and kippers, he thought they had a workable strategy. By the time the coffee had disappeared, the king's personal clothes shopper had arrived. Anso wasn't the one who needed a new outfit. Olivia was being prepared to create just the right impression. The long rack of gowns the consultant rolled into the blue salon caused Olivia's jaw to drop with dismay.

By common consent, not to mention mutual terror, the men abandoned her to the competent hands of Anso's expert.

"*Seriously?*" Olivia complained. "You're all leaving me to my own judgment?"

"We're leaving you to Mrs. Bonn's," Anso said, smiling. "She knows how you need to look."

"I do, Your Majesty," Mrs. Bonn assured her, her curtsey somehow combining friendliness and respect. "Once you've been here a while, you can establish your own style."

Because this would be Olivia's last ambition, James smiled to himself. Because she disliked being rude, he wasn't surprised she allowed the shopper to lead her away.

Twenty minutes later, Olivia stuck her head through the door of the dining room and waved frantically for him to come out. James's wife was decisive about many things, but "dressing fancy," as she put it, wasn't one of them.

"Excuse me," he said to the others.

"I could help," Ty offered, then closed his mouth as Anso laid a hand on his arm.

James looked at them and had a completely surreal moment. Was it odder that he wanted Ty to come, or that the man who'd abducted them was trying to give him privacy with his wife?

He didn't get an answer, but Anso held his eyes the longest. "She doesn't need to look perfect. As long as Mrs. Bonn approves, any outfit she's comfortable in is fine."

"I'll . . . make sure Olivia knows that," James said.

Olivia had already retreated back to the salon. James found her sitting on a silver loveseat in a pair of flowing trousers and a gorgeous Victorian-style bodice top. The pants were gray and the bodice black, the pieces united by a matching embroidered pattern of coral branches. Mrs. Bonn, who stood by the fireplace looking worried, had stuck real diamond pins into Olivia's red hair, securing it away from her face. The freshly brushed waves glowed against the creamy perfection of her skin. Once he got over the extravagance of the diamonds, which weren't tiny, James had to admit her new eyes went with her hair even better than her old ones.

"Wow," he said as she jumped up nervously.

As far as he was concerned, Olivia's figure had been great before. Now, either the boning in the top or the wereseals' infectious genes had worked some extra magic. He swallowed, feeling like a guy from high school who sees his prom date in her ball gown for the first time. The boy parts between his legs were definitely going *sproing*.

Naturally, his speechlessness made his wife more uptight.

"This outfit isn't me," she babbled, her hands fluttering over it. "I mean, it's pretty, and it's less fussy than the others, but it isn't me at all."

Recovered from his temporary paralysis, James crossed the carpet to her. He took her by the shoulders to give her a once-over. She looked as amazing close up as she had from the door, but Olivia wouldn't be satisfied unless he pretended to critique her. He guessed Anso's super-respectful consultant hadn't pulled off this balancing act.

"Turn around," he said, waiting until she did to wink at Mrs. Bonn.

"There was a plainish blue dress," Olivia nattered, "but I'd have to wear heels with it."

"Well, that would be too much. Suppose we had to swim somewhere."

"Those trousers flow beautifully underwater," Mrs. Bonn interjected. "They're not hard to control at all. And the slippers have water straps."

"So you made the right choice," James said. "Plus you look gorgeous."

Olivia turned back to him.

"*Really* gorgeous," he said, his simple affection for her funny vulnerabilities overflowing. "You're the picture people imagine when they think of beautiful queens."

"It's true," Mrs. Bonn confirmed. "I wouldn't be surprised if all the girls want their hair spelled to match to your color."

Olivia covered her mouth and laughed shakily.

"I'll leave you," said Mrs. Bonn, offering them both a curtsey. "I'll be outside if you need anything."

For a minute after she left, he and Olivia simply held each other's hands. He saw she felt foolish for her fashion panic, but also that she knew apologies weren't required. When she'd regained her balance, she sighed out a breath.

"You sure you want me to do this?" she asked. "Aren't we going to make Anso's situation worse when we finally leave?"

"Not if those little dragons are back where they belong by then."

"I'm afraid we'll be leading his people on."

"Some of them will be glad to see the back of us no matter how good an impression you make at this press conference. The important thing is not to make our escape look like it's Anso's fault."

Wryness twisted Olivia's mouth.

"I know," James said. "The part of you that likes the king doesn't want to break his heart."

"I shouldn't be able to. This whole situation is crazy."

James tugged her to him, kissing the hair that swooped back from her temple. Olivia's arms circled him. Maybe his muscles were as changed as her figure. Her weight felt as light as air.

"Look on the bright side," he said. "We'll be traveling out of the palace. I can't pretend to mind that."

Olivia hugged him and snorted. "You just want to sightsee."

"Don't you?"

"As long as I'm not too nervous to enjoy it."

"You'll be fine, Liv. You won't even have to talk. Just stand next to Anso and bat your royal blues."

"You have them too," she said, craning her head at him.

"No one will see mine. I'll be in the back, looking proud my wife got chosen by such an important man."

Olivia rolled her eyes.

"It's not a total lie. You could be a queen if you had to. You have the brains and the heart. And, apparently, the hair."

They grinned at each other, a sense of humor in adversity a trait they shared.

"You're still you," he said. "Nothing can change that. We'll get contacts when we're home is all."

Her eyes softened, and her hands slid up his robe's lapels. "You're still you," she murmured back, "even if you and Ty had sex."

He hadn't told her, but he should have known she'd guess. "Liv—"

"Sh." Her fingers stroked the sides of his neck. "How can I begrudge you that pleasure?"

"Liv, the reason I—"

Her lips pressed his softly. He gave in and kissed her back, part of him wanting to cry with gratitude for her forgiveness, the rest caught up in the sweetness of sinking into her mouth. She kissed him like he was precious, like no one in the world was more important to pay attention to. Her love had never seemed so palpable to him, waves of nearly touchable energy rippling from her to him. He buried his hands in her hair and groaned. How could he love her this much and have wanted Ty so badly? Her body melted into his, his groin hardening strongly in response. He wanted her enough to ache. Lust was a portion of his reaction, but so was the need to express what he felt for her in every way he could. Looking back, he wished he could say lust was the only thing that had driven him to Ty. He just couldn't convince himself of it.

Reluctantly, he drew back from her. Her cheeks were flushed prettily. "I want you to know I've never cheated on you before."

The back of her fingers caressed his face. "Me either." A little smile touched her kiss-red mouth. "I'm pretty sure these qualify as special circumstances."

"Liv, you know how I like to say we've been together in other lives?"

"Sure." Seeing he was serious, her smile faded.

James pulled in a breath. "I actually remember them."

Olivia's eyebrows shot up. "You do?"

"Just pieces, but they're very vivid. Do you remember how on our first date I guessed what you liked to eat?"

"I assumed you'd asked one of my girlfriends."

He shook his head. "I remembered how you liked to be kissed as well. How sometimes you wake up after sex and feel so alone you need to be held. I know more about you than you've ever told me, and I used it to win you."

"What are you trying to say?" she asked.

"Olivia, in one of the lives we shared, you and I were both men."

"Oh." Her hands slid down his arms to his elbows, but she didn't let go of him. "Are you saying that's why you've had daydreams about being with guys? Because you wanted to recreate that memory?"

"I thought so," he said. "Now I'm not sure."

She rubbed his biceps while she considered this. "Does it matter why you're attracted to men?"

"Maybe. It seemed better when I thought it was because of you."

She smiled unexpectedly. "Seems to me even in your fantasies you were trying to be true to me."

"You deserve that," he said.

He practically heard the calculator keys clicking in her mind, his sweet little accountant with a heart. "Maybe," she said slowly, "us being true to each other isn't as simple as we thought."

~

Royal press conferences certainly weren't simple. Another of Anso's staff briefed her on protocol: who got into a transport first, who she was allowed to thank and who only got a nod. Oceanan royals had a dorky public wave the same as the Brits. Olivia privately decided she'd ignore that. She was an Outsider. If Anso's people minded her waving like a normal person, they'd just assume she didn't know better.

The press conference would be delivered underwater. Olivia's ability to breathe that way would provide further proof that she was the king's bloodmate. She made the shift from breathing air to breathing water in Anso's coral garden, to avoid her possible panic being seen in public. To her relief, her anxiety was brief. Anso squeezed her hand, nodded reassuringly, and she inhaled without more coaxing. Once she had, being buoyant and not needing air tanks was quite pleasant.

She was a little disappointed he hadn't had to kiss her this time.

The submarine-gondola they rode in had the option of being filled with air or water. Since they'd already transitioned, water served for today. Always more of an athlete than Olivia, James caught on right away to the trick of moving around inside.

"It's like being an astronaut," he laughed, tugging her down into the seat next to him. "Zero G all the way."

Ty assisted her with the roller coaster-like safety bar, his attention shifting between her and James as he did. Olivia's body tightened as his hands brushed her, though he wasn't trying to flirt. He'd marked her too, so would she get sex-crazed for him? Was that what had happened to him and James? For that matter, would it happen between James and her? James had given her quite a buzz with that kiss back in the salon, so much that she hadn't wanted to stop.

She ought to mind all of this. Instead, she was reckoning the minutes until the four of them could be alone again. Was it wrong of her to hope she'd have a chance to sample Ty as well? Was she like Saint Augustine, who prayed for chastity but not yet?

"You look beautiful," Ty murmured as he checked her shoulder strap. His yellow eyes burned when they met hers. Tiny bubbles clung to the spikes of his fair lashes, though the water in the big royal sub was otherwise crystalline. She supposed they had some sort of magical filter.

"Thank you," she said. "You look very nice yourself."

He smiled. He'd traded his pirate clothes for a crisp uniform, the same black and silver deal the other guards in the gondola wore. His had a few more doodads decorating it. Olivia hadn't missed the fact that they called him *Captain*.

"Don't try to remember every detail of protocol," he advised. "No one expects you to be perfect."

"Actually, I have a good memory. It's the spontaneous public charm stuff that trips me up. James is the one who has everyone in stitches at parties."

Ty's gaze cut to James and then back to her. She couldn't guess what he was thinking as he lowered himself into the comfortable chair across the aisle from them. He had much more of a poker face than Anso.

The king sat farther forward in this aqueous equivalent of Air Force One. He was also in uniform. Guards and advisers surrounded him, plus the elegant older man he'd introduced to her as Lord Noth, the head of his King's Council. Lord Noth's eyes had taken her measure to the millimeter, but Olivia assured herself she'd stood firm. With the exception of Noth and the guards, who were too professional to gawk, everyone here had shot her and James worried looks, as if they were bombs about to go off. She and James had smiled calmly in return, which eventually caused the looks to stop.

She hadn't forgotten what James had told her earlier: that their only real job today was to appear content with their lot. If they weren't seen as a potential source of conflict, there'd be no serious reason for Anso's people to object to him taking her as mate.

Her James had a way of cutting to the core of things.

I can do content, Olivia told herself. She was surprisingly—and maybe shamefully—close to it anyway.

A hum vibrated through the huge gondola as it pulled away from the palace dock. From there, they entered a tunnel through which they traveled at high speed. Though there wasn't much to see beyond the lights flashing by on the wall outside, James still pressed his nose to round window.

"We're clipping along at a hundred knots," Ty said, noting his fascination. "Once we leave the secure tunnel and enter traffic, we'll slow to about thirty."

"Wow," James said in the same wondering tone he'd used for Olivia's outfit. "I suppose it takes a special license to drive these things."

"Very special. The smaller models are easier to qualify on. They're just as entertaining, I think. You feel the speed more when you're a minnow and not a whale."

"*You* could drive this baby," James said, turning back to him.

Ty confirmed his guess with a grin. "There isn't a single vehicle in Oceana I'm not licensed to operate."

"Shit," James said, unabashed envy in the sound.

Boys and their toys, Olivia thought, laughing silently to herself.

No doubt James would have grilled Ty more if they hadn't entered the city then.

"Ooh," Olivia said, leaning across her husband to press her nose where his had been.

Apart from being *underneath* sunlit water, they could have been cruising Venice's Grand Canal. Olivia was suddenly grateful for Mrs. Bonn and her fancy pins, which kept her hair from floating around her face and spoiling the view. The city of Oceana was magical in every sense of the term. Wide boulevards. Graceful historic buildings. A "sky" that was only a slightly deeper blue than at home. Many vehicles joined them in the main thoroughfare. Some were big, some family-sized with faces pressed to their windows, some as neon bright and tiny as scooters. The people who drove these clung to their backs as if riding dolphins with handlebars. Almost all of them were grinning behind their eye goggles.

"Those are Vespas," Ty informed them. "They're cheap to buy and a lot of fun."

"We have Vespas at home," James exclaimed excitedly. "They're little motorcycles. We drive them on the ground."

"A lot of folks who live in the Pocket are descended from Outsiders. Sometimes they like to reinvent a piece of their native land. The majority aren't abducted," he added. "Most wander into our territories on their own. They don't quite fit in your world, and they have enough magic in their nature to hear the call of ours."

"Does it ever work the other way around?"

Ty cocked his head at Olivia's question.

"It would be difficult," she said, "if you were born here and didn't have any special gifts. It might be tempting to try your luck with mundanes."

"I suppose," he said. "But people don't run away very often. Generally speaking, Oceanans aren't fond of dry land. We feel like fish out of water, I guess you'd say."

That scooped a hollow in Olivia's chest, one whose cause she didn't want to examine. Maybe James felt it too. He patted her hand and fell quiet.

Shortly after that, their whale of a gondola pulled up at an anchorage beside the upper level of a basilica—St. Mark's of the Meimeyo, she presumed. The guards sprang into action, including Ty. Before she and James had finished freeing them from their safety harnesses, their uniformed cordon was ready to escort them. Anso swam back through it to her.

"Ready?" he asked, taking her face gently in his hands.

Her eyes stung with tears that immediately washed away. This man was as protective of her as James.

"I'll be fine," she said as lightly as she could. "With all of you looking out for me, how could I not be?"

Seeming to know this wasn't quite the truth, Anso brushed her cheeks with his thumbs. He looked behind her to James.

"We're ready," James assured him. "Olivia doesn't fold when the chips are down."

With that vote of confidence to shore up her shaky nerves, they swam through a frescoed corridor Olivia really would have enjoyed lingering in. She loved the Italian masters, and these paintings looked very much like Giotto's. Sadly, art appreciation wasn't on their itinerary. In no time at all, they reached a stone balcony that overlooked the basilica's broad front steps.

The instant their figures were visible a great roar went up. That was enough of a shock for Olivia, but a million camera flashes seemed to go off simultaneously, blinding her before she had a chance to find the recommended footholds for anchoring her slippers. Between barrages of white strobes, she caught glimpses of Anso and Ty kneeling down on either side of her to help her secure herself—very much like two golden princes preparing to propose. That sent the photographers into a fresh frenzy. Olivia had to press one arm across her eyes until the flares died down, though she tried her best to keep a calm relaxed face. When the worst seemed over, she dropped the shield cautiously.

Anso must have been a popular king. The square beneath them was packed with people, level upon level of them, the colorful, slowly undulating mass stretching out in the distance to either side. A line of easily identifiable green-uniformed police kept anyone from swimming too close. Viewing screens were tacked to some of the buildings, so the balcony could be seen from more angles. Olivia watched her startled eyebrows shoot up her giant brow and firmly ordered them to stop doing that.

At a podium beside her, Anso stood tall and proud. Seeming perfectly calm, his hand came to the small of her back and stayed. In that moment, it didn't feel at all deceitful to lean closer to his support. At these small signs of their connection, the crowd fell quiet. They'd been told their king had taken a mate, so that at least wasn't a complete surprise.

"Thank you, Oceana," Anso said into the microphone. He was very steady, and his voice sounded beautiful magnified. It echoed a bit between the grand buildings. "My queen and I appreciate your interest in our well being. I'll be making a brief statement, after which I'll answer a few questions. First of all, I wish to confirm that I've followed Vitul tradition in seeking a mate with whom I have a true blood bond. Olivia comes to us from Outside. Our courtship has been short but providential. I cannot doubt her sweetness and integrity will bless our city nation and myself.

"In addition, as was the case for William the Second and Conjugus the Magnificent, Olivia has the added commitment of a human spouse."

Anso paused while the crowd exploded again. Intensifying the furor were questions from reporters, who were in the cluster nearest the balcony. He withstood this with more patience than Olivia could have pulled off. The vibrations of the renewed uproar pulsated to them through the water. Anso waited a minute, lifted his hand, then waited some more until he could be heard.

"Thank you," he said, exactly as if they'd cooperated right away. "While no one can deny this situation presents emotional challenges, I have faith that my heart and instincts have guided me truly. Her Majesty's husband is a man of honor and intelligence. Any king would be lucky to have his queen cherished as James Forster cherishes her."

Anso's voice actually broke, which Olivia knew he and the others hadn't planned. This was genuine emotion he was displaying. He was grateful to her husband for loving her. Olivia's eyes flew to Anso's face as he turned to her.

"I feel very lucky," he said to her, though his words still addressed the crowd. "I trust and hope you'll afford us the same courtesies any newly mated couple would want in order to step more firmly onto a path of lasting happiness."

He couldn't have been more romantic if he'd tried. His hand had slipped from her back, but hers found it as it dropped. Their fingers twined together without effort, and Olivia's throat went tight. She had the increasingly familiar and—in its way—increasingly terrible sensation that he was indeed her man. In that moment, she no more could have let go of Anso's hand than she could have looked away. He was the one who broke their eye-lock. This time, as he drew breath to continue, the crowd was pin-drop quiet.

"Finally," he said, his voice still husky, "I wish you to know I share your concern for the fate of our city's beloved guardian dragons. The resources of the royal treasury have been put at the disposal of the Oceanic Wildlife Patrol, so that they can more effectively search for them. Until the Meimeyo are returned to their home, I humbly ask you to join me in praying for their safety, in whatever manner you observe. Love is a power in our fair city. With that behind our rescue efforts, I don't foresee us failing."

He was getting her choked up now. She couldn't have found the voice to pelt him with questions as immediately as the reporters did.

The very first who was singled out asked if His Majesty was going to set up a sexual schedule for all his potential new lovers.

"That's a personal question," Anso said calmly. "I won't be answering those on this or any other day."

If Olivia hadn't known Anso and Ty deliberately chose this journalist to call on first, in order to get him out of the way, the even keel Anso remained on would have amazed her. Subsequent questions weren't as bold, but they all struck her as intrusive.

Because she didn't want to be seen getting upset about it, she tuned them out. She turned her gaze to the marvel-worthy scenery instead. The crowd billowed up and down like a cape, the bright yellow gondola taxis gleamed, and the curving stretch of Venetian buildings provided plenty of distraction. The dome of another church rose above the rooftops a few "canals" beyond them. Scaffolding surrounded its cupola, so she supposed even magic cities required repairs. The silver cross on its roof glinted in the sun, a beacon calling her eyes to it.

Where do faeries worship? she wondered. Did creatures of pure magic believe in gods? She spotted a handful twinkling regally at the back of the crowd against the opposite buildings. They floated hand-in-hand in a line, perhaps to avoid bumping elbows with the regular rabble. Their wings, if they had them, weren't in evidence. Would Olivia get a chance to see some before she and James escaped?

She thought back to her exchange with Ty, about how Oceanans rarely emigrated to the Outside. When their daughter Violet had been a child, she'd sometimes run away as often as once a month, just go into a fury over some perfectly reasonable restriction and take off with her little Barbie backpack full of supplies.

Olivia smiled to remember it. Violet had been so blasted willful and passionate. She was lucky James and Olivia hadn't been able to help loving her.

Violet had always come home, the only exception being the few occasions when she was afraid to. Those times, she'd run away because she knew she'd be in trouble for something she'd done. Violet hated punishment worst of all when she knew she deserved it. Then she'd hang around somewhere close—a fort in a neighbor's yard, the little library down the street¬—until she ran out of juice boxes or judged Olivia's mood had sufficient time to soften. Even at five, she'd been eerily capable of gauging the moment her mother's relief would outweigh her anger.

As annoyed as Olivia sometimes got at her rebelliousness, she'd been in awe of her daughter for knowing this.

Her gaze strayed again to the dome with the construction scaffolding. The newscaster for the original report on the missing sea dragons said they had the intelligence of four-year-olds. That didn't necessarily mean the Meimeyo thought or felt in human ways, but what if some of their reactions were similar? What if they believed they'd be in trouble for running off? And what better spot to conceal themselves than someplace quiet that nonetheless felt like home?

Her grip on Anso's hand tightened at the idea, causing him to falter in the middle of answering a question. He looked at her, but she gave her head a tiny shake and smiled.

When he smiled back, a soft fond glow entering his eyes, she just knew he was going to call an end to the Q and A. She was more important to him than any amount of positive PR.

~

As soon as they were back in the sub, Ty and James bumped knuckles victoriously. Though Anso understood why they were elated, he was occupied with steering Olivia in. He looked on indulgently as they congratulated each other.

"That was awesome," Ty crowed.

"The way his voice broke," James said.

"Olivia's blush when he told her he felt lucky!"

"My favorite was her eyes turning red when he talked about love being a power in 'our fair city.' I knew she'd get emotional if he mentioned those little dragons. You should see her when commercials with puppies come on TV."

As Ty secured himself in a seat with half his attention, Anso heard Olivia mutter *sheesh* underneath her breath. Ty was too caught up in reliving their media coup to notice her reaction.

"The camera *loved* her," he gushed, leaning across the aisle to James. "Wherever she is, Ellice must be shitting clam shells. Olivia couldn't have come off better if she'd been Joan of Arc."

"Guys!" Olivia snapped. James and Ty turned to her with matching startled looks. "If you're done discussing how predictable I am, I have an idea where we might look for the Meimeyo."

"Really?" Ty said. "Where?"

"Yes," James seconded. "Where?"

Anso rubbed the arm he held as she suddenly got self-conscious. "It's only a guess, but I was remembering how Violet—our daughter—used to hide close by our house after she ran away." Olivia's mouth pulled into a rueful smile. "From the age of five until she was around eight, Violet made running away a regular hobby."

"Really?" Ty said, this taking him by surprise. It took Anso by surprise as well. James and Olivia seemed like the kind of parents no child would want to leave.

"Violet was . . . stubborn," James explained.

"Really, really stubborn," Olivia laughed. "We'd tell her she couldn't wear her favorite outfit more than forty-eight hours nonstop and she'd go bonkers."

"Remember when she wanted a pony?"

"A *pink* pony!"

"I think she lit out three separate times over that. Thank God she outgrew that stage, or she'd still be grounded."

They sighed out a laugh together before Olivia went on. "Anyway, I wondered what if your cousenemy arranged for the Meimeyo to be let out but not taken to a specific location? Maybe the freedom went to their heads, and they had a little adventure, and now they're afraid they're going to be considered bad dragons. They could be holed up somewhere together, screwing up their nerve to face their scolding or hoping it will go away. When our daughter was the age they're supposed to be as smart as, that's what she would have done."

"That could be what happened," Anso said, rubbing his jaw thoughtfully. "But we still don't know where to look."

"Somewhere near their home," Olivia answered. "Somewhere like their home, so they'll feel safe. I saw a church from the balcony where we were standing that looked like it was closed for renovation."

"Our Lady of the Waves," Ty supplied. "But OWP checked there already."

"If the Meimeyo are feeling guilty, they wouldn't have come out if they were called. They'd have stayed in hiding."

A thrill of hope skipped across Anso's shoulders. "I'll tell the pilot to change course," he said, trying not to get too excited. "It's certainly worth looking."

Ty flipped his harness open and hopped up. "I'll see if there's any shrimp salad in the stores. OWP would have checked the church a while ago. The dragons are used to being fed on a regular schedule. If they're there, they might be hungry by now."

They both departed so quickly James had to grab Olivia's arm before she floated away.

"Sorry," Anso called over his shoulder.

Olivia waved him on and laughed.

~

The king's desire to join the search party turned out to be a bigger deal than Olivia expected. Ty wasn't inclined to stop him, and the guards took their cue from him, but Lord Noth and the advisers were determined to try.

"The building could be unstable," Lord Noth protested. "We can't risk it coming down on you and the queen."

"It's stable enough for the restorers," Anso countered. "Therefore, it's stable enough for us. We'll use the aquaglides. They've got collision shields built in. And Nico will wear an earpiece. He'll be reachable at all times. Believe me, I wouldn't allow Olivia to come if I didn't think this was safe."

A bit more politely heated discussion followed, but kings weren't easy to overrule. In the end, the four of them plus the better part of the guards went to canvas the cathedral.

Nico, who Olivia was disconcerted to recognize from their abduction, snapped the front door's chain with a big pair of bolt clippers. As he did, Ty and the other guards unloaded their next mode of transportation from the sub's cargo bay.

The aquaglides were shiny black T-bars with football size engines. They were easy to use and ran almost silently, allowing their group to progress down the marble-columned nave while barely leaving a wake. Anso had instructed everyone to be as quiet as possible. If the mini-dragons were here, they didn't want to scare them off. The silence added to the closed cathedral's eerie loveliness.

The electricity was disconnected, and the only light stretched in silvery spokes from the high windows. As far as Olivia could discern, Our Lady of the Waves was Mary, her sad-kind figure featured prominently among the niche statues. Carvings of kelp, fish, and seahorses were also popular decorations, along with a suspiciously muscular looking fellow brandishing a trident. How Poseidon had finagled his way into the New Testament pantheon, Olivia couldn't guess. In one large wall mosaic, he carried a platter of lobster to the baby Jesus in the manger.

Because James was something of a shaky Catholic, he sniggered at seeing that.

They cruised all the way to the choir without spotting their quarry, though plenty of shadows flickered in the side chapels. When they'd reached a respectful distance from the high altar, Anso gestured everyone into a huddle.

"I think we need to go up," he murmured. "The Meimeyo were living in a campanile. They'll probably want to roost high. Nico, spread your men down here and make sure they don't try to sneak back this way. If you spot them, engage the net. They're too quick to chase down individually, plus we'd frighten them if we tried."

"Got it," Nico said. "But take Mark with you at least. Lord Noth will have my nuts if I let you go on without a guard."

Anso made a face but didn't argue. Mark plus his holstered (and slightly mysterious looking) weapon joined their slow upward spiral into the cathedral's dome. A grid of scaffolding covered the mosaics on the vaults, obviously where the church was showing its age the worst. The higher up the aquaglides towed them, the better the light became, due to the many beautiful clear windows. They ascended from the dome into the lantern, passing first through circular oculus. To Olivia's disappointment, not a single dragon tail could be seen.

"Huh," Ty said, peering around the cross-supporting structure that sat atop the dome. "I really thought we were going to get lucky."

Olivia had too—and felt pretty silly for dragging them on this wild goose chase.

"Maybe this church is like St. Paul's in London," James offered. "If the dome was built in sections, there could be cavities in between."

"I believe it was," Anso said, his face lighting up.

"I spotted some holes in the brick around the oculus," Ty said. "They looked big enough for the sea dragons to swim through."

"Not for us, though," Olivia felt glumly obliged to say.

Ty's grin could have been a ray of sunlight. "Right," he said. "That's where the vacuum packed cans of shrimp come in."

With only a bit of jostling, the five of them landed themselves and their aquaglides on the narrow railed gallery that circled the oculus. Ty and the guard called Mark removed a dozen tins of shrimp paste from their uniform pockets. Shrugging at each other, they mutually decided to open all of them, creating a trail that led out from the biggest gap in the aging brick. Then Mark and Ty sat with the others.

Absolutely nothing happened for ten minutes.

Well, crap, Olivia thought, mentally composing her apology. She didn't get a chance to open her mouth. Anso and Ty and Mark suddenly sat straighter.

"What's that smell?" James whispered just as Olivia caught a whiff through the shrimp. The scent was the same flowers-and-spice aroma she'd noticed when she first woke up with Anso, before their latest metamorphosis sidetracked them.

Anso was sitting tailor style next to her, his body taut with attention. "That," he said, "is the smell of magic."

"Hold hands," Ty whispered, clasping both Mark's and James's. "Slow your breathing and think of peaceful things."

He was the last person she expected to be giving new age advice. On the other hand, since they were in a city faeries had created, maybe it would be smart to go along.

Anso's hand was warm and gentle, James's firm and familiar. The instant they were all hooked up, a silent hum ran through the muscles in Olivia's arms. The sensation was extremely nice, like warm blankets and hot tea. Her thoughts naturally calmed. She remembered Violet when she was little, how despite her volcano of a temper, she'd always loved to be cuddled. Their little girl had such a wonderful heart, no matter how hot it ran. Olivia knew she'd forgive her anything.

A small black nose poked out of the nearest hole.

James's hand squeezed hers, but no one said a word. The first nose was joined by a second. Then, as if the entire school had decided it was all right to emerge, dozens of black and gold mini dragons poured from the cavity behind the brick.

They fell on the open tins of shrimp as if they were starving.

"Shh," Anso said when Ty and Mark both began to move. "Let them finish their meal."

That took about five minutes.

The nearest can was three feet from where they sat. The two little dragons who'd buried their snouts in it pushed it around to see if there might be more. Then they looked up at them. Their paws had been as clever as hands, their curly tails adorable. Their eyes were dark with beautiful ruby lights.

Come, Olivia thought to them. Come and have a cuddle now that you've eaten.

The rational part of her nature thought this was a silly thing to think, right up there with pink ponies. To her amazement and her delight, both Meimeyo darted straight to her and twined themselves—paws and tail—around her neck and shoulders.

This made her laugh, but the sound didn't startle them. Before you could say *I believe in fairies*, all the dragons were flinging themselves at their rescuers and clinging like barnacles. Their bodies were slightly warm, their black and gold scales as sleek as silk. The five of them didn't have enough hands to pet them all, but they did their best. Olivia had to nudge two dragons farther up her arms so she could work her aquaglide. The one on her head was gnawing on her hairpins.

They must have looked a sight when they rode with their cargo back to the cathedral's floor.

The remaining guards were startled, but quick-witted enough to drop their net over the dragon-covered searchers as a precaution. The Meimeyo cheeped grumpily at that, but calmed again when they got more petting out of it. Lord Noth established himself as good for more than worrying when the team he'd summoned from the Oceanic Wildlife Patrol showed up in five minutes. Looking thoroughly professional, they brought cages and gloves and shrimp biscuits. In short order, they had all but two of the dragons secured in their carriers. Those final two didn't want to let go of Olivia's neck.

"Oh let them stay," she said to OWP's head wrangler. "I'll ride back to the basilica with you. I'm sure they'll un-pry themselves once they see they're home."

"Yes, Your Majesty," said the naturalist with a bow Olivia didn't think she'd ever get used to.

"We've got a count of thirty-five," said a young plump woman in light blue OWP overalls. "That's only one short of the original thirty-six."

"Send someone to the dome," her boss instructed. "Maybe it's still up there."

"Would you like my aquaglide?" Olivia offered, assuming she wouldn't need it now. The young woman's mouth fell open. "One other thing," Olivia added. "Will the dragon who took my hairpin eat it? I wouldn't want it choking."

"No," the head wrangler answered, shaking off as strange a look as that of his employee. Maybe he thought Olivia shouldn't have let the Meimeyo steal the Vitul jewels. "Dragons just like putting shiny things in their mouths."

"Like kids," Olivia laughed, stroking the two Meimeyo she still held. Her laughter made them wriggle, their cold little noses nuzzling close to her neck.

That was how the paparazzi caught her when they snuck in the church's door: her hair a mess, pieces of net clinging to her clothes, and two Meimeyo snuggled up to her like puppies.

Olivia might not have been an attention hound, but even she knew this was good image management.

CHAPTER TWELVE

AS soon as they made it back to the king's apartments, Ty turned on the TV in the library. It had only been thirty minutes since they'd left Our Lady of the Waves, where they never did find the last missing Meimeyo. Nonetheless, the paparazzi photos of Olivia and the dragons were already being aired along with footage of Anso's speech.

Seeing this, a headache began to vise around Anso's temples. The journalists were in ecstasy, parsing every word and gesture for meaning. Knowing he couldn't avoid it, he dropped to the couch to watch. Ty was standing closer to the screen, flipping through channels with the remote.

"These are good," he said, freezing on a shot of Olivia. "Olivia is beaming, and the dragons could be shy toddlers holding on tight to Mum. Even if people ignore the timing, which makes collusion next to impossible, no one who sees these will believe she knew where to find the Meimeyo because she put them there. The media are calling her a heroine."

"She is one," Anso said, pressing the heels of his hands into his throbbing eyes.

"One thing is certain. That society columnist from *The Daily Current* was on the money. You have to throw a party. The public needs to see you celebrating this and your mating."

"Right. Putting it on the to-do list."

A gentle hand massaged the back of his neck. "What's wrong?" Olivia asked softly.

Simply looking into her new blue eyes calmed him. "Feeling a little hemmed in." He smiled so it wouldn't seem like a big deal. "And since I'm king, I can't just go out and swim it off."

Olivia furrowed her brow sympathetically. "Choosing me as your mate has made you even more of a news story, hasn't it?"

"It's not your fault. It comes with the job."

"But James and I make it worse."

"Your speech is number one on WooTube," James interrupted, strolling in freshly dressed with one of the tablet computers from the guest rooms. "The official video has over ten thousand 'likes.' Oh—" He stopped as he looked up and saw Olivia and Anso's faces. "Did something bad happen?"

"Just a small case of celebrity claustrophobia," Ty quipped. "Occupational hazard."

"We should get out of the palace," James said unhesitatingly. "Somewhere quiet with a lot of space."

His "we" was as welcome to Anso's strained nerves as it apparently was easy for James to say. Anso wouldn't have predicted it, but what he suddenly wanted more than anything was for the four of them to be alone between any walls but these. No ever-efficient butler. No Ellice lurking somewhere waiting to barge in. No Lord Noth calling to ask—or give—his input on this or that. Surprisingly, running off with Olivia wouldn't have satisfied. Anso needed peace and quiet for all of them.

"Q Gardens?" Ty suggested. "They're closed to the public on Mondays."

It was the perfect solution. Donated to the city by a wealthy elf family, the gardens were lovely this time of year. Because they were enclosed in an air-filled structure, the humans would find them familiar.

"Can we get there without being followed?"

Ty's grin stretched across his face. "You leave that to me, Your Majesty."

~

Twenty acres of cultivated parkland made the Q Gardens a favorite destination for school field trips. Generations of Oceana's children had learned their upper world trees and flowers here. A magically reinforced glass structure towered fifty meters above the paths, giving the gardens the look of a conservatory on steroids.

Ty remembered coming here as a boy with other aristocratic students from the palace school. The duck pond had enthralled him, and the rough-trunked oaks with the acorns that plopped on his head. He recalled wishing he'd been an ordinary person so he could have ridden there on the yellow school subs and run wild about the place. To make up for that, he and Anso had snuck off. Anso had saved the crusts from his sandwich to feed the geese. It was one of Ty's first memories of Prince Anso as a real person. God help him, the die might have been cast for him to fall in love with him then.

Today, that stupidity didn't matter. Every cell in his body seemed to have achieved a rare state of peace.

"This is perfect," he said. He was stretched on his back beneath a tree in the wooded area known as the Ramble. The security guard he'd bribed wouldn't intrude on them here.

"Mm," Olivia lazily agreed.

She was a good sport, Ty thought, someone who enjoyed winning but wasn't obsessed like men could be. She lay on the blanket too, with James on her other side. She'd traded her fancy clothes for a nearly clean shirt of Anso's and a pair of lady's button-fly jeans she'd somehow convinced Harrison to scrape up for her. She looked relaxed in them. James's dark head rested on her shoulder, his arm slung across her belly. From what Ty could tell, one of the benefits of being married was being really comfortable with each other.

Ty would have given a lot to rest his head on her other side.

He wasn't sure he had the right to touch her, but her hand was only inches away. Giving her an opportunity to resist, he pulled her fingers gently into his. She squeezed his hand enough to let him know the hold could stay.

"We made a good team," Anso said. He'd been pulling off his boots in preparation for lying down. That taken care of, he reclined on his side. Ty liked how close he was. Anso could see across him to the others.

"We did," Olivia said. "I'm glad the dragons are safe."

"Why did they smell like flowers?" James asked. "For that matter, why does everything in Oceana smell a bit spicy-sweet?"

Anso's chuckle warmed Ty's ear. "I wasn't kidding back in the church. That's the scent of magic. Because faeries created the Pocket, everything smells like faerie dust."

"*Noo*," James said, but not like he really doubted.

"Yes," Anso said. "Species like dragons, which originated in Faerie, carry a stronger scent than half-mundanes like weres. You probably didn't notice when you first came here because your change hadn't fully taken hold. Now you've got magic in you too."

"We're not going to turn into seals, are we?" Olivia asked.

Ty had a feeling if she weren't so mellow, she'd have sounded more worried.

"No," Anso said. "I'm afraid that's a gift we don't have the power to share with humans."

Olivia seemed to realize she might have insulted him. Her hand shifted inside Ty's. "I'm sorry. I didn't mean to—"

"No." Anso reached across Ty's chest to touch her. "You don't need to apologize. Shapechanging must be a strange idea if you're not used to it."

She rolled onto her side to look at Anso, which caused James to grunt and roll after her. Though Ty didn't move himself, he saw Olivia and Anso lock gazes. The atmosphere between them turned more electric, still relaxed but with a hint of the sexual. That hint added weight to his groin.

Anso and Olivia stared at each other for a long moment before she spoke. "The four of us being together feels good. Like when Ty told us to hold hands at the church."

Olivia's left hand had tangled with Anso's right. Both rested on Ty's belly, just over his navel. A tingle ran into him at the point of contact, too strong and too erotic for him not to react. Anso's hand curled farther around Olivia's just as James slung his upper leg over hers. He wore the same buckskin trousers as Anso and Ty. Whether he intended to or not, his bare toes touched Ty's ankle.

He felt as if an electric circuit had been closed. He touched everyone, and everyone touched him. His breathing and pulse came quicker, which both Olivia and Anso had to notice.

"If we're *all* mated," Anso said, the first time he'd put it this bluntly, "it makes sense that we'd enjoy being in a group."

Anso's voice was huskier. Ty turned his head and found a flush on his face. Anso's eyes held Olivia's, but where his hips rested against Ty's, a definite swell was forming.

"Could I kiss him?" Olivia asked.

Ty's heart fluttered in his chest. No way was she asking permission to kiss James.

"Is that what you want?" Anso's voice was even more gravelly now.

"Yes," she said. "Ty's mouth is beautiful."

Ty looked at her, and she looked back. Her eyes were big and solemn, their so-familiar color affecting him physically, as if that deep blue and only that deep blue could reach inside and touch him.

"I want more than a kiss," he said gruffly.

Her smile was unmistakably delighted. "So do I," she admitted.

He touched her cheek and stretched up. He swallowed, because he really didn't want to do this wrong, but the instant their lips sealed together the kiss was pure magic. He made a sound he wasn't sure he ever had in his life. Hunger. Longing. Pleasure at it being completely met. She tasted delicious—like Anso a bit, but also brand new. Her mouth was tender and sleek inside, her tongue a temptation he couldn't resist suckling. She sucked his in return, and all the hairs on his arms stood up.

"You taste like cherries," he murmured against her lips.

"I do not," she laughed. "Why are all the men in my life romantics?"

He loved that she included him among her men, loved that she called him romantic. A pressure welled inside him that was about so much more than sex. He had to roll her onto her back, had to watch the dappled sun hit her face to make *his* mark appear in her eyes. Somehow, James wasn't in the way when he pushed her over. He was making room for Ty to take her.

As Olivia squinted against the light, the yellow inner ring appeared in her irises. Ty's cock stretched so full at the sight it stung. He pushed up on his elbows. Olivia shivered at whatever she saw in his eyes, someone who wanted to maraud her probably. Ty dropped his gaze to her breasts. She wasn't wearing a bra. Her nipples were extremely aroused and pushing out Anso's shirt.

The reaction was trite, but Ty couldn't keep from licking his lips.

"Take this off me," she whispered.

He realized he wouldn't have if she hadn't asked. The bull all the wereseals wanted was too nervous to take the lead with his first woman.

Nervous or not, he couldn't pass up the invitation. He freed her buttons with shaky hands. The other men didn't help. James and Anso lay close enough to touch but were just watching. The sound of their breathing added heft to his arousal. He bared one warm breast and cupped it, his thumb sweeping across her tight red nipple. He tested its hardness with the pad of his thumb, finding the contracted flesh fascinatingly substantial. Wetness trickled from his prick, his excitement already at its edge. He couldn't speak except hoarsely.

"You fill my palm perfectly."

Her hand curved around the ridge of his groin, gently cupping its straining shape. "You more than fill mine, Ty."

Why did her saying his name send his lust soaring? Groaning, he dropped his head to the breast he held, surrounding that tempting peak and pulling greedily at it. This was something you couldn't do with men, a thrill that after so many years of wondering and not doing felt forbidden. Her nipple was warm and smooth, and he knew he'd never get enough of it. His enthusiasm was pretty hard to hide, as were the rooting noises he was making. Olivia stroked his hair and arched closer, so he guessed he wasn't doing it too hard. Giving in to what he wanted, he sucked in more, flicking her with his tongue until she gripped one of his thighs between both of hers and rolled her pelvis against his quadricep.

That nearly made his head explode with triumph. He ran his hand around her taut little waist, under her open shirt. The jeans she wore gapped enough to wedge his palm down around her butt.

Olivia's grip on his crotch tightened. The pressure of her hand felt so good he knew he'd better tug it away.

"Okay," he panted, easing back from her. Her lips were swollen from their kiss and the same red as her nipples, a comparison that momentarily shorted out his brain. "Okay . . . I . . ." He dragged his eyes back to hers, where the swelling of her pupils had once again drowned out the yellow ring. "I know this is my first time with a female, but I'd really like to get my dick inside you before I come."

Olivia bit her lower lip, not quite hiding her smile. "I'd like that too."

The dent she made in her mouth couldn't be resisted. He kissed her again, which led to long dizzy minutes of driving his tongue in and out of her clinging mouth. Each time she sucked him back, he shivered uncontrollably, which would have been embarrassing if it hadn't felt so good. Finally, he remembered he wanted to pull off her pants.

"Shit," he said. "Stop distracting me."

She laughed, then gasped when he bent to nuzzle her soft belly.

Thankfully, his fingers recovered enough of their usual skill to undo her button fly. That exposed more temptations, but he managed to pull the denim and her panties down her strong curvy legs. Then she lay in nothing but Anso's unbuttoned white cotton shirt, the sides fallen around her breasts, the cuffs rolled up many times to keep them at her elbows. Her pubic curls might have been the prettiest red Ty had ever seen, their charm surpassed only by moisture that glistened among them. His chest was tight, his lungs resisting his efforts to fill them.

Olivia seemed to know what the sight of her did to him, and some of the reasons why. She ran her fingers up one side of Anso's parted shirt. "Shall I leave this on?"

Ty shuddered, his hands flying to the leather ties at the front of his own trousers. "Yes," he rasped. "You wearing that after he did mixes your scent and his."

"I know something else that would," she said.

Ty saw from Anso's thunderstruck expression that he guessed what she meant.

"Kneel up," she said to him.

It was an order, but he didn't object. He knelt up, making shorter work of his trouser laces than Ty ever could. His big cock was free and being stroked by her pretty hand before Ty was halfway through undoing his sailor's knot.

The sound of Anso moaning at her caresses didn't help Ty's fingers work. Clearly, the king was in heat again.

"I know you need to come," Olivia panted, her hand small but strong on his reddened skin. "Tell me how to make you come quickly. I want you to be able to watch him take me without your instincts getting upset."

"Suck me," he groaned, his head falling back. "Lick me with the tongue that kissed him."

Ty was staring so open-mouthed at Anso's abandon that he didn't notice James had moved until his hands joined Ty's on his trouser front.

"Let me," James said quietly, his gaze straying to the others and back to Ty. "I used to sail when I was in college. I'm good at undoing knots."

He was good. He had Ty's aching cock in the open air even as Olivia swallowed Anso down. Both circumstances made Ty's organ jerk violently. She was kneeling, and the king was standing, his hips surging into her mouth. This caused the upper half of his erection to disappear. The pleasure he was feeling was obvious. His hands were buried in her gorgeous hair while hers gripped his root and balls, sparing him from worrying about thrusting down her throat too far. Ty could tell his friend would have if she hadn't taken the precaution. Anso's motions were jerky, his expression veering between ecstasy and torture.

Ty had to admit this heat thing was a blinking big turn on.

"She's good at giving head," James said, like a server recommending the best entree. "Somehow she lets you know she cares about you with every suck."

His fingertips touched Ty's cock, lightly pulling up the swollen strut on his underside. His eyes remained on the other couple, his profile flushed but calm.

"Are *you* okay with this?" Ty realized he ought to ask.

James's face turned to him, and for a second all Ty could think was that those cobalt eyes looked amazing with black hair. James's spirit was still behind them: his own individual and somewhat mysterious thoughts.

"More than I ought to be," he answered.

"I *do* love him," Ty admitted, dropping his voice even more.

"You could fall for her too," James said. "Sometimes she's so sweet she's hard to resist."

Ty couldn't tell if this was a warning. James's fingertips had reached the knob of his penis. Along with his thumb, they half plucked, half stroked the sensitive stretched skin. A fat drop of precum squeezed from his slit, the wetness dragging James's attention down. The other man's respiration grew choppy as he watched the effect his hand was having. The caress was very exciting, but Ty didn't tell him to stop. He remembered a time when other men's cocks were all he could think about.

"You're pretty hard to resist yourself," Ty said.

The compliment caused James to release him, or perhaps he was distracted by Anso's cries of pleasure kicking up a notch in pitch. Olivia was making good on her intent to wring a quick orgasm out of him. Ty found himself swallowing in time with her, as if he could help her suck off the king.

"God," James breathed. "God, he's going to go."

He went with a long rough cry. Olivia swallowed the first two spurts, then pulled free and pumped his cock fast and hard directly toward her breasts. Semen shot from Anso's penis over their perfect curves, inspiring all of the men to curse.

Now she'd really smell like him.

Heat crashed through Ty. He was tearing off his shirt as he stepped to her, yanking at the sleeves to get free of them. Her hands fell from Anso, and she turned to Ty on her knees. The blanket she knelt on was blue and silver, the Vitul eel clear on it. He couldn't deny the image exerted power over him. Ty's cock bounced higher, so hard and thick it could have been a weapon. Olivia looked at it, flushed, then tilted her face to him.

"Don't touch my cock," he said, though she hadn't made a move to do so. "It's going in your pussy and nowhere else. Don't touch the seed he spattered on you either. I'm going to rub it in with my chest."

She blinked at him, her blush growing pinker as her lips parted.

He held out his hands to her. She placed hers in them delicately, her skin hot and slightly damp. Ty pulled her to her feet. He loved how little she was, how he could lift her with no effort. "This is my turn with you," he said.

Her eyes were huge. "You're the boss," she agreed breathlessly.

She was fidgeting on her feet. The knowledge hit him that she was so ready to be taken she was having trouble standing still. The scent of her sex reached him a second later, powerful enough to trigger hormonal receptors he hadn't known he had. His entire body broke into a sweat.

"Oh yes," he said. His tone was feral, his grip tightening on hers. "I'm the boss, and I'm going to give you what you need."

She leaped at him and kissed him. His surprise didn't stop him from catching her, from boosting her bare sweet bottom up with his hands. He'd meant to fuck her on the blanket, but the tree was right behind them.

Ty wasn't the sort of lover to ignore a convenience.

He propelled her into it, slanting his head to kiss her deeper, rubbing his chest over her luscious breasts just as he'd threatened.

She made him gasp when she nipped his lower lip. The tiny pain shot like a cannon ball up the nerves of his erection.

"Someday," she whispered. "I'll spank you just like he does."

He gawked at her, panting with increased excitement, scarcely able to believe Anso had told her *that.* She seemed titillated rather than shocked.

She smiled like a siren at his reaction. "Not today though," she said. "Today I know you want something more basic."

Both her hands had been twined behind his neck. One released its hold to slid down the centerline of his heaving chest. On the way, she rubbed Anso's smeared semen into him. When *her* nostrils flared, he thought he'd go insane.

"Olivia," he burst out, his arousal so intense his skin should have caught fire where she touched it.

Her thumb rubbed a circle around his navel, her smile going even more cat-in-the-creamery. She lowered her head to lick a short trail across his shoulder.

"Mm," she said. "Your leopard spots are tasty *and* pretty."

Some other day he might have laughed in simple joy at her silliness, but her fingers cradled his cock just then. They were gentler than they had to be. They bounced his weight, testing it a little, which could have amused him too. Olivia seemed to enjoy men's cocks as much as he and her husband did. Given how little bounce her fingers got out of him, amusement didn't have much of a chance to rise. Ty suspected he was unusually erect. If she found him so, she liked it. Her thumb rubbed pleasure through the steady seep of his arousal. She closed her eyes and shuddered.

"Are you ready?" she asked when she opened them. "I don't want to rush your first time."

James had been right to warn him about falling for her. His stomach dropped, and his heart clenched in a seemingly solid ache. He knew heat was driving her, but her question expressed more than lust. Why was she worried that he was ready? Who was he that she should care for him?

"I'm ready," he said gruffly. "Go ahead and put me where you want me."

He knew this would spare him going astray in unfamiliar territory. She didn't seem to mind. She bit her lip and looked down between them, her fingers adjusting his hardness. Sleek hot flesh closed around his crest, slippery-sweet with wetness. Olivia's hips rocked and she let out a little sound, but she didn't push over him.

That honor she was leaving for him.

"Go slow for the first stroke," she said. "Until you get a feel for how I'm made inside."

Her voice was throaty. He was trembling from head to toe. He got a firmer grip on her bottom and let his brow rest on hers. Then he pressed into his first woman.

He moaned with bliss before he'd gone an inch. The clasp of her walls felt thick, stronger than he'd expected. The flickering movements of her pussy were like a secret she'd reserved for his cock alone. No one else could feel it. The message was his to read or not. Deciphering the code could certainly become rewarding. She drew her breath in sharply as he forged inward, a new gush of cream painting him. He couldn't help but smile at that.

Her big eyes came up to his as he reached her last limit. He was in her all the way, their quickened pulses seeming to speak to each other.

"I like this," he whispered, nudging a touch deeper. "The way my cock stretches you, the way only I know how wet you are."

His words aroused them both. Her tongue snuck over her upper lip. Ty pushed her harder into the tree. A sound tore from her throat that he was pretty sure was pleasure.

Her hands clutched his shoulders from behind. "Please," she said, her head arching back. "Don't leave me hanging."

Ty rubbed his tip on the end of her and groaned. "I don't want this to race by too fast."

"No," she agreed, squirming back at him the same way. "But please make it fast enough."

Her pleading made him shake, but he drew back to fuck her all the same. Being perfect didn't matter. She needed this as much as he did. Any sort of motion was going to be good.

He was right about that. They both cried out when he drove in again.

He couldn't keep it slow, though he tried. She was too hot, too tight, and she rocked herself back at him with an eagerness no man with his killer hard-on could have discouraged.

"Down," she begged, five fervid minutes into it. "Lay me down on the blanket."

He'd lay her all right, and lay her and lay her until they both flew apart.

He cursed as he turned her, trying to keep up his thick deep pumping while he lowered both their weight. He couldn't do it. He had to hug her tight against him to get her down safely. She writhed crazily while he did, her pussy squeezing him as strongly as her thighs.

"God," he breathed in thanks the instant he had her down.

With her braced on the ground, they went at each other twice as hard as before. It was madness: the sensations, the noises, the fact that James and Anso weren't doing anything but watching. The other men were leaving this all to him, leaving *her* all to him. He gloried in it, thrilled at giving them a show, yet also enjoying the stupendous selfishness of it.

He couldn't mind when her fingernails dug into the skin of his back.

"Ty," she cried. "*Ty*!"

She was crying *his* name, and that just plain drove him nuts. He shifted angles, trying to make each inward drive a mallet's rap on her clitoris. He must have done well enough. In a dozen more strokes she came, her passage fisting him with eye-widening strength. The friction on every inch of him heightened. He'd been close to coming for a while now, but that really cranked up the pressure on his gonads. His balls screamed for him to let what they had inside explode.

A little more, he thought, loving the pain of it. *Just a little* . . .

She shoved two fingers between his cheeks into his asshole.

Too many nerves suddenly joined forces to bombard him with bliss signals. Ty's vertebrae seemed to lock, his hips snapping forward to sling him into her. He ejaculated like it was his last chance on earth, the heat rushing from him in hard hot bursts.

"Yes," she groaned, coming around him again.

His vision flashed bright with pleasure, his sensory perceptions narrowing down to just his penis. No thought. No limbs. Just that part of him staking a very copious claim to the matching part of her. In that moment, he was glad Anso thought he couldn't get her pregnant. No prophylactic sheath stretched between them. His seed shot straight to her womb. As it did, their energy zinged together, rays penetrating deeper than flesh to join them. He heard himself gasping with delight, and then—like a pair of fingers snapping —they were separate beings again.

His skin tingled intensely all over him.

"Wow," she said shakily.

He remained jammed in her, supporting himself on straight arms he couldn't recall locking. His chest was dripping sweat on her, his diaphragm lurching in and out with his bid for air. Olivia petted him as if savoring the feel of both.

"You okay?" he asked. He had to swallow after he did. His throat felt as rough as if he'd been screaming.

"Yes," she said, then flashed an eyebrow-wagging grin at him. "You?"

He laughed at her humor, liking her—if warily—more by the second. "Your Majesty, I believe you know exactly how incredible I feel."

Though Olivia rolled to sprawl bonelessly on her stomach, Ty wasn't worn out by what they'd done. How could he be when one of their tastiest members remained unsatisfied? James hadn't beat off while he was watching like he had before with Ty.

The possibility that he wasn't as interested in masturbating if Ty didn't join him closed Ty's throat on itself.

"Come here," he said roughly.

James and Anso had sat cross-legged on the grass for the show. Now James looked at Ty with eyes almost as wide as his wife's could get.

"I want you," Ty said, gesturing him closer.

"You can't."

"I do. In fact . . ." Ty paused to let inspiration gather. "I'd like to take you with your chest laid across her back. I'd like you to hold onto her while I bugger you nice and hard, just like you deserve. I expect she'll enjoy the pleasure noises I wring from you if you're making them an inch away from her ear."

"Oh God," James said, which pleased Ty as much as Olivia chuckling into the folded arms she was resting her cheek on.

"I would like it," she assured her husband. "What Ty described is my idea of triple X."

As stiff as James was from watching Ty's performance, he didn't take much urging. Ty arranged him half on Olivia's back and half on the blanket with a pillow roll shoved under his hips. Then he proceeded to give him what was assuredly the best ass fucking of his life, given that it was only his second. Ty's own energy surprised him, but there was no fighting it. He adored taking James over top of Olivia, her female flesh jiggling and jolting with each determined thrust.

James moaned even louder than he had for Ty in the shower, something about Olivia's presence making it impossible for him to control his responses. Well accustomed to stimulating prostates, Ty pummeled his with unrelenting accuracy. When James came, it was with both hands shoved under Olivia's breasts and his head flung back on a tigerish groan.

Ty discovered he had more come in him.

At this point, they all looked too disreputable to be seen by anyone. Giggling like teenagers, they crept with their clothes and supplies to wash up in the duck pond. This feature of the park wasn't as secluded as the Ramble, so they had to be quick. Olivia couldn't stop laughing as she dressed behind the blanket James and Anso held up for her.

"I'm a sex fiend," she gasped between snickers. "And I can't do these damn buttons."

Ty wasn't sure what one thing had to do with the other. He only knew he was smiling too.

~

In order to slip unnoticed out of the palace, Ty had borrowed a nondescript family van from one of his household staff. Anso wanted to warn him to take extra good care of it, but had run out of energy. Operating on the theory that violating more protocols hardly mattered, Ty was overlooking James's lack of a learner's permit to give him an impromptu lesson at the controls.

They were lurching around in the currents but not too dangerously. Anso and Olivia braced themselves in the separate back compartment, which Ty's good-natured employee appeared not to have had a chance to clean up. Children's toys, ranging from infant to reading age, were strewn across the floor, along with what he suspected was Faerie-O's cereal. Olivia had picked up a teether and was turning it in her hands. Like him, her body language was relaxed but inward turned, as if their physical satisfaction hadn't quite turned off their worries.

Though Anso told himself mated people didn't magically become one person, he couldn't like her being withdrawn from him.

He put his hand on her knee, wishing part of him didn't feel like he needed to ask permission. Olivia turned her head.

"You're troubled," he said.

Her laugh was a breath of air. "I was going to say the same about you."

You didn't though, he thought. And I know there's a reason for that, one I likely don't want to hear.

She placed her hand on the crux of his neck and shoulder, using gentle fingers to soothe the tendon that had gone tense. Still she didn't speak. He guessed if she didn't, he'd have to.

"This isn't how I pictured being mated," he confessed, watching her expression for reactions. "I always thought I'd have my wife to myself. I hoped we'd be each other's bulwark against the storms."

"Husbands and wives can certainly be that." Her eyes were soft but her voice was cautious. Threads of light danced across her face through the van's small portholes. Her skin looked utterly velvety. Anso knew she'd become his definition of beautiful.

"I didn't mind what we did together today," he said. "I mean, of course you could tell I liked it. I just . . . I feel off balance. I don't know how to bond with you the way I want."

Olivia stroked his hair back along his cheek. "You're a wonderful man. You choosing to mate me is an honor."

He was certain she didn't mean to, but the way she put this increased his uneasiness. He realized he wanted her to say she loved him. They'd known each other two days, and already he craved the words. What if she never said them? How would he feel after years and years?

Though it caused his throat to tighten, he reminded himself that her and her husband's love had deepened for half their lives.

"I'm rushing you," he said and looked down between his knees.

She rubbed his back and—God—just that sent sweet waves of warmth through him. "I loved today. You've no idea how much I'll cherish the memory."

"We'll make more, Liv."

She touched his lips and smiled. "I hope so," she said wistfully.

CHAPTER THIRTEEN

WHEN Anso made up his mind to face a necessity, he didn't drag his feet. The process of throwing a giant celebration was set into motion the moment they returned to the palace and were greeted by Harrison. The stiff-necked butler seemed excited about overseeing the menu and invitations, especially when it became clear the king was giving him carte blanche.

"I've seen what you can handle," Anso assured him as he tried halfheartedly to demur. "Use Belikov for the decorations. She knows how to hammer down a theme while looking like she used a feather. Other than that, you only need to call me if you run into trouble. I trust you to make us look good."

Olivia liked that *us*. She sensed it included quite a few people. For that matter, it might have included Harrison.

Anso's a good boss, she thought, a trait she admired as much as being a good leader. As a boss, Olivia thought she was a smidgen better than James. As a leader, he had her beat hollow. Though Anso hadn't been king long, she thought he'd excel at both.

Naturally, a party that was meant to impress required more than food and guests. Media access had to be organized. Entertainment too, both magical and mundane. Different venues were discussed, the winner a historic banquet hall in the old section of the city. Ty had a snake's nest of security to coordinate, including escorts from air to water for foreign guests. That prospect gave Olivia more than one sort of butterfly. Oceana was amazing enough. Who knew what wonders other Pocket territories might provide?

Less thrilling was the super-chic Mrs. Bonn taking charge of her again the next day.

"I swear I'm good for more than looking pretty!" Olivia burst out after the third ridiculously fussy designer pulled his racks in and out of the blue salon.

She didn't usually lose her temper this way. She thought the cause might be that she'd been separated from . . . well, all three of her men for hours. Last night, she and James had slept in a guest room. Sleeping was all they'd done—and not very well, to judge by her crankiness. That aside, she was an independent woman. She adored James's company, but she'd never wanted to chain herself to his hip. She'd better get over this sense of attachment, or going home again would be hell.

"Sorry," she said to Mrs. Bonn, once she'd swallowed the sudden and disturbing lump in her throat.

"Oh that's all right," the older woman said. "Compared to some of my clients, you've been a saint. Wereseal males—especially the aristocrats—can be funny about females. They're a little frightened of us. We seem safer up on pedestals all dressed up."

"My husband ought to know better," Olivia grumped.

"Of course he should," Mrs. Bonn said so caressingly she startled a laugh from Olivia.

"You are good," she said. "Like butterscotch and crumpets."

Mrs. Bonn smiled, pleased to have her talents appreciated. Then her smile turned conspiratorial. "I have an idea, which might be brilliant. There's a royal storehouse of gowns former queens have worn. Some of the older fashions were beautifully simple. Even more important, some of those queens were tremendously popular. Depending on what you choose, you could make a statement without saying a word."

"I might like that," Olivia said. "Unless the dresses are museum pieces. Then I'd be worried about spilling."

Mrs. Bonn tipped her head sideways. "You do realize you're queen, yes? If you spill wine on a priceless gown, no one's going to say boo." At Olivia's look of horror, she laughed softly. "It won't matter, Your Majesty. Your husband can afford to send a boatload of dresses to the magical dry cleaner."

Her husband. The phrase sounded far too normal, considering the woman wasn't talking about James.

"Now," said Mrs. Bonn, clearly thinking the matter settled, "let's make an appointment for your hair."

"You aren't going to do it yourself?"

Mrs. Bonn tapped her nose and grinned. "I'm multi-talented, it's true, but I recently met this three-quarter faerie who can work miracles."

~

Olivia had consulted with Mrs. Bonn in private. When the faerie arrived later that afternoon, the guards Nico and Mark accompanied him into the largest of guest bathrooms, where a stylist's chair had been set in front of one sink and mirror. This seemed a case of chauvinism, though it might have been warranted. Up close, the faerie was lovely enough to make her lightheaded. And he smelled better than chocolate.

Slim as a reed but broad-shouldered, his silky flowing hair was silver. His eyes were a stormy gray, his nose sharp enough to etch glass. His lips were almost as pretty as Ty's, but it was hard to decide in what way they were less. Overall, his beauty stunned. Notably, he was the first person she'd seen wearing glasses. The frames were narrow rectangles with glittering scarlet rims. Maybe she imagined it, but the glitters looked like they were swirling.

"They're spelled," he said, noting her attention. "I can see how you'll look in a style before I work it up."

"Handy," she said, embarrassed that her voice came out breathy.

This was a hairdresser, probably not highly ranked in his race, but she was quivering like a schoolgirl meeting a movie star.

"My name is Lajos," he said, holding out a gleaming long-fingered hand.

"Halt!" Nico barked. He and his brother had drawn their weapons and were pointing them at Lajos. "You don't touch the queen, faerie."

"It's all right," Olivia said, seeing how startled the slender hairdresser was. "He was just—"

"No," Nico interrupted. "Forgive me, Your Majesty, but this one knows he's not allowed to touch you without putting on gloves first."

"He could enchant you," Mark explained. "Faeries carry mojo in their skin."

Fortunately, Lajos was more amused than offended. "I'm only here to arrange her hair. And in case you didn't look up my name in the Magical Registry, I'm not a full blood fae."

"That doesn't mean you're harmless," Nico growled.

Mark holstered what looked like a laser pistol from a sci-fi movie, then held out two elbow-length white gloves. Lajos took them, pulling them on finger by finger with an archly suggestive smile. By the time he'd finished the reverse striptease, Mark was flushed and sweating and gripping his gun again in both hands. He was breathing more deeply than Olivia thought he should, like he'd run up a flight of stairs. It was rude of her to notice, but the guard also appeared to be sporting a large hard-on.

Olivia wondered why she wasn't reacting the same way. Lajos did make her heart beat faster, and his glamour certainly dazzled her, but she wasn't physically attracted to him as she was to Anso and James and Ty.

Perhaps bonding with them gave her immunity?

As if he knew this, the faerie's smile when he turned to her was merely pleasant. "Forgive me for indulging myself. Now and then I tire of anti-faerie prejudice."

Olivia hadn't known there was such a thing. Nico wasn't feeling guilty about it, to go by his eye roll.

"Will you sit, Your Majesty?" Lajos asked politely, swiveling the chair for her.

Olivia slid into it, feeling like she did when interviewing a job candidate who wasn't giving her enough to go by. Were Nico and Mark bigots, or did Lajos have a martyr complex? People could have little chips on their shoulders and still be competent employees. Then again, did it matter? Lajos was here to style her hair. If Mrs. Bonn said he worked miracles, wasn't that likely to be true?

Lajos fluffed her waves across her shoulders with his elegant white-gloved hands. A tingle crept up her neck at the light caress. "You *are* beautiful," he murmured. "King Anso is a lucky man to be able to add you to his treasures."

Lajos's glasses magnified his eyes, their storminess seeming to deepen as she looked into them in the mirror. Like a treasure was *exactly* how Anso had treated her today, one he had to shine up before she could earn points for him. She marveled that this fact hadn't occurred to her until now.

Before she could puzzle out the reason, Lajos began to brush her hair. The steady swoosh of the strokes immediately relaxed her. "You're fortunate your husband is understanding. Most men would balk at sharing a prize like you."

"I'm my own woman," she replied. She meant it to be a statement. Instead, she sounded petulant and unsure.

"Of course you are." His smooth tenor voice was more comforting than Mrs. Bonn's. "I knew that the moment we met. No one could keep you prisoner. Or prevent you from holding to your vows."

It was a strangely personal thing to say. Olivia glanced at the guards to see if they'd noticed. They were standing straight as ramrods with their backs against the Edwardian tile, their eyes forward and unmoving—giving her privacy, she guessed. If they weren't alarmed, chances were everything was fine.

"Do you have family back home?" Lajos asked in his deliciously soothing voice. Listening to it made her feel as if she were half asleep.

"A daughter."

The corners of Lajos's mouth turned down, and hers automatically echoed them. "How sad. You must miss her terribly. And she must miss her mother."

"She must," Olivia agreed . . . or tried to.

The sadness inside her must have been waiting for a chance to get out. How could she have thought, even for a moment, that it would be hard to leave this place? She was a horrible mother. And a horrible wife. Almost before she knew it, she was sobbing too hard to speak.

"There, there," said the beautiful faerie hairdresser, offering her a nice cool hankie to weep into. "Mustn't ruin your looks with tears. I'm sure you'll find a solution to all your troubles soon."

~

James had a deep dark secret: He liked wearing tuxedoes. He especially liked it when they fit as well as the one Harrison had nabbed from Anso's closet so the half-elf royal tailor could alter it fast for him.

James's knowledge that this cloth had lain against Anso's skin gave him a charge he wasn't yet easy with.

Pushing that from his mind, he turned sideways in front of the full-length mirror in the guest room's combination closet and dressing room. The jacket part of the tux draped the back of a chair, allowing James to check the fit of the rest. Being mated to the king and Ty had changed him. He could see as well as feel the difference in his body. His abs were flat as a board beneath the silver eel cummerbund, his biceps maybe an inch bigger. He'd been in good shape for his age before. Now he looked nearly as formidable as Ty and Anso—and maybe the only difference was that they trained harder. Hell, even the sprinkling of gray hair he'd had was gone.

The elation that rose at this told him he was shallower than he'd known. His only regret was wondering how they'd explain the changes to friends and family. Contact lenses would cover their eyes, and he could pretend he'd dyed his hair, since—apparently—he was vain enough. The rest, though . . .

He pulled a twisted face at his reflection. Would people believe they'd taken a extra relaxing spa vacation?

He sighed lengthily, the gust of air making his shoulders hitch up and fall. Part of him, possibly a not-small part, didn't want to go home. He adored his parents, and he liked Olivia's pretty well. If they failed to return, it would cause them pain at a time in their lives they should have been enjoying. Some of their friends he'd miss, but Olivia had always been his favorite companion. Though he was proud of the business they'd built together, he'd leave it in a heartbeat for the sort of fun they were having here.

He knew Violet could take over. In truth, he wouldn't be surprised if, with her at the helm, Forster Media became a world-class firm. Their daughter had the vision and smarts for anything.

Which brought him to the one insurmountable obstacle to staying. James loved Violet differently than he loved Olivia, but he loved her as much—in part because he knew how desperately she needed the unconditional love he and Olivia gave her. Violet could be difficult to get close to. She was prickly and passionate and God help the man who thought he could soften her. She'd have issued that Ellice woman a sharp smackdown—with her fists, if need be. She wouldn't have worried what happened to her for doing it either, not if it helped someone she respected. James liked to think Violet was a true warrior princess.

Smiling wryly, he lifted the tuxedo jacket off the chair and slid his arms into it. Fastening the single button completed the James Bond effect. He assured himself he'd decided. They weren't staying in Oceana. This was just an adventure, the likes of which he hadn't imagined existed, physically or otherwise. James would work his homoerotic interests out of his system, and then they'd go home, hopefully leaving as little damage as possible behind them. If he'd miss Ty for more than the blistering sex—and maybe Anso as well—he'd get over it. Sometimes in life you couldn't have everything.

He glanced at the door to the fancy closet, wondering how long Olivia and that hairdresser would be shut up in the bathroom. He wanted to see what she was wearing, the incomparable Mrs. Bonn having been secretive about it. He wanted Olivia to see him too. She never failed to coo over him in a monkey suit. He realized he hadn't seen her in hours. That was too long. They were in and out of each other's company all the time most days. On the few occasions that they weren't, it made him feel off kilter.

He hoped he wouldn't go through the same discomfort when they parted from Anso and Ty.

Abruptly losing patience, he opened the closet door.

"Liv," he called. "How much gilding does your lily really need?"

He stepped into the bedroom, grinning as he anticipated her scolding him. After a moment, Olivia and her entourage trailed out from the big bathroom. If his eyes went to the faerie first, that was only because the guy was sparkling.

He also smelled incredible, like flower shop baked in a chocolate bun. His hair was a silvery blond that floated around a heart-stopping narrow face. The glasses he wore added charm, but James's cock behaved itself. This reassured him. He didn't need to be attracted to every man he met.

"Hey," he said to be polite before turning his gaze to Olivia.

She was a different kind of heart-stopper.

"Boy," he said, "with an extra helping of *wow.*"

Her draping gown was a blue so dark it probably could be called midnight. Grecian in style, braided silver cords bound the dress between and beneath her breasts. The dark silk fell from there to her feet, where a banding of silver Vitul eels puddled over gladiator style sandals.

"You're a goddess," he said, letting his gaze run up her again. Her new eyes looked amazing with the navy, like sapphires set on fire. Her deep red hair was cool too, piled in gleaming waves on top of her head with an array of pearl pins.

"I could fix your hair as well," the hairdresser offered, his trendy blue glasses winking. "Slick it back so you look as good as her."

For a second the offer tempted. Then James had to laugh. "No one could look as good as her. I think I'd better muddle on as I am."

"It wouldn't take but a minute," the faerie said.

Olivia drew James's attention by rubbing a spot between her eyebrows. She only did that when she was getting a headache. Come to think of it, she wasn't acting like herself. She hadn't said a word about his tux, or blushed when he complimented her. She looked like something had put her in a daze.

"Maybe you should go," James said gently to the faerie. "I think my wife needs a breather. You did a good job. Do I need to tip you?"

The question seemed to startled the hairdresser. "My fee has been taken care of."

This was lucky, because James belatedly remembered he'd been kidnapped without a cent on him.

"Well, all right then." James strode to the bedroom door and opened it. "Thanks so much for your time."

The faerie bowed a trifle stiffly, but he left. James looked back at Olivia and her pair of guards. The men seemed as out of it as she was.

"Jeesh," James said. "Was that so boring you all went comatose?"

Olivia sat on a chair, her hands resting limply in her lap. "What?" she asked confusedly.

James laughed and went to kiss her forehead. That hairdresser must have nattered on but good. "Thanks for looking out for her," he said to Nico and Mark.

"Er. Yes." Nico shook himself alert. "We'll . . . be in the hall if you need us again."

Once the door was shut behind them, Olivia turned to him.

"We can't forget," she said.

"Forget what, sweetheart?"

"That we're only pretending to like them, lulling them into complacence until we get a chance to escape."

She seemed agitated. James crouched down in front of her. "Is everything okay? I know your heart, honey. You couldn't have slept with Ty and Anso if you didn't care for them some."

"I won't be a bad mother. Or a bad wife."

"You couldn't be either," he soothed, wrapping his hands over hers. "We *are* going back. We knew that from the beginning."

Olivia's reminder wasn't that different from what he'd been thinking to his reflection. Agreeing with her shouldn't have made his stomach twist.

"Soon," she said, nodding firmly, her gaze hanging onto his. "I'm sure we won't have to wait long for our opening."

~

Making up her mind on difficult subjects usually calmed Olivia. This evening, she felt more out of sorts.

At her request, James had left her alone in the guest bedroom. She lay carefully on her back on the floor-level mattress, doing her best not to crease her nice outfit. Her dress was exquisite, and she knew she looked nice in it. It was true she didn't live for parties, but she'd have plenty of people looking out for her at this one. Nothing should have troubled her. She *wanted* to go home. If her gut was correct, and the chance to do that came quickly, she shouldn't feel anything but happy.

She turned her wedding ring around her finger, a gesture she hadn't made in a while. The faintest whiff of cocoa and carnations teased her nose.

Happy, she thought. Soon James and she would be as happy as they were before they came here.

A rap sounded on the door and Anso walked in. He was dressed for the celebration in a crisp ice blue uniform, the sort that made women think a wrinkle wouldn't dare come near it. A handful of ribbons decorated the front, so she supposed he must have served in Oceana's armed services at some point. Olivia drank in the sight of him despite her intent to let him go. He carried his straight tall figure with an endearing hint of hesitance. His beautiful worried eyes enlivened his kind face.

He smiled as he looked down at her. "You chose Queen Beatrice's gown. She built Our Lady of the Waves and donated it to the church."

"That's what Mrs. Bonn told me. She said Beatrice also founded a school for music that children still attend today."

"There's a famous portrait of her in their lobby wearing this dress." Anso sat beside her on the low bed. She felt so good with him close to her, especially when he took her hand and pulled it onto his thigh. "James said you weren't feeling well."

"I'm fine. Just a little nervous about spending the night in a crowd of people I don't know."

"We'll look out for you," he said.

Unable not to, she sat up. Anso stroked his fingers around her face. "I'd like to give you a gift."

"A gift . . ."

"It's traditional for a man to give one to his mate. Under the circumstances, this one is appropriate."

"It's not a sardine, is it?" she blurted, making him laugh. She hadn't meant to joke, but she couldn't deny she liked amusing him.

"It's not a sardine." He pulled a small silk bundle from his breast pocket and laid it in her hand. Olivia opened it curiously.

A ring in the shape of a sea dragon lay inside. Tiny rubies glowed in its eyes, and its half-folded wings were so detailed they seemed ready to lift off. Enchanted, Olivia stroked the wings wonderingly. Miniscule gold claws marked their finials.

"My ancestor Conjugus gave this ring to his queen. It's designed to fit on your middle finger. It won't interfere with your wedding ring."

When Olivia looked up, the surface of his deep blue eyes glimmered with emotion.

"You put it on," she whispered, too tight-throated to speak loudly.

He slid the dragon onto her finger, its curly tail cleverly formed into the band. "There. That looks just right on you."

His voice was choked up too. He'd dropped his eyes and wasn't lifting them again. *This is wrong*, she thought. *He deserves to be loved.*

He patted her hand and started to pull away.

Olivia caught his face and kissed him as gently as she could. He returned the kiss the same way. His arms slid around her, his head tilting to the side. His tongue caressed hers, more tenderness in the exchange than sex. His lips were silk against hers.

The kiss ended as gently as it began.

"I'll wait for you," he said softly. "Whenever you're ready to love me back, that will be all right.

"I'll never be the *only* one who loves you," seemed the best thing she could say in return.

He liked the answer, some of the melancholy leaving his eyes as his faint smile grew. "You," he said, "are as wise as you are loyal."

~

James concluded the old Medici would have felt at home in this banquet hall. Lit by thousands of beeswax tapers instead of electric lights, the place was half medieval fortress, half Renaissance palazzo. Thanks to the number of foreign guests, its interior was air-filled. Many round black-clothed tables filled the hall itself, which towered to a dramatic painted ceiling two stories above their heads.

"Saint" Poseidon and his angels cavorted in the murals there.

Belikov, the event's designer, had leaned unabashedly on the mini-dragon theme. Huge museum-quality tapestries depicted the city's mascots in presumably famous scenes from Oceana's history. Ice sculptures were carved in the shape of dragons, ditto for napkin rings. The hors d'oeuvres, which were almost too pretty too eat, offered shrimp (the Meimeyo's favorite snack) in more combinations than James could count. The twelve-man orchestra in the balcony loft, along with all of the servers, were dressed in Meimeyo black and gold.

James wouldn't call this decorating with a feather, but the overall effect was striking.

He munched on a plate of shrimp things as he wandered the chattering crowd. He'd gotten separated from the royal party early on—not that it mattered. Olivia and Anso were the couple people wanted to see tonight. James didn't mind. There was plenty of sightseeing for him to do. He wanted to soak up everything he could while he had the chance.

A pale handsome man caught his attention by leering at him from beside a tall torchier. When James got a better look at his smile, he couldn't restrain a double take. Those were fangs the man was flashing. He must be an actual vampire.

James almost turned to look again when someone elbowed his sleeve.

"Better not," said a pleasant voice. "Vampires take staring as an invitation to make your acquaintance."

A reasonably tall, thirtyish fellow with medium brown hair was addressing James. His clothes were shabbier than most of the people's here, but he looked nice in them. His eyes were gray, his nose crooked at the bridge. All in all, he had the sort of face that made men and women comfortable.

"I won't offer to shake," said the man, holding up his wine glass and plate to excuse himself, "but I'm the mayor of Resurrection."

"Pleased to meet you," James said. "I'm—"

"I know," said the mayor.

James had the disconcerting impression that the mayor knew a good deal more than his name. On closer inspection, the man's eyes weren't gray; they were silver. They were difficult to look away from, but James decided he ought to.

More than vampires might be able to spell him with their gaze.

"So," he said, resisting an impulse to clear his throat. "Resurrection is the Pocket city outside of Manhattan."

"That's right. Because we're drylanders, we don't get many chances to hobnob with wereseals."

What are you ***besides*** *a drylander?* James wondered, but it seemed rude to ask. Not a mundane, he didn't think.

"Those are werewolves," said the mayor, gesturing with his wineglass toward a group of laughing men. "They traveled with me from Resurrection. You wouldn't believe how antsy they were in the submarine." Seeming to enjoy playing guide, he pointed at another table. "Those are the doughty naturalists from the Oceanic Wildlife Patrol. You can tell they're not used to dressing up by how often they tug their collars. And over there, as you can see for yourself, are the crème de la crème of Oceana's fae."

The faeries were impossible to miss. Because they all sat together, their combined glow formed a nimbus around the group, as if they were one big candle flame. Though they drew attention by simple virtue of their sparkling beauty, they seemed reserved compared to the other guests, who were gradually loosening up enough to mingle outside their own races.

"Do they have wings?" James took the opportunity to ask.

"They do," the mayor confirmed. "They keep them folded close to their backs most times, so as not to spoil the fit of their clothes. And for modesty, I gather, like Victorian women not letting down their hair. They extend their wings at home, of course, and they're quite dazzling."

"You've been to Faerie?"

"I have. It's a fascinating land but not as . . . Elysian as many folks presume."

James had a zillion questions then. Unfortunately for his hope of having them answered, the orchestra began to play.

"Ah," said the mayor, gazing up at the balcony. "This is a lovely waltz. I must find the best perch to watch the dancing."

He drifted away, leaving James to stare after him. As he did, he spotted Anso's cousenemy, Lady Ellice. Barring evidence that she'd conspired to release the Meimeyo, he assumed she'd had to be invited. She stood among a group of gorgeously garbed royals, their gowns and cummerbunds as bright as peacocks. Her face was a haughty mask, the rigid pride of her posture easy to interpret. It galled her to attend this celebration honoring not just Anso's mating to someone else but Olivia's rescue of the Meimeyo. Instead of being cast aside by popular demand for bringing a curse with her, Olivia was the city's new darling. Lady Ellice and her clique looked as standoffish as the pureblood fae, and appeared to be having as little fun. James smiled to himself at that. Ruining the bitch's evening was the least they could do.

And then something seemed to entertain them. They put their heads together and whispered behind their hands, their exotically colored eyes turning as one in the direction of the dance floor. Malicious glee radiated from all of them.

Curious, James turned to seek the object of their attention. Somewhat to his shock, he found Ty standing at the edge of the gracefully whirling dancers. A plump young woman in an unfortunate ruffled orange gown had turned her head sharply away from him. The disapproving look on her face said he'd offended her. Ty's cheeks were swiftly going red, his spine as stiff as Ellice's had been.

Her mood was clearly improving. She let out a burst of laughter that turned more than one pair of eyes to her.

"Well," she said just loud enough to hear. "Looks like even the rejects are beginning to reject Otari."

~

Ty was having a very peculiar evening. His comm unit was in his pocket in case emergencies arose, but for the most part he was free to enjoy himself. Generally speaking, he liked parties. There always seemed to be a hookup or three to make. He'd told Anso not long ago that he was one of six on Ty's dance card. The other five were here tonight. Four had approached him with salacious offers, none of which he'd been the least enticed to accept.

Interestingly, they'd been suggesting private assignations. Once upon a time, being seen to share the favors of the future king's best friend would be half the point. Ty guessed his cachet had lost its glitter now that James Forster was the frontrunner to join the king's triad.

Cam Spence had actually had the nerve to ask if Ty thought Olivia's husband swung his bat both ways. Ty had advised him not to attempt running those bases.

"He's married," he'd said. "Outsiders care about those things."

"They don't care on their TV shows," Cam had retorted snippily.

And then Ty had spotted poor Priscilla Bowes near the dance floor. Per usual, she was horribly dressed and even more horribly forlorn. The Bowes, while aristocrats, had committed the unforgivable sin of losing nearly all their money in the stock market. They scraped invitations where they could, Anso being a reliable soft touch. Once Ty had established Priscilla wasn't going to develop a crush on him, he'd made a point of talking to her when their paths crossed. The Otari knew a thing or two about social pariahdom, after all.

He'd never asked her to dance before, but tonight she'd been gazing at the waltzing with so much longing he'd thought: *oh why not?*

He hadn't anticipated being given a sharp set down.

"Don't make it worse," she'd hissed angrily. "I'm enough of a leper as it is."

He couldn't remember flushing this intensely in public since the days when his drunk of a father still left the house. To pluck the pearl from the oyster, his ears were sufficiently sharp to catch Ellice's comment too.

His hands fisted up in knots, stuck at his sides with no one to punch. They had people searching for the link between Ellice and the Meimeyos' release from their roost, but thus far they'd come up empty. Ty was really looking forward to that no longer being true. He wasn't sure how long he stood there, fuming impotently, until a shoulder jostled his.

"I'd ask you to dance," said the male who'd joined him, "but it doesn't look like men do that here. Plus, you probably wouldn't let me lead."

Ty's cheeks blazed even hotter as he turned to James. The surge of blood wasn't all embarrassment. Some was plain old relief at being joined by . . . well, by a friend was what it felt like.

"Beer?" James asked, handing him an icy bottle. "I didn't recognize the brand so hopefully it's not foul. That ruffled-gown girl doesn't know what she's missing, by the way. You're a better man than most I know."

He said this as Ellice had, just loud enough to carry over nearby conversations. James twisted the cap off his drink, clinked it against Ty's, and took a swallow. He choked a little as it went down.

"Hm," he said, eyeing the bottle suspiciously. "This is so not beer."

"Cider," Ty said, finding himself smiling. "Strictly nonalcoholic."

"Then I guess I'll be keeping my head tonight."

Ty put his hand on James's broad shoulder and squeezed it. Suddenly he felt all right, like no one's opinion mattered as long as the people he respected thought well of him. The attraction that had refused to stir for his old partners flared to rich hot life. He wanted this man—and Anso and his wife, of course, but for the first time in his life, Ty's blood and bone comprehended the concept of *enough.*

If those three wanted him, he'd be satisfied. If they loved him, his heart would know peace at last.

The idea felt extraordinary unfolding inside of him. Was he kidding himself? Should he be frightened for the risk to his heart? He didn't think he was. His soul seemed to tilt inside him, then settle into a new and steadier position. *This* was the meaning of being mated, this sense that you were becoming the real you.

"What?" James asked, because Ty was grinning goofily.

"Nothing. Suddenly this party is looking up."

"Damn straight," James said, then gasped like a gunshot. "Holy crap. Is that a unicorn?"

"Newscaster," Ty replied. "She's popular with the drylanders."

The equine journalist and her camera crew were setting up equipment near the dais, an extra clatter being provided by her hooves. Ty knew she'd pre-arranged to interview Anso and his queen.

"Olivia won't be able to say a word," James predicted. "Jeesh, I wish you guys had warned her."

"You could join her," Ty said. "Moral support and all."

"Will you be all right back here? Why don't you come with me?"

Warmth expanded through Ty's chest at his concern. "I'll be all right. Olivia isn't the only one who'd rather avoid reporters."

James touched his upper arm. To anyone watching it wouldn't have seemed a romantic gesture, but to Ty it felt like one.

"See you in a bit," James said.

Ty was pretty sure he meant it.

CHAPTER FOURTEEN

OLIVIA'S headache was getting worse. The interview with the talking unicorn hadn't helped. Caught unprepared to be speaking to a horse, she'd been reduced to the sort of stammering that hadn't plagued her since she'd met James. The lady horse had been nice about it, focusing on Anso after her first two questions to Olivia bombed. Olivia hoped she hadn't said something stupid or, worse, something insulting. The last thing Anso needed was for his queen to appear species insensitive.

A splinter of pain jabbed behind her left eye. *No*, she thought. *You're not Anso's queen. You have to stop thinking of yourself like that.* She closed her eyes to try to get the jabbing to knock it off.

"Sweetie," Anso murmured, pulling her hand into his under the tablecloth. They were seated on one side of a table at the head of the banquet hall, as if they were ye olde royalty. All around the room, candles were being snuffed in preparation for a performance. The darkness should have eased her discomfort, but only Anso's hand did that. Seated on her other side, James clasped her fingers too.

She returned both grips too tightly.

Floor lights replaced the candles as traditional Hawaiian music, or something very like, started up on the balcony. A line of half naked women, each one prettier than the last, swished their hips in mesmerizing figure eights as they danced into the cleared area. They wore teeny-tiny sea grass skirts . . . and not a whole lot else, though their long black hair covered their breasts somewhat. Their green eyes glowed, their hands drawing graceful hula-girl type patterns. Their fantastically shapely legs twinkled with what appeared to be sequins.

Oh my gosh, Olivia thought, momentarily forgetting her headache. *I wonder if they're mermaids.*

She gasped as the dancers' nimble fingertips began leaving light trails behind them. Their hands were literally drawing pictures in the air. Three blush roses appeared between them, with three bright green ribbons to twine their stems together. Olivia concluded this was meant to represent the bonds between her and Anso and James: three blooms for the three of them. She glanced down the table to Ty, who was on James's other side. He leaned back in his chair, smiling faintly as he wagged one foot to the rhythm. Anso hadn't broken the news of their quadruple bond, perhaps because he thought his people had enough to absorb. Olivia wished he'd decided differently. Ty looked wry rather than unhappy, as if the omission neither surprised nor offended him.

She was offended for him. Perhaps she was being rash, but he had as much right to call himself her mate as the other two.

I have it in me to love them all, she thought.

The pain that stabbed through her then stole her breath. Olivia had never experienced a headache like this. Every pin that held up her hair felt as if it were being nail-gunned into her skull. Her vision blurred, and her skin went icy. A whispering swirled in her ears that came from no one.

"Excuse me," she said shakily to Anso. "I'm going to sneak out to the bathroom."

He nodded, not wanting to interrupt the performers, and gestured for a nearby guard to accompany her. Olivia didn't care as long as she got somewhere quiet fast. Fortunately, the ladies lounge was close by. The guard checked the room, found no one inside but a towel maid, and told her he'd wait outside for her.

Feeling slightly better already, Olivia splashed her clammy cheeks with water. Her arms trembled as she braced them on the sink's swirling onyx counter.

"Towel?" the uniformed maid offered.

Olivia buried her face in it, wanting to hide like this for the rest of the night. "I don't suppose you have an aspirin," she said into the soft cotton.

"I have something much better," the attendant replied.

Olivia lowered the towel to look at her. Before you could say *Venus on the half shell* her headache disappeared. "What do you have?"

The towel maid pulled a key and holder from her frilly apron pocket. "Convince your husband to leave the hall. The guard will probably come as well, but we'll make sure he's distracted. Continue along this corridor until you see the door marked 'Deliveries.' Go down the stairs to the two-man sub waiting at the dock. This key will start the engine. The vehicle is programmed to drive you safely through the Helike Tunnel. From there, you should be able to swim home."

"You're a friend of Lady Ellice," Olivia exclaimed softly. "She wants us out of here."

"I'm *your* friend," the maid corrected. "Security here is laxer than in the palace. You and your husband will never have a better chance to escape than this."

Olivia stared at the shiny key the woman was holding out. Part of her wanted to snatch it, wanted her and James to go back to their old life and forget this world existed.

"Take it,' said the maid. "See your daughter again."

Those were the magic words. Olivia took the key.

~

The dance was still going on when Olivia slipped back to the banquet hall. Mermaids, it seemed, weren't known for brevity. Unlike their audience, Olivia had never been so alert in her life. Every hair on her body seemed charged with energy. She was uncharacteristically certain she could pull off this subterfuge. She put her hands on Anso's shoulders from behind and leaned down to his ear.

"I'm so sorry," she murmured. "I'm not feeling any better. Do you think James and the guard could drive me back to the palace?"

Anso craned around to her. "Would you like me to come as well? If you're truly ill . . ."

"No. You've got all these foreign dignitaries here, and it's only a bad headache. Please offer your guests my apologies."

"What's wrong?" Ty leaned around James to whisper.

Shit, Olivia thought, because she just knew what Anso was going to do.

"Olivia's unwell," he said. "Why don't you and the guard take her and James to the palace? Make sure they arrive safely."

"Sure," Ty said, twisting out of his seat without rising all the way. "Come on, James. Let's scoot out before the lights come up."

Olivia tried to look wan but grateful as Ty and James each took an elbow to escort her from the hall. She hoped to hell Lady Ellice's co-conspirators were up for distracting Ty *and* the guard. She couldn't even tell James what was happening so he could help manipulate events. The way he was patting her hand was really frustrating.

They were going the wrong way down the corridor, toward the grand lobby where they'd come in instead of past the bathrooms. Should Olivia pretend she needed to throw up? Didn't people do that sometimes when they had migraines?

A lone woman ran down the carpet in a panic. She wasn't the same woman from the ladies lounge, but she wore a maid's uniform.

"Help," she said, grabbing Ty and the guard's arms. "Please, you two know first aid, don't you?"

"We're on duty," Ty said, but not unsympathetically.

The woman clutched at her hair. "It's the director of the mermaids' dancing troupe. She's gone into early labor back in the dressing room. She's having her baby *this second*."

Now *that* was a story, Olivia thought admiringly. It must have been believable. She noticed Ty and the guard had dropped their hands from their holsters.

"Go," Olivia urged. "James and I will wait here."

"Return to the banquet hall," Ty said. "You can grab another guard at the door."

"We will," Olivia said, already moving in that direction.

They kept moving in that direction until Ty and the guard disappeared down a cross hall.

"Hurry," Olivia said, dropping her halting manner to grab James's wrist and pull him along faster.

"What the hell, Olivia?"

"Sh," she said. "I'll explain when we get there.

She hurried as fast as she could in a floor-length gown until they reached the "Deliveries" door. A metal staircase with peeling paint led down behind it, the scent of briny water washing strongly up the steps. Olivia hiked her dress to her knees and ran down it.

"Is this it?" James whispered, clattering just as swiftly behind her. "Did you find a way out?"

"There." She pointed to a watery loading dock where a single vehicle was moored at a concrete post. The dark blue sub was shaped like a lozenge instead of a gondola. Because it bobbed half in, half out of the water, she supposed it was filled with air. Smaller than the family van Ty had used to sneak them into the Q Gardens, it had a similar working class feel to it. Olivia dug the key from her cleavage where she'd stashed it. "It has autopilot. We can take it almost all the way home."

James stopped her before she depressed the button that unlocked the sub's door. "Olivia, where did you get that key?"

"I didn't steal it. The maid in the ladies lounge offered it to me."

"A perfect stranger gave the new wereseal queen the keys to her vehicle."

"Well, I'm sure she works for Lady Ellice, but honestly, James, who else is going to help us?"

"Lady Ellice! You know she has an ulterior motive for doing this."

"Of course she does. She wants to be queen instead of me."

"What if she wants to kill us? What if that sub is rigged to blow up?"

"We'll check it for bombs before we get in. Come on, James. She didn't kill the Meimeyo, and her plan would have come off better if she had. If she balked at that, why would she murder human beings?"

James's face was flushed with anger, but—as ever—he was willing to hear out a reasonable argument.

"I guess she wouldn't," he conceded. "I just hate going along with anything that woman wants."

"It's not like Anso will marry her even with us gone." Olivia assured herself he wouldn't. The king wasn't that stupid. "This is our chance, James. We might not get another. Not before we're completely embroiled in Anso's life."

James scowled at her.

"I know," she said softly. "Being here hasn't been all bad, but we need to go back to our own world."

"Fine." He thrust his hand out, palm up. "Give me the key. If we're running away, I'm driving."

~

James disliked almost everything about this escape but didn't feel he could object. Maybe it wasn't his gut saying the opportunity was too good to be true. Maybe slightly lower parts were trying to stop him. Olivia wanted to leave, and she had to come first with him.

He couldn't deny they'd been getting embroiled here, though he did dig in his heels about deactivating the autopilot after they'd emerged from the hall's tunnel.

"James!" Olivia said when she saw him switch off the toggle.

"I know how to drive this thing," he said, setting his jaw stubbornly. "And I can find the Helike Tunnel. There are signs for it on every damn corner. Plus, if Anso's cousenemy is planning to kill us, what better way than to have the escape vehicle she supplied drive us exactly where she pleases?"

"Fine." Olivia flopped back in the co-pilot seat. She rubbed her temples, so maybe she did have a headache. "Up there is the turn for the grand canal thingy."

James turned the sub the opposite way.

"James!"

"I'm not taking the obvious route. This way we can avoid police patrols." Privately, he doubted they'd run across any. Most of the city's cops would be posted near the banquet hall for the big shindig. He couldn't help it if he wanted one last look around. Oceana was amazing, and he'd hardly seen it at all.

The streets were different at night, though lit well enough to navigate. He noticed traffic above them and remembered he didn't have to cling to ground level. Once he'd climbed, the bird's eye view of the city was beautiful—like flying over a metropolis in a plane.

From above, Oceana's street grid formed a spiral, loosely resembling a nautilus shell. So many lights twinkled under them, so many exotic little lives, none of which he'd encounter now.

"It's pretty," Olivia said grudgingly, her fingertips pressed to the side window. *She* was pretty, his soulmate and partner.

"I love you," he said. "I'm sorry to go, but I'm not sorry to be with you."

"James." Her voice was soft with emotion, her new blue eyes glimmering.

"You've always been my heart."

James jerked back as a quick black shape darted past their windshield. "Shit," he said, his pulse pounding in his throat. "What was that?"

"A fish?"

It was a big damn fish. The shape darted at them again. This time it was spitting fire. James jammed his foot on the brake.

"Oh my God," Olivia said. "It's the last missing Meimeyo."

It was. As their sub-compact sub drifted to a stop, the mini-dragon landed on its hood. It screeched at them, its three-foot long leathery wings flapping threateningly. James wished they'd found some other way to settle the question of whether dragons could breathe fire.

"Uh," Olivia said, shrinking back instinctively. "This might sound stupid, but do you suppose it doesn't want us to leave?"

The mini-dragon hissed fire at them again, the heat of the combustion leaving a black spot on the thankfully reinforced window glass. James didn't know what to make of this.

"Maybe it's angry we didn't take it home with its nest mates."

The dragon stomped on the hood with each of its rear clawed feet, reminding James of a child throwing a tantrum. One of its front paws threw something at the windshield, which hit it with a clink.

Olivia leaned forward in her seat. "That's one of the diamond hairpins I wore for Anso's speech! How on earth did it get that?"

The oddest sensation came over James, like every millimeter of his skin was tingling on the inside.

"Olivia," he said slowly. "Take the pins from your hair."

"Honestly, James, what good will that do?"

James removed the pearls himself, then stuffed them in the glove compartment for good measure.

Olivia glared at him when he stopped her from pulling it back open. "You're crazy."

"Maybe, but look at the Meimeyo."

The mini-dragon was sitting calmly on the nose of the sub. When it saw it had their attention, it chittered like it was talking and raised its gleaming black and gold wings. This time the display wasn't threatening.

"I think it wants us to follow it."

"James . . ."

"I *know*," he said, "but I think it does. This place isn't ordinary, and neither are we anymore. I have a feeling this is what we're supposed to do."

Olivia gave him a dubious look.

"I trusted you," he reminded her.

"For about five minutes!" She wasn't using the tone that said she was really angry. James tried not to let his smile show. "All right. If it takes off in the next two minutes, we'll follow it."

The mini-dragon immediately flapped up into the currents. With the sense that he'd stumbled into a fairy tale, James put the sub back in drive.

Their escort led them to a section of the city that was mostly warehouses. Big black subs with trucking logos were tied by cables behind the buildings, creating an obstacle course. They steered through it after the mini-dragon to a wall marked PREMIUM STORAGE. Halfway up the expanse of brick, perched on a window ledge, the sea dragon awaited.

"Crap," Olivia said. "We have to go out there."

James was glad she'd given up arguing. He knew how she was about submerging in deep water. "You could stay here while I investigate."

"No point. You'll have to flood the car before you can swim out."

He did this as quickly as he could, to give Olivia less time to grow anxious. Her hand was very cold and squeezed his very tightly before she gave in and inhaled her first lungful of water. She coughed a bit, but then she was all right. They swam from the car together.

Her outfit turned out to be more adaptable than his. She only had to tie up her skirt. He needed to remove his jacket and his shoes. Free to move then, they peered in the window the mini-dragon was waiting by.

"Oh boy," they said in dismayed unison.

Someone had drawn what even they knew was a spell-working circle on the warehouse's concrete floor. Except for a giant pentagram, they didn't recognize the symbols, though they were sufficiently creepy nonetheless. Six or seven men were scattered around the warehouse—hulking, bouncer-looking types. Another man, who wasn't hulking at all, stood within the spell circle. He was naked and had both arms thrust upward in front of him. They couldn't hear through the window, but he appeared to be chanting. Because he was on his feet and not floating, James concluded the warehouse was filled with air.

Most interesting of all, a pair of filmy phosphorescent wings fluttered gently behind the spell caster. Shaped like a dragonfly's and equal to the man in height, the wings gleamed with every color in the rainbow.

"That's Lajos," Olivia exclaimed softly. "Mrs. Bonn said he was three-quarters faerie. He did a super job on my hair."

"I think it's safe to say that's not the only job he's doing."

A vibration shook the building they were clinging to, as if a heavy truck had driven by on a nearby road. The Meimeyo cheeped mournfully and climbed onto James's shoulder, its weight about that of a large cat. Under other circumstances, James would have been flattered. Under this one, he wished its rear claws weren't digging through his tuxedo shirt.

"The faerie made the building shake," Olivia surmised. "He's summoning something nasty with that spell."

James agreed, though he didn't know what to do about it. He was no one-man army, and he doubted Lajos had brought those goons just to stand around.

"Do we have a way to call for help?" Olivia asked.

"There's an emergency beacon in the car, but Ty told me it just notifies their version of Triple A."

The building shook again, harder this time, causing the skin on the back of James's neck to crawl. When he looked down, a jagged crack—maybe five feet long—had split the compacted sandy ground below. He didn't think it was a good sign that the dragon hissed angrily.

"We can't wait for Triple A," Olivia said, arms braced on the brick of the window ledge. "We need a weapon. Or a big distraction."

"Or both," James said. They turned as one to stare at the car.

"There's air in this building—"

"- and this window looks big enough to crash through."

"But what if the glass is too strong to break? What if it's magic?"

"Something powerful could heat it first. Then whatever spells protect it would be compromised."

As James put forth this theory, the Meimeyo stepped around on his shoulder excitedly.

"All right," James said, patting its prickly foot. "I guess you do know what you're doing."

They left the dragon at the window and swam back to the car.

"Safety belt," James reminded Olivia as she pulled her body down into the second seat. God, he hoped this thing had airbags.

Another thunder-like rumble shook the water, this one seeming to originate underground.

"Jesus," Olivia swore. "Is he calling a damn earthquake?"

Suddenly, they both knew that was exactly what the faerie hairdresser was doing. For whatever reason, Lajos was hoping to bring the city down. James's cheeks grew colder than the water surrounding them.

"We've got the car," he said. "We could try to outrun it."

Buckled in now, Olivia shook her head. She looked as white-faced as he felt.

"Olivia, even if we survive this, we'll lose our chance to escape." He had to say it, though he was certain how she'd react.

"You *know* we have to try to stop this," she said. "We couldn't live with ourselves if we let them be hurt."

She didn't just mean the people of Oceana. She meant Ty and Anso. That was clear from the very personal worry pinching her lovely eyes. James turned his own stinging gaze to the warehouse window, where a starburst of scorch marks suggested the dragon had quietly done its work.

"Okay," he said, giving Olivia's trembling hand one last squeeze. "Let's Thelma and Louise this."

~

Ty had never helped a woman give birth before. If he never did again, that would be fine by him. Okay, if Olivia had Anso's child, he'd let her clutch his hand—but only on the condition that the gory bits happened behind a curtain away from him.

Fortunately, mermaids weren't as long-winded in giving birth as they were in their "entertainments." No more than twenty minutes passed between Ty and Kelvin's adrenaline-stoked arrival in the dressing room and Ty carefully cleaning up the newborn. He expected he and his fellow guard were grateful for their training in different species' biology. The baby was small but healthy, the mother sufficiently recovered to be voluble again. Her conversation alternated between gushing thanks and her mystification as to why she'd gone into premature labor.

"My doctor swore I was right on schedule," she said for the umpteenth time. "Sixteen days and three hours from now was my due slot."

"We're simply glad you're all right," Ty said, also not for the first time. He watched the baby nuzzle her pretty breast, the dark fuzz of hair on its head tinged with emerald. Despite the horror of its unscheduled birth, he had to admit the kid was cute.

Unaware of his thoughts, the new mother rocked her blanket-swaddled child and patted its small bottom. "Sixteen days yet. I should fire him. I'm just so glad you were here!"

Given that Ty had run out of ways to say *you're welcome*, the appearance of the EMTs with a stretcher, come to trundle mother and baby off to the hospital, was an undeniable relief.

"*Mermaids*," Kelvin said darkly, watching them disappear down the corridor.

"*Babies*," Ty added.

Both guards, so recently thanked for being heroes, shuddered delicately.

"I need to get back to the hall," Ty said, realizing he'd left Olivia and James to find their own escort.

"Right." Kelvin glanced around the dressing room. "I'll just, uh, finish cleaning up some of this. If you see that maid again, send her here."

Ty slapped him on the shoulder and got while the getting was good.

Two of his men stood guard on either side of the dining room's imposing central doors. One of them was the younger Corlier brother.

"Didn't expect you back so soon," Mark observed.

A single icy finger trailed down Ty's spine. He stopped without going in. "What do you mean? Who took the queen and James back to the palace?"

Mark's eyes rounded. "We thought you did."

"Fuck." Horrible conclusions jumped together in Ty's head. People whose delivery dates were set by the hour didn't go into early labor unless something triggered it. Magic maybe. Or a drug slipped into a water bottle. He thought back to the maid who'd called him and Kelvin to help and then disappeared. Had Olivia and James been kidnapped? Except . . . hadn't Olivia urged them leave and, looking back, hadn't she seemed a tad eager?

"Fuck," he repeated, clutching his head this time.

"What is it?" Mark asked. "Has something happened to the queen?"

Ty gazed at the closed double doors, behind which Anso would be smiling politely for who knew what toast or speech. God, Ty didn't want to tell him this. The king loved Olivia. This was going to break more than his heart.

"The queen and her husband have escaped," he said tightly in a low voice. "They probably had help, very likely from Lady Ellice, but I suspect they went voluntarily."

"Lady Ellice left ten minutes ago," Mark said. "We saw her walk out of here in a rush."

The second guard nodded in confirmation, worried enough by the enormity of this disaster that he'd broken into a shiny sweat. Even the famously unhappy Queen Denise hadn't tried to run away.

"Find Lady Ellice's friends," Ty said. "Any of her clique who are still here. And servants, if you recognize them. Lock them up at the security station. I don't care who they threaten to sue. None of them leaves until I question them."

"Yes, Captain," Mark acknowledged, the guards' spines stiffening now that they had orders.

Ty should have known his course of action wouldn't be this straightforward. Outside the building, Oceana's earthquake klaxons began to wail.

"Jesus," he muttered.

"If it's a false alarm . . ." Mark said.

"We can't afford to be wrong. Help the guests get into the shelters without trampling each other. And don't forget we have visitors who need the air-breather rooms. If you can, separate Lady Ellice's associates, but only if that doesn't interfere with safety."

Ty himself strode into the dining hall, tersely relaying instructions to the other guards through his pocket comm. Inside, guests were queuing up in preparation for filing out to the shielded chambers. Anso must have ordered the men who'd been posted here to get them organized.

One of the visiting werewolves caught his arm. Ty didn't want to stop, but he did.

"We're cops," the werewolf said. "We can help."

"You're air breathers."

The man grinned at him. "Dogs don't mind getting wet."

"Fine," Ty said, making a snap judgment. "Grab mini-air tanks and pair yourselves with my guards. None of you works alone."

The man was a professional, because he nodded and went to do it. Ty found Anso at the rear of a queue in quiet conversation with his Uncle Phoca, Lady Ellice's father. Though the king liked the war hero, Ty doubted affection was the reason for his choice of company.

Anso must have heard Olivia and James were gone.

"I don't know where she is," Prince Phoca was saying querulously. "Sometimes I don't understand my daughter. Those friends of hers and the other folks she hangs out with, they're a strange school of fish."

Anso looked up at Ty's approach. His deep blue eyes were wells of hurt and worry.

"You heard?" Ty asked.

"Mark gave me a brief report."

Neither of them got a chance to say more, because Prince Phoca's e-phone rang. He dug it out of his inside breast pocket.

"Well, that's strange," he said, peering at the little screen. "My security company is sending me footage of a break-in at our family warehouse. In the middle of all this, some fool drove a car through a window and flooded the whole damn place. I thought the strengthening spells protected against that."

He turned the phone to show Anso the video. Anso squinted at it a moment before his expression turned very odd. "May I?" he asked, gently taking the phone from his uncle's hand.

"Do you recognize the car?" the old man asked.

"I think I recognize the people in it." He showed the screen to Ty. The security recording was running in a loop. Ty inhaled sharply as he made out James and Olivia's frightened faces right before they and a massive wave of water smashed through the glass.

"What the hell are they doing?"

"I don't know," Anso answered, "but I think we'd better find out fast."

Ty looked behind him, where the well-dressed crowd was emptying the room in relatively good order. "Okay," he said. "I guess those werewolves will have to make up for us being gone."

~

Anso and Ty were on their own for chasing Anso's runaway mate. They didn't dare pull personnel away from the hall with the earthquake increasingly seeming like it was genuine. All the visiting mermaids claimed to have sensed tremors.

The cadre of faeries who'd attended the feast informed Anso they were withdrawing somewhere quiet to "meditate on the cause of the disturbance."

"Useless bastards," Ty was muttering as he drove. Ty had commandeered a chili red racing sub from one of his men and was currently maxing out its speedometer. Each time they turned, the loose items left unstowed from their hasty flooding swept to a different side. "Why can't the fae throw up extra protections like you asked?"

"They have their methods." Anso braced on the dash at Ty's hell for leather driving. "I can't order them to ignore them. They're royals in their own right."

"Royal dickheads is more like." Ty slowed as they neared Premium Storage. "Holy . . ."

They stared at the place where James and Olivia had crashed through the big window. As the weight of the sea poured inward, it had taken quite a portion of the wall with it. His grudge against the faeries forgotten, Ty allowed their vehicle to glide silently through the gaping hole. A few lights still shone inside the warehouse, those that hadn't broken and gone out. On the opposite end of the building, packing crates and equipment had washed into a jumbled pile, where the surge had pushed them.

Because debris was clouding the water, Anso couldn't locate the car at first. When he did, fear sank cold claws in him. With either admirable aim or dumb luck, the compact sub had landed nose first in a huge spell circle, cracking through the painted symbols along one side. The inrushing water hadn't cushioned the impact much. From front headlamps to driver's door, the cheaply made vehicle was an accordion.

A choking sound broke in Anso's throat. He didn't see how Olivia and James could have walked away from this.

"I see movement," Ty said. "Over by that far pillar."

He pointed, but Anso was already pushing out of the racing sub.

"For God's sake," Ty said. "Wait for me."

Anso really couldn't. His muscles quivered with his urge to keep his bloodmate from being dead. He spared one more look in passing for the crumpled car. The door on the passenger side hung open, and he saw no bodies.

Let them be alive, he thought as he strengthened his strokes. *Just let them be all right.*

When he reached the back side of the pillar where Ty had spied movement, he decided *all right* was a matter of degree. A relief that was more powerful than he expected rushed into him. James Forster was alive. Though cut up and bruised, he was well enough to be holding a very angry naked faerie rather roughly by his wings. Anso had heard faerie wings were sensitive, so this was the equivalent of having him by the balls. If the fae pulled hard enough to break free, he'd cause himself terrible pain.

James seemed to have figured out this vulnerability.

"She'll cut them," he was saying. "Tell your men to put down their weapons, or I swear she'll slice them off a strip at a time."

Anso's heart gave an even more joyous throb. *She* was Olivia, and she also was on her feet. She gripped a shard of broken headlamp glass, which she pointed at the faerie's beautiful glowing wings. Unfortunately, Anso's little queen didn't look bloodthirsty—more like she'd cut the faerie if she absolutely had to. This might have accounted for the six goons who surrounded them not lowering their attack rifles.

"I think you'd better listen to him," Ty said. He'd snuck up behind the faerie's bodyguards. His standard issue guard pistol wasn't as big as theirs, but Anso knew he was crack shot.

Belatedly, he remembered he'd tucked a small gun into his boot tonight. He drew it, slid his foot into a floor clamp to steady himself, and swung into the goons' view as well.

"Yes," he said, drawing eyes to him like he and Ty were playing a tennis match. "Please disarm yourselves."

The goons looked less sure of themselves at this second threat, but still didn't comply.

"Isn't that—?" one goon murmured to the other, likely recognizing his ruler.

Before they could conclude it was, the faerie began whispering in the high tongue of his homeland. Knowing this was the language of enchantments, Ty didn't hesitate. He aimed, squeezed, and got off a killing shot. At least, it would have been a killing shot, if it hadn't bounced off the magical shield the fae was spinning. The bullet ricocheted like it had struck steel, hitting Ty in the shin. Ty cursed and staggered to one knee in a bloom of blood.

Crap, Anso thought. The faerie hadn't used up his juice powering whatever spell the Forsters had interrupted by crashing in. Because there was little point in shooting him, he joined Ty in targeting the faerie's momentarily distracted men. Ty's injury hadn't spoiled his aim. In less than five seconds, he and Anso had dropped them all.

The whispering faerie truly didn't seem to care.

"Shut up!" James cried, wrenching his sparkly wings harder.

The faerie screamed, but what he screamed seemed to be a part of his spell. The air around him thickened and grew darker. James was having more trouble holding him. Olivia rushed in, apparently deciding she'd see what her little manual weapon could do.

She didn't get a chance to find out. A form slipped out of the shadows behind her, dressed all in black leather. The figure yanked Olivia back against it and shoved a gun underneath her chin. Anso recognized the person a second later.

Olivia's attacker was Ellice.

"Hello, cousin," she said.

She was considerably taller and more muscular than his queen. Olivia struggled, but Ellice subdued her easily, even when Olivia tried to slash at her with the headlamp glass. A twist of Ellice's wrist disarmed her, after which she cocked her gun.

That wasn't a sound Anso could enjoy.

"Release Mr. Lajos," she said to James.

Reluctantly, James let go of the faerie.

"And your gun, please," she said to Anso.

He couldn't make the shot, not with her using Olivia as a shield, not even if he'd had the nerve to try. He set down the small waterproof revolver and kicked it behind him. If the faerie wanted a weapon besides his magic, he'd have to retrieve a rifle from one of his fallen goons. Their guns were large and unwieldy. Anso doubted the slender faerie could handle one.

"Cute," Ellice said of his ploy. "That leaves you, Tykon."

"It does," Ty agreed, his pistol still aimed toward her in steady hands. "But I am wondering what you hope to accomplish here."

Ellice smiled at him. "Well, I *was* looking forward to marrying our hot new king. I thought he'd be more receptive to my kindness once his faithless Outsider queen had used the cover of a disaster to run back to dry land. In truth, I was certain I'd find a way to blame the earthquake on her. That curse idea truly was elegant."

She let out a humorous sigh. "Alas, you've foiled that plan. Now I'm just clearing my way to the throne. I am a Vitul, in case you'd forgotten. Next in line after my idiot father. I haven't yet decided who'll be my king, but Mr. Lajos would make a yummy third."

The legislature would never approve of that. Faeries had enough power in the Pocket. By their own agreement, they weren't allowed to govern the territories. This knowledge flickered into Ty's face as strongly as it did Anso's.

"Rules can change," Ellice said in answer to his expression. "Especially when people are desperate for stability. Which they will be once we finish summoning the earth—"

She broke off with a shriek. Olivia had taken advantage of her gloating to jab back at her with some weapon no one had known she had. Furious, Ellice clutched at her thigh, then drew back the hand that had been shoving the gun muzzle underneath Olivia's jaw. Clearly, she planned to whip it against her head.

The opening was all Ty needed. A pop sounded half an instant before a neat red hole appeared in the center of his cousin's forehead. A cloud of blood puffed out, and then Ellice fell dreamily backward. Curiously, a cluster of diamonds glittered on the thigh of her leather pants, as if she'd been injured by jewelry.

Her descent was so picturesque that for a second no one noticed Lajos scrambling away.

Magic notwithstanding, he was a crap swimmer. When a new contingent of faeries—the same faeries who'd attended Anso's dinner—materialized in his path, he didn't have a chance of evading them.

Lajos's wings drooped even before the faerie at the front grabbed him by the scruff like a bad puppy.

"Lajos of Maradrago," he intoned, effortlessly holding him prisoner. "I place you under arrest for unapproved use of magic in a protected territory. Because your offense might have cost many lives, your punishment is to spend the next twenty years in a hell dimension. If at that point you seem to have repented, your case will be eligible for review."

Anso's jaw dropped at the swiftness of this sentencing. Everything considered, Ellice might have gotten off lightly. He shut his mouth with an effort when the lead faerie—just barely—inclined his head to him.

"No need to thank me, Your Majesty," he said. "The fae are happy to provide you this service."

Along with their prisoner, the faeries then blinked out of existence as abruptly as they'd arrived.

"Useless," Ty muttered . . . but not too loudly.

~

Olivia had been *this close* to giving up the ghost. Anso had laid down his gun, James didn't have one, and the best she thought she could hope for was that Ty would blow off Ellice's head not too long after she lost her own.

No matter what the men did, she didn't believe Ellice would let her live. The woman was ready to kill her father to gain the throne! She and James had underestimated her willingness to do violence. Olivia was about to console herself with fantasies of sharks devouring Ellice when she spotted two red eyes glowing among the warehouse's ceiling struts.

For a heartbeat she was frightened. Was some devil glaring down at her? Then she remembered the Meimeyo had ruby eyes. If the mini-dragon was perched up there, maybe it could help. Feeling slightly stupid, she tried to send it a picture of blasting Ellice with its fiery dragon breath. The red glows blinked but didn't budge. Maybe the Meimeyo had used up its fuel weakening the window. Or maybe Olivia sucked at telepathy.

An object appeared from nowhere within her hand.

Despite her intense surprise, she was disappointed. The mini-dragon had sent her the stupid diamond hairpin, the one it had thrown at the car window. Its end was sharpish, unlike a regular bobby pin, but it was hardly a dagger. Ellice was controlling Olivia too well to try sticking it in her eye.

On the other hand, if all she needed was a distraction . . .

Ty's grip was rock-steady around his pistol, his yellow eyes locked with laser focus on Ellice. He didn't need a signal from Olivia. He was ready to plug the bitch the instant he got the chance.

Olivia drew a breath, cocked her arm, then slammed the pin so hard into Ellice's leg that it sank through her thigh muscle.

After that, Olivia's mind checked out. She was aware of people speaking to her, but she couldn't respond. Like a doll, she let them pull her away from the body. She needed to remember something, or explain something, or maybe just wake up.

Sleeping Beauty, she thought with a dreamer's logic. Someone find a prince to kiss me.

Her brain returned to normal working order once the four of them had squeezed into the shiny red sport sub. Ty was at the wheel with Anso beside him. They were speaking by turns into some sort of hands-free phone, giving and receiving status reports from different voices. Olivia's hair was floating around her face.

"The earthquake—" she said, batting at it in annoyance.

"Petering off," James answered, squished in the back seat with her. "It's looking like we stopped the spell in time."

"Good."

The word came out as a heavy sigh. James's arm gave her shoulders a bracing squeeze. She looked at him, startled afresh by his changed eye color. Possibly she'd never completely get used to it. James smiled, but there were shadows in his humor. Neither Ty nor Anso were turning to check on them. All she saw was the back of their light and dark golden heads. No matter how important their conversation, Olivia had a feeling this wasn't an accident.

Ty and Anso knew they had tried to run.

CHAPTER FIFTEEN

THE elephant in the room must have seemed worth avoiding to Anso and Ty. Neither wereseal mentioned James and Olivia had been escaping before they turned back at the warehouse. The men's main concern after returning to the palace was Olivia's well being. Ty claimed her zoning out after he shot Ellice was due to more than shock. According to him, people acted this way when they came out of magical hypnosis, his theory being that the faerie hairdresser had put a whammy on her. This idea gave James a turn, though it might explain his sudden dislike for her hairpins. Ty didn't seem overly alarmed, treating it like a case of the flu she'd recover from. He and Anso had a brief low-voiced argument over whether someone called the Magus needed to be brought in, Ty being for it and Anso against.

"Can he make sure the spell is all the way out of me?" Olivia asked.

"Yes," Anso conceded stiffly, which settled it.

The Magus turned out to be a pureblood fae. James gathered he held some sort of religious post. His stiff embroidered robes resembled a pope's, though James didn't think he was Catholic.

Of course, he also hadn't thought Poseidon was a saint.

Olivia sat like a schoolgirl on a settee in the blue salon while the Magus examined her from head to toe through a large magnifying glass. The process was slightly Harry Potterish and surreal. Sensing Olivia's nervousness, James stood behind her for support. Her shoulders were tense, her hands folded in her lap, as if waiting for a ruler to rap down on her knuckles. The expectation was her own creation. From what James could tell, the Magus was mild-mannered.

Of course, Anso was probably the person his wife feared she'd earned the rap from. That Olivia hadn't taken off the dragon ring Anso gave her didn't escape his notice.

At last, the Magus straightened. He turned to the king to give his report. "It is as I thought, sire. Though Lajos was a minor power for a faerie and only three-quarter blood, he combined a number of smaller spells to persuade the queen to do his bidding. In this way, he avoided setting off the palace's illegal magic alarms. The hairpins were almost certainly used to anchor his enchantment. I'm also sensing vocal hypnosis with a boost from some object he used to store 'mojo'—as the young people say."

"His glasses!" Olivia exclaimed. "Lajos said they were spelled to pre-test hairstyles, but that might have been a lie."

"Indeed it might, Your Majesty," the Magus agreed politely. "Especially if the lenses were real crystal." He hesitated, rubbing long pale fingers over his lower lip. "I do not wish to mislead either of you as to the extent of Lajos's influence. He exaggerated Her Majesty's impulses with his magic, but he didn't create them. Assuredly, you *do* wish to return to your native land. On the other hand, I see by my examination that the part-breed's spells have only recently dissipated. In order to turn back and save Oceana, Your Majesty must have overruled the enchantment with personal force of will. It cannot be denied you've earned your sobriquet of heroine. Because Lajos amped up his power with a spell circle, his earthquake would have wreaked considerable damage. Your Majesty and Mr. Forster faced down a dangerous character!"

He bowed to them both—well, more to Olivia than James, but he was in there somewhere. For her part, Olivia was too unsettled to respond with her usual blush.

"Sir," she said, "why didn't Lady Ellice kill the Meimeyo? James and I assumed she was reluctant to use violence, but clearly that wasn't the case."

"I can only speculate," said the Magus, "but I expect she feared bringing a curse upon herself if she harmed them. Those mini-dragons are potent little beings.

"And now, if you would excuse me, might I suggest you call Pinni to see to your various wounds and bruises? The spirit isn't the only part of a person that needs healing. Lord Otari in particular has been trickling blood from his leg on your nice carpet."

This gentle reminder had all of them turning to face Ty. James wasn't sorry to see Anso put his hand on his lover's arm.

"Old friend," he said, "forgive me for not thinking."

Ty shrugged and turned brick red. "I'm all right. The bullet would have pushed itself out soon enough."

"Eesh," Olivia said, then covered her mouth for fear of having sounded rude.

Because *eesh* was pretty much what James was thinking, he patted her shoulder.

Once they'd been prodded and patched up by Pinni the elf physician, Olivia didn't seem to know what to do with herself. Though they'd averted the worst of the earthquake, downtown Oceana had suffered some damage. Anso and Ty had plenty of relief efforts to take reports from and allocate resources to.

In their absence, the contrast between the emotional wringer they'd been through and its unexpected finish was dramatic. James understood—maybe better than Olivia did—why she wandered the guest-room like a lost child, her fingers trailing over the surfaces she passed.

Readier to accept his feelings than she was, James leaned against the doorway and watched her.

"Olivia," he said.

She stopped walking and looked at him. "I'm fine. I'm just wondering what happens next."

"You know what you want to happen."

"I—" She screwed her face into an expression that pleaded for him not to push.

"You know," he repeated, then walked to her and chafed her shoulders. "You knew what you wanted the moment you agreed we ought to turn back. I don't think you're wrong for wanting it, mind you. I want to stay with them too."

Olivia's chin quivered. "They think we were running away from them!"

"Well, we were."

She laughed and buried her face in his chest. James wrapped his arms around her and immediately felt better. She would always be his touchstone.

"They'll forgive us," he said, rubbing her back gently.

Olivia hugged him tighter. "Will *you* forgive me?"

"Oh sweetheart, that never was an issue."

She tipped her head back to look into his eyes. "Go find him," she said. "He needs to hear from you that we want to stay."

James knew she meant go find Ty. The surface of his cheeks heated. Seeing this, Olivia touched his face and smiled. "How you feel about him doesn't hurt me. I thought it might, but I like the idea of you making him happy."

He could have said so many things. That he loved her. That Ty wasn't immune to her appeal either—erotic or otherwise. He didn't say them because she knew already, and besides she was right. Ty deserved to hear how James felt from James. He'd been treated too often as an afterthought to Anso.

Of course, James was only guessing Ty would be happy about the news. This conversation might be more awkward than he was prepared for.

Laughing softly, Olivia petted his jaw from either side. "Silly man. You're exactly the extra blessing Ty needs, whether he knows it yet or not.

~

The most urgent of Ty's post-disaster duties were carried out. His mind at loose ends, he was uncomfortable remaining in Anso's apartments with the others but couldn't bring himself to leave.

Didn't he have a right to stay? Weren't James and Olivia as much his bloodmates as Anso's? Then again, perhaps the Forsters didn't belong to either of them. They *had* been trying to run away. If Oceana hadn't been in such grave danger, would they have turned around?

He'd drifted to the dining room to grapple—albeit unwillingly—with these questions. A stretch of rare rectangular picture windows gave a pretty view of the coral garden. The upper reaches of the water sparkled with rippling light. Oceana's fake sun was rising. Did James and Olivia miss their real one?

Without warning, a soft and pleasant vibration thrummed through his tired body.

"Ty," said James's voice from the door.

You see, he thought as he turned. There **is** a bond between them and you.

"You okay?" James asked.

God, the man was gorgeous. From his night-black hair to the way his shoulders filled out his shirt to the exotic Outsider accent in his deep voice. Ty wanted to rip off his clothes and ravish him on the table, then maybe lick him all over for dessert. He tried to tighten his groin muscles, to keep his cock from emerging, but the effort was futile.

"I'm fine," he said. "How are you and Olivia?"

James appeared to find this question amusing. He walked in shaking his head, only stopping when he'd reached Ty's side of the long table, where he leaned his hips on its edge. His closeness thickened the air in Ty's lungs. What could Ty say to him? What would convince him and Olivia not to run again?

"You killed a woman today," James said. "One you'd known all your life. And you did it to save my wife."

James's arms were folded across his chest, the cuffs of his plain white shirt rolled up. With an effort, Ty wrenched his gaze from the dark hair on James's strong forearms. "Am I supposed to be sorry about that? Ellice was a shit to me for as long as I can remember."

"That isn't why you killed her."

"No." Ty rubbed his sweaty palms on his casual buckskin pants. He liked that James seemed very sure of this. "It isn't why I killed her, but I won't feign remorse. I wasn't going to let her hurt Olivia and Anso. Or Oceana. I don't care whose family blood she has. Rulers shouldn't act like that."

James dropped his head, his lashes amazingly thick, his mouth slightly curved. Did he think nations with kings and queens were humorous? He watched James uncross his ankles and then look up. Whatever he'd been thinking, it wasn't a judgment. His deep blue eyes sparkled.

"Olivia and I want to stay."

Ty's internal organs were knocked off kilter, heat and chills trying to rush through him at the same time. "You want to stay. Both of you."

"I think we knew we did before we tried to leave. We simply weren't ready to admit it."

"The Magus said Lajos merely exaggerated Olivia's wish to go home."

"I know. And we'll have to work that out. Olivia and I can't be kept here like prisoners. We have to be free to communicate with and see our family as we think best. You and Anso will have to trust us to show good judgment—and to come back."

"The blood bond would call you back," Ty warned. "You'd be uncomfortable without us."

This wasn't the best thought-out response he'd ever made. It sounded too much like a threat. James's faint smile deepened.

"Maybe," he said, "but Olivia and I are fairly stubborn. I think we'd manage to stay away if we wanted to. Of course, you and Anso could join us on dry land, at least for short periods. I know it's not your preference, but Olivia and I might be able to make your stay tolerable. The best marriages rely on compromise."

The best marriages . . . Ty wagged his head in wonder at him using those words. "You're serious about this. You really think we could all live committed to each other."

This was what Ty had come to believe he wanted, but found so frightening to let himself hope for. James took Ty's hand from where it had been nervously rubbing his thigh again. "Olivia always calls me a romantic."

She'd called Ty that too. He wouldn't have thought he was, but he couldn't deny he found James's hold on his hand very sweet. Sex wasn't the only thing Ty desired from him.

"Look," James said quietly. "When people fall for each other, it isn't always even. Maybe you'll always love Anso more than you will me. Maybe Anso will always be most attached to Olivia. That doesn't mean his feelings for you don't matter. This is early days for all of us, but I think it's worth finding out if this foursome can work."

"How can you be so brave?" Ty burst out. "What if Anso or I never fall as deeply as you want?"

He knew these were his own fears talking, but James treated the question seriously. "Maybe I'm naturally optimistic. Or maybe I'm arrogant. I'm accustomed to thinking of myself as lovable. I'd be happy and honored if you fell for me, but I wouldn't be shocked."

And there was the difference between them.

"It shocks me," Ty confessed. "It always shocks me—in either direction."

James straightened from his lean on the table, his arms pulling Ty gently against him. Ty's resistance simply gave. He held James back with his cheek resting on his temple. He wasn't sure he'd ever held anyone like this. Not lovers, not Anso, not anyone. Though the full frontal contact aroused him, he didn't want to move. He was too quiet inside for that. It wasn't even hard to ask his next question.

"Do you believe I could love you?"

"Maybe not *only* me," James said. "But *also* me? Absolutely. Don't you think you could manage that?"

Ty thought about how easy it was to hold him, how welcome his kindness was, and how—when Anso inevitably made James his third—he didn't think he'd sicken with envy. James was a good man, maybe as natural a leader as Anso.

"Yes," he said, the word like a heavy weight dropping from his soul. "I think I could manage that."

~

Anso had just wrapped up a phone call with Lord Noth in his office. Ty had been working at a small antique desk nearby. Along with everything else, he'd set an investigation into motion, to find possible other parties to Ellice's plot. The police would look into it, but Anso and Ty both wanted their own answers. Anso saw Ty was no longer there. Had Anso said goodbye to him when he left? He couldn't remember.

God, he hoped this business wouldn't get much messier.

Knowing it could, he was squeezing his eyebrows along their bone when Harrison appeared at the door. The butler wore his full black-and-white uniform.

"Sire," he said, "might I inquire if you'd like me to order breakfast or if you prefer to sleep?"

"It's morning?"

"Yes, sire. Going on six a.m."

Anso's eyelids felt as if they'd been lined with sand. "I don't think I'm hungry, but you could ask the others."

"Very good. You might wish to know the new shift of guards is posted outside the royal apartments, Lord Otari is in the dining room with Mr. Forster, and I gave the Press Office strict instructions not to accept interview requests until you speak to them yourself."

"Thank you," Anso said. "And thank you for your work on the banquet. It went off well right up to the end."

"I am only glad we were spared a worse conclusion." Harrison started to turn back to the door, then stopped. Despite his as-ever upright carriage, Anso noticed bags underneath his eyes. No doubt the overworked man needed sleep himself. Harrison tugged his stiff black waistcoat and spoke again. "Sire, if it wouldn't be too forward, I'd like to remind you of your father's favorite saying: Seize the—"

"—seal by the tail?"

"That is the one. Her Majesty is in the large guest bedroom. I did not intrude, but her footsteps have been going back and forth for some time."

"I understand," Anso said. "Thank you for your advice."

He didn't want to take it, but he suspected it was sound. Satisfied he'd been heard, Harrison bowed and left.

Anso leaned back in his desk chair and laughed to himself at the irony. *Seize the seal by the tail.* Wasn't that what caused his problems in the first place? He'd seized the seal too tightly, and now she wanted to flee from him. No lesser person than the Magus had confirmed it. Anso hoped Ty was having better luck with "Mr. Forster." Maybe James could convince his wife to stay.

Except that wasn't what Anso wanted. He wanted Olivia to stay for him. He needed her to love him.

He didn't know if he was following Harrison's suggestion, but decision seized him. With only a vague idea of what he'd say or do, he left his office to find Olivia.

~

Olivia couldn't tell James to go to Ty and then be a coward herself. Naturally, she required a longer pep talk than her husband. Of the two of them, he'd always been bolder.

Step up to the plate, Olivia exhorted herself. Grab the bull by the horns and all that.

She literally crashed into Anso as he shut the door to his office.

He caught her, his hands staying on her arms after he'd steadied her. His touch felt like twenty circuits flipping on inside her body.

It had been too long since she'd made love to him.

"I was coming to see you," he said.

"I wanted to apologize," she blurted, her words running over his.

His expression softened, his grip tightening. The glow that began to kindle in the depths of his eyes drew hot sensations between her legs.

"I shouldn't let you look at me like that," he said huskily.

"Why not?"

"Because it's just our mating heat working on you, and you and I need to talk."

"That's the girl's line," she teased.

He stroked her cheek, his warm palm melting much lower parts of her. His eyes were fond but serious. "I know I ought to offer to let you leave, but I can't. I took you against your will. Stole you from a life you loved. I saw what that did to my mother, how every day she grew sadder. Maybe you were smarter than she was. Maybe she should have run away before she killed herself. You owe me no apologies."

Olivia's heart felt like he'd kicked it. "Your mother killed herself?"

"I'm sorry, I thought you— I thought someone must have mentioned it."

"No." She shook her head, then had to do it again. "No one mentioned it. Were you afraid I'd be as miserable as she was? Were you thinking I'd never love you even before you swam up on that beach to claim me?"

"I thought . . . when I saw you and James were married, I hoped bringing him too would make it easier for you."

It had a kind of crazy logic, crazy and terrible. She should have realized how much *not* a game this was to him. "Now I feel even sorrier. My God, I shouldn't have led you on. If I thought I was going to leave, I never should have slept with you!"

"Olivia, with the best will in the world, you'd have had to be a Titan to fight that. Not in the beginning and not after the bond was set. I'm not angry with you for . . . making our time in bed memorable. You thought playing along would help you regain your freedom, which is no more than you deserve. I just don't know how to stop wanting you to love me. I don't know how to stop loving you myself. *That* isn't the blood bond. That's my heart wanting someone I care deeply about to feel the same way for me. My whole life I've longed for a lover I could count on."

This was a whole other kettle, though Olivia saw how one pain led to the other. She took hold of his creased white shirt—the same he'd worn into the water, she realized. He hadn't bothered to change it before he went to work. Just barely, she resisted her urge to give him and the cotton a wake-up shake. "Anso, when I said I'd never be the only one to love you, that wasn't an empty reassurance. Ty loves you back exactly as you describe. Hell, he adores you. And if you think you can't count on him, you haven't been paying attention!"

He seemed caught off guard by her defense of his long-time lover.

"Ty is . . . well, I know he loves me," he said. "And I'm glad he gets along with both of you."

"He has your back, Anso. No matter who else he's slept with, I expect he always has. I can see how his promiscuity might have played into your fears, but in your heart, you know he's there for you. You put your gun down when he was the only one left to defend me. You *knew* he'd make that shot."

Not seeing what she was getting at, his brows drew together in confusion. "Ty is an expert marksman."

"It's more than that." Olivia gathered her thoughts so she could be as clear as possible. "If you don't trust him with your heart the way you were willing to trust me, this isn't going to work."

"This?" he asked.

Olivia screwed up her nerve. "James and I want to stay. We want to make a go of . . . whatever you call four people in a relationship. If it works out the way I hope, someday we'll all have each other's backs."

She supposed it was appropriate to say his mouth fished open. He closed it and swallowed. "You want to accept our four-way blood bond. Voluntarily. Even though you're homesick."

"Yes," she said firmly.

Her eyes hadn't been searched with this particular mix of hope and amazement since she'd accepted James's marriage proposal.

"Come on," she said, giving his hard chest a playful punch. "Me saying yes can't be that surprising. Don't forget I came back before the hairdresser's spell wore off."

"And you think you could come to love me."

"I *do* love you. Right now. No waiting period required."

No one who saw him break into that smile could have thought him older than eighteen. "Right now."

"Right now, Your Majesty. I love you."

He lifted her off her feet to hug her bear-style, his pleasure at squeezing her causing him to growl. "And Ty? You think you'll love him too?"

Olivia thought it nice of him to remember, but kept her amusement to herself. "Ty too," she assured him with only a hint of dryness. "He and I have interests in common."

Without setting her down, Anso drew back to grin some more at her. "God, I love you," he said. "My genes were genius to send me after you."

Ty and James walked up on them just like that. Anso set her on her feet but didn't let her go. Instead, he held her against his side. When Anso and Ty's gazes found each other and glowed brighter, she knew the four of them had a real chance for happiness.

Ty was always beautiful. When Anso smiled, his normal attractiveness became breathtaking. "I guess you got the good news too."

"I did." Ty's grin broadened, then faltered. "You're okay with this, right? Me being in this quartet for real?"

"Ty. Don't you know you've been a part of my dreams of happiness since we first became friends?"

"Well, I hoped so. You were . . . you were always a part of mine."

James and Olivia exchanged eye rolls, pressing their lips together against their impulse to laugh. The king and his captain were too freaking sweet for words. Olivia knew she and James both loved it.

"And Olivia," Ty said, turning to her almost too quickly for her to get her face in order.

"Me?" she asked, trying to sound innocent.

"James is your husband. Do you mind him . . . having feelings for me?"

Olivia didn't want Anso to let go of her, so she reached to tug Ty closer. When he was near enough, she stretched onto her toes, wrapped one hand behind his neck, and laid the most blistering kiss she had in her onto his tempting mouth.

Ty stiffened in surprise for a millisecond, after which he dove into the kiss like he was drowning and she was air. Olivia had hoped he would kiss her back but was rocked by the fervor of his response. Ty felt like he had twelve hands, and they were all over her.

Oh wait, one of those palms contracting on her bottom belonged to

Anso.

When Ty finally let go, she was disheveled and breathless. It took her two tries to speak. "I had something smart planned to say, but you kissed it out of my head."

Ty laughed, a purely happy, purely masculine sound. "Glad I could oblige."

"Oh," she said, jumping a little as his strong hands continued to smooth around her hips. "I remember. I wanted to say why don't you ask James if he minds *me* having feelings for *you*?"

Ty's yellow eyes welled up. "Liv."

"I do," she said shyly. It was odd to be making this declaration with her two other men close by, but certainly not odd bad. "I know it's early days, and my feelings are new, but I'm sure they'll get bigger. You're a wonderful man. Not to mention really hot stuff."

"Plus, I saved your life."

"You did!" she agreed. "Which was very nice of you."

He smiled and kissed her, more gently this time, though the way his tongue stroked hers was exciting. Through it all, Anso's arm didn't leave her waist. If anything, it braced her for Ty. By the end, Ty was rocking his erection into her belly, his arms wrapped around her back while Anso's fingers caressed her side. Both of them were affecting her. Olivia's pussy brimmed with arousal.

Ty seemed to reach his limit just as she did. He rested his mouth against her brow. "I'm about to say something smart, so I hope you'll forgive me."

"What is it?"

He pushed his erection against her harder. "Olivia, *nothing* I feel about you is small."

"I see. You care about me eight inches worth."

"Nine," he corrected, straight-faced. "Because of how we're built, wereseals are hard to measure." He raised inquiring eyebrows at Anso. Having received whatever answer he was looking for, he swung Olivia up into his arms. The ease with which he did it was pleasant. "We're moving this celebration to Anso's room. When you've got servants, hallways are bad places to have sex."

"Thus speaks the voice of experience," James quipped.

Olivia looked at him over Ty's shoulder. Her husband was smiling and unbuttoning his shirt, maybe the easiest of all of them with this.

"My experience benefits you," Ty said with put-on dignity. "All of you should be writing thank you notes to my old lovers."

He said this as if they were history.

"How hard are we going to have to work to keep you from taking new ones?" Anso asked mildly.

He'd opened the door to his bedroom suite. Ty stopped on the threshold to look at him.

"I wouldn't insist on it," Anso added. "I'm simply admitting I'd rather only share the people I love *with* the people I love. I'd like to think we're enough for you."

Ty's body stilled even as his breathing deepened with emotion. Olivia knew he'd heard Anso say he loved him. "You're enough," he said roughly. "If the three of you loved me, I'd count myself the luckiest man in the world."

Anso leaned in to press his lips to Ty's. He probably meant to keep it light, but Ty wasn't a man anyone could kiss halfway. With Olivia still in his arms, the two men got seriously into it. Olivia could feel their groans rumbling in their chests, could hear and see their tongues working greedily against each other. She shivered with excitement, and Ty's arms tightened under her.

"Christ," Ty whispered into Anso's mouth. "I think Her Majesty's temperature just jumped ten degrees."

Anso pulled back and laughed, tugging both of them into his bedroom. "Hey," he called to James. "Why aren't you in here and naked already? I'm pretty sure your wife would enjoy us putting on a show for her."

"I'm pretty sure *your* wife's the pervy one," James said. "My Liv was always a straight arrow."

"Ha!" Ty and Olivia scoffed in chorus.

Still holding her, Ty stopped so they could admire the sight of James shucking off his trousers and underwear. He was hard and getting harder, his erection a steely rod sticking out from a tangle of black pubic hair. His physique might have changed a little, but he was the same gorgeous hero who'd ridden right through her shyness to sweep her up, the same funny adventurous man who made her heart beat harder. Wasn't it a miracle when someone you desired wanted you in return? As James straightened, showing off his abs and chest, Ty let out a happy sigh.

"God, he's sexy," he said.

Amused by the parallel nature of their thoughts, Olivia nipped Ty's earlobe. This drew a secret shudder from him.

"Nice," Anso said, joining them in ogling James's nudity.

"Jeesh," James said, momentarily startled to find all eyes on him. "If this is a peep show, maybe I should charge."

"You're beautiful," Anso said seriously. "You were before, and now you're even more so. Your muscles are more substantial, but you still look lean overall. You could probably survive training with the guards, if that interests you."

James enjoyed competition, and Olivia expected he'd take Anso up on his offer. At the moment, though, this wasn't where his focus lay. He flashed his best crinkling grin at the king. "I thought we were going to put on a show for Olivia, or are you all talk and no action?"

"Those are fighting words," Ty warned and set her down carefully.

To her delight, he and Anso began stripping off their clothes.

"You too," Anso said to her. "Once this gets started, there will be no game delays."

Oh they all knew how to push her buttons, each in his own way. Men seemed to be quicker at getting naked than women, and the king and Ty were no exception. Completely bare-assed at nearly the same instant, they didn't need more than a look to coordinate their attack. They let out matching football player's roars and rushed James in unison.

Yelping in alarm, he tumbled beneath them onto Anso's giant floor-level bed. Three very naked, very aroused men wrestling with each other was a show worth seeing. An all out licking and tickling battle ensued. James didn't have the slightest hope of victory. He was laughing too hard to defend himself—that is, when he wasn't moaning like a foghorn.

Ty would give his cock one long suck, only to have his mouth replaced by Anso's. James tried to grab his attackers, but they restrained his hands. That aroused him more, until a simple nip on his thigh or a lick up his ribs could draw a groan from him. If it weren't for the tickling, he probably wouldn't have fought at all.

"Olivia," he called between gasps as they went at him. "Save me! They're ganging up on me."

Saving him was going to wait. Olivia could have watched them all day: their straining muscles and cute clenched butts, the flashes of long hard cocks being waved around. All of them were hung, but their different shapes and shades fascinated her.

"Bedside chest," Ty panted, catching her eye as he trapped James's wrists. His face was happy, his flush bringing out the pretty pattern of his leopard spots. Anso was nuzzling James's balls in a manner that—evidently—was both erotic and ticklish. James seemed unable to decide whether to protest or shove closer.

"There's lube in there," Ty told her.

In her distraction, Olivia had lost track of his last comment. He jerked his head toward the bedside chest to remind her, then returned his attention to James. Deciding his request was worth her while, she knelt in front of the small mother of pearl inlaid cabinet. The softness of her butt resting on her heels reminded her she was naked for three men, but it felt natural. They were *her* men, and all of them liked her. On instinct, she pulled out the chest's bottom drawer. Inside, she found a cut glass flask filled with clear liquid, plus something else interesting.

A paddle lay on the velvet lining, carved of wood with rubber on one side. This must be the toy Anso used to spank Ty.

"Liv," James gasped from the tangle on the bed, laughingly complaining at her delay. "I need you to take my side."

Of course he did. Olivia retrieved the paddle and hid it behind her back.

"Ty," she said. "I think you need to suck James again. I can tell you doing it really gets to him."

Anso huffed, insulted by this slur, but let Ty take his place when he noticed she was smiling. Ty grinned at her for different reasons before bending back over James's cock. He had no clue what was coming.

Anso's brows rose when she brought out the paddle.

Hold him, she mouthed to him.

Anso grinned evilly and complied. Olivia brought the paddle down in a good sharp smack on Ty's taut rear end. Stunned, he jerked back and looked at her wide-eyed.

"Hoho," James gloated, though the state Ty had left him in had him panting. "Now you're in for it."

"I promised I'd do this one day," Olivia reminded him. "What sort of mate would I be if I didn't keep my word?"

"Jesus," Ty said, the oath shaking with excitement.

Olivia kept her word as well as her swimmer's arm allowed.

~

Good Lord, Olivia was good at this. Never mind how thrilled Ty was that she'd called herself his mate, he'd have admired her aptitude regardless. She hit him harder and faster than Anso did, perhaps because she wasn't afraid of her own strength.

She didn't overwork any spot, but aimed her blows all over. His ass cheeks took on a sweet simmer, the slightly illicit thrill heightened by having three people watch—and hear—him get a charge out of it. Pretty soon into it, James pulled Ty's hips down until their cocks nestled side by side between their bellies. Every time Olivia smacked him, those friction-loving organs jarred together, and every time they jarred together, James gave a little gasp. Ty sensed the reason was more than the nice jostle of their pricks; James liked the idea of spanking too.

Ty had to kiss him even as the paddle's stings rained down, had to thank him for being his partner in freakishness. He suspected Anso could have lived without this game. Chances were, Anso could have lived without male bed partners if his bonding genes hadn't decided differently. That wasn't the case for Ty, and maybe it wasn't for James either. James kissed him back so hard their teeth threatened to cut each other's lips. Ty thought he'd burst with excitement, though the side of him that loved being punished longed to go limp with surrender. The dilemma was delectable, the swelling of his cock causing him to groan his enjoyment down James's throat.

He noticed James's dick was leaking like crazy between their abs, his precum thinner than a wereseal's. The contrast made Ty insane. He wrenched one hand from Anso's grip so he could shove it onto James's cock and rub the warm slipperiness over him. James's veins were throbbing, his glans as full as a plum. He arched and writhed as Ty rubbed him, his breath gasping out with pleasure.

Maybe Olivia sensed how close Ty was to being overwhelmed. Her strikes slowed against his ass, allowing him to appreciate the reverb from every blow. The vibrations slung up his asshole, into his prostate and out his dick. He was so hard, so sensitized he was already fighting not to come. His head arched back the next time she hit him, sexy tingles jolting up his tailbone. Pictures rolled through his imagination of things he wanted to do with these three people—and maybe would get a chance to now. A thick drop of precum squeezed from his slit. This was heaven, but even heaven could get better.

"I want him to take me," he broke out. "I want to be the first man James fucks."

James moaned like this idea suited him. Olivia's spanking ceased. Anso released Ty's remaining hand. The royal bedchamber echoed with hard breathing.

"You're sure?" James asked.

He looked up at Ty from the bed, where a sunbeam from Anso's windows slanted onto his handsome drylander's face. His stubble was darker and rougher than Ty's or Anso's, but his beard wasn't all that glinted in the sunlight. Tiny rays of yellow appeared around the center of his deep blue eyes. Pride rose in Ty: that this man was partly his, that he knew he was starting to love him.

"Oh yeah," he said, his voice gravelly. "The sooner you shove your dick up my ass, the happier I'm going to be."

~

Anso knew the signs that someone was in heat. Foregoing sex felt like torture. Even slowing down was a big challenge. All you could think about was getting more and more of whatever felt good to you, as soon as possible. The flush on James's face, the extreme raggedness of his breathing said more than his attraction to Ty was riding him. Probably he was too hard up to be nervous for his first time, but Anso thought he'd help him ease into it all the same.

He unscrewed the top of the flask of lube. "Hand," he said to Olivia, his voice hoarser than expected.

Olivia held out her palm.

Beside them, Ty was sitting back on his heels, his well-basted bottom making the shift gingerly. He was showing the same high arousal as James, though his might have been due to the surprisingly vigorous spanking Olivia had given him. Anso was considering yielding his paddle to her for good. Each time her lovely arm had fallen, each time the concussion drew a broken pleasure-gasp from Ty, the tip of Anso's cock had tingled. Apparently, for this particular activity, Anso liked watching better than doing.

Thinking about that, his hand trembled just a little as he poured the lube in her palm.

"You liked watching me spank him," she murmured. Maybe the others heard and maybe they didn't. Anso lifted his eyes to hers. He might have changed their color, but her soul shone unchanged behind them. His love for her very essence swelled inside him.

"Yes, I did," he murmured back.

She closed her fingers over the lubricant.

"Get James a rubber," Ty broke in. "This won't be the last thing he wants to do tonight."

"So you wereseals *do* know what rubbers are," Olivia said as Anso turned to retrieve one from the cabinet.

He squirmed at her sardonic tone. Was she going to demand he use one now that she and James had volunteered to stay? Should he explain that this brand was mainly hygienic, that only a spelled condom offered pregnancy prevention—and even that wasn't a hundred percent guaranteed? He didn't want to explain. Every cell in both his bodies wanted her to have his child. Then again, shouldn't he show her the respect of fully informing her?

She laughed at the war that must have been tugging at his expression. "Today you're off the hook. Tomorrow, if I'm still not pregnant, we all talk this decision through."

"Agreed," he said—maybe too eagerly, because the other men laughed at him. "You should know weres don't transmit sexual diseases, nor could we catch them from you."

"No, you only . . . turn people's eyes blue," James said, breath hitching as Ty rolled the thin rubber on.

Olivia was ready to help with the next stage, all but her index finger curled around the lube on her palm. With that one finger, she touched the tip of the condom. It stuck to James's skin when she backed off, the latex caught there by his generous precum. Olivia didn't say a word, but Anso saw awareness pass between them. The couples' gazes held as she wrapped her oiled hand around his dick. James's lids drifted shut for her first downward stroke. To them, sharing these caresses was familiar. Anso wished Olivia felt the same ease with him. The longing that tightened his throat came as no surprise. The realization that maybe he'd enjoy the steps it took to get there did.

"Boy," James said, his hips pushing into her smoothing motions. "That feels *really* good."

"You're in heat too," she said.

His eyes opened. "Not just for him, sweetheart."

She smiled. The curve of her lips, the way the light struck her red hair and face, was so beautiful Anso wished he could capture it forever.

"Be as good to Ty as you are to me," she said.

CHAPTER SIXTEEN

OLIVIA sensed James needed that last permission. He crinkled his eyes at her, one hand caressing the wrist that had just stroked him. They were both aware of Ty stretching out to lie face down on the bed. He lifted his hips to make room for his erection, then settled to the covers.

"Take me like this," he said, his cheek on his folded arms, his voice aroused and dreamy. He bent one long leg up and to the side, his fine golden body hair glinting on his calf and thigh muscles. "This position is the easiest."

"Um," James said, unsure but not unwilling. "Won't I be rubbing against the places Olivia spanked?"

Ty turned his head farther sideways and grinned at him.

"Okay," James said. "I guess that will be a good thing."

"No more waiting now. Get your cock in there, Outsider."

Ty sounded drunk with anticipation. James flushed, then carefully lowered into a position from which he could enter. His cock pulsed hard enough to bounce. He wasn't looking at Olivia anymore. Ty and what he was about to do to him filled his attention. Olivia kept her mouth shut and reached for Anso's hand. He squeezed it back tightly.

James slid one arm underneath Ty's chest. "All right. Tell me if I do anything too wrong."

Olivia doubted that was going to happen. As soon as he started pushing, Ty arched his spine to help.

"Oh boy," James said, the muscles in his ass clenching. "Oh . . . God."

"Mmm," was Ty's answer. He gave a gorgeous full body wriggle as James's cock disappeared in him. His face was toward her, the fist beneath it clenching with pleasure. His expression was nearly unrecognizable. Olivia wondered if she looked that beatific when James penetrated her. It certainly was intimate to have other people witness it.

"Tell me you're okay," James pleaded once he was inside, "because I really want to move."

"Yes," Ty said. "Go."

They moaned together as he did. Anso's hand abruptly grew sweatier in hers.

"Olivia," he whispered, not wanting to disturb the others. "I don't think I can wait until they're done."

She turned to him. His face was flushed, his eyes glowing noticeably. Suddenly, she couldn't wait either. Those twenty circuits he'd flipped on were shooting out energy. She ached with need, her pussy contracting with longing.

"Don't wait," Ty groaned. "Fuck her while he fucks me."

James wasn't fucking him at all. James was stroking into Ty as sweetly as he'd ever taken Olivia. His face brushed the bunched muscles of Ty's shoulders, the arm that wasn't supporting his weight petting up and down the side of Ty's thigh. Even his chest caressed Ty as he went in and out. Ty's body recognized this. It was going looser and looser even as he canted his spine to let James deeper.

Anso seemed to like watching Ty succumb as much as she did. If Olivia's temperature had jumped ten degrees, his had just leaped fifteen.

"Here," he said, urging Olivia onto her knees and over his lap.

She loved the way he handled her, strong and careful at the same time. His scent rose with his increase in heat, different from James's but just as comforting. Anso's hands slid to her waist and rubbed. She bit her lip, wanting to kiss him, but then they wouldn't be able to watch the others.

"Ride me," Anso said gruffly, settling her indecision. "It's been too long since I was in you."

"Wait." Ty's hand fumbled out to hit Olivia's knee. "Go in slow. James and I want to watch you take her."

Ty didn't just want to watch. Despite the awkward way he had to reach, he parted Olivia's labia, pushing up the smooth wet folds and holding them open for his friend. His index finger rubbed once over Anso's crest, then stroked her swollen clitoris. When he put his thumb there too and pinched lightly where she ached most, Olivia couldn't contain a gush of excitement.

Naturally Ty liked that.

"I love this part of you," he said, low and growly. "This is my idea of magic."

It would have been rude to laugh, and besides she was moaning. The dual sensations really got to her: Anso pushing slowly into her, Ty just as slowly frigging her.

"Pretty," James panted, not taking his hands off Ty.

She didn't want him to. Trusting Ty and James were of the same opinion, she kept her touch on Anso, combing through the dark gold silk of his hair, stroking his broad warm back. She rocked herself on his cock as if she had all the time on the world to come. Her body was telling her she was crazy, that it wanted to *come now*, but she honestly didn't care.

Anso shook with need, but he seemed no more inclined to rush. Each of his thrusts was deep, each long entry perfect for savoring. He pushed her breasts up, bending to suck her nipples and groan softly around them.

"Kiss them for me," Ty said.

"Fuck him for me," Anso returned to James.

This seemed to be the signal for Anso to push her backward, tumbling her gently under him to the bed. She couldn't see James and Ty then, though she could still hear them. James had begun thrusting faster, if his and Ty's sped-up grunts were anything to go by.

Anso breathed out a curse, affected by this soundtrack too. She supposed that was the challenge to making love in tandem. The other people got you excited. Anso pushed her hands up beside her shoulders, weaving their fingers together.

To her, that union was as lovely as the other.

"Ready?" he asked, his next thrust already coming harder. It felt like paradise to her aching core.

"Oh yes," she promised him.

He went at her like he'd been wanting to before they started, like this was the real beginning for him. He was so athletic that it was easier to let him take charge than to try to match his pace. She spread for him, arched for him, but didn't get in his way otherwise. Growling his approval, he dug in his knees to give her his all—full length and full throttle.

Olivia climbed so fast it was scary, the noises she was making every bit as loud as Ty's. Her body was more than ready for this.

"*There,*" Ty groaned as James evidently found a good spot. "God, you're so fucking *big.*"

Olivia certainly could have said the same.

Anso dropped his head, his quickened breathing huffing in her ear. He released his hold on one of her hands so he could cup her breast, grunting in reaction as he felt just how tight her nipple was. Thumbing it caused Olivia to let out a strangled sound, her pussy tightening helplessly on him.

She couldn't doubt he liked that. His face went lax with pleasure a second before he set it determinedly. He changed angles and went faster, then changed them one more time.

That angle was the one. He knocked and rubbed the right spots inside and out. Instantly overloading, Olivia cried out and came.

"God," Anso gasped, beginning to go as well.

Energy thickened in the air. The slapping sounds James's groin made on Ty's buttocks turned crazy-fast. Ty groaned, then James did, and then everything Olivia was feeling got extremely intense.

It was as if she was having a four-way orgasm. In fact, it felt like all of them were. Sweet hard shocks ran through her as Anso held deep and flooded her. No one person had this many nerves, nor should they have fired this sharply all at one time. The climax was strong enough that it halfway hurt, though with a sweetness that helped explain why Ty enjoyed being spanked.

When the pleasure-pain finally released her sex, she was completely limp.

The king, on the other hand, not so much. Though it felt like he'd come oceans, his cock remained rigid inside of her. Only his face had sagged next to hers.

"Okay," Ty panted from the other end of the bed. "Are James and I the only ones who want more of that?"

Anso groaned but not in disagreement. "I'm still hard as Hades."

The way they were talking woke fresh quivers inside of her. She squirmed around Anso's hardness to ease her rising itch.

"Um," she said, "if you all wouldn't mind, could I make a request?"

"Oh God." Anso pressed his cock deeper. "Does it involve waiting before the next round?"

"Noo," she said, unsureness creeping into her tone. Asking for sexual things was easier when it was just James and her.

Anso went up on his elbows to look at her. His eyes caught hers in their deep blue magic, but she sensed the others turning as well.

"I recognize that wriggle," James said. "A break isn't what she wants."

She wrenched her gaze from Anso to James and then from him to Ty. All the men smiled at her, silently implying she could ask for anything. What she wanted seemed to come from somewhere even deeper than her desires, though certainly the longing was physical.

"Just ask," Anso said gently.

"I want all of you," she confessed. "I have such a craving to feel your cocks, I can't even describe it. I want you to come in me, one after the other. Maybe it's something to do with this heat, but I don't think I'll be satisfied until then."

Ty's grin was the first and the broadest. "That sounds like a kick-ass idea."

Because Ty had spoken first, he took the lead next with her. Olivia knew his submissive streak was just that: only a part of him. What he showed her then was the mastery of a born sensualist.

He stroked her from head to toe.

Every line of her felt his sensitive fingers. Every curve. Every bend. Every muscle and digit. He kissed her nipples and her knees with almost equal interest. He nuzzled his way up her vertebrae and smoothed his palms up her arms. He turned her into a puddle of relaxation that *still* wanted him to take her.

"I think I'm jealous," Anso confessed laughingly minutes later. "He's never touched me quite like that."

Olivia liked that he wasn't a hundred percent joking.

"I'll pencil you in for next week," Ty teased back the same way.

Done with his exploration, he draped himself along her back like a living blanket. His cock throbbed hot and thick against her, the tip resting in the cleft between her buttocks.

"Mm," he said, one hand wedging beneath her to cup her sex. "Your and James's skin is the best."

"I like yours." She was so relaxed and aroused that the words were slurred. "Your body hair is so pettable."

He chuckled—probably over the condition he'd reduced her to—and licked the side of her neck. "I think you know where I'm silkiest."

She knew, but just in case she didn't, he shifted to let her feel the buttery soft crest against her very wet entrance.

"Mm," he repeated, giving a half push in. "My memory didn't exaggerate how nice this felt."

His whole push made her go *mm*. His thrusts were as luxurious as his all-over massage had been, though they massaged a more intimate place. He didn't grow impatient as quickly as the king had. After a bit, he reared back with her still on him, taking her on his lap while she faced forward. His hands took advantage of the modified reverse cowgirl to roam up and down her front—and even then he didn't speed up. The only sign that he was getting more excited was a greater fullness inside her and a subtle tightening of his muscles.

"Liv," he whispered into her ear. "Would you suck off the king for me?"

The shiver his request inspired was violent enough to see. "Anso," she said throatily. "Ty wants me to suck you off."

He came slowly to his feet, as if watching Ty fuck her the way he was had put him in a similar dreamlike state. He stood before her on the mattress, reaching out—perhaps without thinking—to steady himself on James's shoulder. His cock was fully erect, skin flushed, head stretched and shiny with excitement.

Now that she looked for it, she saw the tight seam in the gold fur around its base. She couldn't dislike the evidence that he was different any more than she disliked any part of James. This was him, and because it was him, it was sexy.

"Come closer," she said, gazing up his beautiful body into his lust-darkened face. Ty's slow thrusts were moving her up and down, shaking her breasts and drawing Anso's eyes to them. He stepped closer, breathed harder . . .

When she lowered her head and sucked him, all of their bodies touched.

"God," James breathed. "That looks beautiful."

Anso made a sound like she was hurting him really good.

"Bring him off," Ty said, his hushed voice breaking, "and I promise you'll bring me."

She took her time about it. She knew this was what Ty wanted, plus Anso felt really good going in and out her mouth. *Silky* didn't cover how smooth he was. The skin of his penis almost seemed delicate. Being protected most of the time certainly made it sensitive. A very little work on her part earned big responses from him.

In the end, watching his friend squirm and strain with pleasure was what snapped Ty's control.

"Damn it," he said, his subsequent thrust jolting into her. He had one arm clamped beneath her breasts, lifting them for Anso's view. His other arm controlled her pelvis, bracing her for his thrusts with his hand cupped hard around her pussy. Despite its newness to him, he'd figured out a couple tricks to working her clit. He used them now as he went harder. "You might want to speed up there, Your Majesty."

She'd been holding Anso by his hips. She held them harder as she caught Ty's urgency. She wanted the king and Ty to go together; wanted to go with them herself. James's hand was steadying Anso's thigh, a handy support when Anso decided to fork all his fingers into her wavy hair.

This was too evocative for Ty.

"Shit," he snarled behind her. "My balls are . . . going to explode."

Olivia's heart felt like it would do the same. She was so close to coming, and his finger had found a spot on her clit that was exquisite. Her orgasm crested between one heart-thump and another. Her neck arched back as Ty pumped and frigged her still more frenetically. The intensity of her pleasure made it impossible to continue pleasuring Anso. He grunted at her letting go, then shoved so close his cock nearly burned the side of her neck. He cupped it there, tight, and she put her hand over his. When he saw that, Ty couldn't hold his climax in any more.

He came with a shout and a tightening of his arms, holding her prisoner for the hot flood that shot from him. Again and again he shoved into her, while Anso did the same underneath her hand, in close to the same rhythm. Ty's chest took most of the king's semen.

Olivia doubted he minded.

"God," Ty said at last, sagging around her.

Anso's cock softened on her shoulder, his hand petting slowly through her hair. *Almost* overcome with lassitude, she turned her face back and forth on his warm hipbone.

"I love you, Liv," Anso said.

Olivia smiled. He was getting used to the words.

"Me too," Ty mumbled in her ear.

"Me three?" James offered, amusement quavering in his voice.

All three men waited for a beat. Olivia burst out laughing. James and Anso she believed. Ty might not know his mind yet, but that he was willing to love her touched her deeply.

"All right, me four," she surrendered, jumping in with both feet. "I love all of you. And I'm not just saying that because you said it first."

"She's polite," James confirmed, "but she takes I love you seriously."

"Good," Ty said, sighing lengthily in her ear.

"Good," Anso echoed after him.

"You *could* let me go," Olivia pointed out. "I do have one more man on my to-do list."

"Really?" Ty said, hugging her like a sleepy child with a teddy bear. "You couldn't use a rest?"

Normally she would have, but her body was oddly energized, as if her two previous climaxes were shots of espresso that whet her appetite for James.

"No rest for the greedy," she quipped, gently peeling his octopus arms from her. "James and I haven't made love together since we came here."

"Really?" This came from Anso.

James smiled at her. He was as conscious of their abstinence as her.

Reluctantly, Ty let her pull free of his cock. "I suppose the other changes in your body have reduced your recovery time. Which is good, because I kind of went at you at the end."

Olivia kissed one corner of his apologetic mouth. "I enjoyed every minute. Maybe my queenly nature is kicking in."

Ty snorted at the idea of her being queenly, then grinned at her. "Go on then. Have at the tall dark hottie. I should be able to stay awake long enough to watch you and your first man do the dirty."

Olivia shook her head at him. Ty had flopped down on his side and elbow with one ear propped his hand. She'd bet her favorite calculator he'd stay awake long enough. His twice-pleasured cock hung thick on his thigh, relaxed and shining with wetness but not retracting into its pocket the way she assumed it would if he were truly indifferent.

Ty didn't miss the direction of her glance. "You keep ogling me like that, and your harem will get jealous."

"No worries," she said, enjoying his humor. "I'm an equal opportunity ogler."

She was, she realized. When she turned from Ty's odalisque pose to her husband, what she wanted to ogle most was the warmth in his eyes.

Like her, he was on his knees on the rumpled sheets, his smile broadening as hers did. In a lot of ways, he'd made this adventure possible. Without him to share it, she'd have been too scared and guilty. With him, it became marvelous.

He tucked a lock of red hair behind her ear. "You and me then."

"You and me," she agreed.

His hands slid down to cover and stroke her breasts. He was very erect from watching her with Ty and Anso, but his caresses were as patient as the others' had started out. His gaze slid down her body, which made her girl parts tingle pleasantly. Her thighs were wet from the other men and herself.

James's breath hitched softly at the sight. When his eyes rose to hers again, his pupils were bigger.

"Feels like it's been a while," he said huskily.

Olivia slid her palms up his chest, loving the way his heart pounded under them. "It's been an eternity since we came here."

He smiled and kissed her, and then they renewed the part of their vows that had always helped glue them together. James slid into her like a hot slow dream. They stayed on their knees—Olivia riding James while he thrust up and held her bottom.

This was how Anso had started off taking her—and how Ty had finished, just backwards. Despite the surface similarities, with each man the act felt different. James's hips were narrower between her thighs, his cock thicker at the head. Most importantly, the way he handled her was absolutely sure. He knew her too well to doubt he'd please her.

They traded old favorite treats: a special touch, a certain way of moving. Though the others weren't obvious about it, Ty and Anso watched what they did as intensely as scientists studying exotic animal behavior. *Here's the devoted married couple, having sex in the wild.* Olivia wondered if they realized they had more than a touch of this familiarity themselves. They too had been lovers for a long time.

Of course, not everything about making love to James was the same. Both of them were changed from before.

She'd known that from his first thrust inside of her.

The sensation of him filling her was a dial spun from ten to twenty—more acute, more pleasurable, even more intense emotionally. She'd had hints that this might happen, but actually experiencing it took her breath away.

By the time they reached the stage where they couldn't go slow anymore, she was mewling for each penetration, and his grip had turned to iron.

"God," he swore, jamming up into her harder. "Fuck."

Olivia twined her arms behind his strong neck, her hips moving faster to speed up his. "Finish me. Come in me."

His thrust went crazy. "Always," he growled in her ear. "Always you're the one for me."

The fit between them got snugger as he swelled for the final drive to orgasm. He felt so good, so hard and so desperate. Possibly his glans was broader. It spread her walls so well. She reveled in his hunger for her, her pussy creaming extravagantly. She wanted to be wetter; wanted to overflow with his seed *and* that of the other men. The craving might not have been rational, but she couldn't resist it.

"Not . . . just me," she gasped in response to his last statement. "The . . . three of us . . . are yours now."

If it wasn't entirely true yet, she had faith it would be. The more people got to know James, the better they loved him. He was the best man she'd ever known.

He made a sound, holding her tighter as she spoke the wish he might not have known he had. "Liv—"

He ran out of breath for words. His cock plunged up into her again, triggering reactions beyond her control. Her thighs vised around him, her pussy tightening in refusal to let him withdraw. She needed him where he was, grinding against her womb.

He seemed to need that too. He cried out and ejaculated, sending her crashing over. Both their heads flung back at the sensations. She heard the others panting, fast and choppy. Someone's come spurted hot on her hip, so Ty and Anso must have started jacking off at some point. The knowledge made her pleasure blaze higher. James squeezed her breast, and ecstasy flared so hot in her it was white.

"God," cried Anso.

"Shi-it," gasped Ty.

James just moaned as they spurted on him too.

As she descended, finally, the muscles of her pussy continued to spasm around her husband.

"*James*," she sighed.

Her tone was slightly astonished. Sex had always been good for them, but that was phenomenal. Laughing, he lifted her gently off him. Ty and Anso were sprawled on the bed, one to either side of the now completed show. Their muscular arms rested in matching bent positions along their sides, their relaxed hands draping but not quite covering their groins. Olivia was surprised either of their seed had hit her from that distance. Maybe wereseal ejaculations had superior propulsive qualities. And maybe James's did as well. She'd seemed to register every burst from him.

"Now we sleep," Anso said, patting the mattress in front of him.

She and James lay down together, for the moment completely biddable. Olivia found herself face to face with Ty, who tapped her nose playfully. "Satisfied?"

"Very," she said and closed her eyes.

They were only shut for a second when an odd sensation enveloped her. Her skin tingled all over, goose bumps prickling as the little hairs on her arms stood up. Was she floating? She couldn't feel the covers under her. Maybe she was falling asleep. If she was, children were giggling in her dream. Three children, she was sure.

Olivia's eyes snapped open. *Oh my God*, she thought. *I'm pregnant. With* ***triplets*** She'd known something like this might happen. In truth, she'd wanted it, and nonetheless it came as a shock. *No*, she thought. *I must be imagining it.*

Anso had sworn he'd sense the instant she conceived, and he wasn't saying a word.

Definitely imagining it, she told herself.

"Hm," Ty said, seemingly in his sleep. Except he wasn't sleeping. His eyelids fluttered up so he could consider her with drowsy yellow eyes. "Hm," he said again, a smile beginning to stretch his seducer's mouth. His gaze dropped down her naked body to where she'd unthinkingly pressed her hand over her belly.

"I'm not," she said, barely breathing it.

"You are," he countered and held up three fingers. He appeared to find her amazement funny, laughing softly as he closed his eyes again. "Boy are we in for it."

"In for what?" Anso mumbled from the other side of James.

"Nothing," Ty said. "Olivia can tell you when we wake up."

Anso must have been too tired to press. They *had* been up all day and all night.

"C'mere," Ty said and pulled her half over him.

Her miraculous—and life-changing—revelation should have kept her awake for hours. Instead, as James rolled closer and Anso rolled after him, a warm and very sweet peace filled her. Men who cared for her, men she felt proud to call her own, surrounded her. Maybe—probably—she was going to have their children, a dream she'd nearly given up on. Surely no woman ever was luckier.

She wondered if Ty's baby radar matched hers in all respects. She'd had the definite impression these children weren't just Anso's. It couldn't be a coincidence that she'd sensed three of them.

I'm a cat, she joked to herself. With a different daddy for each kitten.

The possibility made her smile. Ty's heart beat slow and steady beneath her cheek, the same as James's beat behind her. Ty pressed a kiss to her hair.

"'Night," Anso slurred.

'Night, she thought to the three gigglers.

To her own amusement, she dropped into sleep as easily as an exhausted four-year-old.

~

James wasn't the first to wake. That honor belonged to Anso, as James discovered when he sat up and looked around the rich but comfortable bedchamber.

Olivia and Ty were fast asleep, snuggling together like each other's favorite toy. James smiled at that. Them caring for each other made James caring for Ty less fraught. Besides that, it warmed his heart. Everyone ought to love his Olivia . . . and maybe everyone ought to love his Ty.

We're bloodmates, he thought, trying out the words. Me and Olivia. Me and Ty. In body and spirit.

He didn't remember Ty from another life, but the connection felt as fated as his and Olivia's. He padded to the bathroom naked, his body invigorated but also calm. As he peed without having to work around a monster hard-on, he concluded their four-way heat must be done.

He didn't mind. Taking their time making love, without everything seeming so damn urgent would be nice . . . at least until the next time their hormones went crazy.

Happy about that too, he shaved in the shower, whistling softly to himself through the spray. When his face was smooth, he stepped out, dried off, and pulled on one of Anso's seemingly endless supply of blue and silver robes.

This reminded him he was the king's mate as well.

He doubted Olivia needed reminding. She seemed to have accepted the bond once and for all last night.

Unexplored territory, he thought, resettling his robe's lapels before going in search of his own New World. He was glad Olivia was sleeping. These were waters he needed to navigate personally.

He found the object of his search when he entered the dining room—or rather, he found the other side of Anso. The windows were large here, and there was a long line of them. He had no trouble spotting Anso's seal form swimming sleekly among the coral.

Oddly enough, even before seeing his deep blue eyes, James knew it was the king.

The rosy bars of light declared the hour near sunset. Anso's seal form flickered between the spokes, almost as purely silver as the eels on James's robes. He moved at a clip James didn't think he could match, despite his recent physical improvements. Anso's muscles and streamlining were designed for cutting through water. Swiftness aside, he didn't seem agitated as he undulated around the garden. James suspected this was his version of a relaxing stroll. He was stretching out and enjoying his alternate body.

He shot upward suddenly, joining a school of bright blue fish in rising toward the light above. James lost sight of him for a minute before he torpedoed down again.

Boy, he thought. Liv and I sure got ourselves into something different.

Anso might have been aware of him all along, but only after his velocity slowed did he approach the dining room windows. Hanging there in the crystal water, he stared at James with strange-familiar eyes. Shivers coursed down James's spine, the sense of wonder that gripped him like nothing else he'd experienced.

This is magic, he thought. This, right in front of me.

He wondered if Anso felt this way when he looked at Olivia.

Anso's seal form blinked at him.

"Hey," James said, flattening one hand on the cool window. "Hello again."

He wasn't sure Anso could hear through the glass, but he could see his lips. Anso bobbed his graceful silver head, then jerked it to the left.

"Meet you in your office?" James asked.

Anso nodded again and disappeared in that direction.

Anso was wet, naked, and on two legs when he emerged from the silver-gold changing hatch. Prepared for this, James handed him a pair of towels.

"Thank you," Anso said, wrapping one around his waist and using the other to dry his hair. "Did you sleep well?"

James broke into a laugh. "You're very polite," he said when Anso lifted his brows at him.

"It's how I was raised."

Momentarily abashed, James reminded himself this man had had his mouth on his cock. *Polite* was hardly the sum of his character. "I believe in good manners," he conceded. "When they don't get in my way too much."

"Are they in your way now?"

Anso asked this politely too. James put one hand on the still damp stretch of muscle between Anso's neck and shoulder, squeezing just a bit to coax him to relax.

"No," he said, smiling to ease the sting, "but perhaps yours are."

Anso didn't shake off his hold, though as royalty, people wouldn't have touched him like this often. "I'm not certain I understand you."

"You're a little jealous of me. Because Olivia and I have a history. That evens out, though, because I'm a little jealous of you, for all the nice discoveries you and she have ahead of you."

"There's also Ty," Anso said.

"There is, and I do envy your closeness. But that will even out in time as well. I'm used to taking a long view of life."

The tension in the king's shoulder eased, and James was glad for it. Then his drowning blue eyes narrowed. "There's something else. You want to bargain with me. Does it involve you and Olivia traveling?"

"We can hash that out when Olivia is around. I'd like to discuss this triad thing I've overheard a couple people talking about. I know it's probably an honor, and you might not actually plan to make me your third, but the truth is I don't want the position."

"You don't." Fortunately, Anso sounded more curious than insulted.

"Well, I'm sure you're a decent boss, but I'm older than you, and I've got more experience. Plus, I hate politics."

"What sane person doesn't?" Anso asked dryly.

"Exactly," James said. "So I don't envy you that. The thing is, I'd really rather start a new business here. Ground up. No special royal favors. Just me and whatever interesting idea I come up with. And Olivia, now and then, if you can spare her from queening. She's a great accountant."

Anso was smiling as he folded his arms. His pecs really were impressive. And his biceps. And the rippling abs that dove underneath his towel. "You've thought this through."

"Yes," James said, yanking back his focus. His nerves were fluttering more than he expected. He might be older than Anso, but the man did have gravitas.

Anso lowered his head and shook it as if amused. "You and I."

"You and I?" James repeated, not following him.

Anso looked up and socked him with his blue eyes. James comforted himself that he had nearly the same pair. Maybe his eyes were socking Anso too.

The king cleared his throat. "There's a buzz between us, not just between you and Ty or me and Olivia."

"Yes," James agreed, feeling himself blushing. "I figured we'd work that out as we go along."

"I'd like that." Anso shifted, uncrossing his arms and unexpectedly taking James's hand from his shoulder to hold between both his own. The clasp wasn't what James's had been with Ty, but it wasn't a handshake either. James decided he liked it.

"There's something else you need to know," Anso said. "Something I noticed when I woke up this morning that affects all of us. I hope it's going to please you."

"I'm all ears," James assured him.

Anso's smile broke out like sunshine. "Olivia is pregnant. All of us are going to be fathers."

"*All* of us?"

"I sensed three life energies, each linked to one of us."

"Wow," James said, metaphorically knocked on his ass. "You knew this, and you didn't bust out with it right away?" He realized he was gripping Anso's hand really hard, but couldn't make himself let go. "Wow."

"You're happy about this?"

"Yes," James said. "It's fast, but yes." His knees were wobbly, so he propped his hips back on Anso's desk. He flashed back to the video they'd watched where the little boy turned into a seal pup. "Kids."

"Three of them."

"Will they all be able to change?"

"Very likely. Which will make them quite the handful when they turn five or so."

He laughed. "I can't even imagine!"

Anso bumped his shoulder, their hands now tangled together between their thighs. "Will Olivia be glad?"

"She'll be elated. She's been wanting this. And to have kids with all of us will suit her down to the ground. Olivia really likes making the people she loves happy. To have left any of us out would have worried her. You've no idea how perfect this is."

When Anso blew out a breath, James saw he'd been more nervous than he'd let on. "Good," he said. "I wanted to tell her as soon as I noticed, but I wasn't certain how she'd react."

"Will Ty be happy?"

"He'll be scared to death, but he'll make a great father."

Seeing the look on Anso's face—the fondness, the deep knowledge of his friend—drew such a fount of love up in James that he felt as if he adored the entire world. Since Anso was there, he was who James pulled into a back slapping hug.

Anso returned it with interest. "I'm glad you're here to help. I'm a little scared myself."

They pushed back from each other with matching grins. "Let's go tell them," they said in unison.

EPILOGUE

THE last Meimeyo returned on his own to the basilica. No one knew where he'd been or what he'd been up to since helping rescue Oceana, only that he'd appeared with a wider than usual dragon smile.

By popular acclaim, the city staged a victory parade for Olivia, which she found simultaneously moving and uncomfortable. Oceanans knew James had been right beside her saving the city. They also knew—because careful statements had been issued—that King Anso had formed a four-way blood bond, rather than the simpler historically accepted triad. Evidently, the city felt more comfortable feting her individually. Fertile and pretty queens they knew their opinion on. The rest they preferred to gloss over.

Both Ty and James thought her umbrage on their behalf was amusing.

On the brighter side, the celebration did distract from the dozen of Ellice's friends and employees who'd been sent to jail after a long scandal-laden trial. Happily, Mrs. Bonn was cleared early on of complicity. Though she'd recommended Lajos as a hairdresser, he'd taken her in like others. For a while, the consultant was so aghast at her own poor judgment she couldn't see Olivia without apologizing. Olivia was relieved she'd gotten over that.

She didn't know how she'd have dressed herself today otherwise. Left to herself, she only cared about three accessories: the two rings on her left hand and the three-pearl pendant Ty had given her the day they brought her and the triplets home from the maternity ward. "Our kids are lucky to have you for a mother," he'd said, which made her cry like a baby.

Now all their hormones were under better control—a side effect of nursing, according to Pinni. With that issue settled, they'd traveled to Resurrection, the thriving Pocket city north of Manhattan. It was the family's first visit to dry land since the triplets were born. Before she'd started showing, she and James had spent a weekend with her parents in Flagstaff. Arizona was too arid for Ty and Anso, but the wereseals had accompanied them to Charleston to meet James's folks. Some awkwardness had ensued when James's dad realized the four of them were *together* together, but he'd lost most of his prickle by the visit's end. Anso and Ty might have helped this along by taking him deep water fishing, a sport he loved that his son wasn't too keen on. Olivia didn't know exactly how Ty and the king arranged it, but James's dad had hooked the biggest marlin of his life with them.

"Those boys are all right," he'd conceded gruffly to her at their departure. "I think you and James are crazy, but you all seem happy enough."

She'd hugged him goodbye and thanked her very lucky stars that James wasn't going to lose his folks' affection over their unusual marital status. Lying about it hadn't been an option—at least not for the men.

It wasn't an option when it came to Violet either. Olivia simply wished it were. They were here today to meet her.

Seeing how nervous Olivia was, Ty reached across Anso to squeeze her hand. They'd made reservations at Sardino's, Resurrection's nicest seafood restaurant. Since the day was sunny, they were sitting at the outside tables overlooking the tourist pier. A handful of royal bodyguards were posted here and there, but she barely noticed them anymore. The triplets—who thankfully loved traveling—were sitting quietly in their stroller, thoroughly occupied in goggling at their surroundings with eyes as big as saucers. The moment LoLo started to fuss, Anso lifted her into his arms. She wasn't walking yet, but her legs were strong enough to bounce her on Anso's thighs. She did that while she enjoyed her new and higher viewing perch.

"Daa!" Konnor complained. All the men—and occasionally Olivia—were "Da" to the children. Hoping to head off a full-on wail, Ty extricated him from the stroller too. Ty had gone from being the most worried of their parental trio to the most assured. When all else failed, he was handed a problem child. Usually he could soothe it, a fact he sometimes like to rub in. *I'm not just the third*, he'd crow. *I'm The Man*!

Left by himself in the stroller, Ollie stared accusingly at her.

"All right," she said, "but if you start grizzling because I'm anxious, don't blame me."

"Just how conservative is your daughter?" Anso asked, his steady pat on LoLo's bottom lulling her.

"Not terribly." Clucking her tongue with dismay, Olivia grabbed a cloth napkin before Ollie could drool on her nice silk blouse. "She just prefers her parents to act like parents."

She squinted at the restaurant's roped-off terrace entrance, mentally cursing the "normal" colored contacts that made her eyes feel weird. She still didn't see James or Violet. The suburban train from New York had been scheduled to arrive half an hour ago. James should have collected her by now. She rubbed Ollie's warm little back to calm herself, her towheaded punkin' fortunately oblivious to her mood. Oliver was their only blondie, LoLo was a redhead, and Konnor was russet brown. Ollie was as serious as he was cute.

Perhaps to compensate for his sober nature, he had a scattering of Ty's leopard spots on his adorable chubby butt.

"Do you think something went wrong with the invitation?" she asked worriedly.

Outsiders like their daughter couldn't pass through Resurrection's protective wards without a formal invitation from a resident. One of the werewolf cops who'd assisted during the almost-earthquake had been kind enough to send Violet one.

"I'm sure it's fine," Anso said, rubbing her knee even as he nuzzled LoLo's little ear. "Most likely the train was late, or they ran into traffic. This will be okay, Liv. From everything James has told us, your daughter adores you."

Olivia's eyes burned with sudden tears. Violet was Violet, and you never quite knew how she'd react to big changes. Discovering her forty-something mother had married two more men and given birth to triplets was a lot to take in. Violet had enjoyed being an only child.

And then she was there, striding along the old cobbled street that led through the warehouse district to Sardino's. James was beside her, and they were laughing and talking. Olivia covered her mouth. Her daughter was so beautiful and chic. Taking over as CEO of Forster Media had agreed with her as much as being Anso's third agreed with Ty. Mrs. Bonn would definitely approve of Violet's smart blue suit and heels.

"Mother!" she exclaimed from the hostess's podium.

"Go," Anso said, pulling Ollie from her lap so she could.

Olivia's tears spilled over as she rose. Though her vision was blurry, she saw Violet had no trouble running to meet her in her stylish shoes.

"Mommy," she said, squeezing her tight in that wonderful way she had. Violet was nearly as tall as James and leaned down to her. "I'm sorry we're late. Daddy filled me in on the way and we stopped to talk."

When Violet pushed back, the rims of her eyes were red. Olivia concluded that must have been some talk. However upset her daughter had been, it seemed mostly behind her. Violet smiled at her. "You could have told me, you know. You and Dad must have sent me a thousand emails since I took over as CEO."

"It seemed like something we ought to, er, spring on you in person."

"Spring on me is right!" Violet laughed, but a hint of stress ran through it. Olivia suspected James had taken their daughter's doubts and fears on himself, then talked her out of venting them on her mother.

"I am sorry, sweetheart," she said. "I didn't know how to tell you. I'm aware your father and I have been eccentric."

"You're happy," Violet said staunchly. "And so is Dad. I'd have to be blind not to notice that. You look great, by the way. Are you doing your hair differently?"

"Something like that," Olivia said dryly, glad her daughter didn't think she looked too changed. "Would you like to meet the others?"

"I would," Violet said. "Especially if I can sit down and get off these heels."

There was a predictable flurry as they reached the table, where James had gone ahead. Anso and Ty rose to shake her hand, each with a baby balanced in the crook of his arm. They seemed easier with Violet than she was with them, but that was to be expected. They at least had warning. As deft at baby juggling as the rest, James passed LoLo to Olivia, then pulled out a chair for Violet between them. Her parents might have given her a shock, but they'd flank her as always.

"Would you like to hold Konnor?" Ty offered after she was settled. "He'd probably enjoy it. He's quite the flirt."

Violet agreed to this idea, and Ty passed his armload across to her. Violet stood Konnor on her short blue skirt, which was almost the same color as the baby's eyes. Konnor and Ollie both had an inner circle of yellow in their irises, but unless you saw them in the right light, it wasn't obvious.

"Look at you," Violet said, bouncing Konnor experimentally. "What a cutie you are with your big blue eyes!"

"Gaa!" Konnor agreed before breaking into a throaty chortle and batting his eyelashes. Ty hadn't been kidding about the king's son being a flirt.

Violet laughed in return, because who could resist baby giggles? "You're my little brother," she said. "I bet you didn't know that."

Konnor flapped his dimpled hands and tried to sit down.

"All right," Violet said, turning him around so he could. "I guess I'm holding you for a while."

She looked so natural with a baby in her lap, Olivia couldn't help drawing breath to speak. Surely, she'd explode with happiness if Violet—

"No." Violet cut her off with a scolding finger. "You are not allowed to pester me about grandkids until these three are teenagers."

Reluctantly, Olivia conceded that was fair. "So . . ." she said. "How was your train ride?"

"Fine," Violet answered, a twitch of her mouth the only sign that she thought this question a bit banal. "The funny thing is, no one got off at this stop but me. And there was this taxi driver outside the station who'd painted his whole face blue. Is there a college team around here whose logo is that color?"

"There must be," Olivia said as Ty and Anso exchanged glances. They'd warned her Violet might or might not notice Resurrection's oddities. All Pocket territories were charmed against Outsiders seeing their true nature, but sometimes plain old humans were sensitive.

"Resurrection seems like a pretty city," Violet went on. "It's strange I've never heard of it before."

"It is," Olivia said, "but it's a good place to meet."

Violet picked up her menu. Comically, it looked like both she and Konnor were perusing it. Olivia suspected neither of them read a word. Violet was gnawing at her beautifully lipsticked mouth.

"Venice is so far away!" she burst out. "I know Dad's new transport business is taking off, but couldn't you base it somewhere closer? None of you are even Italian!"

They were something more exotic than Italian, but they'd reached a consensus that sharing the whole truth with Violet would be premature.

"It's not impossibly far," Anso soothed. "All of us are busy, as we're sure you are, but we'll make time to visit. I really want your brothers and sister to have a chance to know you."

Anso's eyes were bright with sincerity. Olivia saw that, as much as he'd prepared himself to meet (and like) her and James's firstborn, Violet hadn't become real until she was in front of him.

"I *miss* them," she said more moderately, clearly trying to contain a pout. "I know I'm grown up, but I do."

Anso smiled at her so beautifully Violet appeared momentarily dazzled. "I'd miss them too, if I were in your shoes. Your mother and father are wonderful people."

"Thanksgiving," Violet said firmly, abruptly all CEO.

"Excuse me?" Anso said, startled by her bossy tone.

Violet didn't know he was a king, and might not have been cowed in any case. She squared her shoulders. "You can have Christmas, but I'm claiming Thanksgiving. The grandparents will want to see you, so we'll meet in Charleston. I'll book a B&B that takes children."

"I don't know if—"

"Yes, Violet," Ty cut in, silencing Anso's doubts with a gentle hand on his arm. "We'll meet you in Charleston with bells on."

"Bybeh!" LoLo loudly announced as she squirmed in Olivia's lap.

Violet's mouth fell open. "Did she just say my name?"

"Bybeh!" Konnor chimed in, smacking Violet's menu onto the table.

"Bababa!" was Ollie's contribution. Anso kissed the top of his downy head. Oliver always had to be different. James petted his golden hair from the other side, his hand stroking Anso's wrist as easily as it did Ty's child.

The moment struck Olivia as perfect: all her men and all her babies, sitting at the same table. She'd experienced an awful lot of happiness since committing herself to her mates, but this golden day had to top them all. This was a gift no one could be sweet enough to deserve. Sharing it was the only way to say thank you.

"This is good, Vi," James said, grinning sideways at their firstborn. "Look how many more of us there are to love you now."

"Hmph," Violet said, but she was grinning too.

ABOUT THE AUTHOR

EMMA Holly is the award winning, *USA Today* bestselling author of more than twenty romantic novels, featuring vampires, demons, fairies and just plain extraordinary ordinary folks. She loves the hot stuff, both to read and to write!

If you'd like to find out what else she's written, please visit her website at: http://www.emmaholly.com. She runs monthly contests and sends out newsletters that often include coupons for new books. To receive them, go to her contest page.

If you like threesomes, her Victorianish demon novel, *The Assassins' Lover*, is also available. If sexy shapechangers are your thing, you might try *Hidden Talents*, which features a werewolf cop and is set in the same general story world as *Hidden Depths*.

Thanks so much for reading this book!

HUNGRY FOR MORE WERESEALS?

"DATE NIGHT"

OLIVIA Forster never dreamed she'd one day serve as queen of an enchanted city beneath the sea—something her three sexy husbands know. Though she adores her shapeshifting mates, she's shy by nature, and they can tell the strain of always being "on" is beginning to wear on her. Sneaking away from their responsibilities won't be easy, but come hell or high water, they'll treat her to a night she won't soon forget!

a digital short story

WEREWOLF cop Adam Santini is sworn to protect and serve all the supes in Resurrection, NY—including unsuspecting human Talents who wander in from Outside.

Telekinetic Ari is hot on the trail of a mysterious crime boss who wants to exploit her gift for his own evil ends, a mission that puts her on a collision course with the hottest cop in the RPD.

Adam wants the crime boss too, but mostly he wants Ari. She seems to be the mate he's been yearning for all his life, though getting a former street kid into bed with the Law could be his toughest case to date.

"*Hidden Talents* is the perfect package of supes, romance, mystery and HEA!"—**Paperback Dolls**

available in ebook and prin

CATS and dogs shouldn't fall in love. Like any wolf, detective Nate Rivera knows this. He can't help it if the tigress he's been trading quips with at the supermarket is the most alluring woman he's ever met—sassy too, which suits him down to his designer boots.

Evina Mohajit is aware their flirtation can't lead to more. Still, she relishes trading banter with the hot werewolf. This hardworking single mom hasn't felt so female since her twins' baby daddy left to start his new family. Plus, as a station chief in Resurrection's Fire Department, she understands the demands of a dangerous job.

Their will-they-or-won't-they tango could go on forever if it weren't for the mortal peril the city's shifter children fall into. To save them, Nate and Evina must team up, a choice that ignites the sparks smoldering between them . . .

"Weaving the police procedural with her inventive love scenes [made] this book one I could not put down."—**The Romance Reviews**

available in ebook and print

DO you believe in dragons? Werewolf cop Rick Lupone would say no . . . until a dying faerie tells him the fate of his city depends on him. If he can't protect a mysterious woman in peril, everything may be lost. The only discovery more shocking is that the woman he's meant to save is his high school crush, Cass Maycee.

Half fae Cass didn't earn her Snow White nickname by chance. All her life, her refusal to abuse fae glamour kept men like Rick at arm's length. Now something new is waking up inside her, a secret heritage her pureblood father kept her in the dark about. Letting it out might kill her, but keeping it hidden is no longer an option. The dragons' ancient enemies are moving. If they find the prize before Rick and Cass, the supe-friendly city of Resurrection just might go up in flames.

"[Hidden Dragons] kept me completely enthralled . . . sexy & erotic"
—Platinum Reviews

available in ebook and print

SEXY fireman Chris Savoy has been closeted all his life. He's a weretiger in Resurrection, and no shifters are more macho than that city's. Due to a terrible tragedy in his past, Chris resigned himself to hiding what he is—a resolve that's threatened the night he lays eyes on cute gay werecop Tony Lupone.

Tony might be a wolf, but he wakes longings Chris finds difficult to deny. When a threat to the city throws these heroes together, not giving in seems impossible. Following their hearts, however, means risking everything . . .

Author's Note: Tony and Chris's book happens in the background of *Hidden Dragons*. You'll enjoy it more if you read that first.

Hidden Passions gets 5 Chocolate-Dipped Strawberries from **Guilty Indulgence**: "Ms. Holly has a special gift."

available in ebook and print

Made in the USA
Middletown, DE
16 April 2017